D1257615

PEACE
in the
VALLEY

Center Point
Large Print

Also by Ruth Logan Herne and available from Center Point Large Print:

Home on the Range

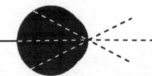

This Large Print Book carries the Seal of Approval of N.A.V.H.

DOUBLE S RANCH, BOOK 3

PEACE
in the
VALLEY

RUTH LOGAN HERNE

CENTER POINT LARGE PRINT
THORNDIKE, MAINE

Scripture quotations or paraphrases are taken from the
following versions: King James Version®. The Holy Bible,
New International Version®, NIV®. Copyright © 1973, 1978,
1984 by Biblica Inc.® Used by permission. All rights reserved
worldwide. New American Standard Bible®. Copyright ©
1960, 1962, 1963, 1968, 1971, 1972, 1973, 1975, 1977, 1995
by the Lockman Foundation. Used by permission.
(www.Lockman.org). New King James Version®.
Copyright © 1982 by Thomas Nelson Inc. Used by
permission. All rights reserved.

The characters and events in this book are fictional, and any
resemblance to actual persons or events is coincidental.

The text of this Large Print edition is unabridged.
In other aspects, this book may vary from the original edition.
Printed in the United States of America on permanent paper.
Set in 16-point Times New Roman type.

ISBN: 978-1-68324-407-3

Library of Congress Cataloging-in-Publication Data

Names: Herne, Ruth Logan, author.
Title: Peace in the valley / Ruth Logan Herne.
Description: Center Point Large Print edition. | Thorndike, Maine :
Center Point Large Print, 2017.
Identifiers: LCCN 2017008789 | ISBN 9781683244073
    (hardcover : alk. paper)
Subjects: LCSH: Large type books. | BISAC: FICTION /
Contemporary Women. | FICTION / Christian / Romance. | FICTION
/ Christian / Western. | GSAFD: Christian fiction. | Western stories. |
Love stories.
Classification: LCC PS3608.E76875 P43 2017b | DDC 813/.6—dc23
LC record available at https://lccn.loc.gov/2017008789

To Zach: Son #3

May you always find your own peace
in the valley, may you always feel
the warmth of God's love
giving you strength and faith
as it shines from above,
and may you be blessed
with all the joys
a roller-coaster life allows.
All of your days.
With love, Mom

One

For once in his life, Trey Walker Stafford had aced his two older brothers. The fact that he had to risk his life and offer up a chunk of his liver to claim the title made it a dubious honor.

The irony wasn't lost on Trey as he drove his packed SUV west on I-90 through Central Washington. The thought that of Sam Stafford's three sons, it was the orphaned-nephew-turned-adopted son whose DNA provided the best possible outcome for his adoptive father fit today's reality TV scenarios too well.

But then their lives up to this point had seemed like a reality television show, so why change now?

The fingers of his left hand thrummed a sense-less beat on the leather steering wheel. He drove the roads he'd known for so long, intent on get-ting back to the ranch and the man who'd rescued him from squalor twenty-five years before. He meant to do whatever he could to help his father. Not because he harbored some kind of death wish. Surgery, painful recovery, and possible death weren't on his agenda. His agent had made that clear multiple times during the past week, and by every possible available media.

"You'd risk everything you've earned, every-thing you have, your home." Ed Boddy ticked off

his fingers as he listed Trey's potential downfall. *"That ranch you love, tucked in the hills of Northern Tennessee, your music, your life. And all to help the man who threw you out of the house because you loved music? You're a better man than I am, Trey. That's for sure."*

He wasn't better. He knew that. He was guilt ridden and fairly vacant inside, like one of those black holes yawning wide in an endless universe. Solid. Dense. Yet empty. And he'd felt that way for as long as he could remember.

Sam hadn't thrown him out because he loved music. He'd cast him aside because Sam had watched the downside of fame claim the life of his younger sister and her husband. He'd seen what life in the spotlight could do. Sam knew it wasn't pretty. But Trey had shrugged off his father's concerns. Growing up knowing the worst of the music industry firsthand had left him with a powerful need to prove it could be done the right way. Clean. Open. Honest. The crazy rich part wasn't something he'd planned. It just kind of happened along the way.

"Poor little boy."

The voice. *Her* voice, the voice of his mother, Sandra Lee Stafford. Beloved on her early country music recordings, that slow-churned alto turned utterly scathing when it came to her little boy.

She'd stood over him, smelling bad and looking hateful, and that's all Trey envisioned anytime

8

someone mentioned his mother. They said a three-year-old doesn't have the capacity to remember actual events, that they might have snatches of recall, here and there. Whoever *they* were, they were plumb stupid, because Trey remembered enough. Too much.

"There ain't no one in this world 'bout to feel sorry for you, Trey-Trey. Least of all, me."

He must have been crying. He couldn't remember the tears, but he remembered the wetness on his face.

And then she was gone, and his father was gone, and the next thing he knew, Sam Stafford strode into that police station. Larger than life, Sam had scooped up Trey and taken him home.

And so it began, and here's where it might end: Trey, donating part of his liver to keep Sam Stafford alive. A good Christian man would go forward boldly, embracing the opportunity. Trey marked that up as another out-and-out failure because he was Christian to a fault on most things . . .

But not this.

His internal guilt spiked like an overwound E string, but Trey spent so much of his life feeling guilty that today shouldn't be any different. But this change—*this summer*—would be life and death. And that, right there, made a difference.

He exited the highway and took the right-hand turn leading up the hill, away from Gray's Glen, the town he grew up in. Broad fields stretched along either side, filled with lush grass and gray-green sagebrush. The sagebrush grew thicker as the meadows climbed. Dark red cattle dotted the upper pastures like a generous sprinkling of cayenne pepper on steamed broccoli.

He was hungry.

Tired.

Nervous?

Yes.

The Ellensburg deejay segued into Trey's newest single in a way that made him cringe. "Ya wanna talk a Cinderella cowboy story? We've got it right here, as Central Washington's own Trey Walker tugs the heartstrings while he rockets up the charts again with 'You Only Live Once.' "

Trey shut the radio off.

He had no desire to hear himself croon sage words of advice to trusting fans. They thought he understood their plight.

He didn't.

They sensed he had a heart of gold.

Wrong again.

They believed in him, in his music, his calling, his faith.

How he wished he could believe in himself. He—

The aged, dark blue van came out of nowhere. Trey hit the brakes too late.

The van shot into the intersection.

Trey cut the wheel and prayed. The SUV squealed in protest.

The van turned too, away from him, in a desperate move to avoid the crash. The maneuver worked, but then the van raced up the embankment and tipped up and over before landing on its side in the small creek running into the glen.

Trey shoved the SUV into park and jumped out. He raced across the two-lane country road, jumped onto the hill, and hit 911 on his phone at the same time. He shouted quick facts to the dispatcher as he scaled the small but steep incline. "We've got a van overturned into Chudney's Creek north of the I-90 turnoff on Buell Road, just past the intersection of East Chelan."

He didn't wait for a response as he crested the creek bank. He leaped into the water and yanked himself up onto the side front of the tipped van. Wet fingers made the grip difficult, but once he gained a leg up, he was able to pull himself the rest of the way. He reached down to jerk open the van door.

It wouldn't budge.

The driver—a woman—was facing away from him.

She didn't move. Didn't wiggle. Didn't—

His heart stopped. He pounded on the door, not knowing what else to do, then realized he might be able to get in through the back hatch. He jumped down and rushed through the knee-deep water, then bent and grabbed the latch on the back hatch.

It opened. He breathed out, glad to have access to the van and the driver.

His relief was short lived. The entire back of the van was filled with floral debris. Upended plants, baskets, planters, and trays of seedlings blocked his way. Utter destruction filled the banged-up van from top to bottom.

"Noooo." The single drawn-out word came from the front of the van, which meant the driver was alive. Knowing that gave his heart reason to keep on beating.

He looked up.

If despair had a face, it was the one he saw right now as the driver spotted the complete wreckage. "Unlock your door," he ordered, then slogged back through the water. He climbed up again and braced himself. The van's angle made opening the door tough. Its weight worked against him, but instinct dictated he needed to get her out of the van. And what if there was a passenger?

He pushed down on his heels and tugged the door upright. It blocked his view, and he didn't have the best footing, but he hung on for dear life. "Can you climb out? I'm afraid to let go of the door to help you; it might fall and hit you."

"I can climb."

Trey prayed.

He doubted the effectiveness, because while *he* believed in God, he was pretty sure God had taken a detour somewhere north of his Tennessee ranch. But then, why wouldn't he?

He and God knew the truth. Trey was here seeking absolution. Seeking . . . something. Something to fill the void left by aching guilt. He didn't know what he was looking for, exactly. He just knew he'd been searching for what seemed like a long, long time.

Nothing yet.

Trey wasn't stupid. The prospects of finding peace in the broad, lush green valley of Central Washington were slim to none. He wasn't being pessimistic. It's just how things rolled these days.

A hand appeared not far from his feet. Then another hand came through the opening, followed by a mass of long gold-and-brown hair. The loose hair tumbled over the side of the van. She turned his way and the hair was now accompanied by a face.

An absolutely beautiful, very angry face.

Great.

He didn't sigh and point out the obvious as sirens approached them from the town below. She should have stopped at the intersection. He had the right-of-way.

A light blue T-shirt emerged, followed by a green-and-blue skirt decked out in swirls. The driver didn't spare him another look. She hopped off the side of the van into the water.

Her skirt billowed, then acted like a wick,

drawing muddy creek water up like a high-priced paper towel. The wet skirt plastered itself to her legs. She growled, wrenched the skirt up with both hands, and strode through the water before stopping at the open back hatch.

He almost couldn't bear to watch, except he couldn't turn away. He'd seen the wreckage inside the van. It was a scene of utter destruction with months of someone's hard work destroyed.

Hers?

Maybe.

Tears streamed down her cheeks as she surveyed the mess. No sobs, no whining, no yelling, just a steady flow of silent outpouring heartbreak.

The urge to help overcame him, but how?

Maybe she was in shock.

That cheered him, because if she was, then the accident hadn't just ruined her life. Shock, at least, was medically treatable.

There were no special warming blankets or mugs of coffee to heal heartbreak. He knew that.

He let the door ease shut, then jumped into the water, as his future sister-in-law, Angelina, rolled to a stop in her new deputy's car. "Trey?" She looked astounded to see him in the creek, but then her eyes widened and her expression changed to one of even deeper concern. "Lucy? Oh my gosh, Lucy, are you all right?" An ambulance pulled up behind Angelina's car.

Angelina didn't waste any more time on Trey.

She hurried to the creek bank and held out her hand to the woman. "Come on, honey, come out of there. What on earth happened?"

The woman—Lucy—took Angelina's hand and let her tug her toward the first dry ledge of the bank before she pointed his way. "He blew through the stop sign in typical Stafford fashion. Fast and furious, with no regard for rules or anyone else."

"Oh, honey." Angelina hugged her, then turned to Trey. "You ran a stop sign, Trey?"

"There is no stop sign." Trey aimed a look of disbelief at the woman, then his future sister-in-law, before he motioned left. "As you can see—" He stopped and stared hard, real hard, when he saw the universal octagon shape. "No." He crossed the road as the medics pulled out a gurney. "This wasn't here ten minutes ago. I swear it wasn't!" He moved down the road, turned, then sighed.

Angelina shook her head. "I come this way all the time and I never noticed how the new growth covered that much of the sign. Probably because I know it's there."

"It never used to be." Trey shifted his attention from the sign to her, then to Lucy. "I never saw it, and when I used to live here, there was no stop sign on Buell Road."

"They changed it up when they put in the Chelan Crossing subdivision a bunch of years back," the second medic explained as he walked across the road and stuck out his hand. "Brian

Mulcahy, I was in school with Colt." He peered closely, checking Trey out while his partner did the same with the van driver. "You okay? Did you get hurt? Shaken up?"

"No. I'm fine. She took the brunt of it." Trey nodded to where the woman named Lucy stood near the ambulance. "I cruised right on through and didn't even notice her coming until we were both in the intersection."

"I'm calling Harv Bedlow to get over here with a chainsaw and clippers and clean this up." Brian indicated the full summer foliage. "I don't know how we missed this, Trey. The growth here impedes the visual of the sign on this side of the road and the oncoming traffic on that side."

Brian was cutting him slack. He didn't deserve it, but for one reason or another, the good people of Gray's Glen had always cut him a leniency they denied to the rest of the family. He wasn't born to be one of Sam Stafford's boys, and that earned him extra points in a community that had borne the brunt of his father's heavy-handedness for too many years. Sometimes it felt good to be favored. Other times? Not so much, and his older brothers never hesitated to keep him from getting a big head.

"I'm fine, Brian, go check her out. Please," he added, swiping at a persistent deerfly that seemed suddenly attracted to his left ear. "And we need a tow truck to haul the van out of the water."

"We have to have a tow truck?" Two blue eyes pinned him, the kind of blue that made the summer sky pale by comparison and a Central Washington summer sky was a mighty pretty thing. She took a step forward, clearly worried. "Can't we just tip it up and drag it out?"

Trey opened his mouth to say something, then stopped.

Money. The wrecked, scarred van, the mess of plants, the tow truck . . . Lack of money put that fear in her eyes. Not him. Well, not *just* him, so that was good. "This is my bad," he told her as he crossed the quiet road once more. "I'll make restitution on everything. And I'm sorry, real sorry." He scrubbed a hand to the back of his neck and shot a quick glance to the stop sign. "I missed it completely."

So Trey Stafford was sorry.

Big deal.

Staffords had a lot to be sorry for in Gray's Glen, and even more when it came to the little farm she owned in the shadow of their wealthy land-baron-type holdings, so Lucy Carlton could just add her total ruination to the lengthy list. The thought of two months' work washed away by five seconds of inattention . . . And he'd walked away unscathed, his big, shiny SUV sparkling in the summer sun, the wide-wall tires thick and new. Typical Stafford good fortune.

17

Her van.

She stared at the narrow strip of blue peeking above the embankment, then gave herself a firm shake. Two seconds later and her van might have hit the bridge abutment instead of the hill, and her outcome could have been much worse. She wasn't injured, and her three kids still had a mother. Reason enough to thank God right there.

But the square-jawed handsome Stafford in front of her was another matter entirely. She faced him coolly, at least as cool as she could be with her skirt dripping midsummer creek water along the road's narrow shoulder. "I need your insurance information."

He shook his head, and when she opened her mouth to protest, his words made her pause. "I'll take care of it personally."

Lucy had learned the hard way not to be anyone's fool. She'd trusted too young and too soon. Now she meted trust out in minute doses, and this guy wasn't about to get even that much leverage. She lifted her chin and refused his offer. "That's not an option. There's protocol involved with things like this. We report the accident."

Angelina raised her hand from where she was filling out the report. "Got that covered."

"And then we exchange insurance information, except that you don't need mine because this was all your fault."

He knew that but still had the nerve to challenge her. "I didn't see the sign, true. But how fast were you going, ma'am? Because you barreled through this intersection in a way that would have taken notice at Talladega. We might have to warn Danica she's got some tried-and-true competition headed her way."

The validity of his question made her scowl. "I had the right-of-way."

He nodded, cowboy style, nice and easy, as if they were comfortable old friends, chatting on the roadside. They weren't, and she'd be darned if she was going to let one more self-absorbed Stafford monkey up her life. This guy's father had managed to do that for years. No more. She folded her arms, stubborn.

He held his ground and didn't look perturbed or particularly guilty. He looked plain good, and she was mad at herself for even realizing that. "You were in a hurry."

"Lucy, were you speeding?" Angelina asked the question gently. She pointed west of the intersection. "There are no skid marks indicating you tried to stop."

"I didn't have a reason to stop until he shot out in front of me," she protested. "How can this possibly be my fault?" She stared at Angelina—her neighbor and only real friend—then turned her attention back to the water-logged van. "I was heading to market and I got a late start."

Angelina looked at her, then the van. "Oh, no. Lucy, was the van full of your flowers?"

She would not cry. Not again. Not in front of a rich, stuck-on-himself Stafford. "Yes."

"Oh, honey." Angelina hugged her, and while the hug felt good, Lucy couldn't afford to get bogged down in sentiment. She'd be bogged down enough in the reality of no money, no van, and the massive cleanup in the back of her vehicle.

The tow truck rumbled up the road. Sal Smith from Sal's Auto climbed out, saw the van, and whistled lightly. "It's been one of those mornings already, and I could've gone for an easy tow, but there ain't a thing easy about pulling that van out of that water. You okay, Luce?"

"As well as can be expected."

Sympathy marked the auto mechanic's face. Then he spotted Trey standing with Brian. "That you, Trey?" He strode forward, stuck out his hand, and gave Sam Stafford's youngest son the biggest smile Lucy had ever seen. "You're here? That's a wonderful thing. I can't wait to tell Gracie. You doin' a concert hereabouts? Or are you here because your dad's ailing?"

"My dad."

"You're a good man, Trey." The older man clapped him on the shoulder, and Lucy expected to see the youngest Stafford soak up the kind words like a sponge on water.

He didn't. A flash of something—indecision?

No, maybe doubt? Yes, that was it—made his hazel eyes wince slightly. "Can you handle this, Sal? I'll help. I'm wet already. No sense having you go down in the water to hook the rig."

"You're wet, sure enough, and if you managed to help Lucy get out of that thing, you did good, Trey. That's a bear of an angle, all straight up and perpendicular-like."

A small SUV pulled up, off the road, a blue flasher marking the volunteer firefighter status. A man climbed out with a small chainsaw, powered it up, and started clearing the brush and branches around the stop sign.

Sal got in his truck, backed it up the hill on a sharp angle, then he and his coworker climbed back out. "Did you mean that about getting wet?" he asked Trey, and Lucy was surprised when Trey nodded.

"I'm in too." Brian moved up the small embankment. "I've got a change of clothes at the firehouse. If we can winch and jerk it upright, then you can pull it up out of there, can't you, Sal?"

"That's the plan, but I don't want one of you hero-types to end up under the thing if she falls."

"Trey, you wanna rethink this?" Brian surveyed the tipped van. "We can call reinforcements."

"No need." He pulled off his outer shirt and tossed it to Angelina, leaving just a plain white cotton knit tee in place. "Let's hook her up." He climbed over the embankment, then into the water. He and Brian followed Sal's instructions and hooked the van. They each fell once, and when they climbed up the slippery slope of the inner bank, they laughed and high-fived one another.

Lucy didn't see a thing to laugh about. This wasn't high school hijinks on a crazy Saturday night. This was her bread and butter. Her paycheck for the month. Her—

She swallowed hard when Angelina slipped an arm around her shoulders. Anger and frustration laid claim to her. Sal fired up the winch, and the whining sound grabbed hold of her just like the hooked assembly clutched her rusty, dented, untrustworthy van. The van jerked, shimmied, then jerked again.

Something broke free and the hook rebounded, then bounced, barely missing Brian and Trey as it ricocheted.

"Rusted out." Brian headed back into the water. So did Trey. They reexamined the area, then Trey went down, under the water, and popped back up, soaking wet. "I've got it. Give me the hook."

Brian handed it over, and when Trey came back up, he gave Sal a thumbs-up. "I think we're good this time."

"All right." Sal started the winch again, and this time the cable held when the van lurched free from the creek bed.

Slow and steady, the truck-mounted motor drew

the van out of the water, then up the bank. A stream of muddy water poured out the open doors, along with mangled plants and flowers. And when they had the van up the embankment, at least a thousand dollars of Lucy's hard work and investment floated downstream in a surprisingly pretty burst of color, almost like it was meant to be. But it wasn't meant to be and her heart pinched tight to see it.

Gone.

Washed away, much like the hopes and dreams she'd had years ago.

The enormity of it all made her want to sit down and hold her head in her hands.

She wouldn't give Trey Stafford the satisfaction, so she stayed focused on business. "I think we're back to insurance information now."

"You live nearby?"

The question irked her because she owned the small farm adjacent to his father's mega-ranch, but then she got a better grip on rampant emotion. The singing Stafford brother hadn't been back for any length of time over the past several years. "Next door to the Double S."

"Let me go get cleaned up, and I'll come right by," he told her. He indicated his soaking wet clothes. "I'm kind of a mess."

He was.

But he was also a raging hot, wet-T-shirt-wearing mess, with one of the kindest smiles she'd ever seen. She'd learned to mistrust smiles, and most everything else, once she married Chase Carlton. "If you give me your info, we can call this matter done. I think that's best."

"Naw."

She wasn't too sure how he could make this decision unilaterally, and yet, he did. "I've always thought if a man makes a mistake, he needs to fix it, best he's able. I'll be at your place within the hour. Ange?" He turned toward her friend. "See you at the ranch."

"I'm done at three, and Mami's running the kitchen."

"And the men, most likely."

Angelina acknowledged that with a smile. "Part of the job."

"That it is. Miss Lucy?" He turned her way. "Can I give you a lift back to your place?"

She'd rather crunch cold snails in her salad than ride with him. She might not know him personally, but she knew Staffords, and musicians, which gave him two strikes. In her experience, Staffords looked out for their own and had done so for decades.

And this one, the country music sensation whose magazine coverage had women of all ages sighing in the checkout lanes? If the tabloids were to be trusted, Trey Walker Stafford liked life on the wild side, and Lucy Carlton had done the wild side once.

With her hand laid flat atop the Good Book, she'd sworn never to do it again.

Two

Trey angled his SUV into a parking spot alongside the near barn, then hopped out of the driver's seat before he got the car any wetter or smellier than he already had. He lifted the small duffel, paused, and looked around, drinking in the sights and sounds of the Double S.

Rangeland. Cattle. Two banks up, someone was working two dogs and a herd, heading up to cooler pastureland, verdant and lush. That meant they'd had a few solid rains, always a variable once you got to this side of the Cascades.

Home.

And yet . . . not home.

"Trey, is that you?"

Trey turned toward the sound of his father's voice and couldn't hide the full shock of seeing Sam's decline. He wiped it from his face, but not before his father recognized the reaction. Would they be in time? Could the transplant really solve Sam's major health problems? And if giving up a chunk of himself did turn out to be the best-case scenario, could Trey willingly walk into that hospital and let them excise a sizable lobe of his liver?

He couldn't think of that now. Facts first. Panic later. Sam had taught him well. He moved forward and opened his arms. "Hey, Dad."

He hugged him gently before he indicated the SUV. "I've got a bunch of stuff in there."

"Bring it in, Son."

"I figured I'd stay in the cabin, remember? More quiet time to write songs."

A blend of embarrassment and frustration crossed Sam's face. "You did say that. I forgot."

"It happens."

"Stupid meds, they fog me sometimes. Some of this, some of that." Sam waved his arm as if he could shrug off the doctor's orders.

"They're necessary, right?" Trey said as they entered the house.

Sam moved toward the good-smelling kitchen and made a face. "These days, who knows? You're soaking wet. What happened?"

"I was wondering if you noticed."

"You smell ripe too."

"Yup." Trey winced in regret. "Creek water. I had a little scrape with a minivan where Buell Road crosses East Chelan. Didn't know there was a stop sign there. I almost clipped your neighbor, and she went into the water."

"The Carlton woman?"

"Lucy?"

"Yes."

"That's her."

"Is she all right?"

Trey followed Sam into the kitchen. "She is. The van isn't."

Sam settled into a chair. Trey had no idea how hungry he was until he was surrounded by the scents of Isabo's cooking. "Isabo, if heaven has a smell, this would be it. Is that a pot of pulled beef?"

Angelina's mother crossed the kitchen quickly. She grabbed him in a hug, then stopped and pointed. "Go clean up, you smell like old moss and decaying matter. And worse."

He laughed and picked up his small duffel. "I will, and I'll throw these right in the wash when I'm done. But I'll tell you what, the smell of that meat and those pies about did me in, walking through. Reason enough to wash up quick."

"Oh, he is your sweet talker, Sam." Isabo bustled back to the counter opposite the black and silver stove. She shifted a simmering kettle to a back burner as she spoke. "Colton got your tough-guy attitude. No one in their right mind wants to mess with that, except my daughter, it seems, and since she is made in similar fashion, it's a good match."

Sam nodded agreement.

"And Nick's about as boneheaded as they come sometimes," she went on, as if dissecting Sam's sons was something she did on a regular basis. In the past no one would have dared say such things to Sam Stafford, even if they were true, but Isabo's open honesty freshened the Double S like new sheets on a firm mattress. "But under all his bluster, Nicholas has a kind heart and now a good woman of such knowledge and warmth, perfection. But this one." She tapped her chin and scrutinized Trey.

And then she stopped tapping her chin, as if she saw too much, and Trey never let anyone see too much. If they did, they'd understand what a phony he was.

"And this one walks in the light," she said softly.

She smiled, but he wasn't sure why, because he hadn't seen the light for quite a while. She studied him gently, and it took a minute for him to break the connection. When he did, he swallowed a lump in his throat and edged toward the stairs. "I'll be back when I'm clean."

"And we'll talk," Sam told him.

His father wanted to talk about the surgery, about the transplant, but Trey wasn't sure how to handle that conversation just yet. Could he admit he was scared spitless by the idea? And yet, still willing to do it?

But what if fear won the day and he backed out? He'd be signing his father's death sentence.

"Trust in the LORD with all your heart and lean not on your own understanding." The proverb meant well, but the lines had grown indistinct somewhere in the last decade. He loved God, he believed with all his heart, but he'd witnessed a lot over the years, good and bad. He understood the thinness of faith through his own facade.

28

If he was faithful in name only, was everyone?

The inconsistency of man bogged down his spirit. He yearned for hope and longed for peace, and that was ridiculous because God had given him a talent that reaped him riches beyond belief . . .

And yet, the craving continued, unabated.

Trey took a long, warm shower, got dressed, and chucked his soaking wet clothes into the new-fangled washing machine. He stared at the buttons, mystified, and when Isabo heard his call for help, she came around the corner and put her hands on her broad hips. "Stymied?"

"Totally."

"I will take over," she decided, and moved closer.

"Can you show me?"

Again she met his gaze, and this time he saw a note of concern in her expression. Not much, a mere flash, but enough. More than enough. "Gladly." She didn't go further, didn't delve, but Trey got the idea that Isabo Castiglione's instincts served her well. Maybe too well. She showed him the buttons to push as he selected the options, then waited, watching. "*Bien!*"

"*Gracias*, Isabo."

Approval shone in her eyes. For his meager attempt at Spanish or his button-pushing prowess? Maybe both, but it felt good, which was down-right silly, wasn't it?

"It is nothing, of course, but I do like to see a

man have a clue about the work entailed in a house, a home. Although with amazing machines like this, it is barely to be called work, no?"

"We'll call it work because while you're running around, managing the house and the kitchen and the men and the kids, the occasional easy machine should be a given." They walked back into the expansive kitchen together. One side of the room was the cook's domain, sacrosanct on a big ranch, and this one was a cook's dream. Cupboards and shelves lined the back wall. Mega-sized stainless steel appliances mixed with rich, honey-toned cabinetry. Broad granite countertops allowed for generous workspace, and the old coffeepot of his youth had been replaced by two coffee systems, a one-cup brewer and a pricey espresso and latte maker. Different, but welcome because he could go for a hot cup of coffee right now, despite the summer heat.

"I will make your coffee." Isabo had seen him eyeing the machines. "Joe was just heading out on an errand."

Joe was one of the younger hands on the Double S. Trey had met him earlier that year when he'd come home to visit and assess his father's deteriorating condition.

"I had him take your things over to the cabin and told him to handle them with utmost care," she continued. "You go sit and talk with your father. He is so happy to see you!"

No mention of how Sam had issued Trey an ultimatum years ago, to either stay on the ranch and help the Double S become an industry standard in beef production, or pursue a doomed music career like his biological mother and father had done.

His parents' choices had resulted in an epic fail. Had Sam been solely worried about that? Thinking Trey would follow suit? Or had he just gotten mad because Sam Stafford liked to be the head cowboy in charge, all day, every day?

Trey had left the ranch, determined to show what could be done in Music City if you lived a good life.

He didn't leave the Double S to pursue music to prove something to Sam, like most thought. He'd needed to prove it to his deceased parents. They'd succumbed to the fast-and-furious drug culture that dogged a broad corner of the music community, then overdosed on laced heroin when he was three years old. He'd left the ranch, loving God and music, intent on making the right choices, just to show it could be done.

And then life managed to prove you wrong, and in the worst possible way.

"You look good, Trey." His father's approval interrupted the old dark thoughts. "Real good."

"I had a few days on horseback as I wrapped things up at my place. Nothing like a good saddle and tight fencing to right things in your head. It's far enough from Music City that I can unwind. Be myself. And then I can get back to Nashville in a few hours' time as needed."

"Why live so far north, Trey?" Sam had never seen his spread along the Virginia border of the beautiful southern state. "Why didn't you buy a place closer to Nashville?"

Should he tell Sam the truth? That he picked the historic ranch in Southern Appalachia because it was the closest thing he could find to this? His home with Sam, here in the rich greens of the sloping Kittitas Valley. "I needed hills." He accepted coffee from Isabo with a smile of thanks, then set it down. "I discovered I'm not much good with flat land."

"Me either." Sam gripped the table's edge so hard that his knuckles paled. "This operation, Trey . . ."

"The living donor surgery that could save your life?"

"That's the one." Sam had never beat around the bush in his life, and Trey liked that he didn't start now. "It might save me. It could kill you. We can't do it."

Shock broadsided Trey because if there was one thing Sam Stafford had never done, it was to put others first.

Isabo brought more coffee to the table. She stood there, silent and strong, a formidable force without saying a word, and Trey was in

32

for another surprise when Sam looked her way, humbled.

The standoff tempted him to run outside and look for signs of approaching Armageddon because Sam Stafford wasn't the least bit humble, ever. Truth to tell, he had to be one of the most egotistically selfish creatures God had ever put on this planet.

Isabo gripped the glass carafe and lifted her chin. "I believe when we profess our trust in God, in his goodness and timing, we should then try to live our lives embracing that belief. Or we can be faithful in word only, not in deed. It is, of course, our choice. More coffee, Sam?"

Sam watched as she poured, as if pouring coffee held him riveted. "If I'd been one of those righteous fathers all along, Isabo, I might see it your way. I wasn't, and putting this off on a young man with his whole life ahead of him doesn't sit right. A fact you know."

That meant they'd talked about this, another frank curiosity, because no one would accuse Sam of being the sharing-confidences type. Had Isabo changed that?

Sam answered as if he'd heard the silent question. "The Castiglione women have a way of prying my business out of me." He lifted his mug and sounded gruff, but the look he sent Isabo wasn't the least bit gruff. It was appreciative. Almost kind.

Trey was pretty sure that falling into that muck-filled creek might have opened a portal that thrust him into a parallel universe, because this wasn't the hard-edged father that raised three boys with a series of housekeepers and little attention.

This Sam Stafford could almost be considered lovable, and that meant he was, most likely, a pod person and the real Sam Stafford had been whisked away.

"We'll talk more of this," Sam told him, with a pointed look at Isabo. "Because there's a great deal to consider, but right now, I need you to do me a favor. If you don't mind, and if you have time."

Trey didn't mention that the old Sam would have just issued orders, because he was really enjoying the gentler motif of this new-and-improved version. "If I can, I will. You know that, Dad."

"Always willing." Sam stared at him, then reached out and put his hand over Trey's in a move so sweet and kind, Trey almost choked up. "I thought that was a downfall once. I was wrong and stupid. It's not a downfall at all, Trey." He looked Trey right in the eyes, and for the life of him, Trey couldn't look away. "It's a strength, and I'm glad you had sense enough to see it when I didn't."

This was getting deep, and Trey was bordering uncomfortable when Sam moved his hand and took another slug of coffee. "This woman next door."

"Lucy Carlton."

"Yes." Sam's frown lines went deeper. "She's had some tough times, and part of that's her bad judgment and part of it's my fault, and there's no doubt I should have gotten around to helping her sooner than this. The liver thing got worse quicker than I thought it would. But with you here now, we can afford to give her the help she needs."

"I don't understand. You've got plenty of money, Dad."

"Money's only the beginning," Sam explained. "She's a widow with kids, trying to make a go of a place without much hope in sight. I owe her and that farm some restitution, and I don't mean just moneywise, but good old-fashioned effort.

"This accident today is the kind of thing that can put a good person like her over the edge, so if you wouldn't mind helping out over there, I'd be much obliged. I want her place taken care of, just in case I'm not here to do it. We've got plenty of people to cover the Double S with Murt back, the summer help on hand, and Colt riding herd."

Sam's request made Trey swallow hard.

With or without the liver transplant, Sam might not be around long enough to fix things with his neighbor. His expression said this was important to him, which made it important to Trey. "You can't just hire stuff done?"

"Some, maybe, but not all. She's too mad for that. She'd run 'em off."

"What makes you think she won't do the same with me?" The thought almost made him smile, because he was pretty sure she would. She'd made it clear he wasn't welcome next door.

"It's like Isabo said." Sam saluted Angelina's mother with his mug. "There's a light about you. Folks are drawn to it. I think it's the perfect solution."

It was about as imperfect a solution as there could be, but Trey had come back to Central Washington for two reasons: his father's declining health and to see if returning to the Double S would fill the emptiness inside.

Therapy had taught him that sometimes you have to go back to move forward. Prayer had showed him the path back began at his father's side, to make peace. Nothing had forewarned him that he'd be starting the journey by dealing with an antagonistic, beautiful neighbor whose life he'd just messed over to a major degree.

God works in ways mysterious.

He paraphrased Cowper's words of wisdom, but was God the puzzle or did the mystery lay in human response?

Trey was pretty sure it worked both ways. He'd come back to Gray's Glen to ease his father's way, whichever path that took. And if Sam asked him to help the woman next door, that's what Trey would do. "I'll head right over and see what's up. I've got to settle with her for the wrecked van and flowers."

"Her flowers were in the van?"

Isabo's anxious tone drove realization further. The flowers were obviously of extreme importance to the Carlton woman, and he'd managed to ruin each and every one of them by missing that stop sign. "Yes." He muttered the word, wishing he could avoid the admission.

Gravity deepened Isabo's expression. She grimaced. "So late in the season for new growth, it is hard to recover such a loss and so many hours of toil."

"I'll make it up to her. I promise." He stood and lifted his hat. "On my way."

"Do you need my checkbook?"

"This one's on me," Trey told him and set a hand on his father's shoulder. "But when it comes to fixing her farm? I'll take your money then. Happily."

He gave Sam's shoulder a light squeeze and waved to Isabo as he headed out the door.

"You have not eaten," she admonished him. She tapped the bright cauldron of simmering beef.

"When I get back," he promised her. "I don't want to keep the neighbor waiting any longer than I already have. It sounds like she's got a lot on her plate already. Wrecking her wheels and her livelihood just made a bad situation worse."

Isabo followed and pressed a basket of warm rolls into his hands. Then she added two quarts of fresh green beans, long and slim. "Take these, and eat a couple of my rolls on the way. Grouchy, hungry men are no pleasure to be around."

He hugged her with his free arm. He wasn't even sure why; he barely knew her from his whirlwind visits in the spring, but he felt like hugging her, so he did. "Thank you, Isabo."

"Go with God, Trey Stafford."

The name sounded funny, like old-funny. In Nashville, everyone called him Trey Walker, his original name, before Sam adopted him, but hearing Isabo use his real name . . .

Hearing it felt good, and that surprised him most of all.

ಬಿಲ

Ruined.

Lucy stared at the small greenhouse that had been lush with promise the night before. Hanging baskets styled with upscale "Proven Winner" combinations had hung from ceiling hooks above boxed planters filled with spillers, chillers, and thrillers. They'd been the kind of displays she loved to create and should have sold well at market. Beside them had been simpler trays of brightly toned marigolds, petunias, and wax begonias.

She'd taken a chance, again. She'd used some of her tax return money to pay bills, and then she'd taken a leap of faith to expand her growing flower-and-plant enterprise into something bigger and bolder. Today's market would have been a litmus test of possibilities. Would local folks lay down the necessary funds for pricier displays? And would they love her work?

Once again, life and time combined to trip things up. If she'd left when she should have, ten minutes earlier, she'd be on the outskirts of Ellensburg right now, making money for her family.

She stared at the half-empty greenhouse, second-guessing herself, a common occurrence these days.

"Mommy, are you so sad?" Three-year-old Belle slipped her tiny hand into Lucy's and held on tight, then laid her head against Lucy's arm. The spill of sun-soaked curls against Lucy's tanned skin was the best reminder.

This was why she did it, why she did everything. Belle and her brothers, two strong, sturdy, slightly boneheaded boys, always tussling. Two boys with too much time on their hands, and not enough cash flow to get them into things boys love—baseball, basketball, riding, and roping.

And then there was Ashley, Lucy's fourteen-year-old sister-in-law, a troubled teen with a drunken, self-absorbed mother and little promise in her future.

Lucy grimaced, wondering what she'd gotten

herself into by opening her home and her heart to Chase's half sister. Would taking the fourteen-year-old in be good for the kids? Good for Ashley? And would Lucy be able to handle it all without murdering someone?

"I can help you with the fwowers, Mommy." Belle squeezed Lucy's arm just enough to show she cared. "I'm a reawwy good waterer."

"You are, darling, but Mommy's not going to water right now. I'm afraid I might lash out irrationally on the remaining plants and that would just add to the list of unsmart moves on my permanent record."

"Huh?" Belle hiked up tiny elfin eyebrows, wondering what on earth her mother had just said.

Lucy hugged her. "Later, okay?"

"Okay."

Cade dashed out of the house just then, yelling his head off. He raced for the first barn.

Cody banged out the dented screen door just as quickly, but with little chance of catching his fast-moving big brother. That didn't stop him from trying. Screaming, crying, and waving his fist, he ran across the dry stone drive, and if he'd had a weapon at hand, Lucy figured he'd be brandishing it now as he promised his big brother's demise.

They didn't get along.

They'd never gotten along.

Was that normal?

It couldn't be, Lucy thought as she hurried to the barn. And yet it was certainly normal enough around their place. She threw the door open wide and barged into the barn.

She'd been mistaken. Cody did catch his brother. He'd caught up with him because Cade had ducked into a stall, but Cade wasn't exactly quiet enough to be good at hiding. Cody had found him and tackled into him.

She pulled one off the other in the dark barn and wasn't even sure who was who initially. But when the sticky feel of blood slicked her hands, she needed light, and right quick. She hauled them both out of the barn, praying no one had managed to impale a vital organ, and when she got into the drive, she felt faint, but single moms don't get to feel faint. She pulled off Cade's shirt, pressed it to the wound on his head, and called Ashley's name.

It seemed like forever before Ashley strolled out of the house, looking bored and annoyed. "What?" Ashley raised the upscale phone her mother had gotten her months ago in a foolish attempt to buy the girl's good behavior. It hadn't worked then and the girl didn't deserve to have the phone now, but that was drama for another day. "I was playing a game."

"You've got to watch these two." Lucy nodded to Cody and Belle. "Cade's cut. I've got to get him to the emergency clinic."

Ashley looked blank, then disparaging. "And

how exactly are you going to do that? On the broken tractor?"

Realization smacked Lucy.

She had no vehicle and her son needed help. She reached for Ashley's phone. "We'll have to call for an ambulance then."

"An ambulance? For real?" The teenager stared at her as if she had a right to question Lucy's judgment, the same expression Chase had used often. "How bad can it be? Throw a bandage on it and let him suffer. He's a brat; he probably deserved it."

"We'll argue that when he's not bleeding out on the stones," Lucy told her. "Make the call or give me the phone."

Ashley huffed and lifted the phone just as the crunch of tires on stone came their way. Trey Stafford's big, shiny SUV rolled up the drive. He parked it, hopped out, and seemed to get a handle on the situation pretty quick for a spoiled Stafford. Of course, the blood-soaked tee might have been a giveaway. His look took in her, the shirt, the kids, and the insolent teen. He hooked his thumb toward the SUV. "Need a lift, ma'am?"

"Thanks to you, yes."

Trey backpedaled and opened the passenger door.

What choice did she have?

None, and that's pretty much what her life had come down to these last few years. Few choices and fewer options. She kept the shirt pressed against Cade's head and helped him into the seat, then climbed in after him.

"You two." Trey squatted low, facing Cody and Belle. "Wanna come?"

Cody and Belle stared at him, then their mother, sitting high in the front seat.

"Ashley can watch them, can't you, Ash?"

"Why should now be any different?" Sullen, with one hip cocked, Ashley looked unhappy and uninvested in the kids' well-being, and Lucy was sorely tempted to send Cade on with Trey and stay home with the younger two. At least that way they'd be watched and cared for.

"I think riding in a big muscle car with a cow-boy sounds way better than staying home with a grumpy teenager, doesn't it?" Trey tipped his hat a little and grinned at the two younger kids. Belle dimpled, instantly charmed. "Do you have boosters?"

"There are two on the porch," Lucy called.

"Got 'em." Trey jogged to the porch, past a scowling Ashley, but then paused on his way back. He said something to her, then hurried back to the car to put the boosters in place. He lifted Belle up and gave Cody a hand in. He made sure their seat belts were snug around the seats, closed the door, and jogged around the hood of the car. He climbed in, tugged his belt into place, and made a full one-eighty in quick time to get the SUV back out onto the road. "Where we headed?"

"The medical clinic in Ellensburg."

He glanced her way as he signaled a turn. "That's forty minutes away."

She knew that. Sure, it would be easier and quicker to go to Quick Care. Or in a glorious moment, she could imagine being able to go to a private practice, but the clinic had been good to her. The drive was tough, especially in bad weather or emergencies. In Central Washington, and with three kids, that was at least fifty percent of the time. "It's what the budget allows."

He tapped the steering wheel with his left hand, then swung the car around on Columbia and made the turn toward Quick Care. "My treat because if I hadn't gone through that stop sign, this probably wouldn't have happened."

"Cody's six and Cade is eight. You had two brothers." She shot him a dubious look. "I have to think stitches were a given."

He rubbed the back of his head and winced, but smiled at the same time, and darn, if he didn't look adorable when he did it. "Three distinct tracks on the back of my head; the reason I don't do buzz cuts. Colt tells me they're a badge of honor, but I'm partial to covering them up." He glanced into the back seat through the rearview mirror. "You guys doing okay back there?"

"I reawwy, reawwy wike riding up high." Belle

44

giggled and placed two little hands over her mouth. "Evwyfing is so big up here."

"World's a big place," Trey agreed, and when he smiled back at Belle, she giggled again, smitten by a guitar-pickin' cowboy, reason enough to lock her in her room from age thirteen on. "What's your name, darlin'?"

Belle held up three adorable fingers, and even Lucy had to smile. "Yes, you're three years old. Can you tell Mr. Stafford your name?"

"I'm Belle." She said it softly, with her hands tucked over her mouth, but somehow Trey caught it.

"It's a pleasure to meet you, Belle." He smiled through the mirror and touched the brim of his hat with one finger. "I'm Trey." He shifted his attention back to the road as he asked, "And who are your brothers?"

She pointed instantly, way more comfortable with this part of the conversation. "This is Cody and that's Cade. He's bweeding."

"I know." Trey's look of sympathy appeared sincere, but he spent a good share of his life on stage, so Lucy wasn't buying into it. She'd learned that schmoozing and flirting were intrinsic with musicians. Burned once, twice careful.

Which brought Lucy to another thought. "What did you say to Ashley?"

"I take it that Ashley is the teen that reeked of reefer?"

"She what?" Lucy turned his way in the seat. "Are you serious? And how would you even know that?"

"I've got groupies that think it's smart. It's not, and she was trying to cover it with that obnoxious smelling oil."

The patchouli oil Ashley loved. Could she be using the heavy-scented oil to mask smoking pot?

Of course she could, Lucy realized, because it wasn't all that difficult to get weed these days, and Ashley wouldn't be the first eighth grader caught with it.

And you were going to leave the kids with her all day, while you sold flowers. What kind of mother are you?

No, she wouldn't ask that question because then she'd have to answer it. She leaned forward to see Trey's face around Cade's head. "You're sure?"

The glance he shot her indicated he was quite sure.

"I'll send her packing. I thought it would help, having her come live with us. I thought I could make a difference to her, that maybe all she needed was a little love and a good example. She hasn't had much of that in her life." Was she talking more to herself or him?

He looked skeptical, but she wasn't after his opinion. In her experience, people with money shrugged off others' needs as nonessential. His father was a prime example, but she couldn't think about all that now, with Cade bleeding beside her.

Trey rolled up to the Quick Care parking lot and pointed to Cody and Belle in the back seat. "Can I take these two to Hammerstein's? I've got some things to grab there, and that would be more fun than hanging out in the waiting room, wouldn't it?"

"Can we see where they're building the new church?" Cody wriggled in his seat, excited. "And the big diggers?"

"Gotta love construction," Trey agreed. He met her son's eyes in the mirror and grinned. "If it's all right with your mother."

Lucy studied him. She'd been about to leave her three most precious gifts with a weed-smoking teenager all day because she didn't recognize the masking oil's purpose. Now she was considering sending two of them off with a virtual stranger who ran stop signs.

The fact that the stop sign had been obstructed put the vote in Trey's favor. "They'd like that much better, I'm sure."

"Give me your phone. I'll put my number in so you can call me when you're done."

She helped Cade down, trying to keep pressure on his head while he maneuvered. Her efforts resulted in more bleeding. She swallowed a sigh. "I don't have a phone. Cade and I will walk your way when he's done. Or just head back here in thirty minutes or so."

"No phone?"

She couldn't afford a phone, and she wasn't about to be on any government handout list to get one, so she shook her head.

"But the teen was holding a mighty pricey smartphone."

"A long story."

He looked like he was weighing her words, her answers, then nodded. He jotted his number on a small scrap of paper in the SUV and handed it over to her. "If you need me, use their phone to call me. And use this. Please." He handed her a credit card along with the slip of paper.

If you need me . . .

Oh, those words. To have someone sincerely offer help or compassion or most anything. It had been over a decade since Lucy Carlton had heard words like that, which made them dear and fairly unbelievable. "Thanks."

She kept her arm snugged around Cade, holding the shirt in place, and walked him into the office. They went through a quick triage, and when she guaranteed payment with Trey's card, the nurse took it, but not without a suspicious look. "If you need confirmation, here's his cell number." Lucy jotted it down on the medical form and passed it through the triage window.

"You just gave me Trey Walker's personal cell phone number." The woman looked at the number, then Lucy. "Oh, man, isn't that every woman's dream? Every woman with a pulse, that is."

It wasn't Lucy's dream. It wasn't even close to Lucy's dream. Her dream would embrace a solid income from the work of her hands, time with her children, surrounded by a beloved community. She'd spent too much time realizing the outcome of poor choices as a teen, then as a young adult. Her dream wasn't to rely on anyone other than herself and God again, ever.

She wouldn't trade her kids for anything. They were her lifeblood, her reason to praise God and embrace life.

But she wished she'd been smarter, more educated, and had waited longer for all those firsts teenagers find so enticing . . . and just maybe she'd have been better prepared to go through life raising three kids alone. Because if she was keeping score based on today's record? She was batting a big fat zero, and that had to change.

Three

Trey Walker Stafford was shopping with kids.

He'd never done such a thing before, but here he was, pulling into a municipal parking space up the road from Hammerstein's Mercantile with two cute kids. He wasn't sure what he'd do if they stopped being cute and started acting bratty, but he'd cross that bridge as needed. "Come here, Belle."

The little girl let him lift her. Cody scrambled out of his own seat and opened the other door. "Mind the road, Cody."

The kid turned and looked at him, suspicious. "It's okay for me to get out?"

"Best way I know of getting into the store is to get out of the car."

"Sweet!" The boy shoved the heavy door, hopped out, and shut the door, then ran to the sidewalk. "Mom always makes me wait, like I'm a baby. I'm not a baby. She is." He pointed a finger and a derisive look at his little sister and started to move ahead.

"Hold it."

The boy turned, surprised.

Trey bent low. "Belle's not a baby."

The kid rolled his eyes, as if he'd heard this all before.

"She's a little girl, and she needs big people to love her and protect her, just like you did when you were three."

"I was brave about everything when I was three," Cody bragged. He scowled at Belle. "She's afraid of water, so we can't ever go swimmin', and Mom makes us watch her like all the time."

"Well, she's three." Trey tipped a smile right into Belle's blue eyes and she grinned back, patted his cheek, and won his heart in the space of mere seconds. "You're twice as old, dude. Cut her some slack, okay?"

"I'm twice as old?" Cody eyed him, then Belle, as if the concept intrigued him. "Like three plus three?"

"Exactly like that."

He looked impressed and less combative. Score one for the country crooner.

He let Cody lead the way up the broad stairs, and when they crossed the wide, Western-style porch, Cody pushed open the door. It swung quickly, and Trey had to do a one-handed grab to keep it from smacking into a freestanding rack, but he managed.

"Trey." 'Ham' Hammerstein waved as soon as he spotted him. He plodded around the seasonal counter to pump Trey's free hand. "It's good to have you back here, young man. You've done us nothing but proud in Nashville."

Kind words, and Trey appreciated every one.

Media speculation had run roughshod over him when he'd lost his wife to an overdose several years before. Rumors of a crazy, swinging lifestyle abounded.

He'd never done crazy, he'd never done drugs, and he'd worked night and day to save Cathy from herself, to no avail.

Was he purely innocent?

No. He could have done more, seen more, been home more.

Or maybe he'd chosen a woman who'd been in drug rehab and seemed to be doing well to prove to his late parents it could be done. If so, it was the ultimate failure because her death had proved them all wrong.

"You've brought some friends along."

"Cody and Belle."

"They're regular visitors," Ham said, smiling. "And they know where the cookie bin is."

"Cookie bin?"

"Gretchen started it a few years back, and it's a big hit with the kids, so long as parents aren't all fired-up worried about little hands in the bin. I set a pair of tongs there to keep the county health guy happy, but no one uses 'em."

He set Belle down. She followed Cody to the bin, and when Cody had pulled out his cookie, he sent a quick glance over his shoulder and deliberately closed the bin.

Trey cleared his throat, nice and loud.

The kid looked up, sighed, opened the bin, and stepped back.

"The polite thing to do would be to offer yours to her, or let her go first. Cowboy up, kid."

"You think I could be a cowboy?" The boy's eyes rounded like saucers. He eyed Trey's hat. "Like, for real?"

"Why not?"

"Well, I don't have a horse." Cody waited until Belle had selected a cookie, then closed the bin. "Or a hat or a saddle or anything."

Trey stooped low. "Bein' a cowboy isn't about what you're wearin' or ridin', my friend."

"It's not?" Cody stared at him, puzzled.

"No sir." Trey shook his head and kept his face serious. "It's about what's up here." He tapped the side of his head. "And here." He clapped his hand over his heart. "The rest is just window dressin', but a true cowboy comes from inside you, in everything you say and do. Being strong, but being nice. Giving directions, but following directions too."

"Like cooperating?" Cody asked. "We learned about that in school."

"Exactly like that."

"But then do I get a hat, maybe?" He eyed Trey's hat and the broad Western display in Ham's front window. "So everyone will know I'm bein' a cowboy?"

"Maybe then."

"I didn't know." The kid glanced around as if he'd just discovered an ultimate truism.

"And now you do. Ham, I need to grab some groceries pretty quick, and I could use a hand."

Ham brought him a cart. Trey picked up Belle and settled her into the seat. "Cody, I'm not sure what you guys like, so I need your help too, okay?"

"Okay!" He started down the first aisle in the grocery section. "We like cereal a lot."

Trey let him pick out four boxes.

"Milk, bread, rolls, meat, fruits, vegetables," Ham muttered as he walked with them. "Otherwise you're likely to get stuck in the candy aisle."

At that moment, Cody spotted the candy aisle. When his eyes lit up, Trey knew the truth in Ham's warning. "Appreciate the tip. Hey, Gretchen."

"Lookee here, it's Gray's Glen's finest, come home to do some shopping." She stepped out from behind the deli counter and gave him a hug. "Gosh, it's good to see you, Trey. It's been a long time."

"Sure has." He jutted his chin toward the deli counter behind her. "Can you hook me up with some cold cuts and cheese?"

"Yes, and how much?"

"I have no idea." He stared at the kids, made a face, and then turned to Ham, pretending not to hear the buzz of conversation as other shoppers noticed him in the store. "What do you think, Ham? Five people, three of them kids?"

"Ham, turkey, roast beef, Swiss and American cheese, a pound of each, sliced on the thin side, Gretchen."

"I'm on it."

"And maybe a couple of pounds, you know, one of those bigger containers"—Trey made his hands into a quart-like size—"of that Italian salad there."

"I'll do it right up and have it ready before you're done."

"Mighty grateful, Gretch."

She grinned when he used her high school nickname. "Glad to help, cowboy."

The murmurs grew louder. People pretended to come around corners as if shopping, but wanting to see him. Ham hung out by his side, almost protective, but by the time the cart was mostly full, Trey read the signs, and he didn't want two little kids unnerved if folks pushed in. He approached a group of huddled women and smiled.

"It *is* you, isn't it?" exclaimed one, and she slapped her hand to her chest. "I couldn't rightly believe it, and we kept looking at you—"

"Did you, now?" he teased, pretending he hadn't noticed, as the second band of customers came in from the other side. "You know I grew up here. Gray's Glen is my hometown."

Some nodded. Some shook their heads.

"My dad is sick. He needs help."

Sympathy marked every single face, including

ones who might not have any reason to like Sam Stafford.

"So I'm in town for at least the summer, helping out."

"Are these your kids?" asked one woman. "Because I didn't think you had kids with Cathy."

His heart bit tight.

She didn't mean to be careless, he knew that, but his life with his country singer wife was like an old, open wound. "My neighbors." He palmed Belle's head and winked at Cody. "Just thought they might like a little shopping trip while we were out and about."

"Oh, that's nice."

"You're just like your music!"

"What a kind thing to do!"

Trey was pretty sure they were going to emerge unscathed when Cody blurted, "Well, my mom is at the doctor with Cade because he's a jerk, and he's always taking my stuff, and I got really, really mad, and he hit his head and now he's bleeding on everything."

Leave it to a kid to shed the dark cloak of honesty on a happy moment.

"Oh my," spouted one woman, distressed.

"You hurt your brother? That's not nice." Disapproval tightened another woman's tone.

"Did you call the sheriff?" asked one stylish and upscale young mother, as if tussling boys should automatically be placed in juvie. If that was the case, half the county would be locked up until they got a clue around age nineteen. Or older.

"The lady sheriff is our friend," Cody assured her, making it sound like they drew special favors from the law. "She brings her little boy over to play sometimes. He's little like my sister, and she doesn't arrest anybody."

"Your sister?" asked one woman.

"The sheriff," Trey assured her, wondering how to backtrack through this now convoluted mess of too much information. "Although I have heard of the occasional arrest, as needed, and those of you with kids know how it is. Boys will be boys. I've got a few brotherly battle scars to show for it, myself."

"Most of which he deserved, and most of which came from Colt, not me." His brother Nick's voice lightened the moment and took charge. To Trey, Nick's presence alone felt like an exit door yanked open on an escape route. "I was the nice big brother." Trey didn't know where Nick came from or how he happened to show up at just the right time, but he was mighty glad he did.

Nick looked down at Cody. "You helpin' Trey shop?"

"He's teachin' me to be a cowboy."

"Is he?" Nick sent a grin indicating Trey might need some reschooling, but he kept quiet. "We ready to check out?"

"Milk, eggs, and butter." Ham looked at Nick, and Nick got the message.

"I'll grab those with Cody while Trey gets everything else tallied up."

"Sounds good." Ham led Trey and Belle over to the seasonal register and called for a bag boy to help out. He angled a subtle look to the shoppers they'd just left. "Love ya or lynch ya, I figured it was time to finish up and avoid the grocery checkout lines."

"It'll take time for folks to get used to seeing me around again." But Trey frowned as he said it. "I guess I just figured hometown was hometown."

"Most likely will be," Ham told him. He nodded thanks to Gretchen when she delivered the bag of cold cuts and cheese. "It's been awhile, and a lot went down with the springtime fire and all. Folks are movin' forward, and your daddy's change of heart is helping that happen. But change takes time."

Ham was correct. Change *would* take time. Sam Stafford had used money and power to undercut some locals and had steamrolled others in the past. Resentment built with time. For a long while, Sam and his money had helped sculpt unpopular decisions.

A spring fire had destroyed the original Grace of God Community Church and several other structures a few months back. The fire and Sam's illness had inspired the older Stafford to be a better person. Now the shell of a beautiful log cabin church stood in its place, the results of Stafford money and community effort. But could they effect change quickly enough to have it matter? And would Sam be alive to see it happen?

Two big questions without an answer.

"Colt's plans for helping rebuild have won a lot of support, but there's some who can't get beyond what your father did in the past."

Trey understood being mired in the past too well. He clamped his back teeth together but kept his face calm. "Forgiveness doesn't come easy."

"And sometimes forgiving ourselves takes longest of all."

Nick's words jerked Trey's head around.

His brother didn't look at him. He simply set the dairy products on the counter and let Ham ring them up. And when Trey proffered his debit card to Ham, Nick gave him a brotherly nudge, one that said too much.

"I've never seen so much food, like ever!" Cody's excitement made Trey wonder if he'd gone overboard, but a family of five would go through a lot of food, wouldn't they? But then if money was tight, overflowing grocery carts might not be the norm.

"Well, I figured it's important to grab stuff while we're in town because your mom's van is broken."

"And all her fwowers." Belle lifted tragic eyes

to his. "She was cwyin' because she missed her fwowers so much."

The thought of causing the young widow strife twisted Trey's heart. One thoughtless moment, one unnoticed sign, and he'd wiped out a significant chance for income. On the plus side, no one was hurt, and he'd called out the pot-smoking teen, so maybe some good would come out of this day after all.

Nick helped him load the groceries and the kids while Trey made use of the ATM, then clapped him on the back. And then he did something the brothers almost never did, something that Elsa, Nick's psychologist fiancée, must have taught him.

Nick hugged him, and Trey didn't know how much he needed that hug until he got it.

"See you at home."

"Will do."

Just that, no long-winded speeches to drag things out, just a hug. And that meant everything.

ຕა

Lucy and Cade had just made the turn toward Hammerstein's when Trey's SUV pulled up. He jumped out, rounded the hood quickly, and opened the door for them, probably being nice while hoping she wouldn't sue him for the earlier accident.

You didn't used to be so cynical. It's a really unattractive trait, her conscience scolded. *Maybe he's just being kind.*

And maybe Cinderella really did cram her foot into that stupid glass slipper.

Nope, Lucy believed in a great many things, but the term "straight-shooting man" had become an oxymoron years before.

"How's he doing?" Trey didn't just help her up into the seat and shut the door. He leaned in, concerned, as if Cade's fate mattered to him, and that tiny bit of interest seemed to stir Cade's emotions. "Stitches or glue?"

"Stitches." Cade peered up at him. "They asked Mom if I was a quiet kind of kid. Quiet kids can have glue. Mom said we better use thread."

Trey laughed, then held his hand up for a high five. The move seemed to deepen Cade's interest. "I hear ya. Better safe than sorry. And you were able to use my card all right?" He shifted his attention back to her, and for a moment, she wished he could just stand there, looking at her like that, for the rest of her life.

Magnetism.

This man had a lock on charisma and exuded magnetism, a dangerous combo. She'd heard that in his music and seen it in his country videos. But those were nothing compared to the real deal, up close and personal like he was now.

She clamped down her errant heart, put a lock on the sweetness of an adrenaline buzz, and answered calmly. "I was able to use it. Thank you. I did have to give her your cell phone number in case they needed assurance, and that made her day. But then she shredded it. And sighed because she said the last thing she wanted to do was shred Trey Walker's personal cell number."

He laughed and gave her a teasing look, the kind that seemed easy and sincere, like they were old friends or new sweethearts.

They were neither, but she couldn't deny the spark of interest on her side. She could, however, control it, because she wasn't one of his teenage groupies, or even a more mature one.

She'd lived a lot of life already. She might be twenty-six by the calendar, but experientially she'd packed on an extra decade. Or maybe it just felt that way.

"I'm glad there wasn't a problem, Mrs. Carlton."

"Lucy."

He was starting to back away from the door when she offered her first name for his use. He paused, made eye contact, and nodded, serious and simple. "I'm obliged, Ms. Lucy." His Western twang drawled out the *Miz Lucy,* and he grinned at her. He touched his hat once more, a gentleman's salute. "And I'm Trey."

She figured her heart started beating again about the time they made the turn into her drive. Ashley was on the porch, zoned out on music and maybe weed, but Lucy would handle that once Trey left.

He pulled in, made a quick turn, and backed the

SUV up to the porch steps. Ashley looked up, surprised.

The hatch went up and Ashley's eyes went wide as Cody raced out of the car and hurried to the back. "I wanna help bring things in!"

"Me too!" Belle worked her latches a little more slowly, but when she was done, she hopped down and scrambled out of the SUV. "I'm big enough."

"I don't understand." Lucy watched them grab some bags. Once Cade had climbed down, she shut the door and circled the car to Trey's side. "What did you do?"

"Just some shopping. I figured you wouldn't have a car for a day or two, and if you were down on supplies, you had no way to get them."

"I'm not a charity case." She stared at him, wanting him to know she understood how things worked. Nothing came free, and no one did something for another person without some kind of string attached. She knew the truth in that. "Things are tight here, but we manage without handouts. Yours or anyone else's."

He considered her words but didn't seem the least bit bothered by them. "Not a handout, just a neighborly gesture since I messed up your day, your van, and all of your hard work. This is nothing more than a stopgap to make up for my carelessness. Not a bit of charity about it."

"I don't need your help."

Now he winced, and he tipped his hat back,

folded his arms, and looked down at her without dropping his chin. "Well, now, that's another conversation, Ms. Lucy."

"Not Miss Lucy. Just Lucy. And please, don't try your country-lovin' stage tricks on me. I'm immune."

"Good to know." He accepted that simply, but Lucy was pretty sure she saw a glimmer of amusement in his eyes before he shut it down. "In any case, it seems my daddy has a debt to settle with you."

"With me and so many others," she muttered, aggravated. "Kids, stop unloading those things right now. I'm sure they can use all of this stuff over at the Double S. They feed a crowd every day."

"Don't you even think of getting me in trouble with Isabo," he warned, as if he was actually afraid of Angelina's mother. "She's running that kitchen now, and anyone who knows anything about running a ranch knows the first rules of the day are to love God the Father Almighty and keep the cook happy."

She tapped her toe, tempted to possibly kick him with it or just keep tapping.

She kept tapping and folded her arms as the kids continued to unload the bags. Squeals of excitement indicated he'd made some good choices.

He directed his attention toward the noise.

"Ham and Cody helped me out. I figured if we go car shopping tomorrow after church—"

"Dealerships aren't open on Sunday," she argued.

He held up his cell phone. "Found one in Wenatchee that we can get to after services tomorrow. I promised Dad I'd go to church with the family, but they don't open till noon so that works out all right. And if you don't see something you like there, then we'll check further on Monday. In the interim, Ange is on her way over here to pick me up. I'm leaving my Jeep so you've got wheels until you've got your own. We've got plenty of vehicles at the ranch, and this one's an automatic, not a stick shift like Nick's and Colt's."

"I can drive a stick." If he raised one eyebrow of doubt or surprise, she might kick him yet.

"Then it wouldn't have mattered which car we left you. I didn't know." He shrugged and handed her the keys and a slim envelope from the ATM. "Tank's full. We can either ride together to the dealership or separate. Your choice. And the envelope is to cover the flower loss. I expect today's sales would have been a big help, so use this as needed. If it doesn't seem like enough, just let me know."

It felt wrong to take the money.

This would be so much easier if it was an impersonal check from an insurance company. Then she'd have no qualms.

But to have this man—this famous country singer/television star personality—slip her cash felt wrong, even though it made perfect sense.

"Ange also said the kids could hang out at the ranch tomorrow if that helps. Rye Bennett's brother and sister are coming over to do some riding, and Colt would be happy to give the kids a chance up top. Plenty of grown-ups around tomorrow to keep an eye out. And to cook food. It might give your teen something to keep her head and hands busy."

Rye Bennett was the local sheriff and Angelina's boss. He'd left a job with the Chicago Police Department to come back to Gray's Glen when his mother lost her battle with cancer. Now he was raising his younger brother, Brendan, and sister, Jenna, a nice pair of kids who'd known grief first-hand.

She should rebuke Trey's offer. She should demand the insurance card and let the two companies wrangle things out, waiting days or even weeks to get a car.

"Pride goeth before the fall."

She understood the words well. She'd let pride trip her up too many times. Hers. Chase's. In such a hurry to grow up, they never quite did until there was absolutely no other choice. "You sure they wouldn't mind having the kids around?"

He shook his head as Angelina's SUV crunched gravel behind them. "Positive."

"Then, yes, if you wouldn't mind. Getting a replacement would take a load off my mind."

"Mine too." He waved to Ange, then turned back quickly. "And about my father . . ."

Oh, she knew his father, all right. A lying, scheming, rich conniver who thought nothing of the consequences of his actions, as long as he gained leverage. She held her ground and the grudge that went along with it. "Yes?"

"He wants to make restitution, but he's not physically capable of doing it, so he's assigned me the task."

"The task?" She returned Angelina's wave, then redirected her attention to Trey. "What task?"

"To get things in order. To help out over here. I guess he got in your way, years back?"

"Not mine, but the Wheelers, which made it mine when we bought the place."

"Well, Ms. Lucy—"

"I told you before. It's Lucy, plain and simple."

"Well, Lucy, plain and simple . . ." He smiled, teasing her, and she wished it wasn't attractive and cute and nice and all those things that cost so dearly in the end. "The Double S has things covered for the next few weeks. I'm on hiatus for the summer, and I've been assigned to you."

"To me, as in?"

"Trey Stafford, fixer upper."

This was too weird. Way too weird. "No."

He climbed into the passenger seat of the ranch

SUV and looked at her, skeptical. "I expect you know my father."

Oh, she did, all right. And it sliced the grace of her spirit to think anything nice about the man.

"There's no refusing Sam Stafford, Lucy, and at this stage of the game, with him being so sick, I wouldn't if I could. If fixing old wrongs over here helps him face these days with a less troubled heart, then that's what I aim to do. I won't get in your way. I promise."

He was already in her way.

He was already a nuisance, a bother, and a temptation.

But his words struck the softer part of her heart, which had long since become the narrower portion.

She'd watched her mother fight and lose her battle with cancer, and she'd seen her work to make amends while healthy enough to do it. And her mother was a kind, soft-spoken woman, who hadn't hurt a soul, ever. Still, she'd tried to strengthen family ties and smooth old regrets, hers and others.

She'd gone home to God gently, probably the same way she'd entered the world.

Sam Stafford didn't deserve to go home gently, or maybe at all, but that wasn't for her to say. That was between him and the Lord God Almighty, maker of heaven and earth. And if Sam was extending an olive branch and she refused it, then the error was hers to own.

Pride again. Her downfall.

She breathed deep and looked off toward the northern hills, rising bluff by green bluff to the mountains beyond. "You won't get in the way?"

"Cross my heart."

She could do this if for no other reason than Sam Stafford owed this little farm a neighbor's respect and a swindler's payback. He'd leased water rights years back, leaving the Wheeler Tree Farm dry as toast during the worst of summer heat. Tree loss was nothing that could be regained in a year or two. It was a decade-long endeavor, and Sam knew that. "All right. We'll talk tomorrow."

"After church."

She almost smiled.

The best music men she knew, or had known, could sing about church. She'd witnessed it firsthand. She'd sung lead next to some of them. They sang about faith and love and God. Her children's father had a voice for gospel music as much as he had for eighties rock, but he hadn't stepped foot in a church or uttered a vestige of prayer for a decade before he died.

He'd talked the talk but could never walk the walk, and she'd found his music-loving friends to be very much the same. So Trey Walker Stafford could take his church talk and bottle it. Either way?

She wasn't buying into it.

Four

"You're home." Colt released his horse into the near paddock, closed the gate, and crossed the graveled barnyard as Yesterday's News trotted off. He grabbed Trey's hand, then thumped him on the back. A big grin split Colt's face, quite different from the taciturn man his brother had been for so many years.

"I'm here." Trey didn't call it home. He had his ranch down south, rolling acres of creek-fed grass, Black Angus cattle, and horses. He'd had the sprawling cabin built big enough to hold the laughter of children and the odd dog or two in an urge to get things right, really right, for once in his life.

They'd had no children. Cathy died, and he wasn't at the ranch long enough to call it home or keep a dog happy, so it had become just another place to hang his hat between gigs.

"Trey, you've got to be starved." Angelina grabbed his arm and drew him forward, toward the kitchen. "Mami said you didn't take time to eat and you've been gone for hours. What kept you?"

He was about to answer when Cheyenne's voice hailed him from the lower paddock.

"Uncle Trey! Uncle Trey! Watch me!" Nick's

oldest daughter waved, and when old Murt scolded her to quiet down from up top a horse, she cringed and nodded. Trey staved off Angelina with his other hand. "I've got to see her run through her paces. Food'll wait. She sounds excited."

"She is." Angelina kept moving toward the house. "You go. I'll make you a sandwich with that beef barbecue."

His stomach rumbled at the thought. He was hungry, for certain, in so many ways. Some of that hunger could be helped with Isabo's cooking. But there was another hunger. One that wasn't so easily assuaged.

Ange aimed for the kitchen.

Colt walked him down to the lower paddock. Trey had learned a lot in this paddock, and from the same old-timer leading Cheyenne around now. "Lookin' good, Murt."

"I miss you, boy." Murt kept his eyes on Cheyenne, but Trey felt the truth in the words. " 'Bout time you came back to hang out awhile."

"Feelin's the same."

"Well, good. Easy now, Chey, go light on those reins, let her feel you relaxed, but in charge. There you go."

"I love this." Nine-year-old Cheyenne beamed at Trey from astride the gray mare. "I feel like I'm on top of the world up here."

"I know that feeling well."

"Uncle Trey!" Dakota, Cheyenne's seven-year-old sister, raced his way. "You came home!" She leaped into his arms, a bundle of frenetic and sincere energy. "I am so glad to see you! There's so much going on! Did you know my dad is going to get married?"

"I heard a rumor to that effect," Trey told her. "Is it true?"

Dakota's bright eyes went wide. "It is *very* true, and Elsa likes to do so many weird things with us, like go into the woods and find frogs, and paint things and make messes, and she taught me how to sit real still while puppies get born!"

"No way."

"Yes way!"

Her sheer delight blessed him in a way he'd forgotten. The joy in her voice, the excitement in her eyes, much more obvious than when he'd been here a few months before.

Colt shoulder-nudged him. "Quite a difference, right?"

"Like night and day."

Nick beelined across the grass, handed Trey a thick sandwich, and took a protesting Dakota from his arms. "Let him eat, kid. He's too skinny. We're going to fatten him up, get him properly prepped presurgery."

"What?" Dakota stared at her father, perplexed.

"Nick." Angelina scolded him with the single word. "Remember if he opts out, you're next in line."

"But not as good a match."

"Nope. I got the straw on that one," Trey admitted.

"Short straw?" Colt wondered out loud, and he directed a pointed look right at Trey.

"Just a straw," Trey told him, and took a bite of his sandwich.

"Genetics can be crazy weird, but I see it in our cattle all the time." Nick set Dakota down, and she instantly scrambled up the fence rail to watch the horses and eavesdrop on adult conversation. "Dominant traits win out, and if they're good ones, that's all fine. Trey, you managed to get all the Stafford brains and niceness, and none of the power quest. Good job."

"Let him eat, for pity's sake. When is Elsa coming back from visiting her mother on Bainbridge Island?" Angelina slipped in along Colt's side and changed the subject.

"When our wedding is nailed down to the last detail," he replied. He braced his hands against the top rail, just like Dakota. "Which isn't soon enough, if you ask me."

"You've got it bad."

Nick answered Trey with a wink and a smile. "Surprisingly so. And yet . . . it's all good."

"And you said you're having the wedding here, at the new church?" Trey asked between bites, and he was pretty sure he hadn't had food this good, or maybe just this *appreciated,* in a long while.

"Ange's fault," Nick explained as he watched Murt work his oldest daughter around the paddock. "Dad was married in the original church. Both times. Ange came up with the idea that it would be good to start the new church off with happy weddings, and it didn't take a whole lot to convince Elsa. Her parents sold their farm up north a long while back, so she doesn't have ties there. So I blame Ange for the delay because I would've just grabbed a preacher and cut time. Ange and Elsa failed to see the romance in that, however."

"I think it's a good idea to continue the tradition with marriages of joy," Ange told him. "Colt and I will be the first wedding in the new church, which gave him reason to build the church quickly between breaks for cattle."

"Trey, you've got Black Angus on your place? A bunch, right?" Murt wondered as he motioned to Cheyenne to go around again.

"I do, but I miss the red." The look of the red coats against midsummer green grass had always drawn him. "Maybe my days of trying to show up my father are finally over."

"I hear you." Colt whistled lightly as Cheyenne spurred the horse into an easy lope around the paddock. "She's got good hands, Nick."

"I know. You mention it every day. I get it, and she's riding now. Shut up."

Colt kept his gaze on the nine-year-old, but he

smirked. Nick had kept his girls away from the business end of the ranch. They hadn't learned to ride or rope or do barn chores, until recently.

They'd worn him down from one side, and Colt and Angelina from the other, until Nick had little choice. The joy on Cheyenne's face said they'd done the right thing. "Murt, how's Annie doing? Is she getting used to having you gone again? Or is she kind of liking it?" Murt had married a local widow two years before. He'd retired from the ranch just long enough to drive him and his sixty-something bride crazy. Then he came back, with forty-plus years of Double S experience under his belt.

"Typical Annie, Trey. She's sassy. And smart. And that woman can bake up a storm, even mid-summer. She sent some of her blueberry tarts over. I had to come back to work, else I'd look like a barrel 'bout now. A man's gotta stay in shape to keep up with a woman like Annie McMurty."

"Annie and my mother have become fast friends," Angelina told him in a low voice. "One tall and Irish, one short and Latina, but cut from the same cloth. And now that they're sharing recipes and quilting ideas, we'll all gain weight. But the blankets will keep us warm in winter."

Trey laughed, and not because it was that funny. It wasn't, but it was normal. Nice normal. He couldn't remember too many days of nice normal on the Double S, but this—

75

He didn't even know what to call it. A new day?

Sure. Good enough.

A new day, governed by cooperation and happiness and faith. The new normal only added weight to his earlier notion of a parallel universe where everyone on the Double S had morphed into kinder, better versions of themselves.

"Make holy, therefore, these gifts, we pray, by sending down your Spirit upon them like the dewfall."

He'd heard that prayer years ago, at a Catholic Mass. It had stuck with him, the imagery, sweet and poetic, imagining grace flowing free, descending like thick morning dew.

He liked that idea even better than the parallel universe, the thought that the richness of God's hand had been laid in full upon the Double S at long last.

"I have brought you coffee and a blueberry tart, and I will take your plate, unless you would like another sandwich, Trey?"

Isabo interrupted his musings with her practiced practicality. He smiled down at her.

She looked at him, and there it was again. A connection, a fleeting moment of knowledge. Did she see the real him? The emptiness inside the shell of normality?

She held his attention and when she handed him the tart and the coffee, her words came softly.

"It is in vain we try to fill ourselves with things other than the One, the Almighty."

"The Alpha and the Omega."

A tiny smile softened the strong line of her jaw. "And it is useless to take on senseless guilt. We are much stronger when we graciously accept God's forgiveness, and forgive ourselves."

If only it was that easy.

"Or"—she accepted his sandwich plate with a firmer look, the one he'd seen in past visits—"we wallow and whine, wasting the most precious gift of all: our time to do good. It is, of course, our choice."

She pivoted and strode back to the house, and when Trey followed her with his eyes, he saw Angelina's look of frank assessment.

She swept her mother, and then him, a glance. "You've met your match, Song-boy. Nothing gets by my mother."

"I see that."

"A trait she passed on to her daughter." Colt's wry tone matched his expression, and when Angelina elbowed him, he laughed. "I wouldn't trade it, darlin'. You know that. And I actually have to leave this little party and get into town. I promised two hours on the church today, and my shift is coming up. Save me some food for later, okay?"

"I will."

Colt leaned down and kissed her, then smiled,

the kind of smile Trey used to share with Cathy, years ago. Pain underscored the sharpness of the memory.

He didn't understand the lure to drugs. It didn't compute in his head, how the enticement could ever be worth the risk. It wasn't. He knew that. He was science-savvy enough to comprehend the logistics, the dance of brain chemicals, the urgent need within.

But why start, ever?

Why take the life God gave, the one body he offered, and risk its ruination?

Weakness? Self-indulgence? Foolishness?

Maybe all three, but if he'd seen Cathy slipping back into temptation, he could have helped. He could have intervened or given her something more concrete to reach for. But he was working, she was working, and then she was gone amid a flurry of inaccurate news reports and computer-manipulated images that made them look like big-time partiers.

She made her choices. She knew she had other options, so why are you excusing her responsibility and taking it on yourself?

Because he couldn't step away fully.

He needed to. He knew that. Folks made good and bad choices every day. His beautiful, talented wife could have chosen health and life. But in the end, it all came back to one thing in Trey's head: If he'd been there, she might have stayed straight. But he hadn't been there. He'd been on the road, and no matter how hard he tried, he couldn't forgive himself, because he'd known she could slip back. He knew better than most because his parents had done the same thing.

And then she was simply gone.

"Uncle Trey?" Dakota smiled up at him with Stafford blue eyes, about as pretty as that Carlton woman next door. Almost.

"Yes, sugar?"

"Will you hold me, please?"

"Glad to oblige." He set down the coffee and the tart and opened his arms. She jumped to him, and he gathered her in. His therapist had scolded him regularly to move on, embrace life, and appreciate the gifts he'd been given.

He understood her reasoning but couldn't quite do it. And yet, standing here, seeing his brothers finally happy, seeing the joy on these girls' faces, and old Murt teaching youngsters the art of cowboying again . . .

He almost felt the urge to try.

ॐ

Lucy had all four kids tucked into a middle pew on Sunday morning. From where she sat, in the choir loft above the congregation, she kept watch over them.

All were fairly clean, fed, and warned to be on their best behavior. If Lucy had been a gambling woman, she'd bet against the outcome, but

Angelina and Colt had promised to sit with them, and Lucy's boys wouldn't dare give Colt Stafford a hard time.

She hoped.

Just as the pianist touched the opening notes of "Amazing Grace," Trey Walker Stafford walked into the church with his father and Angelina's mother. They took the seat right behind her kids and Ashley.

Ashley had figured out who'd "outed" her instantly when Lucy confronted her about the weed the night before. She made a quarter turn, and Lucy watched as Ashley sent Trey the kind of dark look young teens were noted for, country music star or not.

He ignored it and handed Isabo a book.

Nick and the girls slipped into the pew from the opposite side, and if anyone had told Lucy a few months back that the whole Stafford clan would be gathering in church, and sitting with her family by midsummer, she'd have laughed.

And she'd have been wrong.

Lucy listened for the keyboardist to finish the soul-stirring intro, closed her eyes, and began the opening verse.

Her heart soared with her voice. The mellow poignancy of the cherished notes tugged her into a contentment that eluded her most days. And as the rest of the small choir joined in on verse two, she opened her eyes.

Trey Walker had turned right around in his seat.

He stared upward, at her, as if the hymn took him out of his comfort zone.

She found it hard to look away, and not because he was crazy good looking. It was the pain in his face, the empty longing she saw every day in her own mirror.

She did look away then. Purposely. She had enough on her plate, much of her own choosing. Her fault, yes.

But she didn't need more.

She kept her eyes on the sanctuary for the rest of the service, and at the end, she slipped down the back stairs and moved forward.

Angelina spotted her first. "Beautiful music today, Lucy. Absolutely inspirational and lovely."

She felt awkward handling compliments about her contribution to the weekly service. It felt wrong somehow. As if she hadn't sullied her life with poor choices for too many years. But no more, so she worked up a smile. "Thank you. It's always best when I'm singing God's praise. And the acoustics in this church are amazing." She gave the old Catholic church a fond look. The local priest had offered to share space with Grace of God's congregation after the spring fire. "I love the choir loft."

"Which is why Colt had them put one in the new church up the road." Angelina grinned. "Who knew you had such influence?"

"I'm looking forward to singing in the new church, Colt." Lucy shifted her smile up to him. "Thank you for adding the loft."

"I've heard you belt out God's Word, along with a little country twang, now and again," Colt teased. "I think with a set of pipes like that, you can do justice to just about anything, Lucy Carlton."

She loved singing, probably more than was healthy. Giving voice to song sprang from within her, but she had been down that path with Chase. She'd had an insider's view of the music scene. Too many parties, drinking, and drugs.

No thanks. Been there, done that. Living life on the downward side of crazy had never been her choice. She'd stick with the small-town choir. That was enough.

"You guys will be okay with the kids?"

Trey spoke just behind her. The tenor of his voice hailed her, like an altar call on the banks of the river. She longed to turn. Meet his gaze.

She resisted the temptation and gave her kids a warning instead. "You be good for Colt and Angelina, okay?"

"Can we play with the puppies?" Two of the Staffords' Australian shepherds had given birth a few weeks before and playtime with the puppies had become a great motivational tool.

Nick agreed from his side of the pew. "Works for me. Exercise for them, exercise for you. That way I won't be in trouble with Elsa when she gets back here from her parents' place. She called me last night and said we need to socialize the pups, along with a healthy list of other things I should be doing." He made a funny face at the kids. "If playing with the likes of you guys makes those pups more social, I'll consider that a job well done."

"And can we see how big the baby cows are, out in the field?" Cody wondered.

"They sure don't look like babies now," laughed Colt. "But, yes, sure. I'll show you."

"And there are some new babies," Angelina told them. "Special babies that will go live on farms all over our country."

"For real?"

"For real."

The kids looked enthused to be spending time next door. Ashley, however, looked mutinous, and she stayed that way until Trey said, "Ashley, Murt's offered to show you around the ring on one of the horses. We've got boots that will fit if you've got blue jeans."

"I can ride?" She stared up at him, first in disbelief, then suspicion, probably wondering what the catch might be.

"I figured if you know how to ride, it might be nice for Cheyenne to have someone older to ride with. If you stay squeaky clean." He sent Ashley a direct look that meant the outcome was up to her.

"Really?"

"Depends on you."

She was quiet for a moment, and then, for the first time in the three weeks she'd been in Lucy's care, she smiled. "I've got jeans at the house. Can we stop on the way over?"

"We can." Angelina started to herd the younger kids to the door. "Have you got a key?"

"Here." Lucy handed it to Angelina. Then she turned back to Trey to thank him because he didn't have to do that. He didn't have to go out of his way to be nice to a fourteen-year-old with a rock-sized chip on her shoulder. He shifted Lucy's way and looked down at her.

She looked up.

No words came.

She wanted them to, but something held them tight in her throat. He didn't seem to mind. He smiled at her, just her, then cocked his head toward the door. "Shall we?"

"Yes."

The stupid Cinderella feeling came over her again, as if spending an afternoon with a country music star was a date. It wasn't, but his gaze, his smile, and his gentle manner tugged her toward the wistfulness of fairy tales.

She knew better. She'd stopped believing in fantasies when reality beat a path to her young door.

Crossing the wide church parking lot, Lucy

stepped into the shade of a spreading oak, majestic in its size and reach. A soft breeze ruffled the leaves, making the light and shadows partner in a whispered dance. When the dappled light touched her face and her cheeks, she felt better somehow. As if the patchwork sun offered a message, or maybe an enticement to a new day. A new time.

She was being silly, but for this one afternoon of car shopping, she'd allow herself to be a little fanciful.

Cinderella for a day?

Perfect.

Five

Lucy looked a little uncomfortable as they approached Trey's SUV. "Did it drive all right for you?" he asked as he opened her door, figuring cars and weather would make for easy conversation.

"Like a dream," she answered as she settled into the seat. "Smooth and comfortable. It's a nice ride."

"Good." He rounded the front of the car, climbed in, and headed north on Route 97. "If this place doesn't have anything that works for you, we can shop again tomorrow. Or Tuesday. Whatever works for your schedule, Lucy."

"I'm not exactly accustomed to having people or life adjust themselves to my schedule," she told him. "That's never been the norm."

"I broke the car; I should fix it."

"A solid theory, but it's the personal aspects of this." She waved a hand back and forth between them as he accelerated when they got out of town. "Instead of exchanging insurance cards. Being around you is—"

"Nice? Exciting? Fun?" He tossed out the positive adjectives before she could finish, then grinned because teasing her was fun, and he hadn't anticipated that possibility.

"I was going to go with 'disturbing,' but your spin works too."

He laughed out loud. When was the last time a woman treated him as if he was just a normal guy? He couldn't remember. "Well, we're all a little disturbed, aren't we?"

"Within a spectrum, yes. I guess."

He indicated the sophisticated music system above the center console. "If you want music, jump in."

"It looks complicated. And possibly scary. I don't want to break something."

"So complicated it's easy." He hit a button and old-time crooner music filled the air.

"You like Sinatra and the gang? Why did I not see that coming?"

He shrugged one shoulder and kept his eyes on the twisting road. "They set the stage for so much. Why are you surprised? Good music is good music, right? And by the way"—he sent her a quick look of approval—"you nailed the opening hymn today with unsurpassed beauty. When I turned around and saw it was you singing, I was . . ." He paused, then worked his jaw. "Surprised and moved."

"That's mostly John Newton's doing. He wrote it. I just had the privilege to sing it."

"Still." Trey followed the curving road at a relaxed pace. "The delivery commanded attention to the words, and that's clutch, Lucy."

"Well." Her hands moved in her lap, restless. He could see he'd embarrassed her. "Thank you."

"You're welcome. Have you sung outside the church?"

"Yes. A lifetime ago. Nothing I care to do again."

Her answer tweaked him. He started to delve, then stopped himself. The conversation seemed to unnerve her, and if they were going to spend hours shopping for wheels, he shouldn't make her uncomfortable. He opted for a change of subject. "You must have gotten a chance to talk to Ashley about the marijuana. She started shooting me killer looks the minute she saw me walk into the church."

"Sorry about that."

"Don't be. Her choice, not yours. Maybe we can get through to her before she graduates to harder stuff. If I could wipe drugs off the planet," he added in a tone that sounded gruff, even to him, "I'd do it in a heartbeat."

"I expect you would."

Time for another change of subject. Talking about drugs for the next forty minutes of the drive wasn't going to do either of them any good because he wasn't exactly open-minded about the topic. "I need you to do me a favor."

"Me? Do you a favor? As in?"

She sounded skeptical, as if her doing something for him was a preposterous notion. "Stop doubting; it's easy enough. I need you to write me a list of things you'd like fixed around your place. I want your goals to be my goals for the next few weeks. Okay?"

"Listen, I've been thinking about that. It's not really necessary . . ."

It was, but he pretended to listen.

"And you've probably got things to do at the Double S."

"Not until some other unforeseen catastrophe occurs, and hopefully that won't happen. If they need me, they'll know where I am. Right next door."

"And the kids will get in the way, and then I'll get worried, and then—"

"Lucy."

She paused, still looking straight ahead, her hands lightly dancing in her lap.

"Will it help if we change my name for the duration?"

Color darkened her cheeks. "You're making fun of me."

"Possibly." He smiled because teasing her made him want to smile. "If we call me Hank the Handyman, would that make it easier? Because Hank's a great name."

"You're being ridiculous."

"Whereas"—he made the turn toward Wenatchee —"I'd say sensible. You feel weird having Trey Walker hanging around, climbing ladders, and pounding nails. But if Hank comes by because he was commissioned by the evil land baron next door, that's got to make it better. Right?"

"It almost does." She grumbled the words as he pulled into the car lot. "Listen, Hank."

"There you go." He smiled his approval and that made her laugh. And blush. He decided he liked both.

"You were right yesterday. If your father wants to make amends, I'd be wrong to stand in the way after whining about it for years."

"We'll make a no-whining pact. You and me. Sound good?"

She looked up at him once she climbed out of the SUV. Then she stuck her hand out and shook his. "It sounds fine, Hank."

He didn't want to let go of her hand. He stood there, looking down at her, and for a fleeting moment, it was as if their hands were one. Her palm, soft but firm, toughened by work. Her fingers, smooth and small, connected with his.

It felt good.

Then she tugged her hand free and turned away, leaving his hand empty.

She was right to break the connection. A single mom, working to make ends meet, didn't need distractions, and he'd be underfoot for a while.

Still . . . The touch of her hand to his. The feel of her calloused palm, a working woman's hand. Her life was so different from his. A daily struggle.

As a saleswoman approached, he mentally pledged to make Lucy's reality easier by the end of summer. That was a promise he could live with.

"Can I help you?" The saleswoman looked up at Trey, recognized him, and then seemed to make the decision to treat him just like any other customer.

That made him downright happy and ready to spend money, because every now and again, he liked being a regular guy. "The lady needs a van. Hers met with an untimely swim yesterday."

"Oh, I'm so sorry." The saleswoman gave Lucy a sympathetic smile. "Are you all right?"

"Dented pride and a bunch of messed-up plants that were riding in the van. But personally, I'm fine."

"Are you local?" the woman asked. "Will you be driving Central Washington roads in winter and spring?"

"Yes."

"Then have you considered one of our bigger SUVs instead of a van?" She moved toward the right-hand lot. "They'll give you better traction and maneuverability in the snow, or along icy or slushy roads."

"I—" Lucy looked suddenly flustered, so Trey stepped in.

"Can you show us the difference?"

"I'm happy to." The woman reached out and shook their hands in turn. "I'm Winnie Bidlington.

I've been here for nearly fifteen years. Let's head this way while you tell me a little about yourself, ma'am. Kids?"

"Four."

"Hence the van." Winnie smiled. She keyed a modern-style walkie-talkie and asked someone to bring several sets of keys to the lot. She walked them up and down two double rows of upscale SUVs, citing the positives of each. And when Lucy eyed the price tags posted in the windows, she went positively pale.

"Listen." She stopped Winnie as another sales associate came their way with more keys. "I won't get a whole lot back for my van, and these are gorgeous, but they're way out of my league. Do you have a used car lot here?"

"We do."

"But we don't need it." Trey pointed to a decked-out Ford Explorer. "Let's try this first. See how it rides."

"Trey."

"It's on me, Lucy. Go big or go home, right?"

"Then let's go back to Gray's Glen. Sal can hook me up with a decent used van. He's got connections."

"So do I, and my connections say it would be a shame not to try one of these big, safe, well-equipped family vehicles when you're driving four kids and your livelihood around. Doesn't that make sense from a mother's point of view?"

• • •

It did, and his offer went right along with the Cinderella feeling of the day, but she wasn't a stupid, stranded princess. She was a financially strapped single mother of three, with an extra teen thrown in.

She couldn't afford gas for one of these sweet rides, much less insurance and registration and maintenance. And no matter how cute or rich Trey Walker was, she couldn't be bought. Wouldn't be bought.

"It can't hurt to test-drive and get a feel for it, right?" He moved in front of her, coaxing. "We don't have to walk away today with a vehicle, but we came all this way and it would be silly not to check things out. We've got a busy week ahead."

Okay, good point, and she had to start somewhere, but driving one of these beautiful vehicles would make her scoff at lesser offerings.

Winnie handed her the key to a brand-new Explorer. "You don't know if you don't try."

"All right." Lucy climbed into the driver's seat and pretended the thick, cushioned captain's chair wasn't about the nicest thing she'd ever sat on.

Trey climbed in the other side, and instead of coming along, the woman waved them off. "Take this one out, and I'll get another one ready for you. Do you have any favorite colors, Lucy?"

"Green."

"Like the Double S fleet," Trey noted.

Buy a car to match the rich collection next door? Not in this lifetime. She shot him a cool look and said, "Make that red. Deep red."

Winnie nodded as Trey grinned. "I will."

She took the SUV onto the road, then curved left to head uphill. "You can tell better how an engine responds if you're going uphill."

"Good point." He sat back, his cowboy hat mashed a little against the seat, and he didn't seem annoyed to have a woman driving.

Chase had never let her drive when they went somewhere together. He had to be behind the wheel. That became a war zone when he was drinking, a battle that ended when she refused to go with him. She'd called for a ride numerous times, making him spitting mad because he wouldn't relinquish the keys. And in the end, it had cost him his life.

"This is sweet," she whispered as she took in the rise and fall of the mountainous terrain. "You'd never know you were going uphill."

"It's got plenty of power, for sure."

"And so much room. And it smells good. And handles like a dream. I can barely hear the engine."

"Old vehicles get louder as parts age. It's a big difference when you climb into one with the newest engineering."

"I'll say."

He grinned as she came to a stop sign outside of town. "You like it."

"That's a given. But Trey."

"Hank."

She smiled because it was kind of fun to call him Hank. "Hank. You're a working-class guy, just like me. The insurance and gas and tires and repairs on something like this are out of budget."

"Not so." Trey shook his head. "How many repairs did you have for the van this past year?"

Too many, for certain. "A couple."

"Totaling?"

"Over a thousand dollars together."

"So if you're driving something that doesn't need repair for a hundred thousand miles, that's a big annual savings."

It was.

"And sure, the insurance will be higher, but again, that should be offset by the lack of repair bills. How's your driving record?"

"Good. Solid. No problems in years."

"There you go. You're a woman with a great driving record and that makes you low risk."

"I have to think about this. And maybe pray about it because my head is screaming 'Take the car!' while my gut is clenching in fear."

"Take all the time you need, Lucy. I'm here for a while, and you can use my car in the meantime. There's a bigger model that might give you more cargo room for the plants. Should we test-drive that one too? You've still got a bunch of things in the greenhouse to sell."

Her remaining summer inventory should be going to market this coming Saturday, and that would be it until her mums were ready for the September market. "I can't imagine filling a gorgeous vehicle like this with all those plants and baskets. I'd get it dirty."

"It's washable." He sat back against the seat and got quiet, letting her think.

He'd made good points. A lot of them. And she knew he could afford it. He'd made great money singing, and he'd landed a gig on a network talent show three years back as one of the coaches. She'd seen the contract figures in one of the weeklies. If the reporting was accurate, Trey Walker was rich, but that shouldn't matter. Her van was worth a tenth of the cost of this vehicle and that made the whole thing wrong. "I know you're trying to be nice."

He shrugged that off as if nice was a given. Lucy knew it wasn't.

"And you have the means to do this."

"Yes."

"And it's a very generous offer, but I can't possibly accept it." She rushed the refusal, afraid she might cave.

"Can't or won't?"

Candid but pointed. She respected that so she replied in kind. "Both. I don't want to be indebted to you. Or to anyone. Ever. And taking something like this to replace a beat-up, patched-together nine-year-old van would make me indebted to you, so it can't happen."

"Lucy. Pull off in that lot over there for just a minute."

And this is where the nice guy puts not-so-nice pressure on you to do things his way. Why was she surprised? "So you can talk me into this?"

"No." He pointed up. "So we don't spook those two moose. That's a sight I never get to see in the South."

She glanced up.

A pair of huge moose grazed thick green grass along a curved mountain knoll. They moved along easy and content, unworried. Unhassled. Unbothered by lack of finances, rotting porch supports, and leaking pipes. "They're magnificent."

"I miss sights like this. I didn't realize how much until right now."

He focused on the sight with such a look of longing it made her ache to see it. How could someone with so much still yearn? It made no sense in one way and perfect sense in another because contentment had little to do with things and everything to do with faith. She knew that, but as her finances dwindled and her farm fell into deep disrepair, it had been hard to believe at times.

She kept still until Trey made a quiet observation as the big animals lolled their way across the upper range. "This is part of me. Being here, in the valley. Being part of all this."

That seemed like a fairly easy problem to solve when you have a huge bankroll at your disposal. She kept it simple on purpose. "Then come back."

He grimaced. "You know my family. My father."

Oh, she did. Too well. And it irked her to no end that she felt some sympathy for Sam's current plight after all he'd done to hurt so many people, including her. He'd let alcohol and ambition rule his life and left a whole lot of emotional debris to fester along the way. Her late husband had been foolish enough to buy their small farm when Sam Stafford wanted to access it for the Double S. They'd had a good laugh, as if they'd pulled something over on the rich man next door, but Sam wasn't amused.

He didn't like being thwarted and wasn't afraid to make people pay for getting in his way. She'd learned a valuable lesson at a young age: if you mess with the bull, you'll have to deal with the horns. Sam Stafford had power and money on his side of her falling-down fence. Chase's idea of "sticking it to the man" had gotten her nothing but grief and hardship, year after year. "I know your father, all right." She let her tone underscore their adversarial relationship.

"Then you know it's not that easy."

"Who said easy was best? Life gets difficult sometimes. Then we fix it as best we're able."

He shifted his attention to her, and she plowed on.

"It's all about options, isn't it? We go through life with lots of everyday choices and a few of those once-in-a-lifetime opportunities. On a scale, the everyday choices outweigh the others by sheer number. But the once-in-a-lifetime moments can build us or break us. You could have a place here, be close to family, and fly out of Yakima to work. Why be a whole country away from people you love if you don't have to be?"

He grunted, staring at the moose, then slanted her a sideways look. "Family's a weird thing."

"Tell me something I don't know." She sounded cryptic purposely. "It's hard to see the big picture when you're young, with limited experience. So mistakes get repeated." She knew that firsthand. Years of foolish choices had piled on to put her in her current predicament. Some were hers; some were foisted on her by others. She wouldn't trade her kids for the world, but she could have been a whole lot smarter as a teen. Maybe then . . .

"They sure do," he agreed. He'd leaned back against the door, watching her, but more importantly, listening to her as if her simplistic high-school-educated views made sense.

"At some point we have to readjust," Lucy continued, speaking to herself as much as to Trey. "If I prune a tree properly, the new growth will fill in and branch out. In a few years, I have a gorgeous, salable tree that folks will love. But if I don't do my job or animals browse the tender buds, the tree's shape is messed up. The tree has no choice; it grows as it's shaped. But God gives *us* all kinds of choices. Once we're old enough to see that, it's up to us. But it also becomes our responsibility, and that's the scary part. Because then there's no one else to blame."

Her words hit home.

Did taking the blame for his troubled marriage and his wife's death help anything? Or was it just another downward spiral with no end in sight?

"We should get back." Lucy's quick return to practicality didn't give him time to dwell. "Winnie will think we've taken off with the car."

"Either that or they're tracking us via satellite and wondering why a young couple pulled off the road into a farm lot."

"Oh for pity's sake, that's all I need are crazy rumors about me and the handyman." She made a scolding face as she steered the SUV back onto the road.

The face made him smile, and he wasn't sure why. Maybe because she was easy to talk to? Because she seemed so unabashedly normal? "It doesn't take much to feed the rumor mills these days. I stay away from newspapers, grocery checkout lanes, and social media, while meeting the public daily." He tapped his left hand against the center console in a syncopated beat, the kind he liked to back-swell in refrains. "But the trade-off is doing what I love. Writing and singing music. So that's a mighty fine blessing right there."

"You must have people who do that stuff for you, right? Shopping. Cooking. Organizing your life."

"I hire some stuff done because there's not a lot of time, but if I could just go shopping and not create a disturbance, I'd hire less. And maybe that's what I miss most about being here. I can just walk through town, stop at Ham's or the coffee shop or Sal's, and they treat me normal. There are days when I miss plain, old normal, Lucy."

"You're a Stafford, Trey." She shot him a quick look while she waited for a traffic light. "The normal ship sailed a lot of years back. You weren't on it."

That was truer than she'd ever know. Than anyone would ever know, because in a normal situation a mother would love her child. A wife would respect her vows. No one's life should be riddled with this much death and grief, should it? He'd kept his silence about Cathy to protect her memory. He'd taken a lot of flak to do it, and now he wasn't one bit sure why he'd felt the need. Had he failed her? Or had she failed herself, like his therapist believed, and taken him along on the ride?

Lucy pulled into the dealership, parked the

vehicle, then climbed out before he could get around the car.

"So?" Winnie came their way. "How was it?"

"Amazing." Lucy patted the hood, and Trey read the temptation in her expression. "It rides as smooth as it looks, but I'm going to have to think on it."

"Would you like to test-drive another?" Winnie waved toward the row of sleek, solid SUVs. "We've got more keys."

"No, but thank you. I need time." She darted a glance his way, and Trey put his hands up in defeat.

"Take all the time you need."

Relief softened the worry in her face. "Thank you, Hank."

The name made Winnie turn his way. She peered at him, then decided to let it be.

Just as well.

For the moment, Lucy could use his Jeep, and that would give her the time she requested. They said good-bye, and as they moved toward his SUV, an idea flooded him. He tossed her the keys. "Can you drive? I want to jot down a few notes."

"Sure."

He opened her door for her.

She paused. Looked at him, then the door. And then she smiled as if a simple thing like having someone open a door for her was a surprise. If it was, then the men of Gray's Glen were plain stupid because opening a door for a woman like Lucy should be an honor.

He swung her door shut, got in, and grabbed his notebook from the center console box. *Time.* He jotted the words quickly as they came to him, just enough to feed his creative brain later, when he was alone with his thoughts and his guitar. *Lucy. Choices. Home. Mountains. Moose. Loss. Coming back and moving forward.*

"You know the specs for that vehicle are online," she told him after driving five minutes south in silence. "You don't have to remember it all. A click of a button on that smartphone of yours and you're uber-connected."

"Not note taking," he said, eyes down. "Song-writing."

"In the car?"

He nodded, jotting more discordant ideas until the legal pad page was half-full. "If I do it in the moment, then the emotions of the song are heightened. It's hard to recapture the random things that come together in my head if I wait until it's convenient."

She looked dubious for good reason, because if he had to point a finger at one thing that set up the idea, he couldn't. But the combination of things set his brain in motion.

"I'm failing to see a song option in test-driving a car. Or watching someone else test-drive a car. How do you turn that into a chart-topper?"

"And that's the indefinable mystery of the industry," he muttered while he scribbled a few more notes. He sat back, studied the page, then set the notebook down. "I'll play with the thoughts at the cabin later, when everything's quiet."

"You need quiet to write?"

"Sometimes. And sometimes a song floods my brain, and I can write on the tour bus with half-a-dozen yammering guys playing cards."

She didn't act like she thought that was strange. She dipped her chin, gaze forward. "I hear you."

Her response made him look at her more closely. "Did you ever write a song, Lucy?"

She lifted her right shoulder. "I tried a few times. They weren't good."

"And you know this because?"

"My late husband called them silly, sentimental ditties." Her slight wince said the words still hurt. "His group liked deeper stuff. Rage-against-the-machine style. They went pretty dark after a while."

What kind of husband did that to his wife? He refrained from asking and chose his words with care. "That's one man's opinion, Lucy." Trey kept his tone easy. "The best rockers are generally more open to the softer side of music. I'm sorry he wasn't."

"Well, at the moment I'm real lucky to be able to write my name legibly by the end of the day, so it's a moot point."

He jotted down two more thoughts. *Single mother. No time or money.* Then he shifted his attention back to her. "What did you love about the SUV?"

She almost snorted. "Just about absolutely everything."

"Fair enough. What didn't you like?"

"Access."

He frowned, confused.

"A van has side access doors for kids. They stream in, they stream out. I love the SUVs, but the practical issues of access are huge in daily life."

He hadn't considered that. He'd been thinking size and seating and safety. "That's a great point. So let's go to Ellensburg on Tuesday if there's someone to watch the kids. Or we could take them with us."

"Ashley's in summer school, so that leaves us the three younger ones. Three kids test-driving a car." She pretended fear, then smiled. "They'd probably get a kick out of it."

"Is Ashley a ninth grader?"

"She will be if she passes. She's a kid with an attitude, that's for sure."

He'd seen that close up, so why would she deliberately put a kid like Ashley in with impressionable little kids? "Do you ever wonder if Ashley's negative influence might affect your kids? They're pretty susceptible at their age, aren't they?"

"Well, here's the trending issue on that, Hank." She'd come to the infamous stop sign he'd missed the morning before and rolled to a stop. "If no one ever gives you a chance, how do you pull yourself up? And if life hands you a host of negatives, how do you learn to see the positive?"

"You're hoping she'll see your good example and straighten up."

"I'm hoping she'll want to be the best she can be," she corrected him gently. "That she'll see the beauty in everyday things. Flowers. Kittens. Babies. Christmas trees. She was heading down a bad road. I offered her a way out, and hopefully a way up."

"What do you do if things get out of hand? I know it's not my business, but—"

"You're right, it's not." She pulled into the graveled barnyard with the Double S ranch house on one side and the first barn on the other. "Ashley got dealt a raw hand, like so many others, and I believe she deserves a chance. You gave her a chance today, the opportunity to come here and ride."

"She's outnumbered by adults, one of whom is a cop. I was playing the odds."

"And I'm hoping she'll start making better choices. She's smart and intuitive, but she'd rather wiggle her way out of work than get it done."

Trey didn't get it.

He'd always worked, always studied, always

looked forward even when life pushed him back.

"Not to belabor a topic, but even with your crazy family dysfunction, you can't equate growing up here"—she motioned to the beautiful sprawl of the Double S—"to a five-room shack with drunken parents and no rules, a situation that only got worse when her father took off with another woman after my husband died. Losing Chase was the straw that broke his mother's back, so for over three years, Ashley's known nothing but sadness and squalor. Having known a similar set of circumstances, I'd like to change that if I can. I got a chance to clean up my act. So should she."

Would Ashley change? Could she? Could anyone, really, once they'd caved to the allure of drugs?

"Hey, Mom! Look at me!"

Cody's excited voice drew Trey's attention to the nearby paddock. Seeing Cody being led around the ring by Hobbs, another old-time Double S cowboy, took Trey back almost three decades. It was him up top on a saddle, scared to death but pretending not to be afraid because Colt and Nick would tease him unmercifully if he fell apart.

"Keep those eyes right here, on me, son." Hobbs had held his gaze back then. Feeling very small and very high, he'd stared into the cowboy's eyes, and Trey knew he could be trusted. *"Ain't*

nothin' to fear that can't be conquered with time and trust, and that's the truth of it."

He'd held on, watching Hobbs the whole time. Seeing Cody up there now, he began to see Ashley's reality compared to his own.

He'd been surrounded by choices money could buy, yes. But more importantly, he'd been surrounded by people who loved him. Hobbs. Murt. His father, in his own complicated way.

And the trust fund from his parents' death had come to him when he turned twenty-two. They'd messed up a lot, but they'd had insurance, and he'd used that to give himself the Nashville launch Sam had advised against. His father had ordered him to stay here, on the Double S. He talked legacy and responsibility and loyalty.

Trey had understood his legacy. He saw his responsibility fully. He needed to show himself and his late parents that it could be done. A person could live his dream, achieve success, and still be a normal, God-fearing person, no drink or drugs involved.

He'd been right—and he'd been grievously wrong. And here he was, back home. Surrounded by family and still alone. Now there was a country song for you.

"Mommy!" Belle spotted them and raced their way. "Mizziebo let me help make ice cweam, and it was so good!"

"Mizziebo?" The kid's excitement was contagious,

and her face and hands were slick with melted creamy goodness.

"I've got wipes here." Angelina came to their rescue from a porch table as Lucy answered.

"Miss Isabo is what they're supposed to call Angelina's mother. But this one morphed it to Mizziebo, and it's kind of stuck."

"My mother loves it," Angelina added as she gently washed Belle's pink cheeks. "It makes her smile every time she hears it."

Homemade ice cream. Little kids' jumbled words. A whole family, attending church service together like you'd see in one of those greeting-card movies.

Old thoughts of the Stafford's discordant early life mixed with the new reality, and when Ashley came up from the lower paddock with Colt leading the way, Trey longed to see the promise in her. Fourteen years old, with so much ahead, but already embracing a path of dishonesty and lack of self-respect.

She looked their way and flinched when she saw him watching.

He knew that reaction too well. He'd lived it those last months with his beautiful wife, trusting stupidly.

But he'd learned his lesson the hard way. Once a druggie, always a druggie, and Trey was pretty sure you could take that to the bank.

Six

Lucy's kids were living a dream life as they roamed the Double S for the rest of the afternoon.

She second-guessed herself every time she let them visit. For kids to see this grandeur and still be satisfied by their lack of material goods created a mental conundrum. Belle was too little to notice, but Cody and Cade weren't. She should gather them up and take them home. A little went a long way when it came to all things Stafford. She slipped off the fence rail to do just that when Isabo rang the dinner bell.

"Fried chicken!" Cade leaped off the adjacent rail like a shot. "And smashed taters, Mom!"

"I'm so starvin'!" Cody had been playing by the swing set with Noah, Angelina's young son. The two boys raced across the lawn, tagging after Cade, then copying his swagger on the porch.

They were funny, cute, and adorably Western.

She sighed and gave in. She'd missed her moment because there was no way to excise two hungry little boys away from a table laden with Isabo's delicious food. "Wash your hands," she called after them.

"What if I don't l-l-like fwied chicken?" Belle snugged her hand into Lucy's and pushed against her side, nervous. "What if I just want some taters?"

Lucy stooped down. "What are the suppertime rules?"

Belle stared at the ground, stubborn. "I don't 'member all of them."

"You do."

She scowled and scrubbed her toe into the ground before she sighed out loud. "Twy everything."

"Same rules apply here, kiddo. Or no treats."

"You mean like ice cweam?"

"And s'mores. And cookies. You know the drill."

"Ugh." Belle folded her arms tight around her middle and started to stomp off, but a pastel-toned butterfly caught her eye, flitting from wildflower to wildflower beyond the porch. "Mommy! Do you see it? A fwutterby!"

"Butterfly," Lucy told her softly, although the other word made much more sense. "Isn't it beautiful, Belle?"

"Oh yes!" Belle moved closer, then squatted, watching the butterfly flit here and pause there. "It's so vewy, vewy beautiful, Mommy."

"I can catch it!" Noah spotted the attraction from the porch. He set his plate down, jumped down the last step, and made a mad dash across the yard. "I'll get it for you, Belle, just hold still!" He raced into the taller grass, a bundle of almost-four-year-old energy. The butterfly moved up, then out, fluttering well out of reach. And when Noah jumped, the butterfly moved higher yet, in search of safer territories.

Lucy assessed the action to no one in particular. "And there is the difference between two children. The look-and-see variety and the all-boy, let's-catch-it style."

"I found his actions inspirational."

Trey's voice, behind her. He'd been helping with the horses, and he smelled of horse, hay, leather, and something else. Something indefinable and delightfully enticing, but Lucy wasn't there to be enticed. She kept her face placid. "Did you?"

"Sure." He had his hands in his pockets, and he rocked back on his heels slightly. "He saw her gazing in wonder at something beautiful and unreachable. His first instinct was to put down food and race to get it for her. How many grown-up guys think to do that?"

"How many adult males set down a plate of food on purpose? None that I know of," she agreed, and he laughed.

"Proves my point. Chivalry is not dead, and it might actually be inborn, but we've started taking things like that too casually. The polite things. The nice gestures. Folks do it in Nashville all the time. But we should do it everywhere."

"The country crooner starts a trend." She said the words lightly, but how nice would it be for that to be the norm again? Men being kind to women? Chivalry, alive and well in modern society? She'd never experienced such a thing, but her personal choices were partly responsible for that. "Kids sure could use more examples of kind, loving men. Raising boys can be a challenge for a single mom. Telling them how to be strong young men is very different from seeing the example set for them."

"You've given this thought."

She directed her attention to the porch, where Cade and Cody were filling their plates, right alongside Nick's daughters. "I had little choice."

"Good point."

"But it's hard." She watched as the kids crossed the grass to one of the picnic tables in the shaded side of the yard. "Boys do better with an example to follow. I can talk until I'm blue in the face, and they pretty much let it go in one ear and out the other. Elsa says that's normal to a point, but that I'm right too. Boys tend to pattern themselves after a role model, good or bad."

"Then I promise to be on my best behavior at your place," Trey told her as Sam approached them.

"About that," Lucy began, but stopped when Sam stuck out his hand.

She didn't want to take his hand. She didn't want to make peace with a man who suddenly got a clue because he was sick and didn't want to face God with a pile of wrongs on his lackluster soul. She didn't want to be part of his emotional healing, because people like Sam Stafford came late to the party and still wanted a fair share of the meal.

But of course, that was what God exampled and what Christ taught. And then there was that little seventy-times-seven notation about forgiving one's enemies.

Lucy swallowed her pride. It left a bitter taste in her mouth and a hard aching spot on her soul. Old resentments had festered, and she needed to put a stop to that. Sam took her hand, and as she looked into the bright blue eyes he'd passed on to Colt, she read regret. Still, there was the obvious background strength of a man who'd built an empire too, so she wasn't going to buy into the regret too quickly. "Mr. Stafford, how are you feeling?"

"Better." He gripped her hand with a firm but gentle touch. "I wanted to thank you personally for allowing Trey to come by your place and help out. If I could do it myself, Mrs. Carlton, to make up for old stupidity and misplaced pride, I would. But I can't, and Trey's been gracious enough to step in."

"I think 'collared' would be a more appropriate term." Trey touched his open shirt collar, but smiled as if he was okay being collared. "And I'm glad to do it. I need to keep busy, and I'm looking forward to jumping in. Lucy's going to make me a list tonight so we're all set to start tomorrow."

"Good to hear. Did you find a car today?"

Trey shook his head and didn't put her on the spot. "No, they didn't have much in the way of vans, so we're going into Ellensburg on Tuesday."

"A lot of good choices there. Lucy, tell me, did you teach yourself how to trim and train Christmas trees, or did the Wheelers show you what to do?"

"Judd Wheeler gave us a basic lesson, then YouTube videos filled in the blanks. And I messed up a few trees before I got the hang of it," she admitted.

"Don't we all?" Sam reached out and put his hand on Trey's arm.

When Sam swayed slightly, Trey reacted. "How about you come sit with Murt and Hobbs, and I'll get your plate?"

The look Sam shot him mixed frustration with acceptance, a humbling reality for a big, strong cowboy. "Probably a good idea."

He was sick.

He was weakened.

He was sorry.

Lucy didn't want to forgive him, and yet she didn't want to stand in the way of his peace of mind either, and the irony of that wasn't lost on her.

"Lucy, grab food and come over here," called Angelina. "I need wedding advice."

Wedding advice? Not her favorite topic, but she moved to the long stretch of tables set out on the side porch, filled with an enticing array of foods. Isabo had outdone herself as usual. As she filled her plate with chicken, potatoes, salad, and fruit, Lucy considered Angelina's request.

Angelina didn't want her true thoughts on how badly marriage could go, how quickly the light of love could fade.

She'd want thoughts on dresses and prayers and flowers and music, and that's what Lucy would offer, because if she proffered her real opinion?

She'd tell Angelina not to do it.

But as Lucy started down the steps, Colt Stafford came her way, carrying Angelina's little boy. "Hurryin' to a pit stop, ma'am," he told her as he hustled Noah into the house.

He wasn't bothered by interrupting his meal to tend to the boy. He wasn't angry or put out by the responsibilities of fatherhood.

He looked happy, as if helping Noah was good.

Had Chase ever looked at his children that way? Not once the drinking took hold. They became added weight to a baggage-filled life.

So maybe Angelina would do just fine marrying Colt because he wasn't a spoiled, drinking rock-star wannabe. He was a solid man who took responsibility for his actions, and that should make a world of difference. And that realization put the blame on Lucy because she'd brushed smart options aside to be Chase's girl as a love-struck teen.

She wouldn't trade her children for anything. She loved them completely. But her young choices had cemented her family into a difficult situation, and that was as much her fault as her late husband's.

☙❧

"Have you got everything?" Trey asked as Ashley climbed into the back of the SUV with Cade. Once they were in, Cody and Belle took their spots in the middle seat. "Ingress and egress." He studied the SUV and nodded. "I can see how the van layout is advantageous."

"Right?" Lucy checked to make sure the younger two had buckled up correctly. "It doesn't seem like a big deal until you're the one half crawling to get into the back seat."

Sam came their way as Nick took Rye Bennett and his brother and sister down the banked drive to see the setting for his soon-to-be-built house. Trey watched Cheyenne and Dakota run ahead, shouting house specs in excited voices. A few months ago they'd been quarrelsome little girls, angry at the world after their mother had left them. But not now. Their inner light shined through their eyes, their faces, their shared laughter.

"For nothing is hidden, except to be revealed; nor has anything been secret, but that it would come to light."

Mark's words, a repeated message in the Gospels, God's promise that light would repel the darkness.

So much change, *good* change. He was here to be a part of it if he chose the offered role. And even if he didn't, according to Sam. Could he move forward with the surgery? Would he?

Get the facts first. Mull later.

"We had one of those big station wagons when the boys were small," Sam said. Trey couldn't ignore his weakened condition or his slowly healing spirit. "It was sensible, having the big back door so the kids could hop in and out."

"And make faces at drivers behind them," Trey added. "Nick loved to do that."

"It's kind of a shame they don't make a combo, isn't it?" Sam asked, and Lucy shrugged.

"I'm a simple person. If it's in decent shape and runs, I'm happy."

Trey closed her door and stepped back. "I'll be over in the morning."

She hesitated, as if wanting to call him off, but then conceded. "All right." She paused again before saying, "And thank you for a lovely day, Mr. Stafford."

"I'm glad you came, Lucy."

Her jaw softened. "I am too."

"Well." Sam moved back, tipped the brim of his hat, and waved when she pulled away.

Trey looked from Sam to the vanishing taillights

of his SUV. "Thank you for being nice to her."

"Shoulda done it a long time ago."

"Yes."

"But we'll fix things now, Trey. You and me."

Sam sounded almost wistful, another chalk line for the record books because regret hadn't exactly played a major role in his father's early life.

"I won't deny I'm glad you hired the roofs done," Trey told him. "Josh Washington and Benson Adams are coming by Lucy's place in the morning. We'll go over a few things. I know they're both busy working on repairs to the town, but I want to inspect the barn beams for rot, and I'll need Josh's help with that. And Ben can walk us through the reroofing process. For the rest"— he faced Sam fully—"I don't mind doing some bullwork. I haven't had time to just hang out and fix a spot in a while. It'll be a nice change, actually."

"And you don't mind goin' to the doctor's office with me on Thursday?"

Mixed emotions clogged Sam's voice. He obviously wanted to be healthy again, but he didn't want to hurt Trey to do it. Trey understood this part of Sam well. The big, robust cowboy who'd rescued a little boy had always sought to protect his own. Where would Trey be if Sam had shrugged him off? With two motherless boys racing in and out of barns, he hadn't needed an extra kid running around the Double S. And yet, he'd dropped everything and gone to California the moment he heard about Trey's parents.

"We'll get the facts together. Of course Colt and Nick will come too."

"A united front." The pronouncement put hope in Sam's eyes. "It hasn't been like that in a while."

"Ever," Trey corrected in a light voice.

"Well, that. But it's good to be united now."

It was. "And in the meantime, don't do anything else to mess yourself up," Trey warned him. "No more broken bones, cracked ribs, or punctured lungs like we enjoyed a few months ago. Got it?" Trey raised an eyebrow, referencing Sam's unfortunate, painful run-in with a protective mama cow.

"It could have happened to anyone," Sam scolded right back. "Do you want to walk up back? See the new calves?"

"I do."

Trey slowed his pace to match his father's. He knew some exercise was good for Sam, but too much expended energy exhausted the man who used to ride range and rustle and round up for fourteen hours straight midsummer. The difference was a real wake-up call.

ನ೪

By the time Trey got back to the cabin beyond and above Lucy Carlton's place, the midsummer light was fading. He switched on the lamps, settled onto the edge of an overstuffed chair, and propped his guitar. He stared down at the page of discordant words and began to pick at notes.

The notes fought the words. And the words refused to come. He wrote a line, scratched it out, then wrote another.

Slow song? Fast?

He closed his eyes, picturing Lucy and those kids, the run-down farm buildings, the scrubby grass area beyond leading to the dark green thicket of evergreen trees.

Work. Hope. Laughter. Beauty.

The last word gave him reason to pause.

She was girl-next-door beautiful, and that was its own attraction, but it wasn't Lucy Carlton's looks that kept her coming to mind.

She didn't flirt with him. She didn't doll herself up, hoping he'd notice her, and he didn't realize that was refreshing until today.

She treated him like a normal human being. Few people did that anymore.

He liked it. He liked the way she didn't mince words. She spoke frankly, and that wasn't something that happened often in Music City.

He stared at the words, then the guitar, then put both aside when nothing came to him.

Music couldn't be forced. It flowed, like the creek his father had controlled in an effort to gain Lucy's farm long before it was hers. Music found its way, springing from ideas like mountain rivulets, seeking level land. Music melded laws of physics with the hearts of men.

His father didn't get that. He'd never understood the importance of music to Trey's heart and maybe his soul. Had Trey's success softened Sam's stance? Or was it the illness forcing Sam to be a better person?

He caught his reflection in the mirror over the rustic fireplace. The thin light skewed the image slightly, just enough to tweak awareness.

Sam had worked night and day to prove his worth to others, to build his dynasty in the rich soil of the Kittitas Valley. Trey had done much the same in Nashville, anxious to show his success.

It wasn't about money. It had never been about money, not to Trey. But the money was part of it, to launch a successful career, earn a living, and not succumb to the crazy drinking or drugging lifestyle that plagued so many. He'd done it, too, beyond his wildest dreams. But none of it had been enough to keep Cathy from slipping back into her old habits when her career hit a rough bend in the road.

He realized then that his love and support wasn't enough. It would never have been enough, not when the drugs held such power.

Money didn't buy happiness. He got that. But if his music brought happiness to others, he'd sing forever. And maybe someday the right song would come along and ease the yawning ache within. And if it didn't?

He'd keep singing until it did.

He went to bed, knowing the words would flow again, and at the most unlikely time. When they did, he'd pull out his phone and record the thoughts, bit by bit.

He'd be fine.

Seven

Lucy's heart fluttered when she heard Trey's wheels on the gravel. She tamped down the anticipation, but when the boys started screeching his name, her heart resumed its dance.

"Ashley?" Lucy called out. "If you're not up, you should be. Your ride will be here in twenty minutes. Let's go."

A door banged shut upstairs, just loud enough to let her know the teen was displeased with wake-up calls. Lucy set the girl's lunch bag on the table, then followed the noise outside.

A big truck rumbled in behind Trey, followed by another.

"What's this?" She moved forward as Belle danced her way, showing off her floral sundress with spin moves. "You don't even have the list yet."

"We're going to use Benson's crew to do the roof. A good roof is the first step to any building, right?"

A new roof?

She stared at him, then at Josh Washington and Benson Adams as they moved her way. Josh was the most sought-after local contractor and a good man. He tipped the brim of his weathered ball cap her way. "Morning, Lucy."

"Josh." She looked from one to the other and swallowed hard. "You're really putting a new roof on?"

"House, barn, and outbuildings," Trey said. "You explain to Benson what you want in materials and color. I was thinking metal would be good."

Good? Metal roofs were more than good. They were resilient and added solid property value. "Isn't that awfully expensive?"

"Dad's got a lot to make up for," he reminded her easily. "When folks get thwarted making money, there's not enough left over for needed repairs. We aim to fix that."

She'd figured he'd fix broken boards. Paint. Trim.

She hadn't figured on a roofing project that would have cost her tens of thousands of non-existent dollars. "You're serious?"

He turned those hazel eyes her way. He wasn't wearing a cowboy hat today. He'd put on a faded, worn Mariners baseball cap and an old blue T-shirt that had been washed so many times, the words were worn half away, along with loose blue jeans, faded by sun and bleach and time.

He looked like he'd just stepped out of a shot-on-the-farm country music video, the perfect blend of country and cool with a side of downright nice. No wonder women packed stadiums to hear him. See him. Or maybe it was the promise of a new roof that polished his casual appearance. Lucy looked from him to the other men and back.

Nope. The roof had nothing to do with it. Trey Walker was smokin' hot whether he was wearing classic cowboy or farmhand rugged, and she'd have to give her hormones and emotions a stern talking to, later.

"Lucy, I'd go with metal," Josh advised. "It's got long-lasting properties, and it adds to the resale value of the house. As long as he's paying," Josh joked, and cuffed Trey's arm. "But it's up to you. Can I have Benson show you a few ideas and you can choose?"

Show her ideas.

She got to choose.

A flicker of light emerged somewhere deep inside, a miniscule flame that had been squelched too often. Her father, stern and dispassionate, running her mother into the ground with his precepts.

And then Chase, ruling the roost, running the show, a younger version of her father, a young girl's foolish choice in very grown-up matters.

"Whatever you want, Lucy."

The magic of Trey's words set her heart stirring again. She almost asked what he'd advise, then stopped herself, invited Benson into the kitchen, and led the way.

Her choice. *Sweet.*

A car pulled into the yard and parked behind the pickups.

Ashley!

She hurried into the house, called Ashley's name, and when the teen came downstairs, Lucy stared.

Ashley had put on short shorts and a bare-midriff top that left nothing to the imagination. "Go get something else on. Now. They're late and you're not ready, which means you'll all be late for school. Go." She pointed upstairs. "And hurry."

Hurrying seemed to be the last thing on Ashley's mind. "You can't tell me what to do. I can pick my own clothes for school. This is what all the kids are wearing."

"Which is probably indicative of why you're all in summer school," Lucy told her, unimpressed. The car horn tooted outside again, with more force and impatience. "Go get changed."

"Or what? You'll keep me here?" Ashley smirked and didn't seem to care that she was embarrassing Lucy in front of Benson. "I didn't want to go to the stupid classes anyway. I'd just as soon quit school and get a job."

"Not many jobs out there for fourteen-year-olds dressed like streetwalkers."

Trey's voice, from the doorway.

Ashley glared his way.

So did Lucy because this wasn't his affair, and the last thing she needed was a full-of-himself Stafford to run her house.

127

"Mrs. Pedroia left; she said she was running late and couldn't wait. You've missed your ride," Trey went on. "Go get changed and I'll drive you down to school. Or Josh can drop you off."

"You guys don't run my life." Ashley stormed the words, then folded her arms over her bare middle. "I'll wear what I want, when I want."

"Then you'll be hanging out in eighth grade another year, because you're not going anywhere dressed like that." Lucy motioned to the table and was glad she'd gotten the kids' breakfast dishes done early. "Benson, have a seat."

Trey stayed in the doorway, quiet.

Ashley glowered from the third stair up.

Lucy ignored both of them. She turned her attention to Benson. He laid out a folder with pictures, and as she started to ask a question, Ashley stomped back upstairs.

Would she come back down?

Lucy didn't know, but maybe it was time for Ashley to realize the full consequences of her actions. An extra year of school was a desperate move, but if she refused rules and guidance, there wasn't much choice.

She stomped back down two minutes later in longer shorts and a T-shirt.

She grabbed her lunch and moved to the door.

Would Trey make a big deal out of this? Or would he be smart and let it go?

He let it go, and Lucy breathed a sigh of relief

while he spoke. "Josh is waiting. He said he's got to go right by the school on his way through town to order supplies."

Ashley said nothing. She pushed by him and kicked gravel all the way to Josh's truck.

And another day begins . . .

Benson indicated Ashley's retiring form through the nearby window and sent Lucy a look of sympathy. "I've got three kids. Puberty's a killer. And that one's got an ax to grind."

"She sure does, but I keep remembering the sweet kid she was before her life turned upside down. I'm hoping we can rediscover that kid again, the Ashley she used to be."

"Before her dad took off and Chase died."

"Yes."

"What if it's too late?" Trey's voice, from behind her, putting her fears into spoken words.

She didn't want to believe that about a fourteen-year-old kid. She didn't want Ashley's negativity to be a bad influence on her three kids either. She felt called to help. It was why Lucy ran the Overcomers, a church group for people with substance abuse problems. If she could donate time and energy for those folks, surely she could help her own sister-in-law.

"I can't think like that." She moved around the table so she could see Trey and Benson clearly. "If I did, I'd never be able to help anyone out of substance abuse, and then I'd have to live with

129

the consequences of my inaction. So I help where I can. And I pray. A lot."

He didn't say a word. He turned and quietly walked out the door. Why? Did her stance hit too close to home? Were the scandal sheets right, that Trey Walker had a drug problem, like his late wife?

She cringed inside as Trey went back down the steps. "Benson, sorry." She turned back to him. "Let's get back on task here. You think metal's the way to go?"

"I do, and while it's pricey, it's the best. Sam is footing the bill, and he wants things done right." He showed her the different styles, and when he came to one that looked like shingles, she paused him.

"I love this."

"Pretty, right? And then we can use the same for the barn. You'd want them the same color, I expect."

No more leaks. No more wood rot. And with no more wet wood, her carpenter ant problem would be helped. "Benson, I'm a little overwhelmed."

A wide smile split his café au lait skin tone. "You just point. I'll do the rest."

She pointed to the shingle-looking model.

"Color?"

"Slate gray."

"Done." He stood up and reached out a hand to help her up. "I'll send the order right in. As long as the material's in stock, we'll start first thing tomorrow."

"You don't have other jobs lined up?"

"We do. Sam asked for priority status on this."

"So he's paying you extra to make others wait." The thought irritated her, total Stafford money-buys-everything mentality. It guilted her, too, because other people shouldn't have to wait because Sam used cold hard cash to bump her to the top of the list. She was ready to wait her place in line when Benson turned.

"We don't work that way, Lucy. Never did. We're rearranging because he and Trey are on a tight timeline. For Trey to get things done here in a timely fashion, we need the roofs in place. It just makes sense."

Trey was on a tight timeline. Of course he was. He'd be heading south after Sam's surgery, another reason to put a lockdown on the sweet rush of emotion he inspired whenever he drew near. She wasn't a crushing groupie or an awe-struck teen anymore, but it wasn't hard to see and appreciate the guy's allure. Her task was to make sure she didn't get sucked into a single-mom romance under bright summer skies.

"You're not leaving anyone high and dry, are you?"

"I've got the first crew working the other orders. I'm teaming with the second crew here, and it's the first time in seven years I've needed two crews. It actually feels mighty good, Lucy."

"All right." She followed him through the screen door. Across the driveway, on the south side of the barn, Trey was setting up shop. He'd erected a sawhorse table and some kind of a saw. A box of tools sat on the open tailgate of the truck. Thick, orange electric cords stretched from inside the main barn to the table, and three little kids watched, eyes wide.

She couldn't hear what he was saying, but the kids nodded and stared, intent. She called them in to do some quick summer schoolwork.

Cody grumbled instantly. "I don't wanna do stupid number stuff and stupid reading. I want to watch Trey!"

"Mom, can't we skip it today? Trey might need our help!" Cade took a step closer to Trey. "He said there's a lot to do."

"He did, huh?"

Trey put an easy hand on Cade's shoulder. "And there'll still be plenty to do when your school-work's done. I promise."

They could have calmly crossed the yard, making life easier.

Nope.

Always argumentative, the two boys had gotten more vocal since Ashley had moved in, and Lucy needed to nip that trend.

She descended the steps, walked their way, then crossed her arms and stood, quietly.

"Arrggghhh!" Cade didn't need any words. He glared up at her, stomped across the yard, and banged through the porch door.

Cody planted his feet in the stones like a little mule. "I'll do my work tomorrow." He folded his arms, just like hers. "I wanna watch Trey today."

"Get inside and pull out your folder or no treats."

"That's not fair!" He stomped his foot.

"One . . ."

"Come on, Cody, I'll color while you do your work." Ever the peacemaker, Belle urged him forward in a promising tone, as if working with your little sister offered the best of both worlds. Trey had turned his attention back to the cutting table, but she saw his smile while she hid her own.

Cody scowled at Belle, then tipped his stubborn little face up to his mother. "I don't want to work."

"Two . . ." Lucy gave the six-year-old time to make a more rational decision because losing treats this early would make for a long day for both of them.

"Why do you always make us do dumb work?" He uncrossed his arms, still scolding, but moved toward the house. "I don't even like living here with all this stupid work, and I keep telling you that!" He stomped across the yard as loud as he could, banged in through the door, and let it slap shut in his wake.

She glanced at Trey.

He winked.

Not a flirting wink either. It was an I-get-it kind of wink. He turned and slid a board off the truck, from one of the neatly stacked rows.

Barn boards.

A new roof. Repaired siding.

She didn't dare get too excited. She'd had things snatched out from under her before. Disappointment had pockmarked her existence for years, but the steadiness in this Stafford's gaze seemed genuine. "Listen, Hank—"

Trey grinned but didn't look up from his task.

"I'll keep a close eye on these guys so you can work in relative peace, okay?"

"I'd appreciate it." He eyed up the barn, then switched his attention to her. "I'm going to reinforce a couple of structural beams with Josh and his brother before I start replacing the bad siding."

"You know how to do that?"

He shook his head and laughed, and when he did, the day seemed sweeter. More inviting.

"No, they're coming back. I can do simple carpentry, but the sophisticated stuff gets left to the experts. We're going to erect a scaffold too. That way I'm operating from a level ground, not hanging in the air on a ladder."

"The boys will love that."

He winced on purpose. "I thought of that, so I'll make sure to put the ladder in lockup every day. I can just see the pair of them on the scaffold, wrestling. I'm going to try to avoid trips to the ER for you and me if at all possible."

"I concur." She moved a wayward strand of hair from her cheek and tucked it behind her ear. She needed to turn right around, ignore the handsome singing cowboy, and get back to the kids. She knew that—but a part of her liked talking to him. Seeing the thoughtfulness of his expression. "I'll have them busy for about an hour with schoolwork, then cleaning up bedrooms."

"There's a fight for you."

"Did the Stafford boys go at it like this?" she wondered, stepping back. "Because you don't seem like a fighter."

Trey settled the first board onto the makeshift table. "I don't like to fight, that's true. But when the Good Lord saw fit to put me in a family with Nick and Colt, I learned pretty quick to stand my ground."

"I didn't have any siblings, and I'm picking my way as I go with the boys." She started walking backward toward the house when Cade called for her. "How badly can I possibly mess them up?"

He looked up at her. Right at her. "I don't think you'll mess them up at all, Lucy. I think you're real good with all the kids."

Her heart did a merry dance in her chest.

It wasn't so much his words, but his tone, as if he believed in her. Lucy Carlton couldn't remember the last time someone believed in her.

Be careful.

She wanted to ignore the stern mental warning, but she couldn't because a host of bad choices dogged her heels. Yes, Chase had refused to grow up, refused to stop partying, and never put family first. But she'd picked him, which made it her fault too.

She went inside, determined to keep her distance. The whir of the saw repeatedly reminded her of the music-loving cowboy working in her barnyard. She enjoyed talking to him. That was a surprise because she'd painted Staffords with a tough brush of dark antagonism ever since she'd moved next door. As she got to know Colt and Nick, she realized she'd been wrong to judge all by the actions of one.

And now Trey. Different from the others. Deeper. And if her instincts were correct, maybe even more wounded.

Something about him called to her. Maybe because they'd both lost a spouse to substance abuse? Maybe because he was a good-looking cowboy with desert camo-toned eyes that seemed to see too much?

Or maybe she was just plain lonely and tired of being the bad guy all the time, the lot of a single parent.

He started whistling as he worked. The sound invited her to return.

She resisted and sat with the boys, guiding their work. For all of Cody's resistance, he buckled down once inside and did his numbers practice and reading quickly. An avid learner, he was above grade level in all subject areas.

Cade had to work hard to stay ahead of his younger brother. He'd started to notice the difference this year. Lucy had shrugged it off as normal, because it was. Kids had different learning styles and aptitudes. She understood that.

Cade didn't understand it though, and when Cody was done with his work in twenty minutes and moved on to reading a third-grade-level book, Cade dug his pencil into his spiral-bound summer notebook. "Why can't I be done now?"

"Because you still have three problems to finish."

"Cody's done."

"Yup." She'd picked up a pencil to doodle while Cade finished. If she left the table, he'd find something to distract him, so she sat right there, close by, ruing the work she couldn't get done. But this was more important, so she jotted random thoughts while he frowned.

"I'll do one more."

She shook her head. "All three." With Cade, if she didn't make a big deal out of it, neither would he. Usually. And right now things were kind of peaceful. Cody and Belle had gone off to their rooms, and she wasn't naive enough to think they were really cleaning, but it was quiet and that was nothing to scoff at.

Trey's cheerful whistle came through the open windows again. She didn't recognize the tune. It was light. Sweet. Almost humorous as the notes picked up speed and danced.

"Look at them, look at them, slim and nice and pretty." She jotted the words to match his notes.

"All dolled up and workin' in the city.

"Or stoppin' for a latte with their yoga pants on.

"Lord, you coulda made me a coffee shop mom."

"I'm done." Cade made the announcement as she crossed out a few words, then finished the last line.

"Really?" She smiled at him, and he slid the paper her way.

He'd done the last three problems as asked. She went over them, they made a minor correction together, and then she sent him off to read while she checked the progress upstairs.

The creaking stairs should have warned the younger two, but their pillow fight was too loud to hear her approach. When she tapped on Cody's door, he swung around, guilt-ridden, a bed pillow clutched in his hands. A quick meek and mild expression replaced the manic grin. He crossed to the bed and pretended to be putting the pillow in place.

She pointed to the clock on the blue dresser. "Ten minutes. Here's your list." She handed it to him, written in simple printed script. "Clothes put away, toys put away, bed made. Got it?"

"Yes." He rolled his eyes and set the list on the bed.

"You." Lucy reached down and lifted Belle. "Come with me. You are distracting your brother. He'll get things done a lot quicker without you underfoot."

Belle put a hand on each of Lucy's cheeks, stared right into her eyes, and spoke in a monster-type growl. "Can I go to Noah's house?"

"No." Lucy shook her head as she moved toward Cade's room to set his list on his bed. "I'm sure they're busy. We were just there yesterday."

"But Mizziebo said I could come back anytime. And Mizziebo doesn't tell wies, Mommy." She dropped the monster voice. An earnest tone lent credence to her words. "She always tells the twuth. She says it's vewy, vewy important."

"She's right, and you still can't go over. We have to stay here in case Trey needs help."

Her eyes lit up instantly. "I can help him?"

"No." Lucy cringed. She'd dug her own hole with her choice of words. "But we need to be here in case he needs help."

"I think that's wike the same thing," Belle told her, suspicious.

"It's not the same at all. We're being proactive,

but we're actually staying out of Trey's way."

"So we should go!" The logic in Belle's assumption made Lucy smile, but they couldn't go chasing over to the Double S just because she needed to keep the kids out of Trey's way.

"Whereas I think we should practice self-discipline and stay here and follow directions."

"That doesn't sound like fun." Cade glanced up from his book, and when she looked, she realized he'd only read one page—if that—in all this time.

"I'm going to give you a pop quiz on the ten pages you need to read, kiddo. In ten minutes. Get a move on."

He groaned, tucked himself farther into the overstuffed chair, but actually started reading.

Victory. But at what cost of time? A lot, and she had Christmas trees to shape up and the greenhouse to tend. She needed to make sure the remaining planters and baskets were ready for the coming Saturday market. She couldn't do that now though. If she went outside, the boys wouldn't stay on task. Motherhood first.

"Belle, I'm going to get the laundry to hang out. Stay in here until I bring it out so we don't get in Trey's way. Then you can help me hang things."

"Okay."

The phone rang as Lucy carried the basket of wet towels up from the basement. Maude Carlton's number flashed in the display.

Lucy wanted to ignore it. Her former mother-in-law's caustic personality wore on her, but Cade spotted the name and said, "Grandma's calling, Mom!"

"Thanks, honey." She picked up the phone and headed outside. "Maude, good morning."

"Did you give Ashley a hard time this morning about her clothes?"

"I most certainly did, and I'll do it again." Lucy set the basket down and tucked the phone between her cheek and shoulder. "Appropriate school clothing is important, and she shouldn't be going anywhere dressed in things that are too tight, too short, and skimpy in all the wrong places."

"To help keep her on the straight and narrow, I suppose? Like you did in high school? All your uppity ways didn't keep you from bedding with my son, did they? Which means the clothes don't matter all that much. It's what's inside a girl's head that counts."

Maude never let her forget her youthful mistakes, and getting pregnant at seventeen ranked high on the list. Lucy had spent years trying to get along with her because she was Chase's mother. Maude's increased drinking had driven her further downhill after Chase died, and she laid a thick slab of that responsibility at Lucy's door. Even so, Lucy could fight with Maude or move on. She chose to move on.

"Nothing wrong with looking nice and respectable, Maude. Is there a reason for this call? Because I'm working and have to get back to it."

Maude's snort showed what she thought of Lucy's work. "I didn't want to tell Ashley on the phone and upset her before she went to school, but I'm telling you now, so's you can tell her. I'm leaving Gray's Glen."

Leaving?

The Carltons had lived south of the town for three generations. "What do you mean? You and Ashley are moving?"

"Ashley's at your place now, and that got me thinking it's time to change things up. I've spent my whole life sacrificing for others. Now it's my turn."

Sacrificing for others?

Lucy bit her tongue because Maude didn't do sacrifice. In the ten years Lucy had known her, the older woman had never put either of her children first. She'd lost her first husband in a boating accident when Chase was a toddler. More than anyone, Maude should realize how difficult the single parent gig was. She'd lived it until she hooked up with husband number two, a hard-drinking, coldhearted man, reminiscent of Lucy's father.

But not once had she ever offered Lucy help. No babysitting, no hands-on help with the trees or the garden or the house. Not a thing. And if Lucy didn't stop by with the kids to see their only living grandparent, they'd never see her. "You're leaving Ashley? Is that what you're saying? Because if it is, then come right out and say it."

"I've got the house sold, and I'm on my way. Just passed the state line. I'll contact Ashley when I get settled."

She was abandoning her daughter.

She'd sold her house and was walking out of Ashley's life. "You can't do this, Maude. You can't just walk away from a kid. How will she feel? How will this affect her? In a few years she'll be eighteen; surely your adventure can be put on hold until then."

"She's got a place with you, and that's all there is to it." Decision deepened her voice, layered with self-absorbedness. "I've got to look after me. I'm not ready for another winter, and having her gone opened a door of opportunity, so that's what I'm doing. I've signed papers givin' you permission to raise her and do all the stuff she might need. And if you're smart, you'll get her on the pill before time slips away and she ends up like you."

Maude had aimed the sharp words at Lucy's heart, and they made a direct hit. Her choices . . . her fault.

"I left a letter at the school saying you can make decisions for this, that, and the other thing. So you're all set. Good-bye, Lucy."

Lucy opened her mouth and was pretty sure she

was about to rant and rave, but the phone clicked, then offered a dial tone.

Maude had left. Walked out on her daughter and grandkids, thinking nothing of the consequences of her actions except as they affected her. Like mother, like son.

Lucy wanted to scream.

She couldn't.

She wanted to wail about how foolish and ungrateful some mothers were, but Belle came bouncing down the steps just then, laughing and twirling like a music-box dancer. "I'm going to dance just wike this when I gwow up, Mommy!"

Lucy bent low and caught her up. She held on tight, wondering how anyone could callously walk away from their own child. "I love you, Bella-mia."

"I wove you too!" Belle hugged her tight, then wriggled to get down. "I'll do the wittle towels, okay?"

"Washcloths."

Belle nodded agreement as she butchered the word. "Smoshcwoffs."

Lucy couldn't correct her right now. Not with this latest bombshell.

Could she keep Ashley here? Should she?

She'd already seen the heightened disrespect in the boys' behaviors. If Ashley mouthed off or treated her disrespectfully, how long would it be before the boys followed along?

And Belle. Innocent little Belle who loved making people happy. Should impressionable children be around a pot-smoking, looking-for-trouble teen? She'd been on the verge of sending Ashley packing two nights ago. Now there were no options with Maude gone. It was either here with her or out on the streets, and what kind of Christian throws a fourteen-year-old out on the street?

"Be careful for nothing; but in every thing by prayer and supplication with thanksgiving let your requests be made known unto God. And the peace of God, which passeth all understanding, shall keep your hearts and minds through Christ Jesus." Paul's words to the Philippians, to not despair. To pray and believe and put their lives in God's hands.

This wasn't what she'd bargained for when she offered a room to Ashley. She thought—foolishly, it now seemed—that if she set an example of loving and caring, Ashley would see the goodness in it and follow along.

She'd been naive, and now she was cornered.

"What's wrong?"

Trey's voice called her out. He stood nearby, a look of concern on his face. She blinked back tears, firmed her chin, and shrugged. "A surprise phone call that shouldn't have been a surprise. My bad for expecting rational thought from irrational people."

"It gets us every time. Are you crying?"

She wasn't. Damp eyes didn't count, and she had no intention of worrying Belle or sharing the crazy surrounding her with the highly successful guy standing in front of her. "A sentimental moment, something I don't indulge in often. Did you need me?" She kept her voice smooth and her countenance calm, a trick she'd learned years before. At a young age, she'd realized that if she pretended her father's vitriol didn't affect her, she lessened his power. What a shame she'd had to use the same survival techniques on her late husband.

Eight

Something—or someone, Trey decided—had hurt this woman. The urge to fix whatever had gone wrong surprised him. His reaction to her surprised him too. He'd woken up eager to get to work. And maybe eager to see Lucy.

Normally he woke up wanting to get back to an unfinished song.

Not today. Today he'd barely stopped for breakfast when he swung by the ranch to check on his dad, but Isabo had thrust a bulky breakfast sandwich into his hands before he left. He'd driven over quickly, ready to help make things right for the young widow.

"Did you need me?" Her words called to him, even as her expression warned him off.

He longed to say yes, if only to fix whatever put that sorrowed look in her eye, but then, he'd grown up wanting to fix things, all kinds of things. Including people.

Would it be fair to Lucy to grow too close considering his current situation? There was his career for one thing, and . . . what if things went badly in San Fran? Why set someone up when there was no predicting the outcome of this procedure?

He denied his helpful instincts and pointed toward the barn. "I'm having Ham send paint over. This is the brand he's got in stock." He pulled up a page on his phone. "And here is the color chart. Rye Bennett said Brendan and the Battaglia boys could sign on for painting. I kind of like the dark red with white trim to offset your Christmas tree business, but what do you think?"

Frustration deepened twin furrows between her brows. From him? From life?

He understood the combination completely, but that thought gave him a mental smack upside the head, because who had an easier life than him? Doing what he loved, earning good money, making so many people happy?

And still he ached for something indefinable.

Faith? Hope? Love?

He had all three. So why the emptiness?

No clue.

She looked at the charts and nodded. "This red is perfect, and you're right. When we hang decorated wreaths and swags against it, it will be stunning. Hopefully I can get out to the trees soon. They need their summer trim, but it's been crazy these past few weeks."

"You have to trim them more than once a year?" He wouldn't have thought that. He assumed you planted them to grow and they grew, with occasional care.

"They need shaping, and it spurs new growth. It's a busy process, but soothing too. Like being in church, without the walls."

"Or the people."

A tiny smile eased her expression. "That too. A little peace in the valley, just like the hymn says."

He loved that hymn. It defined him. But maybe that wasn't a good thing.

Was it his fault for running off, searching too hard? Or his fault for making mistakes? For not seeing when his wife turned that last, fateful corner back into addiction?

"Do you think those teenagers can paint a barn? For real?"

"Sure." He tapped a text through to Hammerstein's and pocketed the phone. "I'll teach them. And I figured if the little guys want to paint, that chicken house is a great learning experience for their age. They'll get messy, but it would be kind of fun, don't you think?"

"They're six and eight, Trey." She sounded doubtful but slightly tempted, and Trey wondered if she ever allowed herself time to just have fun, or if such a thing was even possible while raising a houseful of kids. "You don't think that's a little insane?"

He winked. "That's part of the fun. How would Wednesday work? We're going car shopping in Ellensburg tomorrow, and I've got an appointment on Thursday with Dad, so if we tackle the coop on Wednesday, Cade and Cody can jump in and feel like they're part of things."

"How do you know that's important for kids?"

He hooked a thumb toward the Double S. "Because Sam gave me a chance to be part of things way back when. And it made all the difference."

She didn't look quite as antagonistic when Sam's name came up, but then her words belied her expression. "That must have been back when he had a heart."

"A broken one, but he had it. And then he forgot to use it for a while." He started to back up, then paused. "Sam Stafford came down to Oakland and found a three-year-old boy, all alone, raised in a hovel, huddled in a police station. And he picked me up, wet pants and all, hugged me, and brought me home. And then made me his own. Yeah, he's messed up big time, and he's been a selfish, money-grubbing, egotistical jerk. But he saved me, Lucy, and I'll always be grateful for that."

He raised a hand in peace. "Not trying to convince you; you've got your own axes to grind. I'm just saying there's good in all of us. Sometimes we just have to look harder. Or be really patient, and I don't do patient all that well."

"Me either."

"It's nice to have something in common, ma'am." He tipped his hat and then made his way back to the front of the barn, but he pulled out his phone on the way. When Rye Bennett answered, Trey jumped right in. "Does Jenna babysit?"

"She took the childcare safety course last spring, and she's had a few jobs. Not much experience with babies though."

"Would she be okay with Lucy's kids?"

"You taking Lucy out, Trey? Because that'll set tongues wagging."

He said no, but as he said it, the thought of taking Lucy out tempted him.

And then common sense untempted him because he wasn't here to stay. He needed to focus on mending her place, and then mending his father. On top of that, it wasn't like she hungered for his presence. Tolerated him was more like it. Barely. And he didn't realize how that bit his ego until just now. "She's got Christmas tree work to do, but you can't watch kids in a grove, and I was thinking if we hired Jenna to keep the kids busy, then Lucy could get her work done and not worry about it."

A short stretch of silence made him wonder if Rye was still there, but then Rye exhaled, long and slow. "Okay, then. I'll call Jenna. When were you thinking?"

"How about Thursday? I'm going to Slater Memorial with Dad for tests. If Jenna's here, Lucy can spend the day in the field."

"I'll set it up."

"Thanks, man."

Trey had filled the week with work purposely. He'd spend time getting things done at Lucy's place and putting affairs in order. He didn't want to think about the Thursday appointment, or the dangerous surgery.

So he shoved it out of his mind with busy hands and hard work, because if he sat around waiting for the surgeon to share the stats Trey had already found online, he'd walk away. And he couldn't do that, no matter how scared he might be. Three decades ago a big, rugged cowboy that smelled of Old Spice and cigars had picked him up, brought him home, and changed everything.

Now it was his turn to do the same thing.

Trey had gotten six rotted boards replaced when his phone rang. His agent's name and number flashed on the screen, and he took the call quickly. "Ed, what's up?"

"You've just hit number one on the country charts for the sixteenth time in five years, and we've got an invite for the fall awards show, even if you're not nominated. Which you will be."

"Did you refuse gently?"

"I didn't because neither of us knows what shape you'll be in then. Have they scheduled anything?"

"We have a surgical consult on Thursday. That should fill in some of the blanks."

"You're a good man, Trey. I don't understand it, and I sure wouldn't have the guts to do it, but you're a good man for even considering this."

"He's my father, Ed," Trey told him, as if that was a given.

"You're still a good man. Belker and Schrief are pestering about a winter tour."

"Tell them no. Spring is good. I'm using my recovery time to write some new songs. I'm not doing anything this winter, except singing and regrowing a liver."

"Luckily we've got a new album to push and new singles to release in your absence."

Luck had nothing to do with it. Trey knew that. God had inspired him to sit down and write his heart out last fall and winter, even on tour, long before they'd learned about Sam's deteriorating condition. With his tour done and the album releasing, this was the perfect time to step off stage and onto the Double S. "God's timing, Ed."

Ed wasn't a big believing kind of guy, and Trey would love to see that change. His next words said that hadn't happened. "It might be God's timing, but you put in the work, so I'm giving you the credit. Junie's agent called. Junie wants you to double up with her to cut a love song for her next album. Your mutual fan bases would go nuts over that, and that's something to consider."

Teen sensation Junie had been texting him the same thing. He'd regretted giving her his number for almost a year. Ignoring her didn't seem to do the trick. "Absolutely not. That's the last place I want public speculation to go. Junie needs to find an eighteen-year-old to hang out with."

"She's blatant, isn't she?"

She was, and Trey wasn't about to get mixed up with teen scene innuendo. Straightforward and focused, he was more comfortable being compared to George Strait than some of the wilder country stars. "Just make sure it doesn't happen, Ed."

"I'll see to it. All right, that's all I wanted to touch base on. You take care, okay? And don't let them touch the pipes, you hear me? Chunks of liver are fine, but leave the vocal chords alone."

"Very funny."

Ed laughed and hung up. Trey set the phone down and surveyed the morning's work. Solid. Straight. True.

"It looks better already, Hank."

The way Lucy said the name made him laugh, and when he turned, she held out a tall clear glass of sweet tea. "Thank you." He took a sip, then looked at her, perplexed. "Orange spice. How'd you know?" He tipped his hat back and teased her with a look. "Are you a secret fan, Ms. Lucy?"

"I called Angelina and asked."

For some reason, that touched him. Doing a little digging had taken effort. "Well, that was nice. Real nice. Thank you. It's perfect."

"I had a sweet orange spice blend I use on ribs. So I used that and the regular black tea, and when it all came together, it tasted pretty good."

"Truth."

"I made a pitcher, so there's plenty." She swiped a lock of hair behind her ear, a piece that wasn't quite long enough to reach the elastic band of her ponytail. "Belle's napping and I'm taking the boys into the vegetable garden for weeding. They'll be less than thrilled, no doubt, so whatever you hear, unless it includes the word *blood,* is most likely normal, unhappy boys whining."

"Want help?"

She paused and looked up at him. "In the garden?"

"I'm good with a hoe, and I could use a break from this for a bit."

"Most people don't equate hoeing and weeding with downtime."

He started walking toward the long, straight rows of the vegetable garden at the back of the property. "A change is as good as a rest."

Her quick smile took him by surprise. "My Aunt Isabelle used to say that."

"Is Belle named after her?"

"She is. Aunt Isabelle was one of those women who would have helped settle the West with one hand, while running the church with the other and rocking a cradle with her foot. She was always getting things done, moving forward. She was a great inspiration."

"She must have been, because you're a lot like that."

"Me?" His assessment made her stop and stare

at him. She wasn't pretending disbelief, and that surprised Trey. "Oh, I'm nothing like her. I've messed up eight ways to Sunday, and in the end, here I am, a single mom with too many bills, a failing farm, three kids, and a miscreant teen. Aunt Isabelle would be appalled."

"Naw, she wouldn't."

"You didn't even know her."

"I don't have to." They started forward again. "The woman you described would be doing just what you're doing. Working on, day by day, getting things done."

Doubt darkened her profile. He stopped and put an arm out to pause her. "Good people don't gain our respect by being judgmental. They gain it by being good. Putting that hand out to help. Your aunt would be right here helping if she could." When she still looked dubious, he moved on. "You can either figure I'm right or wallow in that muck you're carrying around like an anchor in shallow water."

"I don't wallow."

He didn't look back, just grabbed a hoe and started working the first row of tomatoes.

"I don't."

Trey kept working, nice and quiet. Then he started humming a tune in quick time, with up-and-down notes, moving along the row.

Lucy called the boys. They trudged out. They glared at the sun, then her, then moaned.

"Stop whining. You two"—she stooped down, and when she did, that long ponytail gave her a real Western profile, distinctly feminine—"are about to have a fun adventure."

"We are?" Cade and Cody exchanged looks of disbelief.

She handed each of them an empty plastic coffee can. "You're bug hunting."

"For real?"

"Not weeding?"

"For real," she told them, then took them to the tomatoes and showed them what to look for. "These are hornworms, and they can eat a lot of tomato leaves."

"They're green!"

"Just like the leaf!"

"Yup. Green when you squish 'em too. They're green because they've eaten that whole branch and laid a bunch of eggs." She showed them how to pluck the leaf with eggs and the worm and put it into their bucket. "And when you're done with them, I'm moving you to potatoes for a different kind of bug."

"This is great!"

"It's like squishy science!"

They set to their task quickly, and Trey thought they'd rush along the row, missing signs of worm damage.

They didn't. They studied the plants, watched for eaten stems and droppings, and worked their way along, peacefully. By the time the sun was scorching the parched soil, Lucy sent them inside to cool off. "But leave your bug buckets outside," she warned.

They took off inside, a job well done, and Trey motioned after them. "They took care of all of that without you having to use a spray."

"Spraying's expensive and when a plot is this small, it's unnecessary, isn't it? And the work makes the boys feel like you said before, as if they're part of things. Roots and wings are valuable things to have."

Trey almost swallowed his tongue in an effort to keep quiet. His respect for her rose. She was more like her Aunt Isabelle than she realized, but with reduced circumstances. "I asked Rye if Jenna could watch the kids for you on Thursday."

"Why would you do that?" She turned from the first strip of corn, surprised and sweaty. She swiped her sleeve to her brow as she faced him.

"If Jenna's keeping the kids busy, you can work on Christmas trees. That way we can take care of the car tomorrow and the coop on Wednesday."

Mixed emotions crossed her face, as if she wanted to complain, then didn't.

"Is it okay that I did that?"

She looked beyond him, to the house, then made a face. "Yes and no."

"Sorry."

"Don't be." She wrinkled her nose further, then

158

lifted one shoulder. "I get weirded out when people make choices for me."

"Is that what I was doing? Because I thought it was something simple and nice like, say"—he dragged the words out, intentionally—"opening a door of opportunity for a busy working mother."

"Without consulting the busy, working mother."

"Well." He went right back to weeding the last tomatoes, kind of pleased, because he'd forgotten how nice it was to just squat down and weed a garden. "I figured she'd put up a fuss and say no, so I wanted to avoid the fuss."

"What if she didn't put up a fuss at all and you assumed wrongly, Hank?"

He grinned and looked back over his shoulder. "Well, that would be a lovely first, Ms. Lucy."

He wasn't sure if he'd make her laugh or make her mad, and when she *did* laugh, he breathed relief.

Something dogged her, just like him, so if teasing her and making her smile lightened that burden a little, he was happy to do it. When they'd finished the tomatoes and corn, Lucy called it a day. "I've got to change up laundry and check on kids. Thank you for this, Trey." She indicated the barn and the garden with a quick look at both. "I'm still in a state of disbelief that all of this is happening, and I'm very grateful."

"My pleasure, ma'am. Do you have to pick up Ashley from summer school?" Trey retrieved the

159

glass he'd set by the garden, and they walked together toward the house.

"Not today, she has a ride. I'm driving tomorrow."

"I'll come over early to work then, so the kids can stay here. And I'll grab donuts from Cle Elum. I expect all four kids would like that."

"They'd be crazy not to. Are you heading back home now?"

He shook his head. "Supper's at six according to Isabo, so I'm staying put. I should be able to get all the lower stuff replaced before I go." He handed her the tea glass. "This was great. Thank you."

She reached out to take the glass, looking at him. Smiling up at him. And when she clasped the glass, their fingers touched lightly, and then not so lightly.

Beautiful. Caring. Sensitive. Kind, but strong and stoic.

When he was a kid, he'd often wished for a mother like that. When they were little, the three brothers would play a wishing game about moms. What would they look like, how would they act?

Looking back, he saw three little cowpokes, wishing for what they could never have, a mother's love.

"Mommy! I woke up and I stayed dwy again!"

Sheer delight raised Belle's voice. She raced across the yard. Lucy left the glass in his hand and bent low to scoop the girl up, and the vision of her, holding Belle, was exactly what he'd wished for in a mom. Kind, happy, and focused, walking the straight and narrow.

"You sit there."

Sandra Lee's voice broadsided him as he watched Lucy with Belle.

"You sit there and you hush up. Don't need no neighbors comin' round, lookin' after your noise. You sit and be quiet or you'll have reason to cry, Trey-Trey. Good reason."

He'd sat, all right. Tucked in a corner with a TV on, while his parents partied in the next room. Alone in the dark, sleeping and waking, always by himself in the same spot, scolded for even getting up to use the bathroom.

"I forgot the glass." Lucy turned quickly, saw his face, and paused, uncertain. "Are you all right?"

"Most of the time." He smiled at Belle, then her. "It's just nice to see you with these guys." He held on to the glass and walked with her. "I'll bring this in if you don't mind, and can I use the bathroom?"

"Yes." She winced. "Of course you can. I never thought of that. I'm not used to having help. Just come in anytime and grab whatever you need. I have an unusually well-stocked refrigerator right now."

"A wonderful thing." He smiled, held the door open, and let her precede him, thinking she was one of the most beautiful women he'd ever seen. He didn't care that she was flushed and sweaty from working outside. Damp tendrils of hair clung to her forehead and cheeks, testimony to her endeavor.

Her devotion and tenderness caught him, the sheer beauty of living faith to the full. And the tank top and blue jeans were nothing a smart man should take lightly.

As he went through the kitchen, a paper fluttered off the table onto the floor. He picked it up.

"I'll take that." Lucy reached across the table in a quick move.

"Sure." He started to hand the torn-out sheet from a notebook over, then paused when he realized what he held. "Are these song lyrics, Ms. Lucy?"

"Doodles while Cade was working is more like it."

He studied the words. A tune began forming in his head, bouncy and funny, and he could see the irony in her words meld with the riffs of the guitar. "Were you thinking light and funny or deep and poignant?"

She took the sheet from his hands and set it on the counter behind her. "I wasn't thinking at all; I was killing time while Cade worked through his math."

"Then maybe we could think about it together,"

he suggested. His offer drew her forehead into a frown, so he wouldn't push it now.

But at some point in time, he'd like to play with those words and his thoughts about this single-mom life she led. Because if they could blend his thoughts with hers . . . they might have something really good, really special on their hands.

He went back outside a few minutes later, determined to do whatever it took to make Lucy Carlton's life easier. He didn't know much about her, but he knew what he saw, and he liked that well enough. She didn't mind getting dirty, and she cleaned up nice. Real nice.

He scrubbed a hand to the back of his neck, causing instant pain. He'd never thought of sunblock. He'd been in such a hurry this morning that the simple mental checklist of working on a ranch went right out of his head.

Another song lyric came to him, an idea that might mesh her words with his. He grabbed the ever-present notebook from the cab of the truck, jotted it down, and then tossed the book back on the seat.

Josh and his brother pulled in. They braced the beams and set up the scaffold he'd need to complete the southern exposure. When they'd completed the work, Trey glanced at the clock. Six-twenty, which meant about thirteen hours before he would see Lucy again. Somehow that seemed too long.

Nine

"My mom isn't answering her phone." Ashley frowned at her smartphone. "I got some notice text thing that said my phone service was being shut off if I don't pay seventy-two dollars to keep it on."

Maude must have stopped paying for the phone, Lucy realized. She'd left Lucy to explain the abandonment and phone shutoff. Knowing Ashley and Maude's relationship, Lucy was pretty sure the phone would be the initial crusher. Then, when Ashley realized the finality of her mother's actions, reality would set in and she'd understand she'd been abandoned. Half the people in Lucy's Overcomers self-help group saw lack of parental love as their doorway to addiction because parents were supposed to love their children. When they didn't . . . Lucy swallowed a sigh and kept her voice light.

"Try her again in a little while. She might be in a spot with no reception. And my landline works great, kid. Call her from there." She cocked her head toward the cordless phone on the counter. "I'm sure she'll answer if the call goes through."

"Why would she be in a spot without reception?" Ashley moved closer. "Her phone always worked at our house."

"She's not at your house."

A deep V formed between Ashley's eyes, but beyond the frown, something in her expression indicated she wasn't going to be all that surprised by Maude's disappearing act. "Where is she?"

Lucy shook her head. "I don't know. She called me earlier and said she was moving."

"Moving?"

Lucy couldn't go on doing dishes while she broke a kid's heart. She set the towel down and faced Chase's sister. "She left early today. She said she needed to have some time on her own."

"So then I should go back and live in our house so it's not left all empty, right?" Ashley leaned forward. Concern for the house seemed to outweigh concern for her mother. "I heard on one of those HGTV shows, that's bad for a place. You shouldn't leave a house empty."

Lucy knew there were many different ways of seeing a house as empty, and Maude Carlton's place hadn't been filled with love or cheer for years. "She sold the house, Ash."

Ashley went pale as a winter moon. "What do you mean?"

Lucy sat down and tapped the table. Ashley plopped into the seat alongside her and stared, mouth open. "She sold the house and left. She called to tell me what she'd done while you were in school."

"She wouldn't do that." Ashley stared at Lucy,

as if trying to figure out her angle. "She's my mother."

Lucy kept silent.

Ashley got up, smacked the phone down, and paced angrily. At the end of the kitchen, she turned, triumphant. "You're lying. I talked to her this morning when I told her about your stupid rules and my clothes, and she had plenty to say about you and my brother, Lucy." She folded her arms and glowered. "Not exactly as pure as the driven snow, were you?"

Lucy tried to remember the girl was hurting, but Ashley's words and expression made the idea of smacking her a more satisfying choice. It wasn't a choice she could live with. She stood her ground, watching the girl's anguish, wishing she could help. "I'm sorry, Ashley."

"For?"

"Everything?" Lucy shrugged helplessly in sympathy. "That life bites sometimes. That your mom was too busy drowning her sorrows to be a good mother to you. That she walked away without saying good-bye."

"Shut up."

Lucy held her gaze, held it hard. "Don't ever say that to me. You can be angry, you can be disappointed, but there are three young kids in this house and they don't need to hear that kind of thing." She crossed the kitchen halfway, picked up the landline, and offered it to Ashley. "Try her from my phone. Maybe you two can work something out." She went outside to leave Ashley with her new reality.

A broken sob followed her out, but Lucy knew her sister-in-law. She was quick to react, then dealt with things in her own time. But this—

How did a teen deal with being left behind like an old piece of furniture?

Cade ran her way. "Do you see the thing Trey built?" He pointed to the scaffold, studying every angle. "If I could just get up there—"

"Me too!" exclaimed Cody. He shook with anticipation at the very idea of climbing onto the scaffold. "We could do all kinds of things up there, Mom!"

"No." She bent low and locked eyes with her two adventure-seeking little men. "You could be killed if you fell from up there. Look how far up it is."

"Not killed," Cade argued with a skeptical face. "Busted, maybe."

"Yes, killed," she told him. "Or busted. Either way it is not happening, fellas." She pointed up. "Do not even think of going up there. It's dangerous and it's here for Trey to do a job, a very important job. Do you understand me?"

"Yes ma'am." Cade scrubbed his toe into the dirt, but Cody gazed upward with such a look of longing that Lucy figured she might have to lock him up for the next few weeks.

"Cody." He sighed and looked her way. "I mean it. I'd be a terrible mother if I didn't do my best to keep you guys safe and sound. Got it?"

"Yessss." He drew out the word to show his frustration with silly things like rules to keep him alive.

"Cody." She added a note of expectation and warning to his name this time.

"Yes ma'am."

"And you?" She shifted her attention back to Cade. "We understand each other, right?"

"But what if Trey says it's okay when he's here?"

Lucy groaned inside. Raising boys was no piece of cake. They didn't come with instruction manuals, and she knew they needed to explore their surroundings and try new things, but where did exploration end and death wish begin?

She wasn't sure, but she'd talk to Trey tomorrow. The lure of a climbing adventure put the light of exploration in their eyes. Keeping them safe had to be priority one. And once the roofers arrived tomorrow with their various ladders in place?

She couldn't imagine keeping the boys grounded enough to keep them out of harm's way. The expectation on their faces made the thought of the next few weeks stretch interminably. An angry, despondent teen, and boys with a death wish.

It couldn't get much better than that.

"I've got one rule to help make today's car shopping adventure go well," Trey announced as he watched Belle struggle to fasten her five-point harness the next morning. He bumped knuckles with her when they heard that final *click*. "Booyah."

Two dimples flashed in her rounded cheeks, and he'd have to be a miserable thing not to feel great when a cute little kid grinned his way.

"And what might that rule be?" Lucy checked Cody and Cade's shoulder belts before she brought her attention back to Trey.

"Price is off the table."

She shook her head instantly. "Not gonna happen."

"It is because I've given this a lot of thought." He started the engine, accessed the road, and headed toward Ellensburg. "If you sued the heck out of me for missing that stop sign, my lawyer would jump at the chance to settle for the cost of a van. You didn't do that—"

"I might now that you've suggested it," she mused, then smiled.

"So accepting the van without making me jump through silly hoops would be good. And the sooner we find one, the sooner I'm back at work on the barn. And the faster the barn's done, the sooner I can start on the porch."

"The porch?" A quick glance her way said the

thought of her porch being fixed brightened her gaze.

"It needs a doll-up. I'm going to provide it. I want to get at least those two things done before Dad's surgery."

"He'll need care afterward."

"Yes." Trey didn't mention that he'd be in need of care himself. It wasn't like anything could ever be kept a secret in Gray's Glen, but for the moment he was okay being on the down-low. Once folks found out he was donating part of his liver to help Sam, they'd talk the thing to death.

Trey didn't want to think about it, much less talk about it, so keeping it under wraps was fine by him.

"The porch has been needing work for a while." He wished she didn't look so guilty saying it.

"Lucy, there's only so much a parent can do. Or should do. Taking care of kids should always come first." Didn't she get that? How her special brand of love would make all the difference to these kids in the end?

"But then everything else gets let go."

"And that's why Hank the Handyman is here. At your service, ma'am." He pulled into the dealership, jumped out, and circled the car to open her door, then was glad when she let him. "Perfect." He looked right at her when he said it, sending a quieter message, and when she blushed, he knew she understood he meant more than the simple act of opening her door. He meant she was special, even if she didn't see it that way. He gave her a hand down, then helped Cade swing the door wide. "You ready to shop for a van, guys?"

"We can help pick it out? Like, for real?"

"Your opinion is very important to me," Lucy assured Cade. "Let's go see what they've got, okay?"

"Okay!"

Trey had worried the kids might get bored.

They were the opposite of bored from the minute they explored the first van until the time they decided on the third one. "This one is so awesome, Mom!" Cade studied the big forest-green vehicle with the air of a master. "There's room for everybody, and it's got a DVD player."

"And Internet capability," Trey noted.

Lucy scrunched her nose. "Well, we don't have Internet devices, so that's no biggie. But we can borrow DVDs from the library."

The thought of watching DVDs in the car had the boys bumping knuckles, actually getting along for a change. "There's always Ashley's fancy phone."

"Her phone's dead," Lucy told him as Belle explored the third seat of the van. "Her mother left town and cut off her phone account. So Ashley is reeling right now for a variety of reasons."

He hadn't thought too much of the insolent teen,

but Lucy's words made him reconsider. To have a mother who would just take off on you, abandon you to your fate . . . he understood that kind of mothering too well. Time created distance, and maybe understanding, but it didn't necessarily heal those old deep wounds. When your mother didn't care enough to make you important, it left a solid mark on even the toughest hide. "I'm real sorry that happened."

"It's a raw wound." Lucy watched as the kids explored the beautiful vehicle. "Maude, Ashley's mother, didn't worry much about mothering after Chase died and wasn't all that good at it when he was alive."

"A toxic personality?"

"Yes. And self-indulgent, so I probably should have seen this coming."

He keyed in on the last phrase. "Do you always do that?"

She looked up at him while the kids pretended to be camping in the big new van. "Do what?"

"Take on guilt for things you couldn't possibly be responsible for?" He didn't want to anger her, but she couldn't be in charge of the world. "Because Ashley's mother could have chosen differently."

"I know." She kept her tone soft so the children wouldn't overhear. "I'm second-guessing myself about having Ashley come live with us. It sounded like a great olive branch at the time, but I didn't weigh the effect of her behavior on my kids well enough. I've had good success helping teens in the church's Overcomers group. That spurred my action, but I was doing the rose-colored glasses thing and thinking how we could benefit her. Not the other way around. And now with Maude gone . . ."

"You're stuck."

"Yes. I love Ashley," she continued. "She was Belle's size when I started dating her brother. And someplace deep inside she loves me too, but it's not easy to break through her anger."

"It's a tough wall to breach when kids have too much time on their hands. Loose time makes it easy to feel sorry for yourself."

She grabbed his arms with two very feminine hands that shouldn't have a death grip, but did. "That's it." Excitement eased the look of strain. "That's a great idea, Trey."

Trey was pretty sure he hadn't had an idea, but he liked the anticipation in her eyes and the feel of her palms against his forearms. "Glad to oblige. But I'm not sure what I've done exactly."

"A service project," she explained. "Doing something to stop thinking about ourselves. That's the best way of clearing our heads."

She was light-years ahead of him, but he pretended to keep up. "You're right. Absolutely. But what's available to do?"

"People have been doing all kinds of things

since the fire. Providing food and comfort for all the volunteers in town. Helping on-site, being a 'gofer' so the construction crew doesn't have to stop to get things every five minutes. I've got all those nice groceries now, and Ashley loves to bake. We could start with baking things for the work crews. They've got a picnic area set up across from the church. That would be a beginning."

"For all his faults, my father always believed in keeping us so busy we didn't have time to think about ourselves or cause too much of a stir," Trey said, then amended the thought slightly when Cade and Cody started to get into it inside the van. "Unless we were fighting with each other." He reached into the van, collared Cody, and scolded him with a look when he started picking a fight with Cade. He didn't use words. Just gave the kid a look, much like Murt had done with him back in the day. And it worked.

"Sorry, Trey."

"Cowboys only fight when there's no other choice. One way or another, trouble finds us soon enough. Doesn't make much sense to start extra."

" 'Kay."

Lucy had let go of his arms, and he kind of wished she'd grab hold again and talk to him about anything she chose. She didn't. She eyed him and the boys, then him again. "Neat trick."

"Cowboy discipline. Comes from within, ma'am."

"Well, I wouldn't object to more of that self-restraint stuff at home, that's for sure."

"You're one on four, Lucy. Rough odds at times. For all our crazy growing up, we had Murt and Hobbs watching out for us, teaching us along the way. And a housekeeper putting food on the table. And work or fun, morning till night. Your role has more constraints, and that's not easy."

"I'm not feeling sorry for myself."

"Whoa, Ms. Lucy, don't get all up in arms. I didn't mean to imply that," he replied. "I'm just saying there was a whole crew on the Double S to teach us from little up. And plenty of work for idle hands. I think it helped."

"So we've decided?" The salesman had been discreet while they talked. He approached them now with an expectant expression.

Trey turned to Lucy. "Is this the one?"

"Yes." She looked amazed and downright sweet when she sent a smile his way. "It's wonderful."

"It's green." Trey reminded her of their former conversation with a skeptical look. "I distinctly recall—"

"I've grown to like the green actually. And it will look good against the red barn."

"Bring the kids in while we do paperwork," the salesman suggested. "There's a playroom they might like."

They not only liked it, they played for fifteen

minutes without a squabble while Lucy and Trey completed the deal.

Sheer joy came first . . .

And then trepidation.

That's how Trey would describe Lucy's face when the sales manager handed her the paper-work. She looked at the papers, then the van, then Trey. "I'm still not sure this is right."

"It's absolutely right," Trey assured her. He turned toward the excited kids. "You guys want to ride back home with Mom in the new van?"

Cody and Belle jumped at the chance, but Cade tugged Trey's sleeve. Trey squatted to his level. "What's up?"

"Can I ride with you? Please?"

Trey's heart went kind of loose, and he couldn't remember the last time it did that. He nodded, touched by the boy's choice. "Sure. Hop in."

He did. Trey made sure his belt was fastened securely, then turned to open Lucy's door for her. "Can't drive home without getting in, Ms. Lucy."

"Trey, I—"

He leaned close. Real close. Then he touched her hand lightly. "Last Saturday could have been worse. Much worse. Let me do this as a way of saying, 'I'm real glad you were okay,' because nothing is more important than that, Lucy."

She studied his eyes, and for a moment he wondered what she saw, but then she swallowed hard, reached up, and kissed him on the cheek. "Thank you."

No flirting, no teasing, just that, sweet and simple.

His heart stretched wider. He held the door and she climbed in and turned the engine on.

And then he followed her home, with a little cowpoke tucked in the back seat, a boy that seemed to really like having him around. Cade's joy at being with him was a complete surprise and pure bonus because it was the last thing Trey'd expected.

She'd kissed him.

Oh, sure, it was a peck-on-the-cheek kind of thing. He knew that.

But he liked making her smile. He liked inspiring contentment. With four kids to handle and a house and farm, he was pretty sure Lucy had been too busy raising a family to worry about herself. And he suspected her late husband hadn't made it a priority either.

Was he wading in too deep? Cowboy code said you didn't flirt with a single mom unless you meant it. Did he mean it? Like, seriously mean it?

A little soon to tell, isn't it? Stop rushing things, focus on the work you've got to do, and let life and God take care of the rest. You sing about that all the time. Now it's time to do more than sing, cowboy. Time to take your own advice.

The sage advice hit home. He turned onto I-90,

determined to get as much work done at Lucy's as he could fit into the days because if something happened to him . . .

If for some reason he wasn't around to finish what he started . . .

He lifted his chin, determined.

He'd get done what he could before the liver surgery. Sam had always been big on finishing a job, not leaving things half-done. He was right, and Trey aimed to do just that for the next-door neighbor. And if his work earned him more of those sweet smiles?

Well, that wouldn't be a bad thing either.

Ten

Ashley stared at Lucy as if she'd gone over the edge when Lucy proposed her brilliant idea that afternoon. "You want me to bake something? It's like ninety degrees. No one bakes when it's hot like this."

"I agree, and I should have said 'make something' instead," Lucy replied. She kept her voice easy, hoping Ashley would do the same. "They need desserts at the food line for the workers, and you like making things, Ash. You always have." She sent her an encouraging look and opened the nearby cupboard. "You could do a Jell-O dessert. We're stocked up on all kinds of flavors. Or how about those peanut butter bars everyone loves? No baking required."

The idea of the peanut butter bars seemed to tempt the teen, but then she shrugged it off. "I'm not into it."

"What are you into, Ashley?" Lucy kept her voice soft as she faced the troubled girl. "You used to like so many things, making things, doing things, playing with the Murphy girls." The Murphys were Maude's neighbors, and they had three tween and teen girls. "What's changed?"

Ashley stared out the window, then angled a too-tough look at Lucy. "My life. Chase is gone, my mother's a loser who couldn't stay straight for a day if it killed her, and I can't do the stupid schoolwork they want me to. I'd rather die than try, and now I'm stuck here, with you and three little kids who never stop whining. You wanna know why I don't hang out with the Murphy girls anymore?" Angry tears looked close to overflowing, but Ashley brushed them away. "Their parents won't let them be friends with me. I'm a bad influence, and they aren't even allowed to sit near me on the bus."

Should she say something? Or just listen?

Lucy had no idea, but it didn't matter because Ashley turned around and stomped up the stairs, but before she slammed her door, she yelled, "Make your own stupid cookie things!"

Lucy saw her pain. She remembered what it was like to be betrayed by a parent, a father who had no love for his wife or his little girl. She understood the gravity.

Trey had called Maude toxic, and he was right, but Ashley was pretty venomous herself right now. How could Lucy help her without jeopardizing her three kids? Or was she looking at an impossible task?

You have friends, people who know more about this. Call Angelina, see if she and Elsa have any advice.

She took the cordless phone outside. Belle had organized a doll orphanage on the side porch. The boys weren't fighting. They'd actually set up a make-believe "saddle" on a loop of fence and were pretending to be cowboys, like Trey. And Trey was putting the final new board in place on the south side of the barn. The clean, pristine beige of the new wood stood out against the old siding.

"A new heart also will I give you, and a new spirit will I put within you . . ."

Ezekiel's words, so apt.

She wanted that new heart, and the uplifted spirit that went with it. Attaining it was another matter. She dialed Angelina's number before she chickened out, and when Ange answered, she got right to the point. "I need advice from you and Elsa. Is she back from visiting her parents yet?"

"She rolled in a few hours ago. Come over now."

"But—" Now? She couldn't go now. She had kids to watch and things to do.

"Tell Trey to keep an eye on the kids. Doesn't pay to wait, Lucy."

Pragmatic and to the point, that was Angelina, and exactly what Lucy needed. And a touch of Elsa's common sense but gentle psychology as well. "I'll see if he minds."

"He won't." Angelina hung up before she could say any more, and Lucy crossed the stones reluctantly. She hated asking for help. She particularly disliked asking for help from a man.

She swallowed her pride, approached the scaffold, and looked up.

He'd swiped a rag to his forehead and was grabbing a long drink of water.

Amazing. Total male, stem to stern, broad shouldered, narrow hipped, legs braced. Standing there, framed by slabs of golden wood.

She didn't want to think that, but no one looking at Trey Walker on a scaffold, in a white T-shirt and faded, loose jeans, could be immune. She bit back self-recrimination, and when he noticed her, he smiled.

Oh, that smile.

Tune-crooning country cowboy to the max, with a late-day dusting of beard.

"What's up?" He crossed the scaffold, swung down the ladder, then hoisted the ladder and hung it just inside the barn, out of the boys' reach. "You've got that look on your face, Lucy."

"I'm not sure what that means, but I'd like to run over to the Double S and talk to Angelina and Elsa about Ashley. I can't leave the kids. Could you—"

"Hang out for a bit?" He finished the sentence for her. She figured watching out for a bunch of kids was probably the last thing he wanted to do after being up on a scaffold, working in the hot sun. "Glad to. I'll take a seat on that porch with Miss Belle and grab a glass of that iced tea.

Can't think of a better way to end the day actually."

He couldn't mean it, but he looked like he meant it.

So did Chase and just about every honky-tonk and tavern musician you know. Fool me once, shame on you. Fool me twice, shame on me.

"Thank you. Ashley is upstairs."

"She didn't take right off with that whole baking idea, I take it?"

"I believe she was actually insulted by the suggestion."

"Teens can be a tough lot."

Was it memories or sympathy that marked his gaze? Maybe both.

"Go see what the ladies have to say," he continued. "I'll be here when you get back. Mind if I grab a peanut butter and jelly sandwich while you're gone?"

Such ordinary food for an extraordinary man. "Of course not. I should have offered you some earlier. It felt weird offering PB&J to a country star."

He tipped his gaze down. "The name's Hank, ma'am. And I grew up on PB&J not too far from here, true words. That's some mighty fine eats."

Charming. Kind. Caring.

She couldn't help but smile, and he winked when she did, which put her belly or her heart or something midsection into a tailspin.

"You go ahead; I can find the stuff."

"All right." She started for the house to get her keys, then remembered.

She didn't need a regular key.

She walked to the van, climbed in, and started the engine. It purred, and when she shifted gears, nothing clunked.

Smooth and sweet, like the cowboy who bought it. And while part of her was suspicious of anything that came across as *too* smooth, another part appreciated the kindness in everything he did. She pulled into the Double S, not blinded to the irony of coming here for advice, but here she was.

She parked the van and saw Elsa Andreas, a local psychologist and Nick's fiancée, heading her way. Elsa had pulled her blond hair back in a ponytail, and her trusty dog, Achilles, trotted by her side. He'd clearly missed his owner. When Elsa paused, Achilles paused too. Eyes up, he gave Elsa such a look of utter devotion, it made Lucy's heart tug a little. "Lucy, hey." Elsa took Lucy's hand and squeezed lightly. "I hear we've been called for a consultation."

"Off the clock, because I can't afford you on the clock, Elsa."

Elsa laughed and tucked Lucy's arm through hers as they strolled toward the door. "No charge among friends. Ange is inside, Isabo has the girls, and Noah's down at the pond with Nick. What's up?"

Angelina was setting out tea, cookies, and glasses but managed to shoot Lucy a quick cop look. "Is Trey in trouble?"

"Trey?" The question surprised Lucy so much that she stared at her, confused. "How could Trey be in trouble?"

"Ah . . ." Angelina exchanged a look of interest with Elsa. "He couldn't be, of course. Not our Trey."

"Barely know him, but already love him," Elsa declared. She winked at Angelina. "What's not to love?"

The light dawned. Lucy held up one hand, palm out, to stop their speculation. "It's not like that. You two are whacked."

"Of course it's not."

"It never is, dear." Elsa's smile widened, but then she leaned forward. "If this isn't about Trey, then what's going on?"

"Ashley."

Angelina didn't look surprised.

Elsa squinted with confusion. "Who is Ashley?"

"My late husband's much younger sister. She's fourteen. I brought her to live with us three weeks ago, and in that three weeks I discovered she's been smoking pot and her mother left town without a forwarding address after she cut off the kid's phone. Ashley's reluctantly going to summer school because she blew off homework and English class in eighth grade. She wrongly thinks we can ignore the law and let her quit school so she can get a job."

"Because there are so many jobs out there for uneducated, pot-smoking, belligerent teenagers," Angelina noted.

"That's the deal."

"And with her mom gone, you've got little recourse." Elsa tapped the side of her glass and frowned, thinking.

"Exactly." Elsa had nailed the conundrum instantly.

"Don't get me wrong, I love Ashley. We've been friends for ten years, but she's being a first-class brat, and I'm scared that by having her at my house, I'm going to totally mess up my kids. And now I don't know what to do."

"When does summer school end?"

"A week from this Friday."

"And she wants a job?" Angelina folded her hands together. "What if we hire her here for fifteen hours a week?"

"Are you serious?"

"I am. Kids always think they know what they want, but what they need is often quite different. You said the phone was shut off, right?"

"Yes."

Isabo had come into the kitchen for cookies. Angelina put a hand on her arm. "Mami, I think we could scare up some hours for Ashley, don't you? If she works hard she can earn enough money to turn the phone back on. If that's how she decides to spend it when it comes time."

Isabo's lips formed a thin line. "There can be no nonsense here. I will have my hands full caring for Sam and—"

"Oh, that's right." Lucy didn't let her finish. "The last thing you're going to need or want is a somewhat untrustworthy teen hanging around."

"Trustworthiness is a factor of importance, but how does one re-earn trust, if no opportunity is given?"

Leave it to Isabo to sum things up. "You think it would work? And you wouldn't mind?"

"This way she can see if the reality matches the dream. We know as adults that's not always the case."

Lucy knew that, all right.

"And if she likes working here," Angelina went on, "and does well in school, we might be able to extend the opportunity into the school year. As long as she follows the rules."

"Which I will set." Keeping her voice firm, Isabo finished gathering cookies for the kids outside, but kept right on talking. "And then, of course, I will watch. I do believe she liked the horses well enough, and if she's hardworking, we could make that a reward as well."

"That's an excellent idea." Elsa raised her glass of tea in a toast. "And you guys didn't need me at all. I'm kinda bummed by that."

"Oh, we need you, all right." Angelina touched her glass to Lucy's, then Elsa's. "Nick actually smiles now, enough so that Colt makes fun of him."

Elsa laughed.

"And the girls are finally coming around," Angelina continued. "You are very needed here, Elsa. Nick couldn't wait to show people the layout for the new house over the weekend, although he's chomping at the bit because of the delays."

"An impatient Stafford?" Elsa pretended that was unlikely. "Surely you jest."

"Lucy." Sam's voice interrupted their teasing. He walked toward the kitchen from the great room beyond, and Lucy was pretty sure he looked even worse than he had on Sunday.

"Mr. Stafford." Should she stand? Stay seated? Treat him with respect or spit in his eye? *Seventy times seven . . .* She stood and extended her hand. "Would you like to sit with us?"

He took her hand briefly but shook his head. "No. I heard your voice and wanted to see if plans are progressing. Did you find a vehicle today?"

"We did." She blushed to say it because it felt plain wrong to accept a brand-new, off-the-lot, upscale van for her piece-of-junk clunker. "It's parked outside, and it's quite amazing."

"Good!" He smiled at her, a gentle smile. It didn't look like Trey's smile, but it was similar in warmth, and that surprised her again. "I know that will take a load off Trey's mind. And the work is progressing?"

"Trey's working hard," she told him.

He nodded.

"They're beginning the roofing projects tomorrow, they've put in new barn supports, and Trey finished the front side of the barn today."

"Perfect." His smile faded slightly. He grasped the back of an empty chair and took two slow breaths. "I think I'm going to call it a night, ladies."

Angelina followed his progress with a worried gaze. "Good night, Sam."

"Rest well," added Elsa.

Lucy watched him walk down the wide hall. Hesitant steps. Loss of stature. He leaned to the right as if standing straight was simply too painful. And then she couldn't help herself. "God bless you, Mr. Stafford."

He paused and turned slightly. "Thank you, my dear."

"You're welcome."

Angelina covered Lucy's hand with one of hers when Sam was out of earshot. "That was nice of you."

"He looks frail."

"He is."

"And he's trying to make things better."

"Also true," Angelina confirmed. "I know that

fixing things now doesn't erase the past. But maybe it eases some of the sharper corners. The ones that cut deep."

Little voices shouted outside the kitchen window. Lucy stood.

"I've got to get back. It's been almost an hour, and I can't believe I just dumped four kids on country music's finest while I grabbed some girl time."

"It's good for Trey," Angelina told her as she stood.

"Gives him practice for more nephews and nieces," added Elsa. "You're just doing your part to help shape future family dynamics."

"You know he misses living here." Lucy wasn't sure she should say anything, but Trey hadn't said it was a secret. "He misses the hills and the mountains and the ranch. And his family."

"He said that?" Angelina looked surprised. "Trey talks more than the other two combined, and actually says less. A clever trick."

"I'm glad he was comfortable enough to share his thoughts with you," Elsa said. "Eventually we all need a place to call home. Not just a place to store our stuff."

"An imperfect home, but filled with love and hope. Does that sound as corny to you as it does to me?" Lucy asked. "Because I think the likelihood of finding that on a scale of one to ten is about a two."

"Then you need to toughen that faith, girl. Because I'm not settling for anything less than an eight-point-five," Angelina told her as the kids raced across the stone. "I'd go higher, but I am marrying a stick-in-the-mud stubborn Stafford."

"I think eight-point-five sounds solid. I'd be happy with that," Elsa agreed.

Two funny women, jumping into marriage with good-looking, rich cowboys. Maybe it would work for them. Maybe being older and financially secure would help.

Then Lucy thought of Mary and Joseph, trudging to Bethlehem, about to have a child, and realized that stature of heart mattered far more than financial standing. And that's what she'd missed in Chase. He'd fallen in love with the idea of a cute wife and steamy nights, not the responsibility of real life.

"Mommy!" Noah burst through the side door. Elsa caught it on the backswing before it smacked Dakota. "I caught free toads!" He held up three fingers and had to wrestle his pinky down with his other hand.

"And Uncle Nick said we could name th-th-them, so I did. I named them Uncle Nick, Uncle Trey, and Colt!"

"Three toads, huh?" Elsa reached out and hugged Nick's arm when he came in behind the boy. "Out of the mouths of babes," she teased.

Nick laughed, grabbed a handful of cookies,

and saluted Lucy with them. "You've been keeping our country star busy I hear."

"With no effort on my part, he came ready equipped, it seems. I don't think he has an Off switch."

"It's going all right?" he continued, around a mouthful of cookie.

"Yes, thank you."

"Good. Let me know if you need any extra man power to get things wrapped up. I could spare a hand or two for a little bit."

Nick Stafford had been fairly glum for the past several years, so for him to smile, be nice— no, wait, make that *cheerful*—and offer help was about as surreal as Sam's turnaround.

And really enjoyable, which meant Lucy better get out of there or she'd start thinking the Staffords were about the kindest family around. She knew better. She'd experienced the reality, but if she was grading family performance right now, the family next door would be edging toward an A, and that was a sharp step up from the failing grade they'd had for so long.

"Elsa, Angelina, thank you."

"Didn't do much, but we'll be glad to have Ashley on board." Angelina took Noah's hand as she followed Lucy through the door. "Let's try her this weekend."

"And you'll set firm boundaries?"

Angelina pointed toward her mother as she sent

Nick's girls upstairs for a quick shower. "Oh, there'll be boundaries, all right. And the perfect drill sergeant to go with them."

"Saturday at ten," Isabo called over her shoulder. "We have much to do this Saturday and she will be of great help to me."

"All right." Lucy stepped outside and pulled in a breath of sweet, warm valley air. Elsa and Angelina followed. Colt approached from the first paddock, slipped an arm around Angelina, and kissed her. And then he bent, scooped Noah up, and slung the little boy up and onto his shoulders.

"I'm so high!" Noah shrieked in delight, his little hands fisted in the collar of Colt's shirt. "I love this so much!"

"Me too, little man." Colt reached out and swept the curve of his knuckles to Angelina's cheek in a caress so sweet, Lucy ached to see it. "I couldn't be happier."

"Me too!"

She didn't want to envy them. She knew what Angelina had gone through, how she'd left her job on the Seattle police force to keep her family safe from racketeers. And Elsa had sought peace and quiet in the woods outside Gray's Glen after losing two young patients to domestic violence.

They were embracing their happy endings, and that was wonderful, but right now Lucy would be happy with a great floral sale at Saturday's market and the much-needed improvements on her farm.

To have things taken care of in an orderly fashion would be a dream come true. That was more than enough, but as she climbed into the van, Lucy remembered Trey's hazel eyes, all gray and green and gold, bright enough to carry a sweet message of promise. But there was no way that hinted promise held true. Not in the real world.

Trey was a superstar. Women from coast to coast unabashedly crushed on him. He could date, love, marry any woman he wanted, so she was pretty sure he wasn't looking for a long-term commitment with a beleaguered single mother.

He'd had it all once, the nearly perfect profile of a dream come true until everything fell apart. He'd been married to a country singer. They had two great careers going and a marvelous home in Tennessee. And then tragedy struck and his wife was gone after an unintentional overdose at a wild party. The tabloids had a field day. Speculation abounded. News reports had made it sound as if Trey and Cathy were never satisfied, no matter how successful they were. That it was never enough, and they'd followed that high-end slippery slope into partying and drugs.

Lucy had watched what those choices did to her husband, her family, and her marriage. Never again would she risk emotional and physical well-being with a substance abuser. Maybe Trey was straight now. Maybe the papers got it wrong. She hoped so. But she'd risked too much trying to be what Chase needed at the beginning. She'd wised up and quietly grabbed hold of the straight and narrow, and that's where she'd happily stay. And if that meant being single while she raised her children?

Lucy Carlton was okay with that, because she intended to be the person who broke the chain of domestic dysfunction. Kids first. Beyond that, life would just have to be put on hold.

"Lucy. Wait." She'd eased down the first quarter of the driveway when Colt's voice stopped her. He crossed to the driver's side, concerned. "Aren't they starting the roof tear-offs tomorrow?"

"Yes. The big dumpster got delivered today."

"You can't be there with the kids."

"I figured I'd keep them inside."

Colt shook his head. Angelina agreed. "Bring them over here the next few days," she offered. "Kids and construction are an awful mix, and we'd never forgive ourselves if something happened. I'm working, but Elsa will be here with my mother."

Surreal and awkward, but it almost didn't feel awkward to have neighbors care. It felt greeting-card-commercial nice. "Are you sure?"

"Positive." Colt nodded. "Why hole up in the house when the kids can race around over here? I bet Murt or Hobbs will give them some horse time. Neither one can resist showing kids the how-tos of ranching."

It made sense, even though she didn't want to be indebted. "What about your father? Won't that be too much confusion?"

"He'll escape to his room when it's too much, but he enjoys watching the kids have fun," Angelina assured her. "I think it brightens his days. And they'll all be gone Thursday for the surgical consult, so your crew would liven things up."

Thursday. Jenna was coming by to watch kids while Lucy shaped trees. She frowned because having kids underfoot during a roof tear-off probably wasn't the best-laid plan.

Angelina read her expression. "What's wrong?"

Lucy explained the time frame and Angelina waved it off. "I'm off on Thursday, so Jenna can watch the kids here, and you can shape your trees."

"You're sure?"

"Good for all of us. And we'll have Mami bake something delicious and maybe the boys would like to help."

"Instead of riding with Hobbs or Murt?" Colt didn't look surprised. He looked flabbergasted.

"A wise man learns his way around the kitchen *and* the barn," Lucy told him. "The boys love to help in the kitchen, actually."

He laughed and stepped back.

"See you tomorrow then, Lucy."

"All right."

She pulled away in her new dream van, caught

in her neighbors' kindness, wondering if she was about to wake up to the same-old, same-old reality she'd known for so long. When she pulled into her driveway a few minutes later, there was Trey, cozied on the side porch with Belle, reading a story to all three kids. He'd stretched out his long legs onto the porch rail, looking cramped but quite natural as he related the story.

She wasn't dreaming, but if she had been, her dream would look like this. A good man, taking time with kids after putting in a hard day's work. A simple image, really, but experience told her it was mighty hard to attain. And yet . . .

Seeing Trey and the kids on that worn and rickety porch made the impossible seem possible. Maybe some men were good with kids and treated them with patience and humor and kindness. She was learning that her reality didn't always equate with normal, and that was something to keep in mind.

He didn't jump up when she pulled in, as if glad to be done with the kids. He stayed right there, finishing the story, and looked like he was enjoying his role.

Ashley came out the door when she heard the van. She sat down hard on the listing step, still angry with the world, and Lucy's perfect family image fractured, tumbling to the ground below.

Trey stood and hoisted Belle into his arms. She curled in as if she belonged there, which meant she was growing too attached to the soon-to-be-gone singing cowboy. He handed Cody the book.

"Can you put this away for me, partner?"

"Sure!"

Lucy stared at her son as he cheerfully went inside to put the book away.

"I'm going to practice my riding!" Cade raced across the stones, then turned without being reminded. "Thanks for the story, Trey!"

One boy cooperating, the other thanking a grown-up without prodding.

She thought she might be dreaming after all, but one look up into Trey's eyes put her heart into wide-awake mode. "Thank you for staying."

"You're welcome."

"Ashley."

The girl glanced up, clearly discontented with just about everything. "What?"

"You said you wanted a job."

"Yes. Going to school is stupid when you hate it."

Lucy wasn't about to debate that. "Going to school is a necessity; there's no wiggle room there. But if you can keep your grades up, Isabo has offered to take you on over at the Double S to help her with summer chores inside and out."

"You mean, like working there?" She stood up quickly and stared at Lucy. "Like they'd pay me?"

"You'd be on the payroll, yes, on a trial agreement. If it doesn't work out, the job disappears. And the contingencies are you have to follow directions and do whatever they ask you to do—"

"Well, it's a job, of course you do what they tell you to do!"

That was the first common-sense statement Lucy had heard from the girl since she moved in.

"What else?"

"You have to be passing everything, which means getting through summer school, and then high school. Also, half of your wages will go into the bank after the first two weeks. The other half you can spend as you wish, on your phone, clothing, music—whatever, but there can't be any smoking of anything."

She aimed a direct look at Ashley and was glad when the teen flushed.

"No drinking, no partying. One infraction and you're done. You have to be total golden to pull this off."

"I will."

Ashley clapped her hands together, and suddenly she didn't look like a disgruntled, aloof teen. She looked energized. "When can I start?"

"Saturday. I told Isabo I'd have you there at ten o'clock."

"Okay!" Ashley started to turn, then swung back. "You did this for me, Lucy?"

Lucy nodded.

Ashley rarely cried. She'd never been an overly

emotional girl, but her eyes went to water now. She reached out and hugged Lucy hard. "Thank you. All I've ever wanted is a chance to just be me. Thank you, Lucy!"

"Don't blow it."

Lucy hugged her back, but when she stepped back, she made direct eye contact with Ashley. "This might be a good time to start reconsidering those friend connections. A good friend doesn't tempt you to sin or break the law or develop bad habits. A true friend looks out for you."

She didn't mention the Murphy girls by name, but she hoped Ashley began to see the difference. Maybe if she got her act together, the Murphys would let their daughters hang out with Ashley again. "Freshman year is the best time to change up your circle of friends, because everyone's new at the high school, and you'll all be in different classes."

Ashley nodded.

Would she heed the advice?

Maybe, with her new job on the line. And prayer. And support.

"I'm going to call Gracelyn and tell her!"

Gracelyn didn't hang with the wild crowd, and she'd been a friend of Ashley's since elementary school.

"She'll be excited for you."

Ashley hurried inside as Cody came back outside. He whooped and hollered like a wild man and raced across the gravel yard, brandishing an imaginary lasso.

"You got Ashley a job."

Trey smiled approval and pride, then shoulder-nudged her and almost knocked her off the step. "Whoa, there. Didn't realize you were so close to the edge, Ms. Lucy."

She was close to an edge every time he looked her way with that boyish grin and a man's look of appreciation.

"I stay away from edges for good reason."

Understanding lifted his brows, but then he rocked back on his heels. "There's wisdom in that stance, but every now and again you've got to get off the Ferris wheel for a spin on the roller coaster. Something about the wind in your face, the speed, the reactions around you."

"I like roller coasters in amusement parks. Not so much in life."

He grinned and handed Belle to Lucy as he descended the two steps. "We should take the kids sometime. Once Ashley's done with school so she can go with us."

"Except there aren't any in the area."

"The county fair and rodeo, Labor Day weekend."

"You'll be here?"

He didn't look at her. He stared away as if thinking, then gave her a quick salute. "I should be around. If Ashley is doing well with school

201

and work, that would be a nice reward for all of us, I think."

"The kids would love it, Trey." Of course they would. What kid wouldn't? A fair filled with lights and sound, amusement rides, farm animals, food, and historical reenactments. "The boys would be over the moon."

"Consider it a date, Lucy."

She blushed. She didn't want to and could have kicked herself for lack of self-control because when he saw the blush, his smile went wide and he tipped the brim of his hat ever so slightly.

"See you in the morning."

"Yes."

He left, and it wasn't until he'd pulled that SUV up and out of the yard that she started breathing again.

He was flirting with her. She loved it, and she could list a host of reasons why nothing could or should come from it. But, when she was all done listing, she was still thinking about that smile. The touch to his hat. And the September date . . .

And that made her smile all over again.

Eleven

"Trey, we'll have to paint the shed another day. I'm taking the kids to the Double S to avoid possible catastrophes from roof tear-off. The door's open, drinks in the fridge. Lucy."

Trey read the scrawled note she'd left on the front door and frowned.

He hadn't realized how much he'd anticipated seeing her in the morning until he pulled in with painting supplies from Hammerstein's and she wasn't there.

Benson's crew had started on the house roof. The barn was going to be last, giving him a couple of days to finish fixing the exterior siding. And he wanted to install new porch posts before they put the new porch roof in place, so he mentally blocked out time in the afternoon.

The place seemed quiet and lonely, despite the noise of men working. Using broad roof rakes, they slid multiple layers of old roofing into the dumpster below. A conveyor belt stood in the drive, ready to deliver roofing supplies to both levels of the worn house.

Smitten.

He frowned as he started on the barn's east end. He wasn't smitten. He didn't have time or energy to be smitten. And what kind of a word was that anyway?

He turned the radio on, heard his own voice, and turned it right back off again.

Glib words of hope and heart were the last things he wanted to hear. He wanted—

He cut boards and fixed them in place with pops of the nail gun, but he couldn't get images of Lucy out of his mind. Why? After years of enforced solitude, this sudden urge to protect and defend felt alien but good. Real good. And he couldn't remember the last time he felt just plain good.

"Trey?" Josh Washington's voice hollered from out front.

"Round back." He had to yell over the combined sounds from the roofing crew as they scraped away layers of neglect.

Josh gave his progress a thumbs-up. "Not bad for a novice."

Trey laughed. "If it's a straight cut and a nail gun, I do okay. Did you need me for something?"

"Just to touch base. I figured we'd leave the scaffold set up out front so the boys can start painting. Rye said he's bringing them by. We've got some cloud cover today, so it's a good day to put a fresh look on the south face. It won't blister that way."

"Sounds good."

"You've gotten a lot done." Josh tipped his ball cap back as he surveyed Trey's work. "That coat of paint and the new roof will cap this off."

"Can we get the scaffold around back for Friday?"

"Sure. And we'll do the same thing, rotate Brendan and the Battaglia boys in to paint. You wanted advice on the porch, I heard."

Trey angled the freshly cut board against the sawhorse table and walked Josh across the drive.

"I'm handy enough to replace the supports and anchor them, then wrap them in four-by-ones."

"That'll give it a good look. I've got a jack to help maintain support. You got lumber enough for the long braces?"

"To support the roof while I'm working, yeah. But I'm not skilled enough to do railings, and they need to be replaced." Trey pointed out the wet rot from backsplash on the lower wood. "Can one of your guys jump in on those? I've got the new door unit ordered so they'll have a safe, secure porch for the kids, and an entry that doesn't suck cold in and let heat out every winter."

"My Shannon can help with that, as long as someone's around to help balance things if need be."

"Shannon?" Trey pulled back, surprised. "Isn't she like fourteen?"

"Exactly fourteen," Josh told him. "But she's been by my side for years. She's got a knack for detail work and fine carpentry."

He thought of Ashley, with few skills, but

yearning for a job. Maybe hands-on work was part of the answer for kids, like his father believed. He'd taken that Stafford work ethic with him to Nashville, and while others partied or wasted time, he'd holed himself up, writing song after song, playing gig after gig, determined.

"I'll be right here with her," he promised. "Maybe she can teach me a thing or two."

Josh laughed. "She most likely could. And keeping a teenager working means they're not spending every extra moment thinking about stuff best left alone for a few years." He waved to the roofers, then to Rye Bennett as he pulled in with the three teenage boys. Josh took the boys over to the scaffold and gave them step-by-step instructions. When he'd gotten the teens set up, he headed out while the teens set to work, excited.

Rye watched them for a moment, then motioned Trey toward his SUV police cruiser. He indicated the teens on the scaffold and kept his voice quiet. "The older Battaglia brother is the one Angelina saved from an overdose after the spring fire."

Trey didn't do users, ever. He started to step back, and Rye held up a hand. "I'm not saying you have to use him, because I know you're dead set against drugs, but as far as I can tell, it was a one-time stupid mistake, and he's been squeaky clean ever since. He goes to the church's Overcomers group, and Lucy's been a great influence on him. She won't mind him working here, but I wanted to run it by you."

"I don't know what an Overcomers group is, and I have a healthy and understandable disdain for druggies, Rye. I don't tolerate them on my team, in my band, or on my tours."

"Your call. And the Overcomers is a teen self-help group Lucy got started in the church a couple of years back. With weed legally available now, it's become pervasive around the schools. And it's opened up the heroin market, big time. Since the dealers can't make money on marijuana, they upped their games to other drugs. Heroin's become a big problem all over."

Teens and heroin.

Trey hated the very thought of teens and drugs. If they'd seen what he'd seen . . .

"That's a lot of responsibility to put on me, Rye."

Rye didn't press. He stood quietly, waiting for Trey to make the call.

Should he risk it? Could he risk it? He'd already been put through the wringer and hung out to dry once. He scrubbed a hand to the back of his neck, conflicted.

"I figured you didn't know," Rye went on. "And I'd never blindside a friend. Everyone deserves a second chance, but I'll understand if you pull up the welcome mat and want him gone."

"How old is he?"

"Fifteen."

So young to be so stupid. And Ashley, at fourteen, mad at the world and sneaking pot to ease life's sharp edges.

"I think back to our time at that age, and I realize your father had us working so hard, we barely had time to think of girls, much less messing up our lives."

"I resented that then." Trey clenched his jaw, thinking. "But now I see it makes sense, especially raising kids on your own."

"My mom was the same way, and I see how it helps Brendan and Jenna, but it's not easy. Say the word and he's gone, Trey. No one wants to bring trouble down on you or Lucy."

Lucy.

She'd give the kid another chance. He didn't even need to ask. He'd only known her for a matter of days, but he knew what he saw: a kindhearted person, willing to put her faith in others. He'd been that way once and had sworn never to take a risk like that again. Trey kept his tone short and tight, and didn't try to mask the doubt. "We'll give it a try."

"All I can ask." Rye climbed into his cruiser and headed out before he had a chance to change his mind, and a good thing, too, because Trey was close to chasing him down before he made it onto the road.

"For if you forgive men their trespasses,

your heavenly Father will also forgive you."

The words from Matthew's gospel seemed simplistic, as if it was that easy. It couldn't be, not when lives were at stake. When lives were lost.

"Trey, is your phone working? Mine died." Benson approached him, saw the three teens, and turned their way. "Don't you knuckleheads mess up Trey's nice work by being sloppy with that paint! And don't work so slow that it gets tacky before you smooth things out."

"We won't, Benson!" Brendan called down. "My brother already threatened our lives, and so did Colt. Trey would have to stand in line to make us suffer."

Trey could picture Rye and Colt saying exactly that. He grinned. "Before your brushes and rollers do get tacky, change them up. Garbage can is right there for the used ones. I'll be right up to show you what I'm after."

"Got it, sir." The younger Battaglia gave him a little salute, but not in a smart-aleck way.

Benson clapped him on the back. "We're going to be two days on the house, then the outbuildings, then the barn. Does that work with your time frame?"

"Yup."

"And do you mind if I turn on some music? The guys asked, but I didn't want to mess you up if you'd rather have it quiet."

"Music's fine." He climbed up the scaffold, showed the kids how to work from the top down, blending section by section with the big rollers and a light touch, then pointed toward the house. "There's a cooler of drinks on the porch," he told them, "and we've got an outdoor privy coming." Josh had thought of that, so work crews wouldn't be asking to enter Lucy's house. "I'll be on the far side if you need me."

"Okay."

Frustration-fed energy drove him. Trey dove into fixing the north-facing side of the barn, and when that was done, he cut and propped the angled supports for the porch to replace the rotting pillars.

Nick stopped by midday with a huge box of sandwiches and chips, while Trey thought of Lucy, ten minutes west of him, eating with the kids and talking with Isabo.

He thought of her when a sweep of dark clouds rolled in and rolled right back out again, leaving nothing but sunshine in their wake.

And as he settled the first porch roof support into place, he wondered what it would be like to sit on this porch awhile, once it was all fixed up and looking new, with Lucy and the kids, singing songs while he plucked his guitar.

He got all five supports into place before supper. Just before six, Brendan called his name. He turned, and Brendan flagged him over.

The south side of the barn looked good. No, not just good. It looked great. He eyed the white trim, then the boys. "Who did the white?"

The older Battaglia boy hesitated, then poked his hand up. "I did, sir."

"Yeah?" Trey eyed the work, then looked at the kid again. "What's your name?"

"Mark."

"And you're Jacob, right?" He looked at the younger brother.

"Yes sir."

He faced Mark again. "The trim looks good. You scraped it down exactly like you were supposed to and didn't cut any corners. Come back tomorrow, all three of you, and we'll keep going."

Brendan high-fived him. "Sweet! Are there any sandwiches left?"

"Angelina did the ordering, so I'm sure there are. She's not afraid to feed people or spend money. You guys did all right today."

"My brother won't be here to get us for almost an hour," Brendan went on. "Is it okay if we take the food down to the pond out back?"

"Long as you don't mess around."

"We won't."

He followed them down the ladder, put it away, and then had Benson's crew help him relocate the scaffolding to the north side. He asked Benson to keep an eye on things the following day, and the roofer agreed.

Trey had promised Lucy a day to work in the trees, and he knew Jenna would be fine watching the kids up at the ranch, but he didn't like the thought of Lucy having to do the work alone. He knew nothing about trimming evergreens, but he could learn.

Thursday's primary goal, though, was visiting the surgeon. After that, he'd see if he was still in the frame of mind to trim trees or beg God for courage to undergo this surgery.

Did being nervous make him a coward? Or did it make him smart?

Trey was uncertain, but when Lucy drove the van up to the house a few minutes later, it wasn't just his heart that felt good. It was everything about her, making him feel stronger, braver, and bolder.

"That looks amazing!" She climbed out of the van, followed by a scramble of kids, and she took his arm as she looked at the barn. "I can't believe how much nicer it looks, Trey. It's beautiful already."

She hugged him.

A simple hug of gratitude shouldn't have meant much, but suddenly he wished she would just go on hugging him. Talking to him. Smiling so wide and happy when she saw him.

He hugged her back and when she peeked up from the curl of his arm, it was all he could do not to kiss her. He wanted to kiss her.

He wanted to laugh with her, walk with her and spend time with her, and kissing her jumped right into the equation.

"Do you like my mom?"

Cade's direct question pulled Trey back to reality. Lucy's emotions weren't the only ones involved here. Three little kids and an insolent teen were part of the deal. He kept things light as he dropped his arm. "I sure do. I like you too. This one, I'm not too sure about," he teased. He picked Cody up and tossed him over his shoulder. "But he's growing on me. Come on over here and see what we've got done."

He took them into the barn where the new supports shone bright against old, weathered wood. "Nice and solid now. The front's done, although I think it would look real nice with a lean-to coming off from about midway up, don't you? And maybe wrap it around the front for more display space?" He directed his attention away from the giggling kid slung over his shoulder and back to the kid's mother. "Then the front section of the barn could be a shop for folks buying Christmas things to go with their trees and wreaths and all those greenery things."

"A shop?" She looked up at him as if he might have just grown another head. "There's no money to build a shop inside the barn. But it *is* a great idea. I've always thought it would be fun to have a retail area inside, with some fresh baked goods and hot spiced cider. But that kind of thing requires funding, and you know the business climate around here. No one is waiting to hand a single mother a small-business loan."

She lived in a different world, he realized. He'd jumped into his career with both feet, unfettered by responsibilities to others and with a trust fund to get him through the lean times. Single parents didn't generally have that option. "We'll table that discussion." He jerked his head to the left as he set Cody down. "Let's check out my ideas for this porch." He walked them back across the stone driveway and tapped one of the roughed-in pillars. "You've got to use a little imagination here, Ms. Lucy."

She rolled her eyes, and that made him smile wider.

"The new supports have brought the roof back to level again."

"I noticed that as soon as I turned into the driveway. It's a straight line from left to right, a huge improvement."

"I'm going to finish the pillars off and we'll paint them white, then Josh is sending Shannon over to work on the railings."

"Shannon Washington?" Ashley looked surprised and a little envious. "She knows how to do wood stuff?"

"He said he's been teaching her carpentry for years."

"She's in my grade." Ashley studied the porch, doubtful.

"You're getting a job at the Double S," noted Lucy. "You're both growing up."

"But it's not like I know anything," Ashley argued, more with herself than with Lucy, and that was a welcome change. "I didn't know she liked to do that kind of stuff. Like she knows how to work saws and tools?"

"So he says."

"Wow." She sounded sincere. "That's pretty cool."

"There's a lot of cool stuff in this world, Ash," Lucy said gently. "We've just got to open our eyes to it."

Belle reached out her arms for Trey. "Can you carry me up high, pwease?"

"Colt puts Noah up on his shoulders," Lucy explained. "Belle, I—"

Trey picked Belle up and swung her over his shoulders, then waited while she settled herself and wrapped her legs around his neck. "As I was saying," he went on as if carrying preschoolers on his shoulders was an everyday occurrence, "we'll get the porch finished and painted. The house roof should be done by the weekend, and then they're doing the shed roofs. So maybe we can slap some fun paint on that chicken house over the weekend."

"I can't believe how much is getting done, and

so fast." Lucy gazed around. "I can see it, Trey. See what it will look like."

"I'm going to have Hobbs bring the grade scraper over when we're done. He loves running big stuff, so he'll be in his glory as long as he doesn't mow down the house or take out a barn support." He added a wince for dramatic effect. "He can scrape down the driveway here and the lane going behind the barn, toward the trees. I don't think you'll need fresh stone. It's just gotten slogged down into the surface. And that will get rid of those potholes."

No potholes would mean a smooth drive for customers. A new van. Solid porch supports and a renovated barn.

Tears smarted her eyes. She blinked them back as Ashley ran into the house to answer the phone, but when Trey turned to point out something else, he noticed right off. "You're upset."

"I'm not. I'm happy," she insisted. She dashed a hand to her face and breathed deep. "A little overwhelmed. But happy."

"Can we have cookies, Mom?" Cody asked. He grabbed her hand to gain her attention. "Angelina said she sent a bunch."

"She did and I put them on the kitchen table," Trey told her.

She told the boys yes, and they raced for the kitchen like half-starved pups. "They're always hungry."

"Fuel for running around like a pair of crazy kids. Do they play any sports yet, or are they too young?"

They weren't too young, but her options had been limited by lack of discretionary funds. "Money's tight. I'm not complaining," she added firmly. "Or whining. There's nothing wrong with having to make frugal decisions with kids."

"Did they get a chance to work with Hobbs or Murt today?"

She laughed because Sam had insisted that Hobbs let Joe cut hay while he worked with the boys. "Yes. Your father's orders. And the boys loved it, of course. I have to be careful though." She wasn't sure how to phrase her concerns. She paused a moment, then decided to just spit it out.

"This, all of this"—she waved her hand to encompass the barn, the house, the small farm— "is amazing. And I'm grateful for your father's desire to make things right, and for your help. This is huge for me, and I can't find proper words to express my gratitude. What your family has done for us is incredible, but it's not the norm for us, and I have to make sure that I keep these kids grounded. When all this comes to an end, we still need to go on about our daily business, satisfied with what we have."

"Why does it have to end?"

She didn't hear him just ask that, did she? The

sun was in her eyes when she looked up, so she stepped to the right.

He looked easygoing and serious, as he started toward the front of the barn. "Everything comes to an end, Trey. When you're off singing and touring, and our lives go back to normal, I'll be the one picking up the pieces."

"Well, a man's got to work, that's a fact." Half-serious, half-teasing, he kept moving, as if this was only a somewhat important conversation. On her end, dealing with aftermaths took on huge importance, but the frank smile he aimed her way left the conversation open. "That doesn't mean the kids can't learn how to work a ranch with Hobbs and Murt, does it?"

"I think it does actually."

"Why?"

What did he mean, *why?* "Because we live over here and can't impose on their hospitality like that."

"No imposition about it, ma'am. Just bein' neighbors, by and by."

"The country crooner in you makes it sound easy. I know better, and when you're talking kids, it's smarter to hedge your bets rather than set them up for disappointment. Cade was old enough to realize his father's choices. He's young, but he realizes that drugs and alcohol were more important than family, and that's a harsh reality for a kid to bear."

Her words affected Trey. She saw it in his face and heard it in his voice.

"I know the truth in that, but training these boys to the saddle is plain sensible from a ranch perspective. In a few years these guys could be great ranch hands, and they live right next door. That's a plus on any big operation. They'd get the chance to learn from the best of the best, and there's a basketball court set up in the middle barn. A great place for a kid to think, play, shoot hoops, and grow."

"You make it sound like bringing the kids over there is a benefit to the Double S, not a hassle. That is a dubious assumption on your part."

"Well, kids are always a hassle." He grinned when he said it, so it seemed he didn't mind the hassle all that much. "But my father wouldn't pull Hobbs out of the cattle area to help train kids to horse without a plan, and I think having a way to earn some money in a few years is a pretty solid plan for teens, don't you?"

Temptation lured her to think he might be right, but experience taught her to disregard about ninety percent of what men promised. "I'll take this all under consideration," she promised. "My perspective is different. I can't afford to be simplistic when it comes to them."

The boys banged through the inexpensive, dented screen door and raced across the stones to the small, easy-to-climb trees behind the sheds. Lucy continued, "Experience has taught me to handle the ups and downs of life. But if I let them get overinvolved only to have the rug snatched out from under them, I've got no one but myself to blame. I can't protect them from every hurt, but I've got to be the one on the lookout for imminent disaster. Comes with the job description. And I'm not big on being indebted to anyone, Trey. Especially Sam Stafford."

"Then we'll take it step by step," Trey offered mildly. "And in the meantime, I've got to get back to the ranch and spend a little time with Dad. Maybe play him a song or two. Wanna come back over for a campfire, Lucy?"

Of course she did. What normal woman wouldn't want to sit around a campfire on a gorgeous midsummer night, listening to Trey Walker sing? That made it even more impossible. "As wonderful as that sounds, I'm destined to opt for a more prosaic evening."

He furrowed his brow.

She pointed to the house. "I'm going to start some laundry, get the kids settled in, and make sure my trimmers are sharpened before tomorrow morning. A day in the trees." It sounded absolutely delightful to say the words out loud. "I'm sure it sounds silly to others, but I love working in the trees, so I'm looking forward to tomorrow."

Trey looked over her head to the Christmas tree

acres. "A quiet place to think and pray and maybe write some music."

His words surprised her because she did exactly that when she worked the trees alone.

He planted a kiss to Belle's cheek, set her down gently on the drive, and tipped the brim of his tan cowboy hat, a perfect complement to his hazel eyes. "I'll be by tomorrow after Dad's appointment."

"Okay."

"Bye, Trey!"

"Yeah, bye!"

He turned to leave as Brendan, Mark, and Jacob raced into the barnyard.

"I won!"

"Did not, I had you by a hair! Photo finish goes to the bigger brother." Mark slung an arm around Jacob's neck and noogied his head as Rye's cruiser crunched gravel from the other direction. Then the older Battaglia boy spotted Lucy and yelled.

"Hey, Lucy!"

"Hey, yourself. Are you on the work crew?"

The kid grinned at her. "We did the front today, and I did all the trim. Mr. Stafford said it was good. What do you think?" He was a little taller than Lucy, but faced her like a pup waiting on a treat. "Do you like it?"

"You did great," she told him, and the kid relaxed. "I'm proud of you, Mark."

"I know." He shuffled his hands in a nervous way. "And I'm doing better. Not thinking of dark stuff so much."

He said the words softly, but Trey overheard.

"When we push the dark stuff away, we make room for the light. God wants us to walk in the light, and he washes us clean, Mark. Don't you forget it."

"I won't." He smiled at her as he backpedaled toward Rye's car. "See you tomorrow!"

Lucy waved as Rye approached them. "Things went all right, I take it?"

"Fine. They worked hard, did good, and got invited back," Trey answered.

"Glad to hear it." Rye turned to Lucy. "You've made a big difference to that boy, Lucy. And a bunch of others. I know it's not easy, telling your story, setting an example."

"If seeing my mistakes helps one kid from falling into a drug-abuse pattern, it's all worth it."

Her mistakes? Trey didn't just hear that, did he?

"It takes guts to do what you do though. Most of us don't have to air our closet skeletons on a weekly basis. You're a heck of a gal, Luce."

Mistakes. Closet skeletons. Heading a drug overcomers group.

Nerves thrummed Trey's spine. His body tensed. His hands fisted.

He had to work to relax them, and it took more than a little effort.

Cathy had been clean for several years when they met in Nashville. America had forgiven her childish indiscretions and reembraced her as a darling of country music. And when he'd fallen in love with her, marrying her was the testament he'd longed to make to his deceased parents. That they could have cleaned up their act. They could have been decent, moral human beings if they'd tried.

He'd cruised that moral high road for over two years, fist-pumping the air because he'd done what they couldn't do. He'd developed a great career with a wife who'd gotten straight and stayed that way.

Until the lying and cheating of a drug user reared its ugly head once more.

His heart chilled.

The boys bellowed from beyond the house, and Trey might have waved before he got into the Double S truck. He wasn't sure.

But he was sure of one thing. He'd tempted fate before and lost.

There was no way on God's green earth that he was going to tempt it again.

Twelve

Lucy Carlton was a former drug user.

It couldn't be true, but the moment she uttered the words, the light dawned. She'd alluded to mistakes, and when she'd talked about being an example to Ashley, she'd mentioned the Overcomers group . . .

But he hadn't put it together, and now he couldn't pull it apart.

Flames flickered in the high-sided fire pit. No one messed with open fires in Central Washington during summer. The risk of forest fire was too great. Likewise, a smart man who'd already been schooled in the ways of drug addicts wouldn't give them another chance. *"Fool me once, shame on you. Fool me twice, shame on me."* Sam had uttered that phrase often while Trey was growing up, and it made even more sense today.

A drug user. Mother of three little kids.

Former drug user; get your facts straight. And you're being a moron.

Trey shoved the mental scolding aside.

He wasn't a moron. He was smart. Street smart, out of necessity, which meant he needed to put a lockdown on his heart for the duration of the summer. He'd vowed never to be made the fool again. And he'd meant it.

"Now that's a sunset to remember." Sam came

up alongside, looking west, drinking in the vibrancy of bent light. Apricot, coral and gold, rimmed with shadowed violet. With so much beauty in life, why would people turn to drugs? Trey didn't get it, and honestly? He didn't want to get it. Ever. "Everything just so, layered and lit up. A man could work his way through a lot of days, not lookin' up, and I'm guilty of that more often than not. Seems a shame to miss even one, doesn't it?"

Trey shifted his focus back to Sam's new normal because that's what he came home for. He came north to help his father. Not flirt with the woman next door, a lesson he should have remembered the past few days. Romance didn't enter the mix. "It does, but life gets lived and days get hectic, Dad. You had three busy boys to raise and a business to run. We're all doing okay."

"Now." Sam grunted. He propped his feet against the fire pit wall like Trey, but he didn't look nearly as comfortable doing it. Then he swung his feet down and leaned forward. "This appointment tomorrow . . ."

Trey kept his eyes trained straight ahead on purpose. "You worried?"

Sam's words said no. His eyes told a different story.

"We're going there to hear options, Trey, and that's all. I'm no different than any other patient. I can wait my turn for a donated organ."

"And if you die, waiting?" Trey asked. He sent

Sam a skeptical look. "That's not much of an option, Dad."

"If that's the case, we'll call it God's timing and let it go at that," Sam declared.

"Well now, all I can think of is that three-boats-and-a-helicopter joke. The guy who kept climbing from floor to floor, waiting for God to save him." Trey grinned, remembering. "Consider me your first lifeboat, Dad."

"I've been reading up."

So had Trey. The smile slipped from his face. "Me too. The week of intense pain followed by two to four weeks of extreme discomfort doesn't exactly sound like a cakewalk, does it?"

"Then why do it? Why risk it?"

Sam gripped Trey's arm, and there was no missing the true emotion in his expression. Emotion he'd stowed deeply away, but Trey had sensed it as a child. It was good to see that warmth resurface at last.

"We'll go find out the information about a regular transplant and wait. 'Wait patiently on the LORD.' " Sam quoted the words as if he'd spent his life quoting chapter and verse. "That's what the Good Book says, kind of, anyway, and that's what I aim to do."

"You know the system is stacked against you," Trey offered mildly. "There's a bigger need in the heavier populated East and West Coast regions, and not as many donors as in the heartland. So are you going to move to Kansas, waiting on the generosity of strangers? Or sit back, relax, and let me be the hero for a change? Colt's had his shot, helping the town. Nick's done his share by bringing the Double S around to fit your dream, and his. Now it's my turn."

"Nick didn't have to risk his life."

"I've seen him ride," Trey quipped as Nick approached them from the far side. "I'd say both he and the horse are in constant danger."

"Shut up." Nick scowled and took a seat near Sam. "I can ride circles around you, with or without your liver."

Trey laughed.

Sam didn't. "This isn't a joking matter."

"Well, it's not something I want to talk to death either," Trey told him. "We're going to listen to what the doctor has to say, then make our decision. If it will help you get better sooner, then I will gladly donate a sizable portion of my interior. And that's all there is to it." He stood and stretched. "I'm beat. I'm not used to hauling lumber and manhandling saws."

"Are things getting done over there?"

Things were moving along next door, and he'd been a lot happier about that a few hours ago. "You mean at Lucy's?"

Colt had come their way while Trey was talking. Sam nodded while Nick and Colt exchanged knowing looks.

"Yes." He answered Sam specifically while ignoring his brothers. "You've made her very happy."

"Nice kids," Colt observed. "The boys think you're pretty cool," he went on as he settled into a chair opposite his father. "Of course, they don't know the rest of us well, yet, so comparisons will prove inevitable, and that will leave you in the dust. But for the moment, you've got them snowed."

"Part of my skill set," Trey told him, then he got serious. "They're good kids."

"Seems so. And Isabo said the older girl was going to hire on over here to help out?"

"Yes." Trey stretched the word out. "She's been testing all kinds of limits, and her mother left her high and dry. She's got issues, so don't trust her too freely."

"How old?" Sam asked.

He faced his father. "Fourteen and thinks she's twenty."

"A lot to learn, and plenty of mistakes to be made yet. Luckily most of 'em are small enough that we stay out of jail," Sam said with a shrug.

"If you get into the habit of excusing the small mistakes, the big ones come calling pretty quick," Nick reminded him.

"They're likely to do that if you weigh those first mistakes heavy too. Kids need room to grow."

"He's gotten soft," Colt observed to Nick.

"I know." Nick looked positively insulted. "Where was Mr. Nice Guy when we were growing up?"

Colt started to make a smart-aleck remark, but Trey leaned down and faced them.

"I've come to the conclusion that keeping us working night and day was probably in our best interests."

Colt concurred. "It kept me out of trouble. And there's plenty of trouble hanging around, that's for sure. But nothing so tempting as the woman I love."

Angelina laughed as she approached them with a plate of miniature cakes. "Ashley made these with Mami when she got home from school this afternoon. She did all right for the little time she was here. Mami was pleased." She read Trey's warning look and said, "But we'll keep our eyes and ears open."

"Good. It's fine that she's excited about this, but she'd like to hang with a rough crowd. Or maybe she is the rough crowd, and we've got it backward."

"We'll give her time and encouragement. And if she can start making better choices, Lucy is the best thing in the world for her. Nothing like experience to know how to tip the tree so it catches the light. Kids aren't much different." Angelina kept her tone mild. "I'm going to bed, it's an early start for Seattle tomorrow."

Trey slung an arm around Sam's neck, bent, and kissed his father's head.

Nick almost choked.

Colt did choke, but grinned too.

"G'night."

He walked to the SUV, climbed in, and drove to the cabin. He had to pass Lucy's driveway, and he wanted to stop. He wanted to stop long enough to have her say he'd misunderstood the exchange, but he didn't misunderstand. He just wished that were the case.

Kitchen light spilled onto the porch as he went by. Was she working on something? Cooking? Baking? Folding laundry? And how did someone surrounded by the pressures of parenting, working, cooking, cleaning, and juggling bills stay clean when a talented wealthy woman like Cathy succumbed to the allure of drugs?

It didn't make sense, but it wasn't his job to reason it out. His task was to focus his attention on one prize, his father's life. And right now, that prize might lay within him. Tomorrow would tell.

ನಲ

San Francisco.

EKG.

Abdominal ultrasound.

X-rays.

Four to six weeks. And then double that for healing. If everything goes right. And if it doesn't?

230

"Well." Sam had been antsy ten minutes into the consult. As the surgeon wound down his assessment, Sam stood. "I'm on the list for a donated organ, aren't I?"

"Yes." The surgeon didn't stand, and his tone commanded Sam's attention. "But your MELD scores aren't bad, you're managing to get by, and you're way down the list, Sam. Unless you get significantly sicker, or move to the heartland, searching for a cadaver liver, your chances of getting one in our region are slim."

"He has to get sicker?" Colt didn't look any too happy, and Nick was similarly distressed. "He doesn't look sick enough to you?"

"It's a criteria standard, not a subjective assessment," the surgeon explained. "There are baseline measurements, and your father is still in the low twenties. The most critical patients are scoring in the thirties."

"What happens if we wait for Dad to get that bad?" Trey asked. "Will he get a liver?"

"Some do." The doctor looked Trey right in the eyes. "And some don't. On a national average we lose between fifteen hundred and two thousand patients per year, waiting for a liver that never becomes available."

"That's unacceptable," Trey said mildly.

Sam turned his way quickly. "Don't even think it, Trey."

"Don't have to think it. I'd rather just do it."

"I won't hear of it."

Trey made a face at him, like he did back in the day, when Sam was big and brave and bold and Trey could coax him out of a foul mood by being funny. "It's not up to you. My liver, my choice. I'm giving a chunk of it to someone, and I'd prefer it to be you on that second table, but if you decide you don't want it, I'll give it to someone else."

"You're being ridiculous."

"I'm being sacrificial."

That quieted Sam down.

"Like you were," Trey continued softly, "when you brought a snot-nosed little kid, who still wet his pants fairly often, to your home. You made him your own. You taught him how to hang tough, how to see a job through, and how to sit tall in a saddle no matter what."

"Trey." Sam reached out a hand to him. He shook his head. "It's too much, Trey. I can't risk it. I can't risk you, Son."

Trey faced the doctor. "You said the San Francisco transplant center had plenty of experience, correct?"

"Among the best in the nation. Yes."

"And we'd be looking at a fall operation?"

"As long as the hospital and Dr. Nu can put it on their schedule. Often it takes four to six months, but their team is looking at a four-to-six-week, drop-everything-and-show-up deal. They've reviewed the preliminary questionnaires, and once the medical tests are submitted, they'll assess the risk factor for approval."

"And if Dad takes a sudden downturn before then?" Nick asked. "What happens in that case?"

"Sam will remain on the regular transplant list until he undergoes a successful transplant. Or until there is no longer a need."

"A coffin," drawled Colt, deliberately showing the downside of their alternatives.

"And a big, lavish funeral," Nick added, his tone light.

The doctor stared at them, then Sam. "They're being funny," Sam told him. "Because they think I should let Trey do this."

"Well, I'm doing it one way or another, so . . ." Trey sat back down and reached for the pen. "Tell me what to sign, Doc, I've got some Christmas trees in need of pruning, and I promised I'd be back in time to help do it. Yakking this thing to death won't get it done any faster."

The doctor slid the forms his way. Trey signed them, then looked up at his father, waiting. "You either go into this believing God's in control or you go in shaking in your boots. I'm grabbing hold of the whole God-thing, Dad. At least that way we minimize wear and tear on the boots. Good boots don't come cheap."

"You're sure?"

Sam looked him eye to eye, and for a brief

moment he wasn't an incapacitated man waiting for modern medicine to put him right again. He was the old Sam Stafford, owner of the Double S Ranch, a man who saw what needed to be done and did it.

Sure he was a jerk way too often. But that was then, and this was now, and he'd saved Trey's life over a quarter century ago. It was past time to return the favor. "I'm sure. Sign the papers and let's grab the biggest steak we can find. With onion rings and mushrooms. Then I've got some trees to tend."

Sam studied him for several seconds before he clapped a hand to Trey's shoulder and sat back down. He signed the forms, said good-bye to the local surgeon, and they walked out, into a brilliant suburban Seattle day.

"One thing," Trey told them once they piled into the ranch SUV. "We keep this to ourselves. No loose lips."

"We're keeping this a secret?" Colt didn't look convinced. "Good luck with that."

Nick's expression wondered why. "You don't want your fans to know?"

"I don't want anyone knowing," Trey answered firmly. "For however long we have before this happens, I just want to be Trey Stafford, part of the Double S. My agent knows what's going on, and he's respecting my wishes. If Ed can do that, anyone can. Once the surgery's over, we can do an interview or something and the world can find out. But not now. Not yet."

"Angelina will know right off, possibly because I already texted her."

"Elsa too." Nick held up his phone.

"Pair of teenagers." Trey locked eyes with both of them, one at a time. "Wives/fiancées are okay. The rest of the world is not. I'm just hoping I get healthy in time to celebrate two weddings."

"Ange has a late October date picked, but I think we might move it up to early September if we can get the church done in time."

Nick agreed. "That's probably a good idea, if Dad's recovery will take awhile."

"Nothing I do takes awhile," Sam corrected them. "Plan the wedding any way you like, but I'll be ready to celebrate eight weeks after this surgery. That gives you three months, Colt. Don't be messing up Angelina's wedding plans. And besides, that gives me a goal. I like goals."

"Then we stay with late October," Colt agreed. He drove east on I-90 and turned off not far from the city. "Let's get that steak and crunch cattle numbers. Hugh Lacey queried me about expanding the ranch—or at least the concept—into a more southern state, and I've been running start-up costs."

"Gray's Glen is home," Sam stated. The thought of total world domination of anything beef related would have fed his ego not that long ago. Things had obviously changed.

"Maybe we can talk of it more in a few years, Colt," Sam continued. "It's something I've considered, but right now I want to see the town projects finished and polished. I put myself first for a lot of years. Way too many. Let's put the idea on hold for now, and if Hugh finds someone else to run with the ball, so be it. Currently the thought of that steak seems mighty nice. And an ice-cold bottomless glass of tea."

Resignation marked his face and his voice, because Sam Stafford wouldn't have been drinking tea with his steak, back in the day. "I'm even learning to almost like tea."

"I'm buying," said Colt. He held open the first door, while Nick pulled open the interior door for his father. "It's the least I can do if Trey's giving up his liver."

"And we'll all pitch in and help Lucy and the kids while you're recovering, Trey," Nick added. "We'll keep things running smooth over there, like we should have been doing all along."

"When you're off singing and touring, and our lives go back to normal, I'll be the one picking up the pieces."

Lucy. Her words, planning ahead. Mothers didn't have the option of letting life just happen around them. He saw that as she guided events and skirted absolutes. But he saw more too. He knew more. He knew how easily the past could rise up to ruin the present, but Lucy's past wasn't anything he could talk about now, although his family must be aware of it. He was the one left unaware. The outsider, come home to play his part and leave. The heart that had felt real good twenty-four hours before pinched tight. "That would be good."

"I thought so." Nick met his gaze with a sympathetic expression, but not about Cathy this time.

About Lucy. Maybe because he knew her past and saw the impossibility of the situation.

And then Nick smiled, thumped him on the back, and positioned the chairs so Trey's back was to the door and the other diners. Eating in public was rarely simple, but maybe today would be different. Four guys, on their own, enjoying a peaceful, wood-fired steak dinner together. Family, bonding over food, words, and laughter.

He'd missed this. No matter what he did next door, no matter how awkward his work with Lucy might get, the chance to be here with his brothers and Sam filled one hole inside him. Maybe that would have to be enough.

ର

The rasping grind of the metal saw challenged the metallic buzz of pneumatic screwdrivers as Benson's crew applied the new roofing to the house. The combination sounded like a dental office on steroids, the kind of high-pitched noise that put fur on your teeth and goose bumps up your arms, despite the warm midday sun.

Lucy let herself out the back door of the house and circled the barn.

The porch radio was cranking country music. The workmen's voices competed with the sounds around them, but with the kids safely tucked up the road, the grove felt relatively peaceful, and Lucy made the most of it. She trimmed, shaped, and scissored the wide variety of trees in the near section first. A lightweight aluminum ladder helped her reach the upper branches.

The scent inspired her.

Growing Christmas trees was a six-week sale window, mostly compressed into four weeks of insanely busy, but when it was done, there should be a solid uptick in her cash flow. Last year had been the first year she'd been able to open the first two groves for shoppers. Areas three and four would be opened this year, more than doubling her sales potential. And once the weather turned cool in late October and early November, she'd start creating wreaths, boughs, and swags, and then evergreen centerpieces post-Thanksgiving.

The intricate work with spiky needles chapped her hands. Her knuckles would bleed, but in the end, satisfied customers would decorate happy homes with Carlton Trees and Greens, the culmination of eight years of tough times.

She wouldn't think of her dwindling bank account. The envelope Trey had given her made up for the lost flowers. She loved the new van and Trey's generosity, but she had no idea how she was going to stretch one day of market sales into covering two months of summer.

Birds twittered above her, chased from their comfortable perches by her attention. They scolded, reminding her that God took care of them and saw to their needs.

Why wouldn't he take care of her? Hadn't he always, one way or another?

He had, but now there was another mouth to feed, and Ashley would need new school clothes. So would the boys. They'd both shot up an inch or more over summer recess.

She shouldn't worry. Worry was a fruitless exercise. Fretting sapped strength, but objective reasoning went to war with simple faith in the real world. If there wasn't enough money to take care of basic needs, how could she earn more to make a difference?

Maude had made no effort to contact her or Ashley, and she sure hadn't dropped a check in the mail, which meant she and Ashley would have to figure this out.

They'd do it, too, because there was no other choice. She sang softly as her task moved away from the robust sounds of construction, watching the classic shapes spring to life beneath her hands.

ౡ

The poignancy of Lucy's voice drew Trey as he moved into the evergreen grove that afternoon.

The Sirens tempted Odysseus, too, and how'd that work out? You can be nice without being entrenched. You're too smart to fall into this trap again.

He needed to heed the mental warning. He would draw a firm line in the sand because he knew the heartbreak of drug addiction. It would never be allowed to test his soul again. "Pretty song, Lucy."

She hadn't heard him approach. She turned quickly, startled. "You scared me."

"Sorry." He held up a pair of loppers and a hand-held trimmer he'd brought over from the Double S. "If you show me how to trim, I'd like to help."

Concern wrinkled her brow. "You've got enough to do with the barn and the porch, don't you? I can handle this on my own. But thanks," she added.

He did . . . but the thought of her working the rows of trees all by herself didn't sit right.

"Too many people running too many cords right now. They've tripped circuit breakers a couple of times already. No need for me to add to the problem when I can work here."

His explanation must have made sense because she relaxed a little. "I'd like that, then. If you're sure."

He wasn't sure but he couldn't exactly avoid her for the rest of the summer. "Show me how it's done and I'll get started."

"All right." She began nipping the next tree with sure hands. "It doesn't look like I'm doing much, but those trimmed ends will sprout. In three months the tree will look fuller."

"Better eye appeal."

"Yes."

She slanted a quick smile his way and his heart jammed again. Talking with Lucy about eye appeal wasn't in his best interest. Being this close to Lucy probably wasn't smart either, but if he couldn't work on the barn, he wasn't about to slack off because he couldn't trust himself working side by side with her. His problem. Not hers.

The wholesome scent of freshly trimmed pine, spruce and fir filled the grove. The sweet smell seemed to follow her as the warm sun strengthened the aromatic air. He was in the middle of his first attempt when Nick's voice rang out.

"Trey? You back here?"

"Yup." They both turned as Nick came up behind them.

"Lucy, the barn's looking good." Nick grinned and gave Trey's right shoulder a good shot. "Nice to see the kid hasn't gone completely soft with his cush life in Music City."

"Cush. Right." Trey rolled his eyes. "I left you five minutes ago. Why did you chase me down, and couldn't you have texted me?"

"I tried but I think the noise level over here

makes communication next to impossible. Isabo sent me, and you know the unbreakable cowboy rule about the cook. Whatever Cookie wants, Cookie gets. When Isabo says jump, I jump because she's got ribs simmering, and she wants Lucy to come up for supper and hang out for a while. Something about a quilting project? Babies?"

"The Quilting Ministry needs volunteers." Lucy made a face. "I was invited to join them, but once school starts, I need to find part-time work. I don't know how to juggle that and the kids and the Christmas tree business and have time left to piece quilt tops."

"You like sewing?" Why was he surprised? Sewing was normal and nice. Was it because he was trying to blend the drug user with the industrious woman before him?

"I love it." She motioned to the trees. "I love doing hands-on things. Growing food, making clothes, tackling projects. It suits."

"None of that sounds the least bit restful." Nick looked disturbed and Lucy laughed. The sound came like a summer breeze jangling the wind chimes on the Double S porch.

"I suppose you think riding range, driving rigs, putting up hay, and delivering calves is simple?"

"No, but each has its own season. Your stuff is like every day, same thing, wake up, get up, do it again. Like that movie about Groundhog Day."

"I thought it sounded nice."

Trey didn't mean to leap to her defense, but it did sound nice, like the dreams a little boy fashions when he imagines the perfect kind of mother with his two brothers. Kind. Busy. Helpful. Forgiving. The type of mother he'd never known. He shifted to face Nick. "So you had to tell me this in person?"

"Isabo said if I texted you and you forget to ask Lucy, I'm the one in big trouble, and there's a sizable blueberry cobbler cooling that tipped my hand toward personal notification. And I had to make a run to pick up the replacement cutting bar. You guys were on the way."

"Tell Isabo I'd love to come over." Lucy lofted her trimmers slightly. "My hands aren't used to gripping like this, and they'll be aching by tonight. And the food sounds amazing."

"Will do. You sure you trust this bozo with your trees, Lucy? He's not exactly experienced."

"With three sections to go, I'm not about to refuse help, regardless of experience. And he appears to be educable. All right, cowboy."

She turned back to him once Nick left and nodded to a Fraser fir. "Let's see what you've got."

"You're going to watch?"

"Yes."

"Okay." He eyed the tree, then the one she'd just done. It took him a little while, but when he was done, he'd given the fir a trim look.

"You did okay."

He stood back and examined the tree from all directions. "Are you sure? I don't want to mess up your trees."

"I don't want you to either," she said truthfully. "This is my winter budget. If we mess them up, kids don't eat."

He could see she was glad when he took her words seriously. "I'll work on this row while you do that one. I won't be real fast, but I'll do okay. I promise." He'd focus on trees, one by one, and not on the woman beside him. He'd come to do a job and do it well, but with Lucy nearby, humming a tune and smelling of pine-oil summer, keeping a distance might be the hardest thing he'd ever done.

Lucy didn't need a degree in meteorology to sense Trey's cooler attitude. Yes, it burned a little . . . but just a little because she couldn't afford to let it matter. Famous country singers didn't go around falling for impoverished single moms except in made-up lyrics of "today's new country." Not in real life.

"Are you singing in church on Sunday?"

He'd picked a safe topic of conversation. Good. "Yes."

"Reverend Stillman invited me to join the choir while I'm in town."

She'd had a hard enough time paying attention

to the beautiful words and the pastor's sermon the previous Sunday. What would she do with Trey in the loft? "And you said . . ."

"I said I was going to be busy in the pew with three little kids, so I'd sing from the pew while you sing from above."

Her heart sped up despite efforts to slow it down. "You told him that?"

"Someone needs to sit with the kids, right? And Ashley was actually polite to me yesterday."

As much as she hated to admit it, putting confidence in Ashley might not be in his best interests. "She must want something. Or maybe she's starting to grow up. Or she doesn't want you to mess up her job opportunity at the ranch."

"It couldn't just be because she's starting to like me?"

"An unlikely option at this juncture, but think what you want," she assured him. "You're really okay with not singing in the loft?"

He kept right on working as he replied. "A low profile is a welcome change. It's been awhile since I could just walk into a church and sit and pray without ten pews of conjecture going on around me. It's peaceful."

She understood that more than she wanted, and for different reasons. Tongues had wagged at her expense for quite a while. Small towns could be cruel when you messed up. Reearning local respect hadn't been an easy task.

They worked in tandem until two areas were completely done. And when the sound of car engines announced the work crews leaving, Trey straightened and worked a kink out of his shoulder.

"It gets tight, doesn't it?" Lucy noticed him rotating his upper right arm.

"Does yours do that too?"

"Yes. Hot water and muscle cream helps."

"How about this?" Trey's hands settled on her shoulders from behind. He used the heel of his right hand to work out the tension in her right shoulder, with slow concentric circles, radiating comfort to the overtensed muscle. "Better?"

He whispered the words near her ear, and the husky note in his voice said he might like whispering near her ear.

She liked it too. She bent her head back and gazed up into his eyes. "Much."

"Well." He smiled down at her.

She smiled back, and she wasn't sure if she reached up for the kiss, or he reached down, but it didn't matter once they were kissing.

Nothing mattered then.

Not trees or music or clippers.

Just the kiss, a romantic mix of shade and sun and all things good. His mouth on hers, his arms circling her from behind. And when he paused, she thought he was going to end the kiss and apologize for it, but she guessed wrong.

He turned her so she faced him, then kissed her again, snug in the shelter of his arms, held in an embrace so sweet and true it felt like she'd come home at long last.

And then he stepped away. "Lucy. I'm sorry. I shouldn't have done that."

And there you go. The expected apology because the poor widow next door had little to offer except a stolen kiss, here or there. "Neither of us should have, and I can promise it won't happen again." She started for the house at a brisk pace. "Good to know we're on the same page."

"Lucy, stop."

She didn't stop.

She didn't want to hear lame Stafford excuses, and she had to take her share of the blame. She'd wondered what it would be like to kiss Trey Stafford, and the reality was far better than the imaginings.

But she knew better. So did he. From now on she'd keep her distance. Easy enough with work crews and kids milling around. Cozy moments alone like the one they'd just shared?

She'd be sure to make them one hundred percent impossible.

Thirteen

He'd kissed Lucy Carlton.

Trey studied the large stand of cattle in the uppermost pasture, but he wasn't seeing genetically chosen bovine birth mothers. He was seeing those pretty blue eyes, the purest blue he'd ever seen, and he'd kissed her.

It was the best kiss ever under the worst possible circumstances. He was scheduled to undergo life-threatening surgery, and she was a reformed drug abuser, two major negative considerations if he was being sensible. Maybe sensible was overrated.

The romantic songwriter in you would love to think that. Experience tells you otherwise. Why would you take the risk?

Because it felt right, even when he knew it was wrong. What if she backslid? What could he do then? And what if his surgery was unsuccessful? What kind of person put a wonderful woman and kids deliberately at risk of loss? Losing a handyman was sad.

Losing someone beloved was crushing. How could he put her in that situation? And if things went well, was he strong enough to trust again?

He wasn't a fearful man. He hadn't been a fearful kid. But the thought of dealing with another drug user loomed like a thunderhead rolling over the mountains and sinking into the valley like a full-force tornado.

Lucy's not a dark cloud. If a mental voice could sigh, his just did. *She's a woman of strong faith and resolve. She's proven that, and she shouldn't have to go on proving it. Maybe that's the problem. If she falls for you, she'd have to prove herself every single day. No one wants to live life that way.*

"Hey." Colt's voice interrupted his thoughts.

Trey hadn't heard his brother's approach. He turned quickly. "You need me?"

"Nope." Colt braced his arms on the fence and gazed out. "Just wanted to make sure you're okay."

"I'm fine."

Colt snorted.

"I signed the papers, didn't I? I've given this a lot of thought, and I'd be stupid not to be concerned, but I'm doing it, so that's that."

"That's not why I'm here. We already talked that to death."

In cowboy world, talking something to death meant six sentences, more or less.

"I meant Lucy."

Lucy? Trey frowned, concerned. "What about her?"

Colt didn't shift his attention. He kept it right there, on the grazing cattle, a scene of utter contentment.

"You came home like a bull on a charge and headed for the field. There's only a couple of things that make a man that crazy. An angry cow mama protecting her calf. And a woman. And there's not a cow to be seen at Lucy's place."

"I don't want to talk about this."

Colt sighed, nice and loud.

"It's not up for discussion."

"And if it was?" His brother still didn't look at him. He kept his attention on the rolling hills of the Kittitas Valley, filled with nature's bounty.

"You know she was a drug user."

"Yup. When she was a kid. If I got ostracized for every mistake I made as a teen—and then for some time after that—" Colt admitted, "I'd still be making penance. Kids do stupid things. And then most of us grow up."

"And that's a logical argument from someone who didn't bury a wife from a similar scenario."

"Lucy's different."

Trey bristled.

"I'm not about to compare the two women." Colt's tone softened. "I know you loved Cathy. America loved Cathy. She'd won acclaim and fortune at a young age, and her mother took advantage of her good fortune. But she slipped back down the slippery slope the minute she felt like her career was threatened."

"When Blue Ridge Productions wouldn't renew

her contract." The professional rejection should have been a slap in the face, not a crushing blow. But his late wife took it hard.

"Lucy, on the other hand, turned things around and has faced a barrage of obstacles, including our father. She's never slipped once. Three kids, a falling-down farm, a hands-on business, a no-account husband who let her down repeatedly. And still she climbs in the choir loft every Sunday, singing God's praise. Holding weekly meetings to help kids stay off drugs. From where I'm standing, Lucy's got nothing to prove to anyone."

Colt was right. But he was wrong too. "We only met a few days ago."

"I found out the hard way that it's not about the length of time. It's about how they grab hold of your heart and don't let go. And after a while you don't want them to let go. Listen." He turned his back on the cattle and faced Trey. "I'm not telling you what to do. I had a lot of growing up to do when I walked back onto this ranch last winter. But when Angelina yelled at me, it meant something."

Knowing Colt, that sounded about right.

"And when she talked about life and love and forgiveness and moving on, I listened."

"She came along at the perfect time."

"Now you're getting it." Colt slapped him on the back. "We're all here at this time for a reason. God's reason. I don't know the whys and wherefores, but I believe it, Trey. And whatever happens between you and Lucy—or you with this surgery —it's in God's hands. You said that exact thing to your father today."

He had.

"Maybe it's time you applied that to other areas of your life."

"And if something goes wrong in San Francisco?"

"Better to figure out what to do when everything goes right," Colt advised. "There are three kids that need a good man in their lives. And a wonderful woman who doesn't fall at your feet like the tens of thousands of groupies that follow you."

"She's got a mind of her own."

"Just what a Stafford needs. Even if they don't realize it at the time." The dinner gong sounded from the side porch. "Let's go eat. Maybe take a few kids to catch some frogs. Or let the puppies out for Puppy Rumble."

"The kids will miss them when they go to new homes." The seventeen rough-and-tumble baby pups had provided a lot of amusement for children. Adults too.

"Until a new season of pups arrives. And calves. And chicks. I even heard my lovely future bride saying something about miniature goats. That goat milk is great for making cheese and soap and candy."

"What did you tell her?" Back in the day, Sam would have gone ballistic by the thought of adding in nonessential work.

"I took the coward's way out and pretended I didn't hear her. Because Trey," Colt paused long enough to highlight his message, "she's going to do what she wants pretty much, and if sheltering a few little goats makes her happy . . ." He put his hand on Trey's shoulder to mark his words. "Then we get goats."

Small children, dashing around. Miniature goats.

Glee-filled shouts came from the far side of the ranch house. The kids were playing some kind of tag, racing up and down the hills, trying to catch one another. And there was Lucy, holding Belle, talking with Elsa about something.

Peace marked her profile, but then she turned. Saw him. He witnessed the flash of pain in her eyes, pain he'd put there with his rejection.

There was no fixing it now. Not in front of a crowd of Staffords and friends. But tomorrow, he'd try to make things as right as he could because Colt made a good point. If he truly trusted in God, then he needed to live that trust. Not just talk about it.

ରୟ

An e-mail from Ed the next morning celebrated Trey's second week on top of the charts with "You Only Live Once," a nice way to start the day.

Then an early morning phone call from his former mother-in-law reminded him that Cathy's family really knew how to put the "fun" in dysfunctional. He couldn't help wondering if maybe her death wasn't all his fault. Maybe the hot mix of crazy she called family could have worked harder to be less greedy, more kind, and more supportive. He didn't answer the initial call, but when Sallie Somersby texted an SOS with multiple exclamation points, he caved. "What's up, Sallie?"

"Nothing to fret over except that they're throwing me out of my house, Trey! Not that I expect you to do anything about it; you've made it clear that you're moving on. Only when you're the mother . . ." She hiccupped and sobbed, part real, part drama for his benefit, no doubt. "You don't get to move on. You don't get to have another relationship down the road, because your kid *was* your relationship, and God doesn't sell replacement parts."

She sounded drunk. Or stoned. When she started berating the cat for yowling, the slurred words indicated his first guess was most likely. But he wouldn't put it beyond her to use booze and drugs together, an example that took his wife to the grave.

His heart pinched tight, remembering.

Cathy's years of sobriety were wonderful. When not under the influence, Cathy Somersby was sweet and kind and good, longing to help others.

That was the woman he fell in love with, the woman he pledged his life to.

America's Sweetheart, that's what the tabloids dubbed her. Straight for five full years, then gone in a crazy, wild weekend party while he was on tour.

"I miss her, Trey. I miss her so much. She was my baby."

"I know." He also knew that she'd bilked her teenage daughter's bank accounts for almost a cool half million before Cathy turned twenty-one. Stealing from her own kid. Who did that kind of thing?

Sallie Mae Somersby.

"If you choose to let Cathy's mother push your buttons, it's as much your fault as hers." The blunt words of his therapist hit home today. He'd thought her unfeeling at the time because Sallie had lost something precious that day too.

Now he saw the truth in her counsel. "Sallie, I've got to get back to work."

"But you're up here in the Northwest, Trey, and you haven't come to visit."

Nor was he about to. "Helping my dad, Sallie."

"Portland's not that far," she scolded. Her voice took an edge, not unusual when she didn't get her own way instantly. "It's the least you could do, Trey. If you'd been with her that weekend this wouldn't have happened, and I'd still have my beautiful daughter. She'd have done anything for you, Trey. And you know it."

He used to think so. But if that was true, why go on a bender? Why party? Was the chemical lure that intrinsic? The therapist's advice made him square his shoulders. "Gotta go, Sallie. You're in my prayers."

He hung up.

He'd never been able to do that before. Sallie's grief had reined him in every time. He'd sent money, he'd paid bills, and it was never enough.

"Cut her loose," his therapist told him. Clara Johnson had looked him square in the eye when she said it, and she was right. Sallie's greed and grief had been a millstone around his neck. Why did it take so long to see that?

He parked his SUV, grabbed the trimmers, and stopped by the house before heading to the evergreen grove. He knocked lightly on the screened door.

"Mom! Trey's here!" Cade raced to the door, happy to see him, and when he opened the door, the boy hurled himself into Trey's arms.

Lucy came into the kitchen from the basement door. She saw him holding her son. She kept her expression easy but her eyes went stern. "You're here early."

"Couldn't sleep." Did she hear the regret in his voice? If so, she was real good at ignoring it.

Belle came into the room, sleepy-eyed and

dressed in summer jammies, toting a satin-trimmed pink blanket. The sight of her moved him. So sweet. So innocent. And the boys, longing for example and experience. He could fill those roles. That wasn't a question. Not in his head. He'd been rescued by an adoptive father. He knew the drill and could return the favor.

Was Colt right? Should he trust that everything would be all right? Should he trust his feelings? "Hi, sweet thing." He tipped the brim of his baseball cap to the little girl, and she grinned around the thumb in her mouth.

"I'll be in the grove." He stepped beyond the door. "See you later, guys."

He moved off to the third section of evergreens. The sounds of engines and power tools clued him in about the work crew arrival. He heard Lucy join him an hour later. She didn't stop to work in his section. She moved on to the fourth quarter, beyond the small, roughed-up plank bridge spanning a narrow swale branching off the creek. She was giving him wide berth, a smart move. A wise man didn't kiss a woman like he'd kissed Lucy yesterday, then say he'd made a mistake. What woman wanted to be labeled a mistake?

As he neared the last trees, he received an e-mail from the transplant center in San Francisco, confirming the timeline for the upcoming surgery. The message came with multiple signature-requested forms attached.

Lucy was singing three rows over, something soft and sweet. He couldn't hear the words or discern the tune, but occasional sweet notes swept high, then low.

He stared at the e-mail while her song went on.

What right did he have to woo her, with this looming? What if something happened?

He wasn't stupid, he knew the odds, but he also understood the reality behind odds. If everyone who had the surgery survived, there'd be no posted percentages to consider.

How thoughtless it would be to deliberately engage someone's heart, only to risk breaking it.

He pictured the kids, learning and growing.

Sounds of the ongoing farm rehab provided a reminder. He wasn't here to win Lucy's heart and then break it if something went wrong in California. He was here to make her life better.

Focus on her. Let the rest work itself out after the surgery. You're going into this eyes wide open. You can't build a relationship with a wonderful woman like Lucy, then blindside her. Colt's right about trusting in God, but things happen. Protect her first. And then see what happens.

"Trey?" Lucy came his way with her short-handled trimmers. It would be so easy to romance this woman, to follow the sweet path this week had set before him, but could he set her up for disappointment? Or grief?

Not and call himself a good man.

"I'm done over here," she said. She'd tucked the small trimmers into her tool belt. "I'm going to load up the van with everything I need for market tomorrow. Are you okay finishing this corner?"

She kept her tone matter of fact, as if determined to put the kiss behind them. He motioned to the last row of trees.

"I am. Then I can help you."

"No help needed, but thanks. And the trees look great. Thank you for your hard work."

It took everything he had to keep his words casual. "Just being a good neighbor."

His generic words made her hesitate, then she squared her shoulders and walked on.

Focus on the farm, not the farmer.

Wise words, hard to follow.

Lucy was an "all-in" kind of woman. She demonstrated that in everything she did, and Trey was pretty sure no one had gone out of their way to protect her, ever.

He needed to. She might hate him for pulling back, but better a small jab now than a full-on crash later.

"Trey!" Cade came racing when Rye dropped Jenna and the kids off later that afternoon. "I got to ride Pegasus!"

"For real?" Pegasus had been his mount as a teen. Sam had taken pity on the abused colt, raised him, and trained him, then handed Trey the reins when he was ten years old. They'd matured as a unit until Trey left, a pair of castoffs bound together. "How'd it go?"

"So good!" Excitement widened the boy's eyes and smile. "I listened to everything Mr. Hobbs had to say, and kept my heels down super tight, and he told me I did okay!"

Hobbs, a man of few words and fewer superlatives. "That's a compliment of the highest order from Hobbs."

"I've got to go tell Mom!"

He ran back up front, shouting for his mother. Trey greeted Rye as he exchanged three little kids and a teen for the three teenage boys he'd dropped off earlier. Where else but in a small town did the sheriff provide occasional taxi service to help folks out?

Trey put up the ladder and his tools, and followed Cade to the house.

Jenna had Belle tucked onto the weathered porch swing. Belle snuggled a baby doll in each arm while Jenna read all three of them—Belle and the two dollies—a story.

Benson's crew had finished the house roof. The slate gray metal looked strong against the backdrop of a sapphire sky. The clear, clean lines made him want to finish the porch in quick order. A coat of white paint would give the fresh appearance he wanted for Lucy and these kids, and he'd noted several windows in need of replacement. He wanted that done before the weather turned this fall. Lucy and the kids would have a snug, warm house to face the coming winter. Would she think of him then?

She will if you stay. Sell your place in Tennessee and move home. What are you waiting for? A written invitation? I do believe your father has already issued one of those.

From the greenhouse area, Cody's voice joined Cade's as Trey moved up the porch steps. They sounded happy and energized, a wonderful difference.

Ashley was coming out as he was going in. Would she be pleasant or resentful? He held the door wide and waited for her to pass through. "Everything go all right at the ranch after school?"

"You guys have a lot of bossy people over there."

He knew the truth in that. "Pretty much with any job, I suppose. I thought you weren't starting work until tomorrow?"

"Isabo needed help, and then Elsa needed help, but when I went to help her, the pudding burned and the whole house smelled horrible."

"Who would have thought that pudding needed undivided attention?"

She made a face. "Not me, that's for sure."

"They just made more, didn't they?"

"I don't know." She stared down, embarrassed. "I went outside."

"Ah." He didn't say anything more, just waited. Jenna's soft voice, relating a story about a bear

261

who found all kinds of little creatures seeking unexpected refuge in his den, rose and fell on the far side of the porch.

Two teens, so different. One calm and steady, looking forward.

The other restless and quick to battle.

"Maybe I'm not good enough to work at the Double S."

"Are we talking capable good or behaviorally good?"

She groaned and put her head in her hands. Trey found the theatrical move reassuring. If she had enough energy to be dramatic, she had enough chutzpah to handle things at the Double S, as long as she didn't mess around. "Stay away from temptation and you'll be fine."

She frowned but didn't growl. He counted that as a plus.

"And listen to Isabo," he added. "She's no nonsense—"

"That's for sure."

He smiled inside and continued, "But she's smart and fair, and she's tackled into this job like a pro. She'll be a good boss, Ashley."

"If I don't mess up."

He considered that and shrugged. "Well, now, that part's up to you. Everyone makes mistakes. But messing up is a whole other level. Want some coffee?"

"Yeah. I'll make it." They walked inside

together and she withdrew two mugs. "A lot of grown-ups wouldn't let me have coffee." She didn't look at him when she spoke; she kept her eyes on the coffeepot in front of her.

"Cowpokes are raised on coffee from early on. I figured it's got to work the same for future cowgirls, doesn't it?"

"You really think they'll teach me to ride?" She poured his mug first, then hers.

"Stay straight and I'll teach you myself. And how to take care of your mount. How to find your way around a barn."

Her eyes flew up to his. "Are you serious?"

"I said it, didn't I? Unless you'd prefer someone else."

She swallowed hard while adding milk and sugar to her cup. "No. I—umm—" She stirred the coffee as Lucy crossed the porch behind them. "Do you know how cool that would be?"

He pretended confusion.

"To have a big country singer like you teaching me how to ride? The kids at summer school didn't believe me when I said you were here, helping us."

Her tone said more than the basic words, and Trey honed in. "Did they give you a hard time?"

She shrugged. "I just got quiet and figured it would blow over. They weren't going to believe me anyway."

"Coffee smells good." Lucy took an appreciative breath as she opened the screen door.

"It's fresh." Trey toasted Ashley with his mug. "And good. Thanks, Ashley."

"You're welcome. Want some, Lucy?"

If the girl's cooperative attitude surprised Lucy, she hid the reaction. "I sure do. Thanks."

"No problem."

She crossed the kitchen to wash her hands but shot Trey a look of hopeful surprise behind Ashley's back.

"Here you go."

"Thank you." She raised her mug as Trey drained his.

"Is the van loaded?"

She nodded. "And parked in the shade with windows open. It's going to be cool tonight, so that's an unexpected but perfect plus."

"Do you care if I get some time in on the porch before it gets dark?"

"Why would I?" She looked genuinely confused.

"It's noisy and bothersome, and I figured you might be ready for a rest."

"A rest." She drew a deep breath and gazed outside as if seeing something special. So special. "I've imagined what this old house could look like for a lot of years. Seeing things start to take shape is exciting. Plenty of time to rest this winter."

"I'll get on it, then." He spent the next two hours wrapping the four-by-four supports. He wolfed down two hot dogs when Lucy roasted a double pack on the grill, and ate a helping of the best tuna-and-pasta salad he'd ever had.

Simple food.

Simple times.

Simple enjoyment.

Except not so simple for a guy who tours six months of the year.

He considered that as he finished the last beam. Was he ready to minimize touring? Could his career afford that change? Ed would go ballistic at the very idea, but Ed didn't have to leave Nashville very often. He could stay there, tucked in his spacious country home, while the wheels of country music churned around him.

Rye had picked up Jenna. Belle was in bed, and Ashley was stowed away in her room. The boys were lolling in front of the TV, watching a nature show about big cats.

Peace reigned.

He wasn't stupid enough to put much stock in that, because kids and peace didn't exactly mesh, but he soaked the moment in. He found Lucy shaking off laundry on the back line. He shoved his hands into his pockets when he walked up beside her. "Elsa's keeping the kids at the ranch tomorrow, isn't she?"

She treated him offhand, as if their conversation was casual, but after that kiss, nothing he did around Lucy Carlton felt casual. "Yes. It feels like I'm taking advantage—"

"You're not," he interrupted her. He backed up a step, wishing he didn't have to. "We're making up for lost time, Lucy. You're not taking advantage of a thing. There's a lot of payback involved."

Her hands paused near the clothespins as she digested the words and his stance. "And it's much appreciated."

A cool thanks, what he thought he wanted. For both of them to step back to being nothing more than neighbors.

He'd rather kiss her, and then go right on kissing her, but he didn't have that right. And if she hated him later, well, he'd take that chance. It was his turn to cowboy up, no matter how hard it might be. Walking to his SUV, climbing in, and driving away without even a backward glance . . . He hated it. He hated treading water with no clear end in sight. He'd gotten where he was by planning his work and working his plan, every day. Every week. But his personal horizons were fogged, and there was no shore to swim to. Not yet. Not until fate and medicine decreed his outcome. So until then—

He shoved his hat back on his head and scowled as he turned onto the graveled drive leading up to the cabin.

Until then he'd keep his distance, best he was able. But he didn't have to like it.

Fourteen

She'd been shrugged off before, so why was she expecting anything else? Lucy wondered as she drove into the Ellensburg open market the next morning. Yes, she'd been attracted to Trey. Was still attracted, she admitted to herself, but she owned that grudgingly. Who wouldn't be? Between the sweet smiles, the cowboy manners, the down-home affect he adopted so well . . . the country singer had it all.

She'd had a few days of fantasy land before Trey stepped back to reality. She did likewise, trying to convince herself it was better this way.

She didn't need drama. Life came with a generous serving of theatrics, and she'd had her share.

She didn't need sorrow or disappointment either. She had to be at the top of her game to be a good parent to all these kids.

She loved the home improvements, the new van was a dream ride, and if she'd grown a little greedy about the whole Cinderella story and happily-ever-afters, who could blame her? She would cling to these sweet contentments, like Paul when addressing the people of Thessalonica. He understood need and abundance and taught himself to be at peace with either.

So would she.

"Are we going to be here all day?" Cade grumbled from his side of the van. "This isn't fair, you know. Cody gets to go ride horses and I have to help with dumb flowers."

"These flowers help keep the lights on and the mortgage paid," she reminded him. "Families work together."

He scowled and slumped farther into the seat, feeling quite sorry for himself.

That made two of them, but Lucy didn't have the luxury of showing it. She pulled into her rented spot, backed up the sleek, new van, and climbed out.

The cool night was already being chased by a brilliant morning sun. "Time to set things up."

He pouted as he hopped out of the front seat, but when she let him stand on a step stool to suspend the hanging baskets, he forgot to be grumpy. By the time they'd gotten set up, open-air market shoppers were streaming into the fairgrounds.

Cade motioned to the van. "Can I go sit and read?"

He didn't want to read. He wanted to hide. She shook her head. "Nope, I'm going to need your help making change and carrying things to people's cars. Bring your book out here and you can get your reading done between busy spurts."

He groaned.

She ignored his antics as the wide space

between tents filled with avid shoppers. She'd hoped for decent sales and was pleased to be half sold out within ninety minutes. An early drought had nipped folks' flowers, and a fair share of people were happy to pay good money for a fresh midsummer start.

They'd emptied the van by midmorning. As the market prepared to close, they'd sold all but a few stray floral trays and two baskets.

Cade's eyes went wide when he saw the clip of bills in her money bag. "Are we rich?"

She felt rich, especially after last weekend's debacle. "We are considerably more comfortable than we were this morning, my friend. And you did great, once you stopped whining." She laughed and hugged him, then handed him thirty dollars. "Six dollars an hour, as promised."

"For me? Really?"

"You put in the time, you get paid for the time." She finished stowing the last of her supplies and closed the van door. "Let's grab some lunch, okay?"

"Okay!" Accomplishment had erased any trace of the glum kid she'd brought along. They grabbed quick takeout on the way home, and as Cade munched his chicken tenders, he mused at least two thousand ways to use his money.

Hope had replaced disillusionment in the best way possible. Her son was learning to work for a living. He jumped out of the van as soon as she parked and waved the folded bills at Trey.

"I made money today!" Cade fanned the three ten-dollar bills, then raced for the house. "I'm going to put this in a safe place."

"He's excited." Trey descended the scaffold ladder and came her way as she opened the back of the van. He reached in, then paused, surprised. "This is all that's left?"

"I'm as amazed as you are," she told him. She lugged supplies into the back of the greenhouse. He followed with the remaining stack. "We had a great morning, and my grumpy little helper turned out to be a wonderful assistant."

"There's something solid about earning your own money." Trey nestled the empty planting trays into a stack of others. "It's a good feeling to grow on. I gave the Battaglia boys and Brendan the day off because I wanted this side of the barn done, but they're coming after church tomorrow to do the ends. And then the trim."

"It looks wonderful." She kept her attention on the rehabilitated building, not the industrious cowboy at her side. "What a pleasure it will be to look out at a clean, fresh barn when I work in the kitchen this winter. There's something uplifting about a cared-for barn against a background of snow."

"I never thought I'd say this, but I miss snow." Trey studied the barn with her, side by side, but purposely distant. Lucy had to remind herself it was the smarter choice. "When Nick and Colt had to tackle into that storm this past winter, I wanted to be right here with them, heading uphill to bring cattle down."

"But you couldn't be here."

"The tour must go on. But I'm here now, and that's a good thing." A muscle in his jaw tensed, then relaxed. "Duty calls." He touched the brim of his hat and reclaimed his spot on the scaffold. She didn't stand there and watch him go, her heart on her sleeve like a love-struck teen. She was older than that, and smarter too.

What if you woke up tomorrow with only the things you took time to thank God for today?

She loved that reminder. She'd made a poster of those words and hung it in her humble kitchen. She had much to be grateful for. Her faith, her family. Her friends and her home. Her very life. But there were regrets mixed in too, and she needed to face them. One of them lived right next door and was trying to meet her halfway. Sam Stafford had put the ball in her court with his helpful gestures.

She took the wise words to heart, went inside, and baked Sam a batch of her old-fashioned sugar cookies. While they baked, she wrote Sam a note, thanking him for his efforts. As the cookies cooled, she and Cade frosted each one with homemade buttercream. Cade shook bright-colored sprinkles on some, and decorative sugars on others. In the end, they had a tray full of freshly made cookies. She set a plate aside for the kids, tucked the handwritten note inside the bigger tray, and drove up the road.

Sam had been self-centered for decades. Lucy knew that. But if she wanted folks to leave her past settled in the past, she needed to be strong enough to do the same for others. As she pulled into the Double S farmyard, she spotted kids in the distance, fishing on the far side of the pond. A group of cowboy-hat-wearing ranch hands were working a small cattle drive along a long stretch of south-facing hillside. Sam and Hobbs sat on the porch in side-by-side rocking chairs.

Cade raced off to join the other kids as Lucy cut across the grass to the front porch. Construction noise from Nick's new house drifted up the hill, and the laughter of children wandered back their way every now and again.

But the here and now lay quiet as she climbed the steps. "Hobbs, my boys are mighty taken with you and your cowboy ways."

Hobbs's face split in a wide smile.

"They like learnin', them two, and I don't mind teachin'. Of course I'd rather be up top, bossing those young upstarts around, but Sam figured I better let Colt and Nick take lead. That don't mean I'm spendin' my days on this porch, rockin', though." He glared at Sam, and Sam smiled. "You get better, then we can both be up there, showin' them a thing or two about how it's done."

"I'm looking forward to it." Sam breathed short and shallow, then sent Hobbs a droll look. "Once I can breathe again, that is. So, young lady." He turned back to Lucy and smiled a real, personable smile, not something the people of Gray's Glen were accustomed to where Sam Stafford was concerned. "Everything all right down below?"

"It is better than all right." She bent over and set the big plate of cookies on his lap, with the card on top. "I wanted to say thank you for the help."

"We can't exactly call it help if I'm the one who caused the problem in the first place," he reminded her. He looked gruff, then relaxed as he breathed in the sweet aroma of frosted sugar cookies. "But if these are homemade cookies, then I'm pleased to accept."

"They are, and it *is* a help because you're going above and beyond, I believe." She pulled up another rocker and sat right down with the two of them, and who would have imagined she'd be making herself at home on the Double S a few months back? Not Lucy Carlton, that's for sure. "The new roofs. The barn, all fixed up. Trey has started rebuilding the porch, and he's having rails put up, with spindles, pure country."

"He's always had a heart for that sort of thing, and for helping others. He got a lot of my mama in him, a quality that seems to have skipped a generation. But I do remember my sister loving to make these when we were kids." He looked down at the cookies as if surprised by the memory. "She loved doing things like this with our mother. And my mother used to say what a fine mom she'd make someday. I think we both were a disappointment in that department."

"You won't hear Trey sayin' nothin' like that," Hobbs argued. "He's mighty glad you found him and brought him back here. Us too."

"I've got plenty to look back on and regret, Hobbs, and sugarcoating it just wastes a lot of good sugar."

"Until now." Lucy waited for him to look her way. "It seems that you're doing a very nice job of carrying on your mother's kindnesses now."

He met her gaze, read her sincerity, and dipped his chin. "Maybe it was there all along and got hidden by my mistakes."

"Life has a way of doing that to you." She touched his hand, smiled, and straightened. "I wanted the chance to say 'thank you' in person. And nothing says true appreciation like something homemade."

Sam slipped a cookie out from under the plastic. He took one bite and held the plate out to Hobbs. "We'll get our share before that band of rowdies comes in."

"The cowboys?" she asked, glancing up the hill.

"The kids," Hobbs told her as he snagged cookies. "That mess of youngsters can eat a body out of house and home, and it's a whole lot of fun listening to Isabo chase them out of the kitchen."

"They're always hungry, and that reminded me of the boys growing up, and their friends coming by and how much they could pack away in a day. Raising kids is a mighty expensive prospect these days."

"It is."

"Well, that got me to thinking." Sam finished his cookie, licked the crumbs off his fingers, and looked happy to do it. "Now when I'm done you can tell me to mind my own business or just say yes, your choice, of course."

Lucy settled back into the chair. "Go on."

"Trey was explaining your business down there."

"The Christmas trees."

"That and the other, flowers and baskets and things like that. He said you've got a real knack for growing things."

"Ye . . . e . . . s." She drew the word out, wondering where he was going with this line of questions. "I enjoy it and most of it survives, always a plus."

"No one in Gray's Glen grows things like that for resale."

They didn't, so she nodded again.

"And he said you've been taking your things up to the Ellensburg market."

"Yes."

"Well, here's what I'm thinking." Sam indicated

the broad vista of the wide Central Washington valley. "We've got plenty of folks here who'd most likely buy your stuff. And we've got those new buildings going up in town, making it an easy spot for folks to shop, don't you think?"

A town location would be a wonderful thing for sales. "Well, sure, just the traffic getting off I-90 would be wonderful. Gray's Glen is minutes from the expressway. It takes more time and effort to get around the town and find me up here on this hill."

"Just what Sam was saying," Hobbs declared and grabbed another cookie. "Make it easy for folks to buy, and they'll do it!"

"But I don't—" Lucy was about to explain that she didn't have enough greenhouse room when Sam interrupted.

"You'd need more greenhouse room."

He had, perhaps, read her mind.

"And that can be accomplished before winter sets in so you're all set for spring. And with that extra acreage behind the new street of shops and apartments Colt's arranging, we could put a couple of greenhouses right there too. That way you can restock from the farm as needed and run three seasons of business in town. Folks could grab precut trees there, and if they want to cut their own, they drive out to the farm."

"You're saying you'd like to lease me a shop front in the new building?"

"We'll talk leasing after you're on your feet. A new business is nothing to take lightly, and it's hard work, easily messed up. So if you'd like to give it a try, Lucy, I'd like to see that northernmost shop become a farm market store."

A farm market store.

A place to sell everything she could grow.

A respectable business for a single mother whose life had been tattered and torn.

She studied Sam.

Could she trust him?

Sure, he'd had a change of heart, but was it long lasting and sincere, or would he turn back to the same old land baron mentality once he was back on his feet?

"I think it would be good for the town and for you." Sam sat back and ate another cookie. "You'd be stocking things no one else has, so you wouldn't be stepping on Hammerstein's toes, or hurting someone else's business."

Lucy was glad she wasn't eating a cookie, because she'd have choked. Sam Stafford was aiming *not* to step on toes. That had to be a first for a man who generally plowed full steam ahead, regardless.

"You think on it, but if you decide to do it, I want to add an outdoor covered area to the end of the building, and it would be good for the project engineer to know that now. A farm market should have an open-air feel to it, don't you think? And you could market local fruits and vegetables in season, and outdoor things like that." He pointed to the wind chimes hanging from the porch beams.

She didn't know what to say.

She wanted to jump up, hug him, and shout yes, because wasn't this a dream come true?

She didn't dare. Not without thought and prayer, because owing Sam Stafford could spell destruction. Yes, she wanted to forgive his past trespasses, like the Good Lord said.

But she couldn't forget how fast he'd pulled the rug out from under others. Old stories now, but true enough because Sam had always looked after himself first and foremost. "I have to think on it, Mr. Stafford. That's a very generous offer, but a lot to consider."

"I respect that."

Once again she was surprised because Sam hadn't respected much of anyone besides himself and managed to anger a good share of the town because of it.

"You let me know as quick as you can because I want to take advantage of the good weather. We've had Josh's crews working on multiple projects, and I've never built a greenhouse. I expect this upcoming surgery will keep me down awhile, but not forever, and I'd like to see this done over the fall. The Town Center plaza is slated for a May first opening if all goes well, and that would be just in time for your spring arrangements."

"Perfect timing, actually."

"You think on it. My hurry is not knowing when California's going to call and say come on down, we've got room to do your surgery. We're scheduled in four weeks, but if they get an opening, they could call any time. Knowing that pushes me to hurry, but I don't mean to rush you. If I'm down and out, Colt can see that things get done."

"I will. And thank you for the offer, Sam. I'm a little overwhelmed."

"Me too." He leaned back in the chair. Pride brightened his profile as noisy kids streamed their way. "But in a good way now."

Hobbs laughed and grabbed two more cookies before the kids reached them.

Joyous and loud voices surrounded them. Noah, climbing onto the rail, with Belle following right along. Dakota retelling the story of the fish that got away, while Cheyenne showed off a turtle. Cade and Cody joining right in, as if they belonged.

Neighbors. Friends.

She'd never had that luxury. Not as a kid and not as a teen, nor as an adult living next to the Staffords.

She'd wisped through life alone in a crowd, letting few in.

Just because you've been that way, doesn't mean you have to stay that way.

The little voice made perfect sense. Maybe she needed to change as much as Sam Stafford did, in a different way.

By the time she got the kids in the car and back home, it was past suppertime.

Trey's truck was gone. Quiet prevailed. She had money tucked away, enough to get through the next few weeks. And she had an offer from Sam, a proposition that sounded too good to be true.

Maybe that meant it *was* too good to be true. Could she risk being under Sam's thumb, developing a business in one of his sites? What if it all went bad?

"Refrain from anger and turn from wrath; Do not fret—it leads only to evil."

The old psalm held good advice.

Sam seemed sincere. But a smart woman learned to put everything in writing, which meant she wanted a contract before getting into any kind of deal with her wealthy neighbor. She might not have much, but what she had needed protection. A contract of terms could give her that.

She'd talk to Sam after church the next morning. He'd either agree or end the discussion. In any case, she'd know right off, and Lucy was more comfortable having things nailed down than left in the air.

Fifteen

Trey waited at the edge of the Catholic church parking lot, watching for Lucy's van while minutes ticked by. She'd told him she was singing today, but maybe he'd misunderstood. Maybe he'd messed up the dates. Perhaps—

Her van turned into the small lot with scant minutes to spare. She had to go all the way to the back to find a parking spot, which meant a long hike back up to the church.

He jogged the length of the parking lot and got to her van just as she was stepping out. "Guys, come on, I am ridiculously late. Ashley, can you get Belle? Cody, Cade, I—"

"Go." Trey put a hand on her arm and pointed toward the church. "Head up there. Ashley and I've got this."

She hesitated, then nodded, but didn't look any too happy about doing it. "Thank you." She hurried across the broad parking lot while he corralled the boys.

"Trey, can we come to your house today?"

"Can I ride Pegasus again?"

"Is Isabo making a big supper?"

"With corn on the cob?"

"You're being rude," Ashley scolded. "It isn't polite to invite ourselves places, and your mom would be embarrassed to hear you guys begging like that."

"Ashley's right." He took each boy by the hand. "You wait for an invitation to be given, and the first person to talk to is your mother, which means you better behave in church. She's more likely to say yes if you're good."

"I'll be so good, Mr. Twey." Belle peeked up at him from Ashley's side. "I told my dowwies that if they were good while we were gone, I'd give them a tweat when I get back. If you want tweats, you have to be good!"

"Suck-up." Cade scowled.

"Cade." Ashley frowned right back at him. "She's little, and you shouldn't talk like that."

"I learned it from you," he retorted. "You say mean stuff all the time. I've heard you on the phone, lots of times."

"More witnesses around when you can't text things," Trey reminded her softly. "Oops."

Ashley glared at him, then Cade. "Listen, you stinking little eavesdropper, you don't know anything, all right? You've got no business listening in on private conversations. Butt out."

Cade started to reply, but Trey bent low. "Stop now. Mind your manners and be nice to your little sister and to Ashley."

Ashley's brows shot up, probably surprised that he was taking her side.

"But—"

"No buts. Belle needs your protection and Ashley deserves respect. Being a cowboy isn't fun and games and showing off rodeo moves once you know how to ride. It's being respectful of others and trying our best, every day. Caring for people and not looking for thanks."

"Just being nice, right, Trey?" Cody squeezed his hand to gain his attention. "Like you told me last week. Work hard and be nice."

"Yup. And that starts with being polite and respectful to family. Got it?" Cade groaned out loud and stomped up the steps. He calmed down inside, sparing Lucy embarrassment up above.

"He's such a brat." Ashley crossed her arms, staring after her oldest nephew. "He tries to be annoying on purpose, just to see what you'll do."

"He's eight," Trey reminded her. "It will get better."

She rolled her eyes and followed Cade into the church, looking just as unhappy.

Belle reached out and took his free hand. "I'll twy to be extwa good, 'kay?"

"And I'll help her," Cody promised. "We'll be so good you won't even have to notice us."

His words touched Trey's heart as bells began tolling overhead.

He'd done exactly that as a small child. He'd tried to be so good that no one would notice him. It was a hateful existence, imprinted on his brain like a brand on an Angus hide. "I'll notice you," he promised, bending low. "I'll notice how hard you're trying and how good you're being, okay? Because we should always get noticed for being good, especially if it's hard to do."

"Thanks, Trey!" Cody's grin lightened Trey's mood. If he'd been asked about his childhood a few months back, he'd have shrugged and said he was over it.

He'd have been wrong.

Being back in Gray's Glen, among family and old friends, made him realize how blessed he was that Sam came looking for him. He didn't have to. As an adult, Trey knew that many kids went into the county systems, overlooked by family, shrugged off by friends.

Sam hadn't let that happen. Being home made him grateful for the good of that decision, but it brought back that handful of Oakland memories. The smells. The voices. The derision. And being constantly hungry, while needing to be constantly quiet.

The choir began singing, a soothing harmony of welcome and rejoicing. When Lucy's voice took lead on the first verse, Trey's pulse sped up.

The notes called to him. Her voice beckoned him with a warmth and clarity most singers strove for and few achieved.

A bank of candles flickered in the right-hand alcove, votive lights in amber glass, lit for intentions.

Hearing Lucy's voice, he understood his own intentions real well. He was falling for this woman, a totally surprising circumstance at the worst possible time.

He wanted to spend more time with Lucy Carlton and her fun, crazy, grumpy crew of kids. It made little sense. He'd been purposely off the radar since losing Cathy, but if his reactions to Lucy were anything to measure with, his radar was working just fine again. He wanted to make her smile. See her relax and laugh. Give her the gift of time, ease her work burden. Was he man enough to overlook her past and do it? And could he juggle an out-of-state career that he loved and still be present enough for a family?

Those were big questions.

Six weeks. Plus recovery time. He'd have thought he could do anything for six weeks, but when he turned and saw Lucy coming their way after the service, his palms itched.

Colt picked up Noah, waved to Lucy, and headed for the left-hand door.

"Sam's not here?" she asked.

Trey shook his head. "He wasn't up to it today. He's home and Isabo is watching over him. Did you need to see him?"

"I did, but it will wait." She reached down and lifted Belle, and when she kissed the little girl's soft cheek, the image of a loving wife and mother rocked him.

That's what he'd wanted. Maybe because of his mother, his early life, or maybe because he was a simple country boy in love with baseball, hot dogs, and apple pie.

But the image made him yearn, then smile.

"Bring the kids over and have dinner with us. Or supper, or whatever Isabo's got planned. That way you can see Dad, and the kids can play. I've got to supervise the teens at your place, so if you're tucked up at the ranch, I can power-wash the porch and get the primer on those posts so they're ready when Josh and Shannon start the rails."

"I don't want to impose, but I do have to talk to your dad."

Which most likely meant his father had talked to her about opening a town store. Sam had made it clear there wasn't time to waste, and he'd meant it.

She started for the door, and he fell into step alongside her. Sunshine bathed the front of the church in dappled gold as the broad old oak spread cool shade across faded grass. The boys and Ashley had gone ahead with Nick, Elsa, and the girls.

"Lucy."

"Yes?" She kept a fair distance between them purposely.

"Have you ever done much riding?"

"On a horse?"

He touched the brim of his hat. "Exactly that."

"No."

"Would you like to learn?"

"To ride?"

"Yes, again." He paused and so did she.

"Someday, yes. If it works out. There's little time with the kids and all."

"How about this afternoon? I'll get my chores done at your place, and we'll leave the kids with Angelina and Elsa for a spell. We'll take a ride up the old trail and across the ridge. I haven't had my seat in a saddle this entire week, and I'm curious about what Colt and Nick have going up along Schuyler's Pass."

"I don't think that would be considered a beginner's ride."

She was right, so he abbreviated the plan. "We'll just do the ridge, then. Angelina's been learning, and she and Elsa have gone off exploring more than once. It's a good skill to have."

She should say no. Why put herself in an impossible situation? She was attracted to Trey, and the kids were growing fond of him. He'd even managed to break through Cade's dig-in-your-heels nature. Cody gave affection easily. Not Cade. But he liked Trey, and that was a positive change.

If things were different, she'd simply keep her distance, but he was slated to be at the house every day, helping with this, fixing that.

Keep it light. Keep it simple. Or just say no.

"No strings, Ms. Lucy. Just a chance to see the valley from up top a horse."

Those hazel eyes, so sincere. His hat, tipped just so. And when he winked, waiting for her answer, she couldn't refuse. "If things are good with the kids, then that would be nice."

"It surely would, ma'am."

Oh, be still her heart. She knew he was flirting with her on purpose, but knowing it didn't make her more immune. He gave her a leg up a few hours later, coached her around the paddock, then brought his horse around and opened the gate.

"What if she takes off?" Lucy eyed the gate, Trey, and then the horse.

"It's Betsy. You're lucky to get her to walk, much less run."

"Are you sure?"

"Exceedingly. Peg will be chomping at the bit once we get through those upper gates and Betsy will plod like a plow pony, half-asleep."

"You're exaggerating her gentleness to keep me calm while on top of a thirteen-hundred-pound animal that can toss me around like a tennis ball before trampling me with sharp hooves."

He laughed. His horse pricked an ear and nodded, almost as if he was glad to hear Trey laugh. The singing cowboy didn't laugh often. It sounded nice.

"If I'd wanted to give you a wake-up-call kind

of ride, we'd have switched horses. Peg used to like to barter with me for the lead, but he's mellowed."

"Maturity has a way of doing that to us."

"And responsibilities. Schedules. Pausing to smell those roses, now and again."

"I love roses."

"Yeah?" He closed the gate and looked up at her as he remounted Pegasus. "I don't see any at your place."

"Fancy house gardens take precious time with no financial return. And the boys would probably wage dinosaur wars between the plants. Right now I'm better off growing flowers I can sell."

"Understandable. Do roses even grow up here?" He swept the rugged rise a quick look. "We get some sharp cold snaps midwinter."

"The hardy varieties do. They don't mind the cold, but they're sensitive to wet roots."

"I would have supposed that wet roots are conducive to plant life."

She laughed softly as he got down to open the second gate. Betsy walked through, then Trey led Peg into the upper meadow and relatched the gate. "They love water in doses. But if they're wet all the time, they rot."

"Too much of a good thing."

"Yes. They can be finicky, so it's just as well I don't have any. Keeping aggravation to a minimum has been a mainstay the past few years. Self-preservation of the single parent kind."

"Have you heard anything from Ashley's mother?"

"No." She grimaced. "Ashley pretends it doesn't bother her, but of course it does. And Maude must have changed her phone number. Ash tried the old one last evening, and it's been disconnected."

"That's harsh."

"That's Maude. When I was a newlywed and a young mother, I used to feel sorry for my husband. Having to deal with Maude couldn't have been easy. And about the time I realized I was expecting Belle, I realized something else. That Chase was a carbon copy of his mother. No matter what happened, he'd come first. It was a rude awakening."

"The mistakes of youth follow us."

"I made plenty, but I learned a lot. My choices were similar to the ones my mother made, and I was determined that my children weren't going to suffer from a similar fate. When I told Chase he had to cut out the drinking and partying, he said he'd sooner ditch us than his music and his friends. He let me know that his weekend highs were what got him through the drudgery of marriage and fatherhood."

"Lucy." He said her name in a deep voice, rich in sorrow, layered in empathy.

She wasn't telling him her story to gain his consideration; it was more to paint him a picture of what had been and why she kept stringent rules now. "He died in a one-car crash a few months later. He was wasted and angry that a weekend gig in Wenatchee brought in no money. He took the curve on a mountain road doing at least eighty, and lost control."

"I'm sorry."

He sounded genuinely sorry. She grasped the reins lightly like he'd shown her, and shrugged. "He was unhappy with everything life offered. He loved power and had none. He loved money and had none. And his mother had little to do with him or any of us, but when he was gone, she carried on something awful and made Ashley's life so hard.

"I traded bitterness for bitterness, from my father to my husband, but I learned a valuable lesson. I'll never settle for anything again. I've got my little place and my kids and my faith, and that's honestly all I need. Although Sam's help will make that a whole lot easier to grasp, with things looking so much nicer."

"It's coming along." He stayed fairly close to her side, not enough to worry her horse, but close enough to be truly present. "Has Ashley been straight this whole week?"

She thought so. "As far as I know. She knows I won't tolerate drugs or drinking. One more week of summer school, and then my hope is she turns a new corner once she's in the high school after Labor Day. There are plenty of nice kids to be friends with. I'm hoping she'll turn back to some of them."

"She and Cade don't get along."

She knew that. What she didn't know was the best way to handle it. "It's dicey, isn't it? I feel like I've got to protect Cade, even when I know he's being annoying, because she's older. She's usurped his position as the oldest kid, and he's resentful of the intrusion."

"Hobbs would say that's a lot of gobbledy-gook for something that just is what it is, and that Cade needs to get over himself."

"That sounds like Hobbs," she acknowledged. "And it makes sense. Which means I'm probably too soft and I'm going to mess them both up."

"Well, it's only been a few weeks, right?" He moved slightly ahead and angled her an amused look. "I expect there's time to get it right, yet. Turn that horse around here, Ms. Lucy, and check out the scene behind us."

She did and sighed.

Verdant beauty waved across the broad, lush valley below them, dotted with farms and fencing. The town lay to the right, shrouded in tall trees, but she could see the spire from the old Catholic church, and now the bell tower of the new, log church. "I can see Grace of God from here."

"My father's directive. He said he wanted that bell tower high enough to see all four seasons, to remind him to be a better person."

"Sam Stafford said that?" She looked at him, then regretted her action when their eyes met.

Gorgeous eyes. Short, clipped dusty blond hair. A rugged face, square-jawed, but gentle too. Trey Stafford had a kindliness that drew her, but she couldn't afford to be drawn.

"He said it all right. I used to pray for him when I was young. Nick and Colt didn't bother much with church; they went because they had to, but something about faith and hope got to me. The wanting to be a better person. A nicer version of me. And I saw Sam as this amazing benefactor; he'd rescued me out of squalor and brought me to all of this." Trey waved a hand to the sprawling ranch above and below. "But he couldn't find happiness no matter what he did, so I used to pray for that. For my dad to be happy. And now he is, despite his health issues."

He lifted one shoulder. "No matter how long he's got, I'm pleased to see him happy at last."

Selfless.

Was he really, or was it just plain easy to seem selfless when you're raised with money and acquire your own at a young age? Lucy had never had that casual regard for funds, so how could she know? "And yet you're not happy, Trey."

His jaw tightened and he kept his eyes on the valley below.

"I often wonder what goes on inside of us, that we're rarely satisfied," she said. The horse moved left unexpectedly. Trey reached over to steady her reins, his hand on hers in a quick protective move. "When do we have enough?" she asked quietly. The peaceful scene below them showed a land of plenty. "Why do we always long for more? And are we unhappy with what we have or are we more dissatisfied with who we are?"

"You said you made mistakes."

She sure had, but as long as God gave her breath, she wasn't going to wallow in a foolish past. "Big ones. But I'm not the first person to make mistakes. And I won't be the last. Still, right now I'm trying to be the best person I can be for the sake of my kids. That's my goal."

Trey was quiet for a moment, then pointed. "See this ridge?"

She nodded.

"When I was little, Murt used to tell us this story, about how the Yakama Tribe would pause on this ridge, thanking God for the rich valley below, then come down the hill to gather for the fall festivals, a custom they did every year. I think about that sometimes, how vast and open it all must have looked before the settlers moved in."

"It's hard to blend such different cultures. And

then, of course, both were led by men," Lucy added.

"Meaning men cause problems?" His voice teased, but the men in her life fit this mold easily.

She turned toward him. "You know how the Bible says that man is as inclined to sin as the sparks to fly upward? There's something in us, in all of us, but I think you see it more clearly in men, that they need to assert their power. Their influence. Their ways. Not all, of course, but it's as if when men get power, they need more power."

"The lack of satisfaction."

"And lack of humility. It's not a situation I ever care to be in again. I like making up my own mind, Trey. Leading my own life. It suits."

"Well, this is a mighty interesting discussion, and I'm taking your words and your warnings to heart."

She blushed because she had been warning him off, and he didn't let it slide.

"But here's the whole of it. Women are just as confusing in what they say they want and what they really want."

She couldn't deny the truth in his words because she was at odds with herself fifty percent of the time.

"If you can find me a woman who knows her own mind and is comfortable in her own skin, I'd like to meet her, because it seems to be a rarity. If men are lusting for power and money and might, women seem to be chronically searching for a way to impress other women. And I don't get it."

"That makes us sound a little crazy."

He didn't say they were crazy, but he didn't say they weren't either. He simply settled a skeptical look her way.

"We're not crazy; we've just got a lot of pressure on us to be the best we can be, in all things and all ways."

"And who puts that pressure on you? Because I'm here to tell you that most men could care less about that."

"You're not going to give me the 'little woman at home in the kitchen' speech, are you? Because these days I think that's a myth and men want a full-time wage earner, who is also at home in the kitchen while nursing a baby and making soup."

He laughed, reached over, and tweaked her hair, but then his hand stayed there. Right there. Cradling her cheek, her ear, touching her hair. "Oh, Lucy, we've got a lot to talk about." He smiled and then sighed. "But not today. Today we need to head back down the hill and hang out with noisy kids. And tomorrow, back to work for the day."

He was drawn to her. She sensed it. Felt it.

But he hesitated too, just like her.

"But they that wait upon the LORD shall renew their strength . . ."

Isaiah's words, potent, yet simple. To trust God's timing, his ways, his paths.

She had a hard time with that lately. A part of her longed to run full force toward the future, charting her own course, her own way. Was there really anything wrong with that? Shouldn't women take charge of their own lives?

They should, and yet . . .

Trey created a longing in her, a yearning for fulfillment. Togetherness. Building a family, a home, a life.

She was being ridiculous. Trey Walker Stafford could most likely have any woman he wanted. Why would a rich, successful country music star be attracted to her?

It made no sense, but when he looked at her . . . When his rough palm touched the soft pad of her cheek . . .

She sensed the same longing in him.

They descended easily, with no need to talk, and if Trey smiled a little too long when he unlatched the gate, she chalked it up to a handsome guy flirting with the only available girl, and that happened to be her. As they came across the last shallow field, Trey paused. He stared ahead and then motioned his horse forward. "We've got unexpected company."

She peered ahead and spotted an older SUV and a fairly buxom, bleached-blond woman standing nearby. They moved forward. Trey didn't quite slow down, but he didn't encourage the horse to move faster either.

The woman braced her hands on thick hips. When Trey dismounted, she crossed the stone drive, eyes narrowed, her mouth drawn. "Just like I said, isn't it, Trey Walker?" She gave Lucy a dirty look, then raised a finger Trey's way. "I told you how it was, and you scoffed at me. It's different for you, Trey, and shame on you for letting folks think it wasn't. You get to move on, even though your wife lies in a cold, dark grave. You get to have your songs and your guitar and your little flings from town to town."

Little flings?

Trey reached up and gave Lucy a hand down before he turned. "What are you doing here, Sallie?"

"You said you'd come see me."

"I did not. You asked me to come, I said no, and I refused to give you money. I kept it simple. Showing up here isn't helping anything."

"Of course it ain't, if you're not the one who needs help. When you're the one standing still, with your hand out, well, that's different, isn't it? If Cathy was still here, she'd help me. And you know it."

Trey started to respond, but Lucy beat him to it. "Cathy was your daughter?"

"Yes."

The blonde stared at Lucy, trying to intimidate

her, but Lucy didn't scare easily anymore. That ship had sailed years ago.

"The one you bilked hundreds of thousands of dollars from when she was a teenage superstar?"

Trey looked surprised by her words, but maybe a little pleased too. There wasn't time to tell because Sallie Somersby glared at Lucy, absolutely furious.

"You can't believe anything you read in those papers. Cathy loved me. I loved her. She was my everything."

"If by 'everything' you mean meal ticket, then I can understand your angst, but at least be honest about it. If nothing else, people should at least be honest about their greed and their selfishness."

"Why, you little—"

Lucy backed up a step. "Trey, it was nice riding with you, and I know you've got a heart as big as they come, but don't let her hoodwink you out of another penny. She could always try getting a job, like the rest of us do."

She strode away, leaving him to deal with his former mother-in-law.

Regret smacked her before she got twenty steps between them. She should go back and apologize. She should make amends. But then she remembered the look on the woman's face, and the long court battle that had entrenched Cathy Somersby in a media feeding frenzy for years. Cathy's parents had stolen nearly ninety percent of her earnings. And then they'd tried to wrangle money out of Trey after her death.

Lucy had seen it in the magazines, and with Trey a hometown hero, the local newspapers had covered the melee. The courts had found against the parents and ordered them to make restitution, but that never happened because they'd spent every penny on gambling and high living.

Lucy's father had put himself first, always. And then her husband had done the same thing. Seeing it in Cathy's mother touched all those old anger buttons, but that didn't give her permission to spout off at a complete stranger. Satisfaction mixed with regret.

"Take a breath and tell me who to kill. I'm ready, willing, and able. And armed." Angelina fell into step next to her, and her willingness to back Lucy up made her laugh.

"Then we'd both be in jail, and who'd raise the kids?"

"A valid point, but just so you know?" Angelina shoulder-bumped her. "I've got your back. I take it you met Sallie."

"Wretched person."

"Yup. But I think our Trey can handle her now. Coming home has toughened him up. Your cookies were amazing, by the way."

"Good change of subject. Innocent. Innocuous. Baking. Safe."

Angelina laughed and hugged her arm. "Let's let Trey deal with Sallie and the horses. Come on in the kitchen with me; cool off mentally and physically. Elsa's made tea, and Mami is showing us how to piece quilt tops for those needy babies. Peaceful, calm, and quiet, while the men watch the kids."

"It sounds just right, Angelina."

Angelina held open the screen door and gestured inside. "It is."

ॐ

Music. A campfire. Tired kids, marshmallows, and a pretty girl. Trey could get used to this.

Murt strummed his old acoustic guitar from the far side of the fire pit. Approval shone in the older man's expression as he surveyed the sight, a measure of peace and joy for the Double S Ranch. He glanced toward Trey, then Trey's SUV, and arched a brow.

Trey knew that look. He wanted Trey to fetch his guitar and join in, like old times.

Noah grabbed Angelina's hand and pulled his mother up to dance with him. Cody did the same thing with Lucy, and the sight of two little boys dancing with their mothers blindsided him.

He glanced toward Colt and Nick.

They saw it too. It was there in their faces, their expressions—the mix of emotions.

They saw what they'd missed, what they'd all missed, growing up. A mother's love. A mother's guiding hand, advice, the hugs and kisses and scoldings.

They'd grown up without any of it, a grievous loss. But seeing Lucy and Angelina move in step with their little boys, and Elsa snuggling a sleepy Dakota on her lap, awareness washed over Trey.

This was a time of second chances. Of new beginnings. And if all went well with Sam, Trey wanted a chance to start over. A chance to be whatever God intended him to be, with the love of family surrounding him. Fame wore mighty thin in an empty house.

He crossed the yard, longing to be part of this new normal. When he got back to the fire, he sat, propped a knee, and faced his mentor.

Murt played timeless, familiar notes from his guitar, a beloved spiritual that had marked Trey's life for years. He'd been tired and weary, like the great hymn's opening. And he'd trusted, believing in the light of Christ, the Lamb of God. And yet, that spiritual calm still eluded him.

He wanted the peace in the valley he sang about at every concert. The tranquil, the serene, the everyday normal he'd never had.

He bent his head and plucked along with Murt, and didn't look up when he launched into the deep-toned vocal.

He sang from more than his heart. He sang from his soul, and as the verses went on, he could see the opportunity before him. Maybe he wasn't free to grasp it yet, but he could envision it, a future, God's plan, laid out for him here in the broad, lush valley of Central Washington.

He closed the last plaintive notes and paused, then looked up.

Lucy's eyes met his.

She knew. She understood.

He didn't know how or why, and didn't much care, because what he saw in her eyes matched what he felt in his heart.

"Nice way to end the night, Trey." Colt stood and stretched, then offered a helping hand to Sam. "But morning's coming early, and there's a lot to be done. We've got those Nebraska buyers due in and a second cutting to put up. They're calling for rain midweek, and the horse hay needs to be under cover."

"It was a pleasure, Trey." Murt tipped his hat from across the flames. "Like old times."

Only better, thought Trey. Because he was finally beginning to get it, the understanding of accepting with grace and not chasing for more.

He picked Belle up, carrying her in one arm and his guitar in the other, then faced Lucy. "I'll walk you to your car."

"Thank you, Trey."

The combination of the pliant child in his arms and Lucy's winsome smile made peace in the valley seem close. So close.

They got the kids settled in. Ashley slid into the front seat. She glanced up at them, excited, then held open her hand. "Isabo paid me for this week. She said I did well and I can work Wednesday after school and then next weekend. If that's okay?"

"Keep your grades up, and it's fine," Lucy told her. She smiled at the girl as Trey opened her door. "It feels good, doesn't it?"

"It feels amazing!" Ashley grinned. "And I did it myself!"

"Yes, you did." Lucy turned back his way once she settled into the driver's seat. "Thank you for the song. For the day." She shrugged and smiled softly. "For everything, Trey."

"Weren't much, ma'am, just a pair of old cowboys, pluckin' away. And I wanted to thank you for standing up to Sallie today. You surprised me. You surprised her, even more," he added lightly. "And I think she's finally gotten it through her head that the free ride is over."

"I shouldn't have said anything, but I took one look at her and saw that selfishness. It hit every old button I've got, and I spouted off. But it wasn't my place, Trey, and I'm sorry."

"Those buttons can mess us up. Or they can be a big help to keeping us on track. One way or another, it's all right. And I wanted you to know that."

Her smile deepened. She reached up and

touched the back of his hand, just that. "Thank you."

He watched her go, then climbed into his SUV and drove to the cabin.

He hadn't found much inspiration to write since being home, but tonight was different. Tonight the notes and words and emotions moved him, and he stayed up half the night, working. When his alarm sounded a few hours later, he didn't fight waking up.

Waking up meant seeing Lucy. Helping her get that old place back into shape. Watching her smile and scold as she taught young boys good manners. And the way he felt when she turned that smile his way, as if anything was possible.

Sure it was quick, maybe too quick, but it was too right to be wrong. God's timing, that wonderful, simplistic belief, was being played out before his eyes, and for the first time in years, Trey trusted the tangibility of the intangible. And he began to truly believe.

Sixteen

The next two weeks flew by for Lucy. Ashley passed her summer school classes with two solid Bs and a clean slate to start high school after Labor Day.

The boys were getting antsy when they weren't at the Double S, but they couldn't be over there, underfoot, every day. Belle caught a cold from Noah and needed snuggles more than medicine, but she wasn't happy with Ashley snuggles. She wanted her mommy, and no one but her mother would do.

Lucy had approached Sam about a contract, and he'd presented her with one forty-eight hours later. She went over it carefully, found nothing objectionable, and signed on the dotted line.

Lucy Carlton was going to open her own business in town.

The thought thrilled and terrified her because what if she failed?

Then don't fail.

She ordered books from the Ellensburg library and studied while caring for Belle. She read up on greenhouse production, maximizing profits, and resisting the urge to increase overhead by overstocking.

It all made wonderful, perfect sense, but of

course the unknown variable was the consumer. Would people shop there? Would they lay down hard-earned money season after season? And did she have what it took to run a business and build her own version of the American dream?

Trey had finished the barn repairs the previous week. The painting was done. All the buildings wore their new roofs like church ladies wore spring hats, shining softly in the midday sun. Josh and Shannon had installed the porch rails, and the look of them, clean and white, made her feel like anything was possible. The three teen boys were working daily to put a new coat of white on the faded farmhouse, and where run-down had ruled the day, fresh and new surrounded her.

Cade had dashed out when he spotted the mail truck. He raced back up the driveway, looking taller and lankier than in years past. He jumped the two steps, dropped the mail in her lap and ran off again. Trey had promised them an afternoon at the ranch once the lower fields of cattle hay were baled, but she'd given the boys two old stalls to clean and sweep. If the stalls weren't done, they went nowhere, and she hoped that was impetus enough to keep them working.

She set aside two bills and three advertisements, then paused.

In her hand was a greeting-card type envelope, in unfamiliar writing.

She tore it open, smiled, and sighed.

Roses covered the face of the card, trailing along an old farm fence. Pink, yellow, and red, the flowers bloomed against the rustic backdrop, old and new, beautiful together. She opened the card and her smile grew. *"Saw this at Hammerstein's and thought of you. I could deliver it in person, but there's something real nice about getting mail. Trey."*

Just that.

Her heart stretched wider. It shouldn't, because she understood the time frame and the meaning of "temporary" better than the kids, so she knew he'd be leaving once Sam was better.

But today, with the late-summer sun slanted more southward, Lucy let the sweetness of the gesture tempt her. Belle had dozed off. She carried her inside to the couch, tucked her in, then crossed the drive to the single greenhouse. Josh Washington was coming by to sketch a plan for the new greenhouses. Trey was coming to pick up the boys and Ashley. Lucy's world, which had seemed out of whack two months before, had taken on new life and new goals.

She examined the area and the path to the Christmas tree fields, then paced off enough space to allow a transport vehicle access to the new greenhouse area as Josh pulled in. He grinned when he saw her and came her way. "We've got another project going, Lucy. Who'd have thought?" He pushed back his hat and crossed his arms over his chest. "I like the sound of this idea, real well."

"Unbelievable, right?" She could say that to Josh because they'd lived in Gray's Glen for many years. Not much had changed until everything changed, and that took some getting used to.

"My friend Trey would say you've got to make hay while the sun shines," Josh drawled, half-teasing and three-quarters serious. "And that's how I see all this. Your farm and the town and that sweet new church rising in the midst of it all. The sun is finally shining on Gray's Glen, and that's because it's shining like a beacon in Sam's soul."

"It feels almost wrong to take advantage of that," she admitted as Trey's SUV pulled in. He parked alongside Josh's truck and came their way, looking way better than a cowboy ever should. When he smiled at her, her pulse absolutely, positively refused to behave.

"It's not taking advantage," Josh told her. "It's what folks do to rebuild what's gone wrong before." He turned toward Trey, noticed his sunburned neck, and winced. "You might have wanted to use more sunscreen up on that hill. Ouch."

Trey grimaced. "The fire-breathing skin on the back of my neck is a steady reminder today, and it's the second time I've done it this summer. You'd think I'd learn. Hello, Lucy." He smiled down at her, as if seeing her made him forget sunburned necks and long hours working hay. "Is it still okay for me to grab the older kids?"

"It's wonderful," she told him. "The boys are in the barn. They needed to clean up those first two stalls. If they're done, they're free to go."

"And Ashley?"

"Hopefully Ashley is just finishing her summer book report on local history. It's due the first day of classes next week."

"I don't want to mess up your time with Josh," Trey said, "but the Ellensburg Rodeo is this coming weekend, and if you guys would consider heading that way with me, Ashley could come face to face with some local history. The Yakama Indians will set up their old-style encampment outside the grounds, and then they open the rodeo with a show on the tribes and how they descended into the valley every autumn. Have you ever gone?"

She didn't say there had never been enough money for her to even think of such a thing. How easily life flowed for people of means. Even through hardships, the kind everyone faced, people of means didn't have to slog and worry about every single penny, and that was a luxury she'd never had. But now, with a new business, with regular money coming in next year, maybe she could join the normalcy of middle-class America. If she could achieve that, she'd never ask for anything more.

"I expect the kids would love that," Josh added. "Cade and Cody have caught a real fine case of cowboy fever being up at the Double S."

Lucy hesitated. If she immersed them in too much Western cowboy lore, how would they react when Trey was gone and the regular invites to the ranch stopped coming? She started to refuse, then caught herself.

She was being irrational. Why shouldn't the kids have a day to remember? She'd never been able to afford vacations with them, so a day at the rodeo, surrounded by bulls and broncs and Columbian plateau history would be wonderful. "I'd love that, Trey. The kids too."

His smile grew. "Thought for a minute you were going to turn me down, Ms. Lucy."

"And if I had?"

"I'd find another invite to issue," he promised. "But I'm glad you accepted this one. I haven't been to the Ellensburg Rodeo in over a decade. Even in the busiest of seasons, Dad found a way to get us to the rodeo every year. This will be like old times. Only new."

"And a great time for all four kids," Josh agreed.

Trey backpedaled to the barn. "I'll see you later. Is it all right if we give them supper at the ranch? Isabo's marinating chicken for the big rotisserie. With salt potatoes, from the back garden. And corn."

"You had me at rotisserie chicken."

"Good." He paused, smiling at her, and drat if she didn't stand there, stuck in one spot, smiling back.

"Back to greenhouses." Josh tapped his old-school spiral-bound folder and brought her back on track, as Trey rounded up kids. He showed her basic plans, and they worked out square footage and walking room between the rows of plants, along with a storage area at the end with water and electricity access.

"This is taking a simple greenhouse design and turning it into something beyond the expected," she said.

"That's the fun of a new build," Josh replied. "We can do it right from the beginning, making sure everything's in place for successful growing. Cuts down on your time, and that helps your profit margin. Sam said he wants two of these done here, and then he wants me to go the next size up for display at the Town Center shop. That way you've got plenty of work space here and good display space there."

"It's wonderful, Josh."

Josh bumped knuckles with her. "That's exactly what Sam said. Now that we're all on the same page, I'm going to order the materials. Then we'll have the topsoil stripped here so we can begin construction." He turned and pointed toward the house and the inviting front porch. "And here's a thought, Lucy. I'd like to move some of that topsoil over in front of the house, along the porch to create a green space."

"For a garden?"

He nodded. "What do you think?"

What did she think? She loved the idea; the bland stone drive edging the house went beyond austere. An old farmhouse should always have a little yard and garden, with some clothesline strung for hanging wash. It ought to be a rule. "I've always wanted a garden there, but it's full of stone."

"I'm bringing the Cat in to break ground, so we can use it to dig that out. I can use that stone to fill in the rough spots along the tractor path, then backfill along the porch with topsoil. That gives us a garden, right?"

It did, and she couldn't believe how absolutely delightful that sounded. "Yes."

"Sounds like a plan."

She wanted to ask if Trey had talked to him, but what if he hadn't? Josh was a sensible man; he'd understand the importance of her place looking nice if she wanted to sell flowers and plantings to others.

Still—

Maybe Trey did put the idea in his head after they'd talked, and if he had? Lucy was grateful.

༺ༀ༻

"Will there be cowboys there?"

"Yup." Trey kept his eyes on the busy road to Ellensburg, but he smiled. "And Indians."

"Real ones?" Cody's eyes rounded and he let out a *whoop!*

"Cody Michael, don't do that." Lucy twisted around in her seat and scolded him. "What if you scared Trey and we got into an accident?"

"Don't scare easy, ma'am, but thank you for lookin' out for me." Trey touched the tip of his hat but paid attention to the highway. I-90 was nothing to mess with on rodeo mornings. The traffic thickened and slowed as they approached Ellensburg, and the kids' anticipation heightened.

"Ashley, have you ever been to something like this?" Trey asked.

She shook her head. "Chase promised to take me when I was little." She shrugged and stared out the window. "We never got to go, so this is my first time."

"There's a lot to see," Trey told her. They'd stopped as cars crept off the exit, so he met her gaze through the rearview mirror. "The retelling of the Yakama tribal customs might be stuff you can use in your book report."

"But it's not in the book." She didn't look intrigued but she didn't look annoyed either. "I can't use things that aren't in the book."

"Sure you can. You just have to say that it's independent research outside the book." Trey winked. "Teachers love that kind of thing. If you find any of it interesting today."

"You mean she'd like me to do extra?"

"What teacher wouldn't?"

"So this is like a field trip under the guise of being fun?"

Trey laughed and thumped the wheel. "I guess it is. But we'll sneak the fun side in so the teacher doesn't know we found learning enjoyable. And if there are funnel cakes or fried dough here, I'm a happy man."

"Fried dough?" Cade sat up straighter. "Like Bob gave me at the market?" Lucy's old neighbors brought their fried dough wagon to every county event.

"Bob and Jaycee's booth will be here. They always cook for the rodeo."

"Will we see the cowboys and Indians right off?" Cody strained forward in his seat, scanning left and right as if expecting to see a face-off along the interstate.

"First there's a parade. And the Frontier Town and the Indian encampment. And the county fair. The rodeo is in a few hours, after lunch. That's where we actually see and hear the Yakama history in more detail."

"It's not like I brought a notebook with me." Ashley sighed out loud. "How am I supposed to remember it all?"

"You paid your phone bill with the money you earned, right?" Trey glanced back again.

"The notebook feature!"

"All that money for a phone that's actually

like a minicomputer, a girl ought to be able to take some notes. Or even a video," Trey suggested.

"I never thought of that."

"There you go." He smiled at her through the mirror as he slid on a pair of sunglasses. "And we're here." The parking attendants directed them where to go, and by the time they'd toured the two historic reenactments and watched the parade, Lucy thought they'd be hungry.

They were, but when Cade spotted the agricultural booths and the farm animals on display, he headed straight that way. "I hafta see the animals first," he insisted. "This is cool, to have all these farm animals right here, right?"

Belle wanted to ride the carousel. Cody wanted to lasso a bronc. But Cade wanted nothing more than to check out the animal pens. "I'll take Cade in if you guys want to catch some rides before the rodeo," Trey offered. "I like the barn exhibits too."

Lucy turned toward Cade. "You don't want to ride anything, Cade?"

He looked torn initially, then shook his head. "I want to learn about this stuff. I want to learn *a lot* about this stuff." He pointed to the barns. "What if Mr. Sam wants workers someday?"

"A big ranch like that needs help, that's for certain."

Cade folded his arms, a little smug and a little

excited. "So if I know stuff, I can do more on the ranch."

"Can't argue logic," Trey agreed.

"Then I want to stay too." Cody slipped from Lucy's side and stood by Trey. "I can ride things another time, right, Trey?"

Lucy handed Ashley some money for the ride tickets. "Can you take Belle on the carousel and the little kids' rides?"

Ashley didn't pout or make a face, a welcome change. She tucked the money in her pocket and nodded. "Sure. I haven't ridden a carousel since I was real little. Do you want a horse or a seat, Belle?"

"A horse!"

"That would be my choice too," laughed Ashley. "When should we meet you guys?"

"How about twelve thirty near the rodeo gate? Well, actually . . ." Trey slipped his hand into his pocket and pulled out two tickets. "Take these just in case it's busy at the gate. That way we can all meet inside, and we can have lunch while we're watching."

"Are you buying us lunch?" Cody's eyes grew wide, and right about then Lucy was hoping he'd stop talking. Of course he didn't. "We never get to have lunch when we go places." He turned toward Lucy, eyes shining. "This is like the most special day ever, Mom!"

Before she even had time to push away her

embarrassment and wonder if she was setting her beautiful children up for bitter disappointment, Trey tucked an arm around her shoulders.

"Cowboys and burgers." He tipped his sunglasses down to grin at her. "We sure know how to party, don't we, Ms. Lucy?"

She laughed.

She had no choice.

He was funny and normal and endearing, and while she knew this wasn't slated to go anywhere, Trey made it easy to laugh again. At herself, the kids, the times . . . even at him. To keep a low profile at the fair, he'd replaced his signature cowboy hat with a scuffed-up NYPD baseball cap, and he'd let his beard grow for a few days, just enough to look scruffy. With the whiskers, the cap, and the dark shades, he looked more like the guy next door and less like a superstar. She liked the guy-next-door persona. The superstar status seemed too far removed from anything she'd call normal.

"We're wild and crazy, all right." She waved good-bye to Belle and started for the animal exhibition barn. "Let's see what they've got."

Alpacas, goats, lambs, calves, cows, and horses. They browsed from barn to barn, and when Cade fell in love with an orphaned miniature donkey, Trey scratched the back of his neck, then winced.

"The sunburn." Lucy cringed. "Don't touch it. Ouch."

"It's better. I was just being dumb." With his phone, he took a picture of the farm info posted on the rail.

Lucy poked his arm. "I don't have fencing or money for hay. Don't do anything rash."

"Plenty of fencing and hay next door," he said easily. "And every now and again, being rash is mighty nice. Don't you think?"

Easy to say when money allowed such things. "When you're on a budget, rash decisions can make for long regrets," she continued. "There's nothing wrong with weighing decisions carefully. Even when longing eyes implore us." Cade was stroking the little donkey's head and smiling. When he withdrew his hand, he stood up and squared his little shoulders.

"I know we can't get one, Mom. It's just he doesn't have a mom or a dad, and I thought he needed someone to love him. For just a little while."

Sweet emotion rose up inside her.

"Trey." Cade reached out and put his hand into Trey's. He tipped his head back and gazed up. "Even if I don't have animals at my house, I can read about them, right? About how to take care of them? And then maybe I can have a job at your house when I'm bigger."

Trey longed to make lame promises he might not be around to keep, but he didn't. He squatted to Cade's level. "I think that's a great idea, actually. The more we know, the more valuable we are in the workplace."

"Great." Cade clung to the big guy's hand as if they'd just sealed a deal. "I'll practice when I'm over there and read about stuff when I'm not. Okay?"

"Okay." Trey stood back up, nice and easy. He nudged those glasses down, smiled at her, and she was a goner. Maybe she was foolish to build walls against all this. Perhaps the thought of Trey Walker falling in love with a struggling single mom wasn't a stretch. Maybe it was God's timing being played out before her.

And maybe it's you being played.

She hushed the internal doubt. Trey wasn't like that. Sure, she'd seen the tabloids after Cathy died. They'd plastered his picture and suppositions in every grocery aisle checkout lane.

Not locally, of course. Folks around Gray's| Glen and Cle Elum loved Trey.

But other places, yes. Her late husband had scoffed at Trey and his success, then used the tragedy of Cathy's overdose to make fun of Trey and country music. He'd been jealous of another man's success and cheered his downfall.

Except Trey hadn't fallen. He'd kept his silence, ignored the gossip, and moved forward, writing and singing songs filled with heart, soul, and longing for better times. Sweeter times.

"And what have we got here?" Trey asked as

they moved into the cattle section. He spotted her expression and offered a friendly frown. "You're thinking too much for what is supposed to be a fun day."

She blushed because she'd been doing exactly that.

"There's no time for thought when you're eyeing a beauty like this." Trey paused before an award-winning Angus heifer. "That's Double S lineage right there. Gorgeous, right?"

"She is!" Cade climbed the rail of the empty stall adjacent to the contented young cow. "Is that why she looks like your cows?"

"Yup. Bred true, and a prize winner." He nodded toward the blue ribbon fastened to the stall.

"How come you don't bring cows here to win prizes?" Cody wondered, eyeing the ribbon. "Because that's cool."

"I would if I had some young 4-H folks around," Trey told him. "If we had some kids interested in raising and training and keeping animals for a 4-H project, I'd be all over that, Cody."

"What's 4-H?"

"It's like a special club of kids and leaders who want everyone to know about the best way to do things for animals on the farm. It's very cool."

"Like kids our age?"

"You're getting to just the right age," Trey told him.

"Wow."

"Except let me go back to the lack of funds for the necessities." Lucy tugged Trey's arm and when he bent her way, she whispered a warning into his ear and tried to ignore that he smelled amazing, even over the surroundings of penned animals. "Let's not make promises we can't keep, okay?"

He didn't move his glasses this time. He didn't have to. She felt his gaze, without seeing it. "I never do, Lucy."

Her heart, a ridiculous organ, began skipping beats and behaving in a most undignified manner.

He smiled.

So did she, even if she shouldn't, because she wanted to smile with him. At him. And when he shrugged his arm around her shoulders and drew her alongside, Lucy Carlton was pretty sure she could just stay there forever and be perfectly, wonderfully happy.

"Trey? Trey Walker?" A high-pitched voice screeched his name.

He turned, and half-a-dozen girls mobbed them. "It is you!"

"I saw you outside, but I wasn't sure!"

"Oh my gosh, oh my gosh, I might faint! I cannot possibly even believe this! Can I have a picture with you?" A pushy teen budged into Trey's side and extended her arm and a smart-phone as far as she could. "I can't even! A selfie with Trey Walker! And I love your music, your newest hit, and everything about you! I don't believe this!"

Her voice carried beyond the end of the stock tent. People moved their way, surrounding Trey.

Another teen girl pushed in, nearly knocking Cade to the ground. Lucy corralled Cody to the outside of the group, then sought Cade's hand.

Trey looked her way. "Have you got him?"

"Yes."

"Give me ten minutes to do pictures. Then we'll find our seats."

"Okay." What choice did she have? None really.

She herded the kids out of the stock barn and sought shade beneath a broad, wide-leafed maple. "Who needs to use the bathroom before the rodeo? This would be the perfect time."

Cade tugged her hand. "Why are all those people pestering Trey? And taking his picture?"

She steered them toward the restrooms as she answered. "Trey's a singer. Lots of people buy his music and go to his concerts. And he's on TV."

"He is?" The boys both stopped, surprised.

"I've never seen him on TV." Cade shoved his hands in his pockets, disgruntled.

"His show is on too late for you guys."

"So he's like those famous people? Like in movies?" Cody looked impressed and surprised. But then his little face darkened as he realized what just happened in the cattle barn. "They didn't want a picture of us," he muttered. "They just wanted us out of the picture." He scuffed his toe along, chin down.

"Nobody wants your dumb picture anyway," Cade scolded. "You do that dorky smile thing, and it looks weird."

"Cade, stop that. Your brother is adorable. You're mad because we had to move on before you wanted to." Lucy stooped to their level. "I'm sorry about that, but I want you to be grateful for all the time you *did* have, looking at the animals. Not to focus on the last couple of minutes that didn't go like you wanted. Be positive, little man. It will get you further."

"It doesn't matter." Cade refused to buy into her logic. Stubborn anger toughened his chin. "I was done with stupid old animals anyway. No sense in reading about 'em if we can't ever have anything at our dumb, dumb house." He started to trudge off to the men's room.

"Cade, you can't go in there alone."

He spun around when he caught her drift. "You want me to go into the girl side?" His eyes shot wide. "When I'm a boy?"

A woman shot her a sympathetic look. So did a middle-aged man, but what could she do? "No one will know."

"Except all the people here." He stared around at the two bathroom lines, and if embarrassment had a color, it was Cade's face right now. "I'll hold it."

"Cade."

"I will," he insisted, stubbornly.

She was not going to have a bathroom fight with him in public. "That's fine, then, but you still have to walk inside with me and your brother. You can't stand out here alone."

"Whatever." He stared down for slow ticks of the clock as the line moved forward, then raised angry eyes to her. "If I ever, ever, ever get a dad again, he will always take me to the boy bathroom. Like every single time. Okay?" The last word wasn't asking permission; it was demanding understanding, and Lucy understood, all right.

Life minimized a lot of her choices, but she wasn't about to send an eight-year-old into a public restroom alone, and no amount of histrionics would change her mind.

Nearly twenty minutes had passed by the time they met Trey. She spotted him near the rodeo entrance. He was scanning the crowd, looking for her, and when he spotted her—

He smiled.

Oh, that smile.

Easy and calm and happy to see her. To see them. He ruffled Cody's hair, then spotted Cade's face. "Hey, partner. What's up?"

Cade said nothing.

Trey looked to her for direction, but Cody beat her to it. "He didn't want to use the potty in the girl's room, and he made mom sad."

"I'm sorry to hear that." He didn't console Cade. He didn't side with him. But he reached out and took the little guy's hand in his. "Lucy, I'm sorry you were sad. Are you all right now?"

He was modeling the sweet nurturing she'd love to have had as reality at pretty much any point in her life. She nodded. "I'm fine now. I'm going to let it go so it doesn't spoil our wonderful day."

"Great idea. And if you don't mind, we've got just enough time for me and this little cowpoke to hit the men's room before the action starts. Is that all right with you?"

She flashed him a quick look of gratitude. "That's a great idea. Thank you. We'll meet you guys inside the arena."

His phone rang as he handed her the tickets. He scanned the display, tapped the screen, and slid the phone back into his pocket. "I'll call him back. Let's go, partner."

She led Cody through the ticket gate, then scanned the rapidly filling seats for Ashley. She didn't spot her, so she let Cody pick their seats. They settled mid-high and toward the bull-riding chutes, a typical boy choice. Ashley found them a few minutes later, then Trey. He took Ashley and Cade out to the food vendors, and they brought back lunch on thick paper plates. Burgers, nachos, and fries. He saw her raised brow and he grinned. "Rodeo food, ma'am. Delicious and fun. And your friends said they'd deliver fried dough a little later if everyone eats their lunch."

"I love their fried dough like crazy," Cade exclaimed. "It's the best."

Nothing like food to quiet kids down, and when Trey took the seat just below her, she leaned down. "The phone call went okay?"

She couldn't see his face, and he didn't look back. "Fine."

His voice didn't seem fine or as lighthearted as it had been a quarter hour before. He stayed facing forward, but when the opening show chronicling the Indian traditions began, he withdrew his phone and drew Ashley's attention.

"I'll record it too. That way one of us should have a solid shot."

"Thanks, Trey."

He dipped his head in that classic cowboy style, even without the hat, and smiled at Ashley, but the smile wasn't as easy as it had been an hour before.

Ashley wouldn't notice. She was quite caught up in having Trey help her, be nice to her, encourage her.

But Lucy noticed. And she noted his silence too. He was entitled to his privacy. She understood that. But she'd been schooled by men who said one thing and meant another all her life. She'd learned the hard way that secrets were rarely good, and that was a red flag of the highest order.

She knew little of Trey's professional life, and a mega-star's schedule held numerous factions and temptations. Some good, some not so good, and some downright immoral.

She couldn't imagine Trey that way, but she'd only glimpsed one small corner of his existence, leaving a large margin of error.

She didn't like movies where the heroine made foolish choices and ended up making the same mistakes repeatedly. Their weakness annoyed her, even while she was tempted to trust Trey's sweetness. His kindness. His warmth.

But red flags flashed warnings for a reason, and a mother of three couldn't afford to ignore them. Not for herself, and certainly not for her precious children.

ରଔ

A long, wonderful day.

Trey parked his SUV along Center Street and walked to the small inn. He didn't have to climb the steps. His agent came down them at a quick clip and clapped him on the back. "You look good, Trey."

"Because I am good, Ed." Trey jerked his head left. "Let's walk." They moved east toward one of the construction zones Trey's father had commissioned. Josh Washington and Colt had offered the town a new possibility after the fire, an altered layout to rebuild homes and jobs for the people of Gray's Glen. Beyond the churches and the small-town playground stood the beginnings of four new homes on staked-out lots. Not big or fancy, the bungalow-style rentals fit the low-key Western town. When they got to the construction area, Trey faced Ed. "This should be a good place to not be overheard."

Ed glanced around. He looked uncertain, but Ed was born suspicious. "You're being nominated three times on Wednesday."

Wednesday was the announcement day for several of country music's biggest awards, awards Trey had won in the past. In country music, winning awards kept you on the fast track.

"Don't ask how I know, let's just say I got cut a special deal because of your circumstances."

"My circumstances?" Trey crossed his arms and glared because Ed knew better. "My circumstances that are supposed to be kept secret, Ed?"

"They're secret enough, but we need to have you healthy enough to walk onto that stage in November and hit the ground running with a winter tour. Momentum, Trey. It is, was, and will always be about momentum."

"Momentum equates money. I've heard it a million times."

"Momentum pays the bills, and I'd be a lousy agent if I didn't look out for you when you refuse to look out for yourself."

Ed had been good to him, and good for him. He knew the business, and he had connections.

"I can't push the surgery schedule, Ed. It's out of my hands. We'll just take things as they come."

"That's a senseless way to do business and you know it."

"Life intervenes, and doing the right thing isn't always convenient, but it's always right."

"Are you sure you've got to do this?"

Ed locked eyes with Trey in the cool dark of the early September evening. "Have you truly explored all of your options? Your father is rich, Trey. You're rich. There's got to be a way to turn that into a donated organ."

"You're talking about buying an organ that might save someone else's life?"

"Black market cadaver organs aren't a rarity." Ed spoke frankly. "I've looked into it. If we go that way, your father gets a full organ and you don't have to undergo life-threatening surgery. And the donor is deceased, so I don't see a big hang-up about supporting some hospital's cause with a hefty donation while saving your father's life and sparing yours.

"It's a no-brainer, Trey," he continued. "And if that doesn't appeal to you, I've got a guy who can hook us up with people willing to take your place for fifteen grand. That's like a drop in the bucket, and then your future is ensured." Ed stepped closer. "Your father wants you to think about this, Trey."

"My father?" Trey reached out and grabbed Ed's shoulder. "What do you mean my father wants me to think about this? You went to Dad and offered your self-serving ideas to plant doubts in his mind? I might have to punch you for that, Ed."

Ed shrugged off his hand. "*He* called *me,* Trey. He's worried about you. And he's scared. So he called me to talk some sense into you."

Trey should have been surprised, but he wasn't. He'd watched Sam's worry grow as the days wore on. More than once, he'd caught him watching Trey out of the corner of his eye, wondering. Worrying.

Was he being foolish and stubborn? Was Ed right? Did Trey's naïveté help or hinder this decision?

Jesus was led into the wilderness and tempted by the devil. In Christ's hour of need and hunger, Satan's offers must have sounded good. But just because something was easier and affordable didn't make it right.

"Seek the ways of the righteous always because the path to perdition begins easily, with small steps. Once taken, it is readily taken again."

Religious studies, his sophomore year at Oregon. It made sense then. It made more sense now. "I'm sticking with my plan, Ed."

Ed blew out a breath, aggravated. "You don't have to, though. That's what I'm saying. And if we go the other route, your father worries less, and isn't that what this is all about? Helping your father?"

Trey was kind of impressed at how quickly Ed turned that around. And if Ed had been a totally selfish, egotistical jerk, Trey would have fired him on the spot.

He wasn't though. Trey knew he actually had a good heart and a keen head for business, but his lack of faith was showing now. "I'm helping my father twofold."

Ed sighed on purpose.

"I'm offering him a part of me that he needs to survive, and I'm saving him from slipping back into the abyss of trying to buy his way out of everything. Money's not the great equalizer you're making it out to be, Ed." Trey stuffed his hands in his pockets and headed back toward the inn. "It's a great destroyer, making life too easy. We're doing this my way, and I'll make sure my father knows that. And I expect you to respect my decision." He paused and looked Ed straight in the eyes. "No matter what my father says."

Ed studied him for drawn-out seconds, and Trey knew when he'd won the battle because Ed rolled his eyes. "I tried."

"You did, and it was a valiant, if misdirected, effort. When do you fly out of Yakima? Or did you come into Seattle?"

"Seattle, of course. I don't do small airports or cheap wine. Tomorrow afternoon, four oh five."

"The whole family's going to church at ten right there." Trey pointed to Our Lady Queen of Peace. "Father Murphy's lent us their building until our church is finished."

"I can't believe your family is building the town a log cabin church," Ed said. "I thought it would look ridiculous, but it doesn't. It's kind of awesome, actually."

"Colt's idea. He's the smart one."

Ed laughed. "Church, huh? Tomorrow morning?"

"You should join us," Trey told him. "Meet us for services and then come up to the ranch for food. Meet folks. Then I'll drive you back to Sea-Tac."

"What time did you say for that?" He indicated the church across the green.

"Ten o'clock."

"I'll be there. Maybe I can pray some sense into you." He said it fierce, but he didn't mean it, and Trey laughed.

"I'll do the same. And quit talking to my father, you hear?"

"I hear."

"Good night."

Ed waved. He paused on the upper steps, pulled out a cigar, and lit it. "I'm going to take advantage of this cool weather and enjoy a smoke. Nashville was close to one hundred and humid when I boarded the plane." He took a deep breath of cool, clear Washington air and sighed. "This is real nice here."

"It sure is. See you in the morning."

Head down, Trey walked back to his car in the small municipal lot.

So his father was worried? Seeking alternative answers?

Trey was worried too, and if they could have just marched into that operating room that first day and been done with it, he'd have more peace of mind now.

But he wouldn't have accomplished all the good things they'd gotten done at Lucy's the last couple of weeks, and that meant something. He drove up to the cabin, let himself in, and prowled the small rooms, restless.

He tried to write.

Nothing came.

He tried to pick out notes on the guitar.

Same result. He put his head into his hands, thinking.

Was he truly a man of conscience, or was he simply seeking God's favor? And if that was the case, did his sacrifice make him a lesser man?

He thought of the widow, with her meager coins. She gave what she could, and that's the kind of faith he embraced. Give what you can, when you can.

An old image of Sam came back to him, driving

a big red pickup truck, with a scared little boy tucked into a booster seat beside him.

Sam had pulled into a restaurant, taken Trey's hand, and walked him inside. The place was full of people, truckers and travelers. It was big, loud, and teeming with action. He'd taken Trey to the men's room, made sure he washed his hands, then ordered food.

But Trey couldn't eat.

He'd been mesmerized by the lights and the people and the sounds, a kaleidoscope of color in a cacophony of sound.

He'd sat there, staring, surrounded by so much input that even though his belly had been empty for days, he couldn't imagine biting into the pieces of sweet-smelling chicken or golden, hot fries.

Sam didn't yell at him.

He didn't scold. He looked down at him, scanned the crowd, and pressed his lips into a tight, grim look. "Can you box this up for us, please? And how about two of those frosted brownies too?"

"Sure enough!" The woman had put everything into neat little boxes, tucked them into a bag, and handed them over. Sam had paid the bill, retaken Trey's hand, and led him out to the truck. He'd lifted him up and set him in the seat.

Trey's stomach had gurgled. He remembered it so clearly, as if it was a new memory.

He'd looked over Sam's head at the bright

blinking sign, the smell of good food surrounding them. He'd spoiled it. Spoiled it all, and now Sam was taking him away from the food, from the place.

He'd blinked back tears, so tired and so hungry and so alone.

Sam had climbed into his side of the truck. He'd reached over and turned on the engine, then the radio. Soft music filled the cab. Then Sam turned on one small light, and he flipped down a ledge between their seats and smiled. "Who needs all that crazy noise in there when we've got a perfectly good dining room right here?"

Then he laid out the food in the quiet of the cab and didn't scold when Trey ate so fast and so much he'd probably get sick.

He'd seen a little kid's desperation and acted on it. He'd read Trey's distress and fixed it. Despite all of Sam's faults, when he saw something wrong, he fixed it, and that was what Trey meant to do. It wasn't payback.

He could never give back enough for the life Sam had offered him.

But he could do this one thing out of respect for his father. And that's how it had to be.

Seventeen

Lucy pulled into the church lot, late as usual, and when she spotted Trey waiting, relief washed over her. She parked and hit the button to open the side door.

"May I take a couple of kids off your hands, Ms. Lucy?"

Lucy could have kissed him on the spot, and while the idea was tempting, the actions would have sparked a lot of talk. "If you could separate the warring factions, I'd be much obliged."

He grinned as he greeted Belle. "Lookin' mighty sweet this morning, missy."

He didn't jump in and hurry her out of her seat. Lucy was grateful for that. Teaching independence took time and patience. Trey had both qualities.

"Cade and Ashley, I don't want to hear another thing about the phone, got it?" Lucy leaned over the seat and scolded Cade while Cody followed Belle out the driver's side door. "Cade, it's not yours, don't touch it. And Ashley, threatening his life will get you nothing but trouble, and you're working at the Double S today, so cool it. If you want to have a job, act responsible enough to keep a job." She turned as an older man approached them from the Center Street side of the parking lot. Trey waved him over.

"Ed, come here. I want you to meet our neighbors. Lucy, this is Ed Boddy, my agent."

Lord, have mercy, how did she go from plain old Lucy Carlton, the somewhat impoverished woman next door, to standing side by side with a big-name Nashville agent? She decided not to overthink it, put out her hand, and smiled. "A pleasure to meet you."

"Same here." As the older kids scrambled down from the car, his eyes widened. "All yours?"

She wasn't sure if he was impressed or insulting. "We're a family."

Cody strode right up to him, the family ambassador. "Trey took us to the rodeo *and* to the carnival *and* to see the Indians and people dressed up like the old people that used to live here. It was really cool, but I mostly liked the big animals, just like Trey." He stuck his hand into Trey's and held tight, as if holding Trey's hand was the new normal. "It was the most fun ever."

"Just like Trey, hmm?" The agent looked at Trey, then Lucy, then Trey again.

"Lucy, do you need to get inside?"

"I do." She handed him Belle's hand. "I'll see you after service, and you're sure you don't mind riding herd on this bunch again?"

"Reinforcements have been sighted as we speak." He directed his attention to the big Double S Jeep as Colt parked two rows back.

"We've got them covered, and this is nothing Ashley and I can't handle."

Ashley's expression softened when Trey included her. Lucy saw him notice that, and he looked satisfied.

Strong enough to be gentle.

That was Trey Stafford.

She hurried off, not as late as last week, but later than she should be. How many times had she pondered giving up her spot in the small choir until the kids were older?

So many . . .

But she'd resisted even though spare time was nonexistent. Getting to practices was hard, and half the time she had to bring the kids and hope they'd behave because hiring a sitter wasn't a possibility.

She'd stayed with the group for her sanity. Singing God's praise and leading worship music kept her focused on all that was good and holy in the world. Praise. Grace. Warmth. Worship.

She'd lost all that as a teenager. She'd taken the slippery slope into self-absorbed and self-destructive behaviors. She'd used bad choices of escapism purposely, and the musical crowd she'd embraced ran hard, fast, and heavy in all the wrong directions. Alcohol. Sex. Drugs.

She'd wised up finally, but not before she'd set a course of action that brought her to this point of life.

But now it was different.

Now the music healed.

Chains of notes provided prayer and solace, sweet and pure, a solid win for a frenzied single mother.

She ran through scales softly with the choir director, and when she launched into the soprano of John Rutter's "For the Beauty of the Earth" as a prelude, her heart danced with the quick notes and praised with the long ones.

And just like before, Trey turned and smiled up at her, as if the music touched him. As if she touched him.

And then the agent turned.

He turned gradually, as if measuring what he heard. As if assessing. And then as if contemplating.

He looked up.

This big-time, well-heeled, famous-in-music-circles agent looked up at her.

And he nodded slowly, then with more definition.

She read his look. It was the look she'd hoped for as a younger woman, singing with Chase's somewhat derelict band.

Approval. Promise. Hope. Action.

She read all of that in his gaze as he took in the choir, the loft, and her.

And when the service began, Trey's smile shared an inclusive joy, an emotion she'd never truly known. And Ed's expression indicated an interest she'd longed for years ago.

You're letting your imagination run wild. Stop it.

She took the mental advice to heart. She was crazy to be standing in the quaint, old loft, imagining the Nashville agent's interest.

Trey's affection must have turned her head to delusions of grandeur, to "what-ifs" that hadn't been and could never be. She scolded herself internally and focused on the reverend's words of peace, hope, and love, three things that were finally coming to fruition in Gray's Glen. She'd promised God that would be enough, and Lucy Carlton never went back on a promise.

"Brilliant." Ed Boddy seized Lucy's hand once the service concluded, and she was pretty sure he wasn't about to let go. "Listening to you sing was a gift, Lucy. Have you ever sung professionally?"

"She used to, all the time," Ashley informed him. "With my brother and his band before he died."

Why did Ashley pick now to be open and forthcoming? Lucy gently extricated her hand and pasted an uneasy smile on her face.

"Now I just sing in the choir."

"What if that were to change?"

Ed stared at her, right at her, his voice serious.

341

"Have you ever thought of giving music a try as a career?"

Trey came their way just then, holding Belle. The two of them were laughing about something, a pair, a unit, so joyful. Lucy focused on the simple pleasure of that.

"Long ago. Not anymore."

"But you're perfect."

Trey overheard Ed's praise. He paused, looking back and forth between them.

"I can't disagree with Ed's assessment, ma'am." He touched the brim of an imaginary hat. "And while perfect is a bit of a stretch for us mere mortals, I'd say the Good Lord knew exactly what he was doin' when he created you, Ms. Lucy."

"Thank you, both." She pretended to swoon. "I'm not sure what I did to warrant this kind of attention, gentlemen. All this fuss and bother could turn a girl's head."

"I'm serious."

The deep note in Ed's tone paused her. It paused Trey too.

"We don't have to discuss this here and now, but, Lucy, you have a gift."

She looked at her kids. "Several of them, in fact."

"Talent like yours is special." Ed held up his hands, palms out. "Listen, I won't browbeat you, I'm just overwhelmed that I strolled into a tucked-in-the-hills church and discovered one of the most beautiful voices I've ever had the pleasure to hear."

Who could resist a compliment like that? "Thank you. What a lovely thing to say. But now I've got to get these kids on the road."

She hooked her thumb toward the vehicle and called Cade's and Cody's names. "Gotta go, guys. Ashley has to get to work."

"And Mr. Hobbs promised to take us for a ride up the hill!" Cody shouted the words as he and Cade raced their way. Cade beat him, but not by as much this time, and they scrambled into the van, then into their seats.

"I love Hobbs," Lucy noted to no one in particular. She turned toward Ed as Trey watched Belle climb up into her car seat. "Ed, it was good meeting you."

"Ed's coming up to the ranch," Trey told her, but he didn't look her way, and he didn't sound excited. He kept his attention on Belle as she tucked herself into the seat. "I'm taking him to the airport later today."

"You should drive to Seattle with us," said Ed. "That would give me over an hour to crunch numbers and details with you."

"Ed." Trey looked up from checking Belle's clasps. "Stop pushing."

"You're right." Ed backed up a step. "I don't mean to be rude. We can just talk at the ranch."

"Or not." Trey met Ed's eyes with a firm look

once he straightened. "We can table the whole thing right now. Lucy's not interested. Are you?" He looked her way then, and darn if she didn't just become interested because he said she wasn't.

"Stop. Both of you." She climbed into the driver's seat of a van filled with her current reality—kids—and faced Ed. "I'm flattered, of course, but I honestly have no idea what this all means and where flattery ends and cold, hard business begins. And with everything I've got on my plate"—she flashed a glance into the rearview mirror—"I'm not up for any more dead ends in life. I've got a plan of action now, thanks to Sam and Trey, and that's plenty."

It might have ended there, Ed might have accepted her dismissal and moved on, but then Trey added his two cents.

"It is. More than enough, most likely. Our thoughts were to make things easier for Lucy. Not tougher."

A burr formed between her shoulder blades, an old wound, rubbed raw by a mean-spirited, self-absorbed father and a similar husband. She'd been belittled and demeaned for too many years, until faith in God had created faith in herself, and no one got to call the shots anymore. Except her.

Yes, she'd promised herself she'd sing simply for the Lord. But she'd also promised herself that no one would ever again bully her into decisions she was loathe to make. She didn't look at Trey. She couldn't. She faced Ed once she started the engine. "We'll talk later."

Ed's face relaxed instantly. "Good."

Trey's didn't. His face went flat. He stood there wearing a guarded expression, as if her words threw him off.

Ed's queries had thrown her off, too, but in the end the decision was up to her and only her. She'd learned to stand her ground because appeasement didn't work, not in the long run. And Lucy was done having other people make decisions for her.

ɷ

Trey drove back to the ranch, grim faced. Ed was too busy texting Nashville movers and shakers to notice, and Trey knew what that meant in the industrious agent's world. He was already sending out feelers, wondering what label might want an amazing new talent wrapped in a drop-dead beautiful package. He parked the car, let Isabo take charge of Ed, and headed for the barn.

He wanted to punch someone.

The peacemaker of the three Stafford boys was aching to have a knock-down, drag-out fight with the next available person.

She didn't mean it, did she?

Remembering the expression on Lucy's face, he realized she might mean it. She absolutely, positively meant it, and the minute she said that, his gentle, easygoing plans flew out the window.

Thoughts of Cathy crowded his brain.

She was an amazing talent too. A child prodigy. Born to please. Born for the stage, a musical entity in and of herself. And by her fourth year in, she was so dependent on drugs that she could barely function without them.

She'd straightened herself out before they met, and all Trey could see was the innocent beauty of the woman she was. He knew her past. He knew what Sallie and Rich had done to her. Embezzled her earnings and lied their way into her accounts. Everyone knew it; the scandal was front-page news.

He'd fallen for her quickly, and she'd done the same. He'd even accepted that her past was in the past, and knowing she'd overcome a drug addiction was like a crowning glory. His parents had never been able to dig their way out. Maybe they'd tried, maybe they hadn't. It didn't matter. Cathy had fought her way through the darkness and into the light, and he loved her for it. And she'd loved him back, making her love a vindica-tion and a benediction, all at once. The drugs hadn't won. He did.

So when she succumbed to the lure a few years later, he'd seen the truth firsthand.

He hadn't been enough after all. He'd never

been enough. Maybe nothing was enough once the brain got a taste of drug-induced highs.

He'd been left on his own by his parents and his beloved wife. No matter what, the drugs came first, and his heart was left to wither into nothingness.

"You are a sorry sight."

Trey swung around as Nick came his way.

"Don't let the girls see that face," Nick continued. "They'll never be able to sleep tonight."

"Shut up."

"Hey." Nick didn't shut up, but he stopped teasing Trey. "What's wrong? What's happened? I'll be glad to punch out someone's lights for you. Say the name and consider it done."

"Lucy."

Nick rolled his eyes. "Well, I can't punch Lucy. First, she's nice, and she's got cute kids, and I think the Double S has done enough in the past to mess her up, don't you?" He stood square in front of Trey, blocking him into a corner. "What's going on?"

"Her singing impressed Ed."

Nick looked confused. "Her singing impresses a lot of folks. How is that bad?"

"He's talking to her about a career." He punched the nearby stable wall with his fist and got nothing but really sore knuckles for his trouble. "In music. In Nashville."

"Lucy going to Nashville? For real?"

"If Ed has his way."

"With all the kids?"

Trey scowled.

"Oh, man." Nick crossed his arms and contemplated Trey. "It's not the going to Nashville that spooked you. It's the idea of Lucy having a singing career like—"

"Don't go there."

"Cathy's," Nick finished. "You're letting this push a lot of buttons, Trey."

"I'm not the one pushing the buttons. She could have just told him no. Do you know what the odds are of making it in Nashville, even with a good agent? Slim. Real slim. Almost none actually. Every label has cut back with record sales down. There's no getting around digital sharing, and it's a night-and-day kind of job to make enough money to just scrape by for a new artist."

"Did you assess that risk when you left college and headed to Nashville?"

"No, but I didn't have four kids to raise either."

"That raises the stakes."

"And multiplies the risks."

"Talk to her about it," Nick suggested. "She'll listen to you. I think she actually likes you, though I can't figure why." He grinned when Trey glared at him. "You've got two choices. Pout in the barn like a four-year-old or talk to the girl." He fake-punched Trey's arm. "Take it from a guy who's been in your shoes not too long ago. Talking to the girl is best."

He couldn't.

Oh, he knew the drill. He needed to step back and assess what emotions were getting pushed and why, then disengage them mentally. He'd gone over it in therapy with Clara. He'd witnessed it in others. Nick was right. But there was no way he could approach this subject right now and not come off like a complete and fairly insecure jerk. "I can't. Not right now."

Nick sighed. "Why do Staffords always have to be the slowest learners on the planet?"

Trey said nothing.

Nick jutted his chin toward the yard beyond the barn. "When does the city slicker go to the airport?"

"Midafternoon."

Nick eyed Ed's designer suit and his Italian leather loafers through the broad barn door. He didn't sigh again. He didn't have to. He kept his face placid. "Can't be soon enough."

Right now Trey was feeling the same way.

Sam had purposely invited Ed to the Double S to dangle doubt and money in front of Trey. He'd thwarted that volley the night before.

Today's barrage wasn't so easy to dodge.

Lucy had parked the van nearest the driveway, as if keeping an escape option open, and he couldn't blame her. Belle and Noah came racing out of the house as he and Nick crossed the driveway. They'd changed into play clothes, and as they dashed for the playground equipment at the far end of the yard, they set an example of unfettered joy. Sweet and pure and uncluttered by grown-up mistakes. If only it were that easy.

He went inside.

Sunday morning smells filled the air. Cinnamon and apples, a September staple. Coffee, rich and robust. A pot of potatoes covered one burner of the stainless steel stove, and a pan of barbecued beans sat waiting to go into the oven.

The four older kids hurried through the kitchen, ready to claim the outdoors for the last few days of summer vacation. Lucy and Elsa followed, chatting, with neatly folded church clothes in their hands.

Lucy saw him and stopped abruptly. She'd been talking easily.

His presence made her hesitate. She looked at him, then dropped her eyes to the plastic bag Elsa held out. "Great, thanks. I'm going to put these in the van now, so I don't forget."

"I'll walk you."

She didn't answer, and her face looked sad, which only added to the weight he carried.

Elsa backed toward the opposite kitchen entrance. "I'll be out in a few minutes. I'm going to get changed myself."

Trey held the kitchen door open for Lucy. They

crossed the broad side porch, then the graveled drive to her car, silent. She opened the back of the van, set the clothes inside, and then just stood there with the hatch raised.

"Lucy, I'm sorry."

She kept her attention on absolutely nothing in the van.

"That whole talk of Nashville, of you singing." He thought about what to say, then confessed, "It caught me off guard."

"Caught you off guard?" She turned now, fast. "Your agent compliments me, says nice things about my singing and my appearance, and you take offense. That says one of two things. Either you can't handle your agent's split attention, or you have absolutely no confidence in the idea that I can make it in Nashville. So which is it? Your wounded superego or my lack of ability? I'm dying to know."

"Neither." He went to rub his hand across the back of his neck, made the sunburn sting even more, and scowled half at the pain, half at her assumption. "You're more talented than a lot of folks making money in Music City, and Ed has lots of clients who've managed to make him a very comfortable living. I'm friends with a bunch of them. It's not about Nashville, not really. Well . . ." He stared off at the rising hills to the north. "Some, I guess."

He rocked back on his heels. "It's a great city. I

love it. But being a newbie in Nashville isn't an easy path, and there are four kids to consider."

She stepped back and closed the hatch harder than needed. "So now I'm selfish and inconsiderate of my family. Somehow that's not making this better."

"I didn't say that. I'm just saying it's hard, Lucy. It's hard to get a grip on a musical career and keep that grip."

"You wanna know hard?" She faced him now, and those pretty blue eyes blazed hot. "Being raised by a miserable man who belittled you and your mother at every turn, blocking every normal thing a kid would like to do. That's hard. Then making stupid teenage mistakes and ending up married to a man who was a younger version of your father, only you were too young and gullible to see it. That's hard.

"And then being a single mom to three impressionable kids, stuck in a hand-to-mouth existence because of your own choices, and wearing that guilt like a yoke across your shoulders. So don't spew rich-man nice-isms at me about tough times and difficult choices. I've lived them. I've survived. And no one will ever do me the disservice of making my decisions for me, ever again."

She didn't wait to hear his response. She strode off, tough and angry, insulted by his reaction.

Anger rose like A.M. mountain fog.

He wasn't trying to hurt her. He was trying to protect her. Her and those kids.

She didn't know how tough things got with late-night gigs every night, and the label pushing you to extremes. Sure, the money made it easier if you made it big, but if you didn't?

It was taking whatever job you could, with whatever crazy hours were offered, day in, day out.

It can be, his conscience reminded him in a somewhat snarky voice. *But that's not the real reason you're upset. Tell her about Cathy. Talk to her. And then be man enough to leave it alone.*

He took Ed to the airport a few hours later. He didn't ask Lucy to come along, and she was doing a real good job of ignoring him, so that made his escape easy. Too easy.

It was a quiet ride to Sea-Tac, and a quieter ride back to the Double S. When he pulled into the ranch drive, Lucy's van was gone. The kids were gone.

He glanced around, decided he didn't want to answer questions, and drove right back down the driveway. He passed Nick's new house, just begun. He passed the arched sign at the ranch entrance with the two wrought iron *S*s centered at the top.

He drove to the cabin, but didn't go in.

Restlessness spurred him to work. He hauled an ax out of the shed, sharpened the blade, and split firewood for as long as daylight allowed. He didn't want to think right now, and he sure as heck didn't want to remember. Bone-wearying, mindless activity suited the moment, and when he finally fell into bed, he knew he needed to fix this. But with old emotions tying him in knots, he had no idea how.

ᘒᘒ

Lucy tucked Ed Boddy's card behind a refrigerator magnet the next morning.

He hadn't pushed or prodded the previous afternoon, but she caught him watching her from time to time. When he did approach her to say good-bye, she'd extended her hand, knowing Trey was nearby. "Nice to meet you, Ed." Just that, pure and simple. Trey hadn't invited her along on the ride to Sea-Tac, and she wasn't about to ask.

But then the agent took it further of his own accord. He slipped her the card with a promise. "The pleasure is all mine, Lucy. I'll be in touch."

Years ago, those words would have spurred hope in her heart.

Now consternation mixed with the hope because she'd matured. Trey was right. The music industry wasn't easy. But what was? "All right."

She didn't encourage him, but she wasn't about to slam the door shut either, because sometimes

354

God opened doors for a reason. And a door like this deserved prayer and thought.

The crunch of Elsa's tires said she'd have to think about this later. They were taking Dakota, Cheyenne, Cade, and Cody back-to-school shopping in Ellensburg. Ashley had been invited to work with Isabo for the day, and Angelina was keeping Noah and Belle at the Double S.

"Boys. Elsa's here."

"Do we have to go do dumb clothes shopping?" Cade hooked his thumbs into his front jeans pockets like he saw the ranch hands do and faced her. "Can't I just go help Trey?"

"Cowboys need an education," she told him. "And to get one of those you need new clothes. And if you give me a hard time, we won't worry about visiting the Double S for a while. Got it?"

"Yes." Head down, he scuffed his way to the car.

Cody had already climbed in. He'd grabbed the middle seat with Dakota, so Cade had to climb through them to get to the back seat.

Cheyenne was reading a book. She set it aside when Cade sat down.

"Do you wish we could just stay home and ride too?"

His face lightened instantly. "Yes!"

"Same here. I'd much rather be in the barn, taking care of the new baby calves. I loved having the puppies around. They were so much fun."

"I miss them," Cade confessed, and Lucy caught Cheyenne's nod in response.

"Me too. But Dad says you have to get used to the comings and goings on a ranch if you're going to work it. Animals come, they go, and then there's more. But I sure hated seeing that last puppy drive off down the road."

"I've never had a dog." Sadness gripped Cade's voice with the admission. He kept his voice soft, but Lucy heard every word. "I want one someday. Just a nice dog to roll around with."

"Like Achilles." Elsa's big, hairy mixed breed was quite at home on the Double S. "My dad didn't let us help with the dogs before. And we couldn't do a lot of stuff. But now we can, and you get to come over a lot. If you can't have your own dog, you can share ours, okay? No one will mind."

And they wouldn't, Lucy realized.

She'd mind, because she didn't like feeling obligated, but that shouldn't become the kids' problem. Cheyenne had shed light on the issue from youthful simplicity.

"Elsa, can we have the radio on back here?"

"Sure." Elsa hit a button as she pulled out onto the road. "Are you ready to tackle this?" She kept her voice low and light, so Lucy did the same.

"Looking forward to it actually. There hasn't been a lot of girlfriend time the past few years."

"I hear you. Me either. Of my own accord," Elsa

acknowledged. She hit the interstate and eased into end-of-summer traffic. "And I've never taken kids back-to-school shopping before."

"A novice."

"Of the highest order. Which means feel free to offer advice as needed."

"Me?" Lucy kept her voice soft but filled with question. "Advising a psychologist? There's a role reversal for you."

"How about friend advising friend?" Elsa smiled her way. "I like level playing fields."

"I do too, but they can be a rarity in the real world."

"Your past with Sam underscores that." Elsa pondered the thought as she shifted lanes. "But sometimes that imbalance is our own doing, isn't it? When we apply skewed reasoning?"

Was it?

"God doesn't assess land holdings or bank accounts. He sees us. Our hearts, our souls. He sees the person we strive to be. That's pretty level."

"Well, he's God."

"Exactly. So we can't expect humans to be omniscient. We need to allow ourselves—and others—time to figure things out."

"You're talking about Trey."

"Or not."

Yesterday's emotions rose within her. "I don't like being told what to do."

Elsa kept driving. The kids in the middle seat were busily making pictures to illustrate a story they'd made up the day before, and the older two kids were quietly talking horses, dogs, cats, and cows in the back seat.

"I made a promise to myself years ago. That I'd make my own way in this world, me and God and good choices. And that's what I intend to do."

Angelina would have made a cryptic remark here. Elsa stayed quiet, and Lucy decided she might have preferred the snarky reply. "I'm not being stubborn." The minute she said it she realized she was being purposely stubborn. "Well, I am, but for good reason."

"Our reasons always seem good to us." Elsa switched lanes again and signaled for the upcoming exit. "But when we examine them from other perspectives, the view can be quite different."

"Trey told you that Ed approached me about singing."

Elsa nodded.

"He seemed insulted by the idea."

"Insulted or worried?"

"I wasn't about to take time to find out." Lucy clutched her small handbag with both hands. "Years ago I would have been thrilled by an agent's interest. My husband thought that making it big would be the end to all of our problems. In retrospect I realize that nothing could be further from the truth. Problems dog our steps no matter where we are. But that's for me to decide. Not the gorgeous guy next door who's never had to worry about food on the table or shoes on kids' feet."

"Did you ask him why?"

She hadn't. She'd gotten angry and treated him like an outcast for the rest of the day.

"I don't know Trey well, yet," Elsa said.

Neither did Lucy, not really. She knew Hank/Trey, the kind, funny, hardworking, unafraid-to-get-dirty cowboy next door. Superstar Trey seemed to be a different thing entirely.

"But he's suffered traumas. His parents. His wife. Trying so hard to show what can be done is an exhausting task because it never really ends. With no endgame in sight, it's got to be hard to balance what was with what is." She pulled into a parking space and turned Lucy's way. "You make choices based on experience, right?"

"Life can be the world's best and harshest teacher."

"Yes." Understanding softened Elsa's tone. "Trey's got such love inside him. He's a true tender heart; those songs he writes come straight from who he is. Who God created him to be. But there's another side to Trey, Lucy, the side he doesn't let the world see. The side that fears loss and abandonment and love not being returned. That's a gaping hole for a grown man to fill."

Trey feared nothing. He'd said so often enough,

but the minute Elsa said the words, Lucy recognized the truth in them.

"He's looking for peace, Lucy. Just like the rest of us. And it's an elusive hunt, especially when the world thinks you have it all. That makes the loneliness even harder to endure."

Like the hymn, a few nights back, the poignant words about finding peace in the valley. He'd brought those words to life in the emotions of the song. Why didn't she see that he wasn't just singing a sweet old song, but that the words poured out of him, about him? Was she that self-absorbed? "Elsa, I—"

Elsa waved her off as the kids scrambled to get out of their seats. "Just something to think about when there's a quiet moment. Which"— she made a doubtful face as Cheyenne and Cade climbed out of the back seat—"probably won't be for a while."

Eighteen

Lucy would have never taken Elsa as a shopaholic. Clearly she was mistaken. By two o'clock she was ready to drop into a chair, put her feet up, and stick earplugs in her ears because the boys had started getting grouchy an hour before, and grumpy boys were loud.

"One more stop," Elsa promised. "And then ice cream."

The ice cream soothed the ruffled kid feathers, but Lucy kept thinking of things she needed to get done at home. By the time they'd finished their ice cream, it was nearly four o'clock.

"We got so much done." Elsa seemed pleased. Really pleased.

"We did. And I even got Belle the things she needed for fall, so that's another good thing to check off the list."

"She's going to look adorable in that pink-and-gray outfit," said Dakota. "I think that was my most favorite, Lucy. What about you, Cheyenne?"

"I'm wiped out." Cheyenne laid her head back and acted like Lucy felt.

"You're all set for a new school year," Elsa told her, and when Cheyenne exchanged looks with her in the rearview mirror, Elsa smiled. "And it will be a wonderful new beginning."

She turned left onto the two-lane, then put her signal on to make a right into Lucy's yard. Except it didn't look like Lucy's bare, graveled yard anymore. It looked positively, radiantly beautiful.

A tapered garden stretched the length of the refurbished porch. A natural wood trellis shaded the near end of the porch. The tawny hue of the wood complemented the white railings, and a pair of raspberry-toned climbing roses hugged the trellis's bottom.

Small bushes and more flowers dotted the garden plot. Zinnias and mums brought fall's rusts, golds, and cranberry into the mix, while two golden euonymus added all-season spots of color. At the far end, a pyramidal yew offered a natural high point. Thick Washington stone provided a barrier from the driveway and busy little boy feet.

"Is this why we stayed out two hours longer than expected?"

Elsa came around the front of the SUV and smiled. "It's quite possible that I received a text or two asking me to keep you away a little longer than expected. And it turned out wonderful."

Ashley came through the side door. "Do you love it?"

"I love it so much!" Lucy told her. She climbed the steps and hugged Ashley. "You knew about this?"

"I helped Trey do it." Pride brightened her voice and lifted her chin. "He said I did great," she added. "He did all the digging, and then a guy from Cedarwood brought the black mulch for on top." She held out her stained hands. "I hope it washes off before school starts."

"Oh, Ashley." Lucy gripped her hands. "Thank you. Thank you so much. And two new rockers."

The handcrafted rockers came from a family business outside of Ellensburg. They'd seen them at the fair, which meant Trey must have made the drive back to buy the matching chairs. "This is beautiful. So beautiful."

The kids scrambled from chair to swing, then back to the rockers again, trying things out. "Did Trey leave?"

"He got a text right when we finished, and had to head out. You just missed him."

Elsa raised her phone. "I just got a similar text. The surgical team in San Francisco has an unexpected opening. The men are heading to San Francisco first thing in the morning."

"All of them?"

"Yes. Girls, hop in. We've got to go give Grandpa and your dad a kiss good-bye."

A kiss good-bye . . .

Two days ago she might have had that right, the right to kiss Trey good-bye and wish Sam well.

She wished she could smooth things over. Talk to him. Maybe if she'd given him time to explain, time to share his feelings, she'd have understood his reaction.

But she didn't, and this time should belong to his father. "We'll be praying. And I'll be happy to jump in and help at the ranch with anything you guys might need."

"Isabo would love that, I'm sure." The girls had hurried into the SUV and fastened their belts. "See you soon." She pulled the SUV around and disappeared from view a few moments later.

"Do you like it, Mom?" Cade came up alongside her. She saw more than just the question in his eyes. She saw concern. She nodded and took his hand.

"I love it. It's like living in a fairy tale, isn't it?" The outside of her little farm glowed with care. Clean, freshly painted outbuildings met slate-gray roofs with a trim of white.

The freshly painted house and shutters gleamed in the late-summer sun. Hobbs had regraded the graveled portion of the yard, and he'd eased out the bumps and holes in the Christmas tree path. Trey had staked off a parking area on the far side, and he'd lined the walking paths with wood chips. He'd created an inviting entry into the tree area, perfect for holiday sales.

"It's so vewy beautiful, isn't it, Mommy?" Belle dashed out the door.

"Angelina dropped her off at naptime," Ashley explained. "I hope that's okay. I made sure the monitor was on downstairs so we could hear her if she woke up."

"That's fine, Ashley." Lucy reached out and put

her palm to Ashley's smooth, soft cheek. "It's just fine. And I was thinking that you and I could get some shopping done on Friday if we leave right after school gets out. We could drive down to Union Gap and get a solid few hours in. I'm going to see if Jenna can come by and watch the kids. That way we can spend the evening together."

"Just you and me?" The thought deepened Ashley's smile.

"Just us."

"That would be awesome."

"I think so too." Ashley moved ahead of her, started to open the door, and then paused. She turned back and scanned the yard, the clean, fresh barn and sheds, then the pretty garden. "Are you worried about Mr. Stafford?"

She'd be lying if she said no. "I am, but they're in good hands. Elsa told me the transplant center is among the best."

Ashley stared out at the flowers, then turned toward Lucy. "I heard Angelina talking to Elsa about forgiveness."

Lucy stood quiet, listening.

"She was talking about God forgiving us, but then about forgiving ourselves."

Lucy understood the difficulty in that firsthand. "That's often the toughest of all."

Ashley gripped the door handle hard. "I don't want to mess up anymore, Lucy. I want to start high school and be normal."

Normal. The thought of being normal seemed minimal, but Lucy recognized the gravity of the wish. When your entire life had been dysfunctional, normal seemed just plain nice. "I hear you."

"Anyway that's my goal. Angelina said it was a good one."

"She was right."

Ashley pulled the door open, but then she let it go and hugged Lucy, like she used to, years ago. "Thank you, Lucy. Thank you for taking a chance on a kid like me."

A kid like her.

Lucy hugged her back, good and hard. "Right back at ya, kid."

She went to bed that night praying for Sam's full recovery. He had to recover. He'd spent months trying to undo the damage he'd done over the years. Was he buying God's love?

No. Salvation wasn't for sale and grace wasn't a commodity. It was freely given.

But he was working to atone for his sins and mistakes. The compensation couldn't fix the pain Sam caused to so many, but it showed heart and soul. Whatever life held in store for Sam Stafford now, Lucy was truly pleased that he'd gotten right with God. She'd put a note on the fridge, reminding them all to pray for Sam's return to health.

"Where two or three are gathered together in my name . . ."

Christ's promise would be fulfilled, right there on Lucy Carlton's little farm. A family, praying for their neighbor, together.

For once in her life, things felt beautifully, absolutely right.

ನಲ

Trey pulled into Lucy's yard shortly after seven the next morning. He jumped out of the SUV and paused.

He didn't have time to pause. He knew that, but seeing the progress around Lucy's house and yard, the barn restoration, and the overall improvements made him breathe easier. If nothing else, he'd given her a lighter, prettier view of the world. No matter what happened in the coming days, he'd helped create a more soothing environment for Lucy and the kids. And with the changes he'd made to his will, he'd ensured their future if—

There is no if, and they won't need a bequest. This is all going to be fine. Just fine.

He wanted to believe the internal scolding. And it wasn't like he felt doomed or had a premonition. He just wanted to cover all the bases, because that's what a man did. He took care of things, just in case.

He'd made arrangements to make sure Lucy was okay financially if something went wrong. That wasn't fear talking. That was Western common sense. He started for the house as she came out the door.

He paused again, drinking her in. So beautiful, so special, standing barefoot on the freshly painted porch, framed by clean white pillars and bright-toned flowers. "Nice garden, Ms. Lucy."

"Prettiest I've ever seen, Trey." She moved forward, slightly. "Thank you so much for doing that."

"Just a little yard work, ma'am. That's all it is."

"It's almost too beautiful to be real," she whispered.

It was, and he wasn't talking about the simple visual. He was thinking about more. Much more. "Came to say good-bye for a bit."

She stayed where she was, as if glued to that spot on the porch. "Sam's lucky to have you. All of you." She took a deep breath. "I'll be praying for him, Trey. I'm real glad he found peace with the Lord, but I think it would be nice for God to give him some time here, on the planet, to enjoy it with his family." Hope infused her voice. Grace deepened her soft smile. Right then, Trey could imagine a lifetime of inspiring that smile. A full and beautiful lifetime. He started up the steps as the kids poured out of the house.

"Good-bye, Trey! I hope your dad is okay!" Cade grabbed hold around his waist and didn't let go.

"See ya soon!" Cody grabbed hold from the other side, a pair of entwined monkeys, clinging tight.

"I made this for Mr. Sam." Belle handed him a

coloring page of pretty flowers in an interesting array of somewhat drastic colors. "I fink he'll wike it a l-l-lot," she told him earnestly, trying hard to pronounce things correctly like Lucy showed her. "It's so pwetty, isn't it?"

"It is. Like you." Trey bent low and hugged them all.

Fear gripped him as the kids piled in.

What if he didn't come back? What if things went bad? Was he a fool to resist seeking alternative choices and risk the chance at happiness with these children? This woman?

How often was Christ tempted in that desert? Those other choices had to look good. Real good. But in the end he did the right thing.

The right thing.

The words both tore and healed. He knew how to do the right thing. He'd always known. His biggest fear was having others choose the wrong thing.

"You'll let us know how he's doing?"

"Of course." He wouldn't be making that call, of course. But she didn't need to know that now. "Keep prayin', guys. And keep it real over here for your mom, but not too real. Okay?" Ashley came onto the porch as he stood. He reached out and bumped knuckles with her. "Chin up, eyes forward, Ash. One day at a time."

"That's the plan, Stan."

"All right, then."

He started to leave, then couldn't. Not without holding Lucy one more time. A hug . . . just a simple, life-affirming hug, an embrace that needed no words.

Her hair smelled of ripe berries and vanilla, a summer mix of home sweet home. Like silk, her hair touched his face, swept his cheek.

She folded into his embrace as if made to be there, as if molded for him. Never had timing seemed so utterly important and sharp-edged cruel.

Did you mean all that stuff you spewed about God being in control? Or were you just doing lip service?

Colt's words came back to him. He hauled in a breath and let Lucy go as Cade took hold of his hand.

"You're comin' back, aren't you, Trey? You promise?" The question went deeper than the simple phrasing allowed. It wanted a pledge, a pledge he couldn't be sure of, and he remembered another little boy, longing for love, begging assurance.

He bent low, not wanting to lie. "I'm going to do my best."

"But I'll miss you so much if you don't come back." Cade's voice pleaded. He gripped Trey's hand in a hold Trey remembered like it was yesterday. A little fellow, grabbing hold of a hand and a heart and never letting go. Cade choked out the next words, as if speaking them was hard. So hard. "Please come back."

Trey's heart went tight. So did his throat. He reached out and hugged the boy close. "You be good, okay?"

Cade's jaw quivered. He studied Trey, and when he didn't find what he was looking for, he stepped back, reading between the lines. "Sure. Whatever." He rubbed the back of his sleeve to his nose, trying to pretend it didn't matter. That nothing mattered.

Lucy tuned in on the lack of promise too. She put a loving arm around Cade's narrow shoulders. "You've done a great deal for us, and we're grateful for it. For all of it."

He longed to explain, and if all went well this week, he'd be back in a few weeks, ready to begin anew. And if it didn't, he'd have done his best, and that's all a man could do. "Good-bye, guys."

"Bye, Trey! We love you!" Cody climbed onto the bottom rail, waving madly. "See you soon!"

"We wove you, Twey!" Belle's sweet little voice, calling to him. "We wove you so much!"

He couldn't help himself. He turned and faced them all. "I love you too. All of you."

He didn't look at Lucy's face.

He couldn't.

He couldn't face the disappointment he sensed when he didn't make the promise she longed for and deserved, but he'd made a pledge to himself years back. A vow to be honest and true. More than anyone, Lucy deserved that absolute honesty.

Trey climbed into the car and headed back to the Double S where his family waited.

He'd left things bittersweet at Lucy's place. He'd have to deal with that post-surgery.

For now, Sam's timeline ruled the day, and there was no telling how things might go. If Trey had his way, his father would fully recover and enjoy a nice long life in his treasured valley. And if everything went well, Trey would join him there, all of them, making Washington home again. Maybe like it should have been, all along.

ಬಬ

Colt drove the big ranch SUV to the airport. Angelina rode shotgun, jotting notes in her phone as he issued orders, until she finally punched him in the arm.

"Hey." Colt shot her a look of dismay. "What was that for?"

"You think we're suddenly incapable? You think because you're gone for a little while that everything will fall apart? Might I remind you that Murt and Hobbs will keep everything in hand on the outside, and Mami, Elsa, Lucy, and I will keep things running smoothly on the house, yard, and child end of the spectrum. I don't need instructions from you on things I do every single day. Got it?"

He didn't scowl. Colt grinned. "Man, that felt good. When you start being too nice to me, I start to worry that you're worried."

"So yelling is better?" She threw up her hands as if he made no sense whatsoever.

"Well, you scolding me for something or other is normal, Ange." He flashed Trey, Nick, and Sam an amused look in the rearview mirror. "Normal works."

She muttered something in Spanish under her breath, but then she laughed. "Normal is always good."

They got to the airport with barely enough time to make the plane.

Angelina didn't prolong the good-byes. Trey would have been more anxious if she did. She hugged them all, and when she got to him, she paused. "Your courage and God's will, Trey. I think that's what this has all been about, from the beginning. You completed this family circle once, when you were a little boy. And now you'll do it again."

She hugged him and stepped back toward the running car. "Call, text, whatever. And do not give the doctors and nurses a hard time. At all. Any of you. You hear me?"

"Half the airport did, darlin'." Colt grinned and waved from the door as the others walked through. And a little while later, an unusually quiet group of Stafford men boarded the plane.

Nineteen

You were silly to get your hopes up and leave your guard down. Be grateful for all the good that came of this summer, and let the rest go.

Great mental advice, but not so easy when Lucy was surrounded by reminders of Trey. The sharp-looking barns, the neat walking path, the house, the porch, the bright new garden.

She couldn't afford to let her heart ache. He hadn't led her astray or led her on. He'd been nice, pure and simple.

And kind and good and funny and gorgeous, but was that his fault?

Yes, she decided, as she got the kids' things together for the first day of school. His fault or hers, she needed to shelve the raw emotions laying claim to her from within.

"Every good gift and every perfect gift is from above, and cometh down from the Father of lights, with whom is no variableness, neither shadow of turning."

The wise words from James were a great reminder.

God wasn't fickle. He didn't play games. He stood strong and resolute, now and forever. She'd cling to that simple truth.

Belle and Cody went on with their day, eager to

race beneath the warm September sun. Cade tried to join in, but then he'd pause and his eyes would stray up the hill, toward the Double S.

He missed Trey already, and that guilt was on her for letting down her barriers. Her son followed her lead, which meant his aching heart was her fault.

"Trey said he'd try to come back and see us. Right?"

"He said he'd try." She refused to let her voice break. "He's probably got a lot of work to catch up on after Mr. Sam's operation. He's been here, helping us for half the summer. Right?"

Cade nodded, a tiny V ridged tight between his brows.

"It's probably a good time for all of us to do a little catching up. In school, on the farm, and Trey's job too."

"I just miss him."

Her chest went tight, hearing the pain in his voice.

"That's all."

"I know."

He looked at her then, and she couldn't blink the tears back quickly enough. He crossed the pretty porch and leaned his head against her upper arm. "It's okay, Mommy. You take care of me, and I'll take care of you. Just like Trey said."

Her throat went tighter than her chest, and she didn't think that was possible. More tears fell of their own accord, despite her toughest efforts to stop them.

She wasn't a crier. She hadn't had time to cry in a long time. But right now she couldn't seem to help it.

"Hey, Cade." Ashley came through the front door with a minnow bucket. "Want to go catch some bait with me? Trey showed me how to set up that back trough like an aquarium so we can have live bait anytime we want. Then maybe Lucy will let us go fishing at the big pond."

His eyes lit up. "You want to take me? For real?"

"Yup."

Ashley didn't look at Lucy. She looked straight at Cade, the kid she always found bothersome, and raised up a plastic bucket. "Let's see if this idea works, okay?"

"Okay!"

He raced over to her, and the pair went off toward the creek for the first time ever.

Trey's influence, again, in such a good way. On Ashley, on Cade. Lucy needed to count the blessings of having had him around—getting to know him—and appreciate those good effects, because he'd helped all five of them.

She wouldn't trade that for anything, she decided as she hung sheets that had soured in the washer and needed to be washed twice.

She would take all of the goodness of summer and appreciate it. She'd been silly to dream of other things, but that wasn't anyone's fault but her own. Now it was simply time to move on.

Her message light was flashing when she got inside. Ed Boddy's number showed bright in the screen.

She held the phone, staring at the number, then replaced the handset.

She couldn't call him back. Not just yet. She needed to know herself and her answer before she picked up that phone. If she called him back now, the lure of an old dream might burn too bright.

She'd made a deal with Sam for the new shop in town. Was it too late to take it back if she decided to give Nashville a try?

Probably not.

But the teenage singer who'd longed for love and attention had grown up. And just maybe her dreams had grown up with her.

※

Focus forward.

Trey pulled out the old mental stability tactics he'd used following Cathy's overdose, dusted them off, and put them back into play as they went through the presurgical rigors in San Francisco.

Medical tests. Private interviews to assess mental capacity and understanding. And then the play-by-play explanations of what to expect.

Nick blanched when the surgeon explained the follow-up pain in stunning, gut-clenching detail.

Colt gripped Trey's arm when they calmly went through the statistical odds of survival.

And when all was said and done, father and son signed the necessary documents and were admitted.

He didn't dare think about Lucy.

He couldn't let his mind wander to the risk of losing her and that precious family. One way or another, he had a task at hand, and that promise needed to be fulfilled first.

Caring for Lucy was special in the very best of ways. Falling for Lucy had been fun. Natural. Unfettered. When was the last time any aspect of his life had simply happened? Not since he was a kid, sitting saddle, working his father's ranch.

Helping her rewarded him, and he wasn't sure how that worked, but it did. And kissing her? Imagining a lifetime of kissing her?

He'd come so close to making that leap until Ed showed up, going all gung-ho warrior agent over Lucy's voice. *"And ye shall know the truth, and the truth shall make you free . . ."* John's gospel, Christ's words.

Ed's proposal hadn't just irritated him. It scared him outright, because how many parallels could he embrace? Lucy had a past she'd overcome, but the rigors of Nashville—and the partying in some circles—tempted so many.

Shame bit deep.

He'd wanted his chance in Music City. He'd

wanted a chance to show what could be done, how success could be won if you stayed clean and clear of the self-indulgences. But he was quite willing to have Lucy forego that opportunity out of fear. His fear, not hers.

What kind of man put himself above others?

A scared one.

"If God be for us, who can be against us?" Paul had reminded the Romans to stand tall. To be brave and true in the face of adversity and persecution.

Paul was right.

Trey needed to live the faith he claimed. He needed to . . .

He swallowed hard, because this was the toughest one of all . . .

He needed to trust.

He needed to trust God. To trust his timing. To trust that God alone was in charge of him. In charge of Lucy. And in charge of the looming operation.

"Whom shall I fear?"

The beautiful words of the twenty-seventh psalm flooded over him. Words of pleading and promise, of hope and healing.

And in the end, the psalmist promised to wait upon the Lord.

Nick and Colt came in to say good night. They looked nervous and even a little guilty. "We just saw Dad, and they've given him something to help him sleep." Nick clutched his hat in his hands, crushing the nicely rolled brim.

"You're manhandling that hundred-dollar hat. Hobbs would smack you right now."

"It looks stupid to wear it in the hospital."

"Not if you wear it right," drawled Colt. "Darn sight better than rolling it up like a cheap cigar."

"I bet Elsa thinks he's cute when he's nervous." Trey made the observation knowing he was in a hospital bed and less likely to get wailed on because of it.

The very thought made Nick indignant. "I don't get nervous."

"Or mad," added Colt, rolling his eyes.

"Or worried," Trey agreed while Nick began to sputter. "I've got two things to ask of you guys."

"Name it." Colt, quick and to the point, as always.

"Pray for me. Pray for me to get beyond my fears once this is all behind us, and to move on with my life. Pray for me to be strong, like you guys are strong."

"Shoot, Trey." Nick didn't get all sentimental. He frowned instead. "You've been the strongest all along. The one who held on to your faith and your beliefs and your career. The one who rises up from the stinkin' ashes like that dumb bird, again and again. You just don't see your strength, so you think it doesn't exist, but it does. Always did. Always will. And if you get a little worried about things now and again, who doesn't?"

Nick had never been a hugger. He'd been too busy being mad at just about everything in the world to reach out to others, but he moved closer, leaned down, and hugged Trey. Hugged him hard. "You're strong, Trey. To the bone. And I'll help you any way you need once we've got you back home."

Normally Colt would take this moment to make fun of both of them.

Why should life-threatening surgery be any different?

He looked from one to the other, faintly horrified, then growled, "The littlest doesn't get to be the strongest, just because you've gone all romantic and mushy on us." He reached in from the opposite side of the bed and clenched Trey's left hand. "We're Staffords. No matter what else we mess up, we practice what we preach. Go in there and kick butt, okay? And we'll keep an eye on things at Lucy's place. No missing the way she was looking at you lately, and I expect she's worried sick right now."

"I didn't tell her."

"You what?" Colt wasn't faking stress this time. "You didn't tell her about the surgery?"

"I figured I needed to do this myself. If things don't go well . . . ." He shrugged. "I didn't want to make things worse for her and those kids."

"Well, that's about the dumbest thing I've ever heard." Nick's "Mr. Nice Guy" persona faded quickly. "If ever God put a woman on the planet that can take charge of a situation, it's Lucy Carlton. That woman figured out how to make stuff out of nothing a long while back."

"I can't believe you left her in the dark, but on the other hand, I get it." Colt still sounded grumpy, but understanding too. "This self-sacrificing stuff is new to me."

The truth in that made the other brothers smile.

"We'll watch out for her. No matter what, okay?"

If his brothers said they would, they would. He nodded as a nurse came in to kick his brothers out.

Nick turned at the door. He didn't say anything, just turned. And then he smiled like he knew it was all going to be okay.

And for no reason in the world that Trey could think of . . . it helped.

ॐ

Lucy didn't expect him to call. She told herself that, time and again. She hoped for it. Longed for it. But she wasn't foolish enough to expect it.

And still, when it didn't happen, her heart broke a little all over again.

She got Ashley and the boys off to school while she and Belle worked to get the barn ready for a wreath-making area. She tried not to look at the beautiful garden, growing brighter and bolder as the plants took hold. She averted her eyes as best she could because each time she looked at it, she thought of Trey. *"Just a little yard work, ma'am. That's all it is."*

Her heart went hot and cold, wondering how things were going and yet unwilling to place the call to ask. If he wanted to share news about Sam, he'd call.

No call came, even though she brought the landline into the barn with her, just in case.

She worked. She sanded, swept, dusted, and swabbed white paint on the barn stall, then sanded some off to give it the stressed, old look she wanted. She watered rows of mums, just breaking bloom.

She painted the concrete floor of the barn entrance a soft gray while Belle napped, and when the kids got home from school, she helped them with organizing their folders and filling out emergency-contact cards, and then she went online to fill out the same thing she'd just done on paper.

A little later that evening, she received a quick text from Angelina, via Ashley's phone.

Surgery complete. All is well so far.

She kept her reply simple too.

Happy to hear this, thank you!

Nothing more came. Not a word. Not a text, not a message, not a voice mail.

She'd hoped for some kind of contact from Trey.

Nothing.

As she handed out lunch boxes the next morning, she gave the kids Angelina's message. "Mr. Sam's surgery went well, but we should still pray for him to recover completely."

"Then Trey's coming back!" Cade leaped out of his seat. "If his dad is doing all right, then he'll be back. I know it!"

She hated to be the one to burst his little boy bubble, but his assumption wasn't based on fact. "I don't know what Trey's plans are, honey. I'm not sure he knows what his plans are. And it will take awhile for Mr. Sam to get strong enough to come home."

Cade blinked, confused. "But I know Trey wants to be back here, with us. With all of us. I know it, Mom! I can, like, feel it."

"Cade." She knelt down beside him while he tied the laces of his well-worn sneakers. "I'm sure we'll get to see him when he comes home for holidays. And you've got Dakota and Cheyenne to play with now. They'll be living right next door, on the ranch. We'll have friends right here, close to us, even if Trey has to work far, far away."

He stared at her. His eyes went moist. "You don't know anything."

Great. Now she'd be sending him off to school upset, and that was the last thing she wanted to do. "Cade."

"No." He slipped off the chair and grabbed his

384

things. "I don't think you even know how to understand boys, ever. I know he's coming back because I feel it. Like right here." He patted his hand against his heart. "Nothing you say will change it, and even if you want to change it, you can't because Trey wants to be here. I can tell. I can tell he wants it the most. Like the most *ever!*"

He slung his bag over his shoulder. A tear slid down one cheek, then the other. He brushed them aside with one swift motion and went out the door quickly.

Cody followed. He glanced back at Lucy, but he didn't speak. He didn't smile. He dropped his chin and followed his brother to the end of the driveway, waiting for the school bus.

They needed time. Time to get used to this new normal, without Trey's laugh. His voice. His work, his smile, his light whistle.

Cody would be okay. He'd bonded with Trey, but he'd been tiny when Chase died, and he'd never known or really bonded with his father.

Cade had seen enough of his father to know something was wrong. He'd been just old enough to realize Chase liked booze, women, and heavy metal music far more than his family, and even at such a young age, he'd tried so hard to win his dad's favor. To secure his love. It never happened and then Chase was gone, leaving an empty, aching space inside his oldest son. A space that had seemed fuller when Trey was around.

Twice that morning she picked up the phone to call Trey and rail at him. Tell him what his absence meant to a sad little boy.

Both times she stopped herself, because she wasn't one hundred percent sure who she was defending. Cade's feelings? Or hers? And when she decided it was both, she set the phone down and got back to work organizing mums for an upcoming weekend sale while Belle set up a pretend nursery school on the freshly painted porch.

A car pulled into the driveway midday. Lucy heard the crunch of the tires, and for just a moment, her heart leaped . . .

But then she heard Angelina's voice. "Lucy? Where are you?"

"In the barn." She set down her tools and moved toward the door. "Hey." She met Angelina and Noah halfway across the driveway. Belle grabbed her little buddy's hand. The two preschoolers took off for the porch instantly, then inside to gather some stuffed-animal playmates. She waited until they were out of earshot, then noted Angelina's worried expression. "You look worried. Has Sam taken a turn for the worse?

"Not Sam. Trey."

"Trey?" Lucy stared at her, not comprehending. "Why would we be worried about Trey?"

Angelina studied her. She drew a breath, bit her lower lip, then sighed. "He didn't tell you."

"I have no idea what you're talking about."

"Trey is what I'm talking about. Trey was the living donor for Sam's liver."

"He was what?" Angelina started to repeat herself, but Lucy waved her off. "No, I heard you. I just can't believe this. He never said a word. Not one of you ever said a word. Who keeps something like this secret?" She didn't mean to raise her voice, but she did and when she was done, she wasn't at all sorry.

"Now he's off in a California hospital, probably in dreadful pain, and no one even bothered to say a word to me. Except that I really have no right to know, so I guess it doesn't matter anyway. Except that it matters to me, Angelina!" She thumped her chest.

"Well, anyone with half a brain can see that, Lucy, and the other half of the brain says the feeling's mutual, and just as stubborn. But he's taken a bad turn. He developed a postsurgical infection. Nick and Colt are staying right there. Sam is beside himself because Trey risked his life for him, and Trey is fighting for his life."

Fighting for his life.

The adrenaline rush started somewhere around her heart and surged throughout her body.

Trey in trouble.

Trey, near death.

Trey, the kind, gentle cowboy crooner, sacrificing his life to save his father.

Her heart beat harder. Her fingers tensed, then thrummed. "What can I do? There must be something, Angelina. Tell me what I can do to help."

"Pray."

It seemed like so little, yet hadn't it been her mainstay for so long?

"Pray hard and I'll keep you informed. They're fighting the infection with antibiotics, but it's a deep wound."

"And that makes the situation more dangerous."

"Yes."

Oh, Trey.

She stared around the empty yard once Angelina left. Trey sick. Trey fighting death. Donating a part of himself so his father could live.

She'd loved him before knowing that. He'd crept into her heart and her life with constant acts of kindness and candor.

But standing around wasn't what Trey would expect her to do. He'd get things done while waiting. She prayed while she worked in the barn. She prayed while she made signs for the upcoming Christmas sales season. She prayed while the boys did homework, willing the phone to ring.

And when Angelina's number finally flashed in the display, she grabbed the phone up, hopeful, only to hear there was no change.

"Then we'll pray and work until there is," she told Angelina. "Do you guys need help over there?" It sounded odd to offer help to the Double S, but nice too. Like somehow they'd evened the playing field over the summer.

"I'd love for you to bring your kids over after church and hang out here on Sunday," Angelina told her. "Everyone here is restless and anxious. With the men all gone, the house feels empty, even though it's filled with kids, women, and the occasional dog or cat. It's like there's a shadow looming over everything, and it's a shadow that won't go away until we can sound the all's well. You and the kids would be a welcome addition."

"I'd like that," Lucy told her. "And in the meantime, we keep railing the heavens."

"Amen to that."

Twenty

Hot lights burned Trey's eyelids and cheeks. He struggled, trying to edge away from the incessant beam, but he couldn't move. He was trapped on stage, with too many lights and nowhere to go.

He couldn't sing.

He couldn't talk. He tried to see the crowd, but the lights blinded him.

He heard them though. Calling out, yelling his name.

Crowds of thousands, tens of thousands sometimes, paying money to see him. He tried to see the crowd again, but his eyes refused to open.

All those people. So many people clamoring, and for a split second, he wondered if Lucy might be there.

His brain recoiled at the thought, then stopped recoiling.

He wanted Lucy there, didn't he? He peered through the light but saw nothing. Nothing at all.

The noise of the crowd diminished slowly. The lights faded, then dimmed.

He slept.

ରୋ

Lucy parked in the church lot, running late as usual. It felt funny to be on her own again, bringing the kids to Sunday morning services. She'd have to trust them to behave themselves for a few minutes until Angelina and Elsa arrived.

The unlikelihood of their good behavior wasn't lost on her.

She took Belle's hand and hurried to the sidewalk.

This day the music was for Trey. For his recovery, his strength, and the medical team working on him. While Sam improved daily, Trey's battle continued, so today's music, today's service, would be her prayer for him, and with every beat of her heart she yearned for God to hear her plea.

Cade seized her hand before he followed Ashley to their pew. "I'm gonna pray extra hard today, even when it's the boring part." He clutched her hand tight in his, and his eyes implored her to understand his mission. "I think if I do that, God will hear me real clear, no matter how far away heaven is, and he'll want Trey to be okay. And then he will be."

Should she tell him it didn't always work like that?

No.

No, she'd let him storm the heavens from the right-hand pew while she did the same from above. And when the pastor said a special prayer of healing in Trey's name, Cade didn't look up.

He sat, head down, his little hands folded tighter than tight, begging God for Trey's life.

The simple faith of a child.

She wanted that. She wanted that simple belief, and the trust she'd lost long ago. Trust in people, trust in men, trust in anyone other than herself.

As the congregation prayed for Trey as one, Lucy made God a promise—a pledge to follow Christ's command to love one another. To forgive and move on.

And if she could do that moving on thing with Trey Stafford, she'd be the happiest woman in the world.

ဢ

Soft, sweet music tempted Trey to waken.

Wait. Not music.

Humming.

Lucy's voice came to mind, humming in the trees, softly singing hymns of faith and songs of love.

Her voice, sweet and pure, going soft, then rising into a crowning long-breath crescendo. In the background, children's voices called his name. Laughing, playing, they called for him to join them.

And then the music came again. Soft. Soothing.

He opened his mouth to harmonize with her but couldn't. He struggled, trying to talk, wanting to sing with her, but his arms wouldn't work, and his voice wouldn't work, and he couldn't move to save his soul.

"It's all right, Trey."

Another voice, not Lucy's. Deep. Strong. Gruff and sweetly familiar. He paused his struggles, straining to hear.

"It's all right, Son. I'm here." The voice choked just then, and Trey felt a firm and gentle touch to his right shoulder. "Daddy's here."

Sam's voice.

Sam's touch, on his shoulder, just like he'd done so many times in the past. Trey had been alone in a crowd of druggies for his first three years, but when Sam Stafford had hauled him up into those big, strong arms, he wasn't alone anymore. Ever. Even through their ups and downs, he'd never been truly alone once Sam brought him home.

"You're going to be fine, Trey. Just fine." Sam's voice cracked slightly, as if he stumbled over the words. "The doctors and nurses are taking good care of you and me. We're going to be riding herd in no time, with your brothers pestering us morning, noon, and night. Okay?"

The blast furnace heat came again, surging within, from the bottoms of his feet to the hair on his head, rising heat even though the lights were gone.

He wanted to tell Sam he heard him. He wanted to say so much, to tell him how glad he was to be his son, to be a Stafford, but when he tried to form words, nothing came.

Later, he promised himself, succumbing to sleep.

He'd tell his dad later.

ಬಿಸಿ

Fever spiked again. Doctors are worried. Us too. Dad's distraught. Pray. All of you. Just pray.

Lucy clasped her hands together tightly as Angelina read the text from Colt out loud. Her heart squeezed, and she tried to steady her breathing.

Angelina didn't try to control her voice. She didn't blink back tears. She let them fall, then wiped a hand towel across her face in an impatient gesture. "So, he thinks we're not praying? That we need to be told?"

"Or he needs to feel he's got some control over the uncontrollable," said Elsa softly. "If he asks for prayers, at least he's doing something. When I talked to Nick, I was pretty sure he was set to punch someone, he was so mad."

"And do you think he did it? Punched someone?" Lucy asked.

"He went downstairs instead. To the chapel. And for just a little while, he sat, all by himself. Quiet."

"When Stafford men sit, quiet, then you know there is a crisis." Isabo set out a deep pan of warm apple dumplings, one of her favorite crowd-pleasing recipes. "I used to make big trays of these for the Seattle mission," she told the women as she slid the pan onto the large wooden trivet. "People needing help, needing warmth, wanting to get out of the rain for a little while. To talk, to share, to eat . . . The reasons did not matter when they sat and ate these dumplings. All that was bad suddenly wasn't so bad. And that was good, no?"

"Comfort food, an ageless cure-all," Elsa noted as she awkwardly pinned a pattern over gold-brown material at the opposite end of the table. "I have to make this look like an oak leaf by Wednesday, and the last thing I want to do right now is struggle with slippery material and dull pins. What do you think my chances of a successful completion for Dakota's science class are?"

"You cut, I'll sew," Isabo told her. "You are better at keeping big kids amused with games. I am fast with a needle, and it will keep my hands busy. Busy is good. Busy keeps my head from wanting to explode with worry when I know I must trust in the Lord our God, but it is possible that in this instance, he could move at a speed I find more pleasing when someone so beloved takes ill."

"We work and wait as one. Like you taught me long ago, Mami." Angelina touched her mother's shoulder.

Wait as one.

"Where two or three are gathered together in my name . . ."

That's why Lucy had come here after church. She couldn't stay home alone with the kids, waiting for a phone call. She needed to be here, with the other women.

Ashley was working on a project for Isabo in the near barn, and the older kids were under Murt's and Hobbs's watchful eyes while Noah and Belle raced tricycles across the graveled drive. The place might look normal, but to anyone who'd been part of the past summer . . . there was nothing normal about it. No bold men swaggered across the yard. No laughter echoed from barn to yard and back again. Despite the gathering of women and children, the broad, sprawling ranch seemed wanting.

Much like them. "Lucy, you must tell me what you think of this pastry. Too wet, too dry, not flaky enough?" Isabo slipped a plate in front of her a few minutes later, and Lucy read the message behind the older woman's kind words.

She wanted Lucy to eat something. She wanted to soothe the worry with warm food and gentle words.

Lucy accepted the plate of warm wrapped apples and met Isabo's eyes. She didn't think she'd be hungry, but she was, and not just for food. The friendship and empathy in this house filled her with hope and strength.

And when the landline phone rang just before six kids raced inside looking for supper, Isabo scanned the display, then raised a hand for quiet. The raised hand held a wooden spoon she'd been using. The other reached for the ringing phone while the rest of the women waited and watched.

Her face crumpled. Her jaw went slack. And when she then gripped the phone tight with two hands, both hands shook.

Angelina stood slowly. So did Elsa.

Lucy couldn't stand. Her legs refused to hold her. Her chest went tight and her palms grew damp. But when a broad, damp smile broke through Isabo's overwrought emotions, Lucy's stopped heart began beating once again.

"He is better! He is to be fine, they think. His fever is down, and he was talking to Sam just now! Oh, praise be to God, the Father Almighty, creator of heaven and of earth!"

"Mami, you nearly gave me a heart attack!" Angelina scolded, one hand to her heart.

"Ditto," chimed in Elsa.

"It is most compelling news," Isabo told them, and she waved that wooden spoon around again. "I have great emotion over things; this is never a bad thing, is it, my daughter?"

"Mami." Angelina moved across the room and grabbed her mother in a big hug. "I wouldn't trade you and your slightly overdramatic sensibilities for anything. You're wonderful just the way you are, and I'm too happy about Trey to be the least bit annoyed. Lucy." She turned her attention toward Lucy. "I'm so glad you were here with us."

She was too. No matter what happened next, if Trey was all right, that was enough. "I've got to tell Ashley and Cade."

She crossed to the barn. Chill nipped the night air. She crossed her arms against the cold and went through the barn door.

Ashley wasn't cleaning the office in the front section of the barn like she expected. "Ashley?"

"Back here."

She followed the voice, then paused.

Ashley had tucked herself into a stall with Trey's horse. She was grooming the gelding with long, slow, even strokes. "With Trey gone, I figured nobody had time to let the horses know how much we love them. So when I finished the office, I started brushing them."

"Like Trey showed you."

"Yes." Ashley worked the brush down in smooth, rhythmic fashion. "It's hard when you don't know how to help. You know?"

Lucy knew that feeling too well. "I think you took the best possible way and just did it. I'm proud of you, Ashley. We just got a call from the hospital. Trey's doing better. They think he's going to be all right."

"For real?"

"Yes."

Ashley leaned her forehead against the horse's neck. "I prayed for him. And for Mr. Sam, but Trey mostly. Because he knew I was being dumb and gave me a chance anyway." She breathed deep, brushed her sleeve against her eyes, and went back to grooming. "Not many folks would do that."

Lucy knew the truth in that too. "No. I've got to go tell Cade."

"He loves Trey. A lot."

Lucy knew that, and she heard what Ashley wasn't saying too. That Cade wasn't the only one who'd fallen for the kindhearted country singer. "I think we all do, darlin'."

Ashley smiled through more tears before swiping her face again. "Happy tears this time. Much better."

"Agreed."

Cade found her before she found him. He came dashing into the front of the barn and threw himself at her. "Trey's feeling better! I knew it! I knew it all the time, that he wanted to come back to us and it was hard, and so I kept telling God to help him, to show him the way back, and he did it! He did it, Mom!"

"He did. And I'm so glad you didn't give up, little man."

Cade shook his head hard. "He wouldn't give up on me. Not ever. Some people do give up, or they do bad things, but not Trey. He wants to do good things, and he wants me to do them too. So I will. Will he come home soon?"

She had no idea how to answer that question.

Home was a relative factor. Would Trey head back here to the Double S, or would he need to finish his recovery in Nashville?

"I'm not sure, so for right now, let's just be glad he's going to be okay. And your letter to him should get there tomorrow, so that will make him smile, Cade."

"And then maybe he'll call us."

She couldn't promise that, and she didn't want him disappointed. "Recovery first . . . and then cute, pesky kids. Okay?"

He grabbed her in a hug, a hug of huge proportions. "Okay. And I'm going to practice my reading extra hard so I can read to Trey when he comes back. Like you do when I'm sick. I think he'd like that a lot."

Of course he would. If he were here. "That's a great idea."

They ate a quick supper because it was a school night, and as Ashley helped get the kids into the van, Angelina and Elsa both gave Lucy much-needed hugs. "I am relieved beyond belief," Angelina said.

"Me too. I hated being here when I felt like I should have been there, at his side. Even though there's no real reason for me to be there."

"Emotions don't always need a reason.

Sometimes they are the reason," remarked Elsa.

"And I'm pretty sure Trey shares those feelings," Angelina told her.

Lucy wasn't nearly as certain. He'd been careful to make no promises. "None of that matters."

Angelina snorted.

Elsa sighed.

"It doesn't, not really. As long as he's going to be okay, that's the important thing. He's done wonderful things for us, more than I ever expected. I can be content with that."

Angelina faced Elsa. "Did you hear that?"

"I did. Classic denial and measured acceptance."

"What's your prognosis?"

"Some quiet time with the cowboy in question could help move things along. Once the poor guy can lift his head without seeing stars."

"Stop. Both of you. You're ridiculous."

"While that might be true," Elsa conceded, "we've walked in these shoes already, and we recognize the symptoms. I'm pretty sure that Trey Walker Stafford is going to have a true shot at happiness at long last. You can sing duets at the Grand Ole Opry together."

Lucy shook her head. "Not that. I'm pretty sure God's directing me down a different road, straight and simple. Right here, with my plants, the little store in town, the choir, and my Overcomers." She paused and looked out over the view of the ranch for a moment. "When Ed was talking up the music business, I was thrilled. Who wouldn't want to hear that kind of thing, the thought of being a star, a real star?"

She looked from Angelina to Elsa and shrugged. "But it's not me. It's not me at all. I've had enough crazy in my life, and no desire to test more. Now, the store in town?" She waved a hand in the general direction of Gray's Glen. "Having a place to sell flowers and plants and baskets, all those fun things that make the world a prettier place to live? That's enough for me. More than enough."

"So if Ed calls you back, you're turning him down?" Angelina asked.

"He did, and I refused the offer. It's not the kind of life I want for my kids. Right now we've got it good. Better than I've ever known. And that's enough."

"Of course if a certain country crooner cowboy sidles along and pops the question, well, that's never a bad thing," Elsa supposed.

Lucy knew that wasn't going to happen, but she parried the observation with grace. "Trey has taught me so much. Given me so much. And between him and Sam, I'm on my feet, exactly where I always wanted to be. Normal. And normal isn't just good, ladies." She climbed into the van. "It's great."

Twenty-One

Home at last.

The long-winded discharge, made up of a host of instructions, a ream of papers, advice given to his father, and referrals to local labs for regular blood draws, and then getting to the airport, going through security, and boarding the plane exhausted Trey, but sleep would come soon enough.

He was back in the valley, *his valley,* the place he loved most.

Angelina, Isabo, and Elsa stood waiting on the side porch as they pulled in midafternoon. They hurried to the car, excited. "You're back!" Isabo went straight to Sam's side of the car and opened the door. "It is so good to have you home and looking well! And now you must do as the doctor instructed each and every day, Samuel." She gave him a hand to hold as he stepped out. "All of this drama and effort will be for nothing if you do not do as the doctors say."

"Did you miss me, Izzie?"

She flushed, then frowned. "Of course, you know this already, there is no need to ask."

"I missed you."

Trey wouldn't have thought Isabo could blush. She did.

Sam looked down at her and slung an arm around her shoulders as he slowly walked to the house. "And I expect you'll be real good at keeping me in line, Izzie. When I let you, that is."

She rolled her eyes but she smiled too, a bright, womanly smile that said more than words.

"It's so good to be back, to be out of that hospital, to be home." Nick hugged Elsa close, then just stood there, unmoving, holding her awhile, but this was Nick, so the questions started pretty quick. "How's everything going? Did Murt handle that Oklahoma deal? And how's the house coming? The shell looks good, but did they start the inside? And have you been checking it daily?"

Colt didn't waste time talking.

He took his own sweet time kissing his future wife, reveling in a homecoming moment.

Who's here to welcome you, Trey? Who's here to tell you they missed you? That they longed for your return?

He shrugged that off and moved toward the house to get his keys.

Angelina stopped him before he made it halfway up the walk. "No welcome home hug?"

"Of course." He hugged her and winked at Colt over her head. "It's good to be here, that's for sure. After the past couple of weeks, it's good to be anywhere."

"Let's get you inside and resting." Angelina wasn't about to take no for an answer, which made Trey realize a take-charge woman was a real gift from God. She moved forward and opened the door. "There will be no going up to the cabin until we're sure you're okay. I don't want any relapses to grab hold of you with no one around to take care of things."

"I'm fine, Angelina. And I don't think that sleeping here is conducive to anything I'd call rest. Have you counted the kids around here lately?"

She laughed. "Isn't it marvelous? But they're back in school now and not underfoot like they were all summer. Except for Noah and Belle, of course. When she comes to visit."

So Lucy still brought Belle over.

His spirit rose, just a little.

He'd had time to think once he could think again. And time to pray. And time to imagine what it would be like being a dad, the kind of dad he'd dreamed of being if he made it through the surgery.

He needed to see Lucy. See Cade. Talk to them. There was so much to say.

"Lucy's kids are dying to see you, but we decided you needed some rest after the trip home. Is that all right, Trey?"

She'd actually asked a question instead of bossing him around, and Colt laughed out loud.

"Aw, isn't that sweet? You must have been near death for Ange to treat you with kid gloves like that." Colt grinned at him. "Normally she'd just tell you what to do and expect you to like it."

"I know." Trey pretended worry. "Maybe I'm not doing as well as they say."

"Stop. Both of you. You." Angelina pointed inside. "You are going to use the downstairs bedroom near your father's. There is to be no arguing in this matter. I have a wedding in six weeks, and I expect everyone to be there, healthy and hearty. And you." She tipped her face up to Colt's and was rewarded with another kiss. "Thank you for staying there with your father and brothers. For trusting us to handle things. Which we did."

"Never doubted it for a minute, darlin'." He winked at Trey over her head. "Not one single minute."

"Well, the kid gave us enough to worry about for a while. But he rallied in the end and did okay." Nick brought Trey's bag from the car. "We were almost proud of him."

"Key word: *almost*," Colt added. "We sure don't want any of this savin' lives stuff to be going to his head. It's big enough already."

There had been no teasing when he was near death. There hadn't been too much of anything he could remember, but the soaring heat, Sam's voice, and a little guy's voice, calling him home.

He went inside, determined to catch nothing more than a quick, revitalizing nap, and managed to sleep for fourteen straight hours.

And when he woke up later that next morning, surrounded by the sights and sounds of the Double S, happiness washed over him. But there was still a job to be done, a visit to make, and once he managed to pull himself together, he grabbed the keys to his SUV and headed down the hill.

Worry had made him hesitate before he went to San Francisco, but two weeks of conscious recovery after a near-death experience taught a man a lesson or two.

He wasn't a quitter.

He wasn't a fool.

Life came with opportunities and chances, and a man needed heart and gumption enough to seize both. Sure, things could go wrong. And if they did, they'd figure it out and put them to rights again, like Lucy had been doing all along. He'd just been too wounded, and maybe scared, to see that clearly.

Not anymore.

But now the question was, would Lucy be interested? He'd have to see about that, and he wasn't afraid to pour on some old-fashioned wooing if needed. A woman like Lucy was worth whatever it took.

"You heading out, Trey?"

"Got a stop to make, Angelina."

She didn't look surprised. "You haven't taken any pain meds, have you?"

"Nope."

"Didn't your papers say no driving for another two weeks?"

"I'm pretty sure they didn't realize how close we are to the farm next door. Otherwise they'd have written an exception."

"I could just call down there and have her bring Belle up here," Ange said softly. "Relapsing on my time isn't how I want this to play out."

"I won't be long."

He caught Colt's grin and headed to his SUV. He'd rest again later, in a nice, comfortable bed with no bells or whistles or whirs or beeps to wake him on a regular basis. Just a bed, clean sheets, and a good pillow.

Simple worked best.

He pulled into Lucy's yard a few minutes later and paused at the upper end of the driveway.

The garden had grown in the weeks he'd been gone. The cool September temps and gentle rains had created a lush corner of paradise, vibrant against the snow-white porch. To the left of the path leading to the Christmas tree fields stood twin greenhouses, sharp and new in the September sun. And in the first one, framed between the panes, was Lucy, moving this, adjusting that.

His heart didn't twist.

It soared.

Watching her, he finally saw the difference that made all the difference. Lucy had made mistakes, sure.

But she'd accepted her mistakes and moved on. She hadn't fallen down the slippery slope repeatedly. She'd taken on a new, mature life and clung to it, through thick and thin.

She was strong and wonderful, and the thought of being without Lucy Carlton was far tougher than having half a liver.

He parked, climbed out, and shut the door. The noise made her look up. She saw him.

Her hands stopped midair. Her mouth, her pretty, sweet, and very kissable mouth, opened slightly. She stood there, staring; then her face changed.

This is it, he realized as he approached the propped greenhouse door. *The moment of truth when she lets you have it, both barrels, and well deserved.* He stepped across the threshold.

She met him there. She gazed up at him, watching him with the prettiest cornflower blue eyes he ever did see, and then she reached up one soft, sweet hand to his cheek. "I've never prayed so hard or so long for anything in my life, Trey Stafford, like I did the past few weeks. Welcome home."

"Lucy."

She smiled softly and kept her hand there, right there, against his face.

"I've missed you, woman."

A quick sheen brightened her eyes as she nodded. "Me too."

He opened his arms, wanting to say so much, but mostly wanting to hold her, cradle her against his heart.

She laid her head against his chest, and when she did, when his arms closed around her and drew her close, that yawning, gaping hole in his heart closed itself right up.

He breathed in the sweet smell of her hair, mixed with the aroma of potting soil and plastic packaging she'd been unpacking. "Lucy, I—"

He stopped talking when she stretched up for his kiss, and he'd be okay not talking for a long, long time if he could just keep holding her. Kissing her.

"Mister Twey!"

Lucy intervened before Belle launched herself at Trey. She bent quickly, caught her up, and hugged her, then turned her to face Trey. "Belle, we can't jump on Trey right now."

"We can't?" Twin tiny brows shot up in surprise. "Why not?"

"Because he has an ouchie in his tummy."

"You do?" Eyes wide, she stared at him, then his midsection, then him again. "You got an ouchie? Why?"

"Because he helped Mr. Sam get better, honey. But we've got to be really careful of Trey and Mr. Sam right now, okay?"

"Oh, Mommy!" Belle turned a most serious gaze her way, then aimed it right back at Trey. "I will be so careful of everyfing, okay? I pwomise so much!"

"That's perfect, darling. Now why don't you run and grab your shoes . . ."

Belle shot a guilty look to her bare feet.

"And we'll get Trey back up that hill and resting comfortably. Okay?"

"I can be his doctor!"

"I've had more than my share of them," Trey muttered when she was out of earshot. "But none so cute. Lucy, listen." He turned back to her, needing to clear the air before the rare moment of privacy came to an end. "I have to apologize."

She waited quietly, listening.

"You scared me."

The face she made indicated this wasn't exactly how she saw this moment going.

"Not you, per se, but the situation."

"Single mother, former substance abuse, lots of kids, errant teen, stacks of bills. What on earth could you possibly find scary about that?"

Funny, the kids didn't scare him at all. Maybe that was his naïveté talking, but the thought of a family actually sounded good. It was the fear of disappointing that family that made him think

411

twice. But no more. "Put that way, a smart man might turn tail and run, but here's the thing." He bracketed her sweet, soft cheeks with his two hands. "I was wrong. I kept singing about faith and peace and hope and falling in love forever, but I couldn't let myself just sit back and live that peace. I had to prove to myself that I was worthy to be loved. I was the hamster on the wheel, trying so hard and still going nowhere."

"Please tell me you're over that now." Lucy reached up and put her hands over his. "That's not what God wants for you, and it sure isn't what I want. I want you, Trey Stafford, just the way you are. Which, I suppose if you throw the rich and famous parts into the mix, seems gratuitous on my part, but Trey"—she leaned up for another sweet, tender kiss—"I'd want you without the rich and famous too. It means nothing to me. It never will."

She meant it. He heard it in her voice, and saw it reflected in her expression. "I messed up big time years ago, but that was then. This is now. God doesn't want us wallowing in those old mistakes. When I was a child, I spoke as a child . . ." she paraphrased the old verse softly. "And then we forgive ourselves and move on."

He needed to do that, he realized. Not because he felt guilty, but for so long he'd been trying to fill that lack within himself. That aching, yearning hole that had gaped wide for so long.

The emptiness didn't come from lack of love.

He realized that now.

It was because he thought he must be unlovable, despite all the adoring fans and records and accolades. For all this time he'd been trying to earn what didn't need to be earned, but what was freely given by good people: love.

He'd been loved and lovable all the while, despite what his biological parents led him to believe.

God loved him.

Sam loved him.

And now he could pass those two beautiful examples of a father's love on to four kids who needed exactly that.

God's perfect timing.

"I love you, Lucy." Quick tears wet her eyes. Her chin trembled, and she looked like she was about to stop him from going further, but he gripped her shoulders gently and went right on. "I love you. You and these kids make everything I do seem better."

"Trey, I—"

"Hush, woman."

She hushed and smiled through her tears.

"Lucy Carlton, I can't get down on one knee right now, and I don't have a ring in my pocket, but I intend to get one, if you don't mind giving me a little time, that is. Will you marry me, Lucy? Be my wife and let me help raise these kids and any more God might send our way?"

Her eyes went wide, then soft. She blinked and looked him right in the eye. "Can we keep our home base here in Washington?"

He nodded. "This valley's my home. First, last, and always. I'll fly into Nashville as needed, but I think Colt's already got a Realtor checking things out. But what about Nashville, Lucy? And Ed's offer? I don't want to be the guy who stood in the way of your dreams."

"How about if my dream is running that sweet store in town and growing pretty things for folks to put in their gardens?"

Had he heard her right? "And that's all right with you, Lucy?" He needed her to be sure, quite sure, because his old fears should never be allowed to govern her goals. Her dreams. "You're sure about that?"

"One set of crazy is more than enough for any family," she told him softly, and then she cradled his face in her hands, leaned up on tiptoe, and kissed him. "I would be honored to be your wife. To have your children. To run our home here and make it a place any man would long to come home to. So, yes, Trey. I'll marry you."

He kissed her long and slow until Belle's excited voice pulled them apart.

"If you guys are done kissin', can we go? I've got a pwesent for Mr. Sam!"

In one hand she held a mitt full of flowers with very short stems. In the other she held a coloring page of a cowboy, riding up a hill from a sweet green valley. And up the hill stood one small young cow, waiting to be gathered and brought home.

Trey stared at the imperfect coloring of the most perfect image and smiled down at her. "He'll love it, honey."

He reached for Lucy's hand, then paused as a school bus rolled to a stop at the top of the drive.

The door opened wide. Two boys hopped off. They began running for the house, but when Cade spotted Trey's SUV, he skidded to a crunching stop.

He turned, and when he spotted Trey with Lucy and Belle, he raced their way with Cody following. "I knew it!" He let his backpack slide to the ground as he fist-pumped the air. "I knew you would come back, Trey. I knew it all along!"

Lucy ran interference so that the boys wouldn't barrel into Trey. "Trey's hurt, remember? So we can't grab him and hug him right now, okay?"

The boys nodded, but there was no missing their matching grins.

Trey put a hand on Cody's buzzed head, then bumped knuckles with Cade. "You knew it, huh?"

Cade nodded firmly, unafraid to claim bragging rights. "I always did. Because when you *really* love somebody, then you always try your hardest to come back to them. Because it's the best ever. Right?"

The boy's faith went beyond right. It went straight to trust, the kind of trust every child should know firsthand. Trey tugged Cade carefully into his side and wasn't ashamed to blink back emotion. "Absolutely right, Cade."

Lucy took his other hand. She gripped his fingers lightly, with meaning, and they drove back to the Double S, nestled in the rich, sweet valley of Central Washington, and Trey Walker Stafford knew he'd finally come home . . . again.

Epilogue

"A fall wedding, a winter wedding, and a spring wedding!" Isabo put the finishing touches on a bridal shower cake and beamed. Then she spotted Sam as he tried to slip out the back door. "Sam, have you forgotten your appointment?"

Sam stopped in the door, head down. Then he sighed, aggrieved. "I'm fine, Izzie. Just fine."

"And that's the reason we have scheduled these checkups for the first year," she prattled, "because a man does not know to make sure he is fine until he is not fine, and when his carelessness messes up his son's beautiful April wedding, he is certain it is not his fault."

"I wouldn't argue with her, Dad." Nick walked through the kitchen, tested the icing, and grinned approval. "Great icing, Isabo."

"Lucky for you I have already frosted Lucy's celebration cake. Do you want to set up tables for tomorrow's shower or take Samuel to the lab for blood work?"

"That's a no-brainer," he whispered to Sam. Louder, he said, "I'll take Dad. Trey's due in by supper. He'd be glad to help with the tables."

"Ashley and I can do the tables," offered

Cheyenne. "They're not heavy and we want to help get things done. I can't believe this will be our third wedding in six months!"

"And a baby on the way." Ashley and Cheyenne exchanged grins. "I hope it's a girl, and that Angelina lets us babysit for her."

"She will be blessed with much help, no doubt." Isabo finished the lower cake border and nodded to the girls. "I would love your help setting up, so thank you, girls. And you'll find the tablecloths on the chest in the great room."

"You sure you'll be okay here, Izzie?"

Isabo lifted her eyes to Sam's. Spring birds chorused behind him, and a new generation of Double S signature cattle lowed in the broad pasture, crossing the valley. Elsa's dog barked in the distance, as if welcoming folks up the drive. And outside the doors of the rambling ranch house, kids, cats, and dogs ran free in the soft Cascade spring breeze.

"I have never been better, Sam. I am at peace here, with you. With them." She gestured to the noise outside. "With all of this. You are healthy and God is good. This is all I need. All I will ever need."

She smiled at him. Just him.

And that smile was enough to make him want to be more cooperative, keep his appointments and stay healthy.

He'd brought Christine to this valley nearly

forty years before. A lot had changed. A lot had happened.

He'd made mistake on mistake, but when he most needed forgiveness, God had issued it . . . but with more than one reminder for atonement.

Nick pulled the SUV up to the porch. "If we hurry, we might be able to grab a box of maple bars. We've got to go right through Cle Elum."

"Sounds good to me, Son."

They pulled out of the drive easy-like. With kids and dogs running amok, no one approached the ranch with any speed. Not anymore.

And as Nick drove by his newly finished house, they could glimpse the skeletal framing of Trey and Lucy's new house up the hill.

Two years before, Sam had dreamed the impossible dream. To have his family reunited, here, in the lush Kittitas Valley, snugged between the rising forms of the Cascade Range. He knew it wouldn't happen. He knew it couldn't happen. He'd done too much damage in his time, and there were no quick fixes in sight.

And then he got sick. Illness threatened his time frame and his life. And for long months, he couldn't imagine how he could bring his dream about. How he could fix things, just so. Make things right.

Now he realized he didn't have to.

God fixed things.

God offered chances and choices, and this time

Sam chose wisely, even when he didn't much like the offerings.

And now this.

Three sons, three precious boys, now beloved men, were back home finding their place in Central Washington.

It was everything Sam Stafford dreamed it would be.

And more.

From Lucy's Kitchen

Lucy took the time to make a personal thank-you for Sam Stafford. It was her "olive branch," a hand of forgiveness, extended.

It's so hard for someone who is strapped for cash to "give back" to a person of means, but Lucy's heartfelt effort to make frosted sugar cookies for Sam showed her desire to move beyond their past difficulties. Homemade cookies are a great conversation starter!

(This recipe is adapted from an old Betty Crocker recipe the author used growing up and has used ever since!)

LUCY'S SUGAR COOKIES

3 cups powdered sugar
2 cups butter, softened
2 large eggs
3 teaspoons almond extract
1 teaspoon vanilla extract
5 cups flour
2 teaspoons baking soda

Blend sugar, butter, and eggs together until smooth and fluffy. Mix in extracts. Add flour and baking soda and mix thoroughly.

Roll out one-half of dough on flour-dusted table to about 1/4-inch thickness. For softer, chewier cookies, don't roll too thin. Cut out shapes and place on cookie sheet. Bake at 350 degrees for 7 to 9 minutes, until edges just start to hint "gold." Let sit on cookie sheet for a few minutes before removing to finish cooling.

These tender, delicious cookies are then topped with old-fashioned butter icing, thinned slightly and flavored with almond and vanilla, the perfect pairing to the cookies.

LUCY'S BUTTER COOKIE ICING

1 stick butter, softened
4 cups powdered sugar
3 teaspoons almond extract
1 teaspoon vanilla extract
1/4 cup milk

Mix all ingredients in a large mixing bowl, then beat on high speed for several minutes. Add a little more milk (don't thin too much; you want a slightly fuller frosting, more like cake frosting) and beat until frosting is the consistency you like.

Frost cookies and shake on sprinkles or sugar quickly before the icing firms up and your sprinkles all fall off!

The most delicious sugar cookies we've ever made . . . or eaten at the Double S Ranch.

LUCY'S SIMPLE MACARONI
AND TUNA SALAD

Lots of folks have tight budgets these days, and this simple salad is great for those on a strict budget . . . and those who aren't! A picnic pleaser, this is the kind of salad Lucy can bring to a summer barbecue and feel like she's adding to the table without breaking the budget.

1 pound pasta, cooked al dente, drained and
   cooled quickly
2 cans white tuna, drained
3/4 cup chopped celery
3/4 cup chopped carrot
1/2 cup minced sweet onion
Mayonnaise
Salt and pepper to taste

Cook pasta in salted water according to directions. Don't overcook. Drain pasta, rinse with cool water, drain well again.

Put pasta in a bowl with tuna, veggies, salt, and pepper. Add mayonnaise to desired moistness. (Pasta will rob mayo of some moistness while it sits in the fridge.) Garnish with parsley, and if fresh veggies are free in the garden, it's a pretty touch to ring the top of the salad with grape or cherry tomatoes and sliced green pepper rounds.

Center Point Large Print
600 Brooks Road / PO Box 1
Thorndike, ME 04986-0001 USA

(207) 568-3717

US & Canada:
1 800 929-9108
www.centerpointlargeprint.com